MW00677214

L♥ve Lessons

A novel by

Terren Grimble

Library of Congress Catalog Card No.: 2003094096
ISBN 0-9742423-0-6

Madada Publishing
P. O. Box 7186
Largo, MD 20792-7186
www.terrengrimble.com

Printed in Canada
10 9 8 7 6 5 4 3 2 1

PUBLISHER'S NOTE:

Cover Design: Stacy Luecker

Layout Design: Terren Grimble

Editor: Chandra Sparks Taylor

acknowlegements

First, I want to thank God for giving me the gift of imagination and creativity among my many other blessings He has given me throughout my life.

This book would never have come to fruition without the help, support and patience of so many people.

To my husband, Tres, I know I jokingly said you wouldn't get a thank-you because you didn't read my chapters when I wanted you to but you and I both know that if not for your love and support, this book would still be an idea in my head. Thanks for living our vows, not just saying them.

To my babies, Brianna and Brittney, thanks for forcing Mommy to learn the difference between writing time and playtime. I love you both more than words can express.

To my daddy, thanks for always supporting me. You've always been my greatest cheerleader, even if you didn't necessarily agree with me. You're the best daddy in the world!

Ma, thanks for trying every day to be the best person you can be. You have become a great friend.

Kristie "Krusty" Reynolds-Scruggs, I love you more than you can imagine.

Monique Plater, God blessed me with another sister. We may not be biological but you are my sister nonetheless. Thanks for all the laughs.

My girl, Tracy Malone, you just don't know how much I love you. We may not talk every day but you are always in my heart. Thanks for all the encouragement.

To all the people who read my manuscript and gave me such valuable feedback: Katrina Wright-Ductant; Vicky Jenkins; Jessica Artis; Tara Brown; my cousin Jeanette McDuffie; and my girl, Romona Jackson.

To Chandra Sparks Taylor, you are more than a great editor. You went above and beyond to help me translate my vision into words on paper. Thank you so much.

A very special thanks to Nancey Flowers. Girl, I don't even know how to begin to thank you enough. You are a great inspiration to me. I know I probably sent you hundreds of email with thousands of questions. Thank you so much for having such a giving spirit.

To Ms. BJ and 4 His Glory Productions, thank you for helping me learn PageMaker and letting me bounce ideas off you. I also want to thank you for being as excited about my book as I am.

I couldn't write a page without my music so I have to thank all the artists who helped stimulate my thought process: Rahsaan Patterson, Donell Jones, Blackstreet, India Arie, Vivian Green, Jill Scott, Rachelle Ferrell, Ruff Endz, Ginuwine, Public Announcement, Anthony Hamilton, Alisha Keys, Lyfe Jennings and Avant, just to name a few! Maxwell, thanks for adding a little sumthin', sumthin' to Stacey and Ronnie's love experience. Also, thanks to Dru Hill for the beautiful song, "Never Make a Promise," which actually inspired much of this book.

I want to thank all those authors out who kicked open the door for people like me, as well as the up-and-coming authors who are my inspiration: Bebe Moore Campbell, E. Lynn Harris, Nelson George, Omar Tyree, Eric Jerome Dickey, Sheneska Jackson, Michael Baisden, Connie Briscoe, Terry McMillan, Zane, Nancey Flowers, and many, many others.

If I've left out anyone, please charge it to my head, not my heart. E-mail me at *terren.grimble@yahoo.com* and let me know what you think of the book. I look forward to hearing from you.

Peace & Blessings,
Terren

Summer '99

the perfect "10"

stacey

Number 10—Ronnie Morgan, the six-foot-five forward and co-captain of the Howard University men's basketball team—he led the Bison in scoring and rebounds, averaging six steals per game, shooting eighty-five percent from the free-throw line. And on top of all that, he was fine! Ronnie was so fine that he made my eyes water.

My knowledge of Ronnie wasn't limited to his basketball stats. Ronald Steven Morgan, Jr., was from Brooklyn, New York. He was a senior and a hospitality-management major. He had an older sister, Raina, who was twenty-seven and a younger brother named Robert, who was eighteen. His parents owned two restaurants and a nightclub.

Howard's football team was alright but the basketball team had been to the Mid-Eastern Atlantic Conference (MEAC) finals the past three years, so that made Ronnie a big man on campus. It also meant every girl on campus wanted him. I guess I fell into that category too. All the attention never seemed to go to his head though. He was real cool about it.

Since I was a finance major, Ronnie and I both took most of our classes at the School of Business, and I would always see him around campus. I finally met him one night sophomore year after one of our home basketball games.

My best friend, Erika had set her sights on David Washington, the other co-captain of the basketball team. She finally decided to make her move that night. She wanted to wait for the team to come out of the gymnasium and of course, I had to wait too. We were sitting outside on her car freezing our butts off. It had to have been almost thirty degrees that night. After waiting about a half hour, I was about to leave.

"C'mon, Stace, five more minutes," Erika begged.

Five minutes came and went.

"E, it's cold as hell out here. I'm 'bout to be out." Dave was a nice-looking brother but not all that for me to be freezing.

Just as I was getting ready to leave, he and Ronnie walked out of the door. Now Ronnie Morgan was a reason for me to freeze. Dave smiled at Erika, noticeably happy to see her.

"Sorry I took so long. I was waiting for my boy Ron," Dave explained.

"That's okay," Erika responded, smiling widely.

She was so busy being in Dave's face that she didn't even introduce me. I nudged her to make sure I would get my introduction.

"Oh, ah Dave, this is my best friend, Stacey."

"What's up, Stacey?" Dave said, shaking my hand. "This is my man Ron."

Ronnie said, "Nice to meet you, Stacey," and extended his hand. When my hand touched his, it was the first time in my life that my knees actually buckled.

"Nice to meet you too," I replied, smiling almost uncontrollably.

After that night, whenever Ronnie saw me on campus, he would make it a point to speak. I loved the way he said, "How you doing, Stace?" with his New York accent. He made my name sound so sexy.

That was the extent of our relationship until the summer of 1999. I had been going out with this guy named Patrick Smith almost two years but was growing more and more confused about my feelings toward him.

I met Patrick at the beginning of my sophomore year. We were both registering for some business classes when we literally bumped into each other. Well, he actually bumped into me. At the time I didn't mind much because I thought he was kind of cute. He had just transferred to Howard from the University of North Carolina at Chapel Hill. He had a falling out with the basketball coach there. Apparently, Patrick thought he was good enough to be a starter but the Chapel Hill coach didn't. It wasn't that Patrick didn't have a little game but he was in school on an academic scholarship so he was a walk-on for the team. There really wasn't another starting spot for him. He still argued the point though. When the coach didn't budge, Patrick transferred. I guess he figured since he was coming from a big-time Atlantic Coast Conference (ACC) school that he was a shoe-in to start at Howard...*wrong!* Much to his surprise, he rode the bench for a whole season before he became a starter. He was really salty about it but he knew his parents, well mainly his father, wasn't going to let him transfer again.

Patrick was an only child. He and his mother were really close, but he was a carbon copy of his father in every sense, right down to their need to be the center of attention. Just as with Patrick, many people perceived Mr.

Smith as conceited and arrogant. A lot of people, including my twin big brothers, Devin and Kevin, couldn't stand Patrick because of this fact. I have to admit he did know he was nice looking and had no problem letting everyone else know. That conceitedness was some kind of persona he felt the need to keep up for people on campus, especially his Alpha Phi Alpha fraternity brothers. But Patrick was cool with me because when we were alone, he wasn't like that at all. We would study together a lot and sometimes go to the movies. After a while, I really started liking him and, eventually, we started going together.

When Patrick was born, his father had high hopes for his only son. He wanted him to follow in his footsteps. Mr. Smith had attended the University of North Carolina at Chapel Hill and played championship basketball with Michael Jordan. So when Patrick had his little issue with the coach at Chapel Hill and transferred to Howard, his father wasn't too happy. Then Patrick's 3.0 grade point average didn't sit well with his father, since he had been a 4.0 student throughout college.

Mr. Smith had very high expectations and Patrick wasn't meeting them as far as he was concerned. The only thing he was happy with Patrick about was becoming an Alpha just as he had.

During a trip home to New Jersey one weekend in October, Patrick found out his mother had breast cancer. He was devastated. What hurt him more was he found out that both his mother and father had known about the cancer for a while, almost a year. His mother said she didn't want him worrying about her, and his father said he had to respect his wife's wishes. That decision on his father's part added to the deterioration of his and Patrick's already strained relationship.

Patrick wasn't planning on coming back to school but his mother insisted that he return. His body was there but his mind was in New Jersey. He walked around like a zombie most of the time. Then on November 11, 1998, at 3:45 p.m., his whole world came crashing down when he got the call from his uncle. His mother had passed away.

From that time on, it seemed like Patrick and his father drifted farther and farther apart. His father had lost his only love, and Patrick lost his beloved mother. But neither of them could find a way to acknowledge the other's lost. Mr. Smith threw himself into his work; only calling Patrick to chew him out about his schoolwork, and Patrick started not caring about school at all. His mother was the person who always encouraged him. With her gone, he was skipping classes and hanging out with his frat brothers more.

The relationship between Patrick and his father continued to go downhill and by spring semester of our junior year, things had gotten really bad. Patrick had been relatively low maintenance up until that point. But as things got worse between he and his father, he turned to me for comfort and support, which was natural since I was his girlfriend. My problem was my feelings for him weren't the same as they had been. I was secretly still holding out for Ronnie Morgan. But Patrick and I had been through so much together up to that point that I couldn't bring myself to leave the relationship even though I knew we were growing farther apart every day.

I'm convinced that God definitely has a sense of humor because around the same time that I was going through those changes with Patrick, I began noticing Ronnie staring at me. I had been at Howard for three years with not so much as a second look from him, but since I was seeing someone, now he decided to show some interest. Yeah, I was convinced; God was getting a big kick out of that.

Erika and Dave were pretty serious by this time so Ronnie and I found ourselves in the same company a lot. When I would catch him staring, he made no effort to stop. But with all the stress Patrick was adding to my life, I just brushed it off.

When summer break came, Patrick reluctantly went back home to Jersey to work at his father's accounting firm, like he had done every summer. I thought that was kind of strange because the two of them hadn't been able to stay in a room together for more than five minutes without arguing since his mother died. But I was so drained emotionally that I was glad he was going to be gone for the whole summer. At least I wouldn't feel so suffocated by him for the next three months.

Ronnie stayed in town to take a class his adviser had suggested, and Dave had gotten an internship downtown, so Erika and I ended up hanging out with the guys a lot. We went to the movies, to the park and out clubbing. It gave me an opportunity to really get to know Ronnie better. One afternoon we all decided to meet up at Hains Point, a popular summertime hangout spot in D.C.

Erika Matthews had been my best friend since we were five years old. She was the first person I met when my family moved to Upper Marlboro, Maryland, from Northwest D.C. We were more like sisters than friends.

Growing up in a house with three brothers, it was nice to have someone around to talk to about girl stuff.

"What would you say if I told you Dave and I we were thinking about moving in together?" Erika asked as we headed up I-395 toward Hains Point.

"For real? When did this come about?" I asked.

"Well we're just talking about it now."

"What do you think Ma will say about that?" I asked.

She laughed.

"Oh, we both know what Ma will say about it. 'It's a sin to live together out of wedlock,'" she said, mocking her mother's high-pitched voice. "But, you know, I'm on my own, and I'm going to make my own decisions, and I will deal with my own judgment. When the time comes, she ain't goin' be the one held accountable, I am."

"Yeah, you're right but just don't rush into anything, girl."

"Oh, I won't," she assured me.

If Erika was talking about it, she had already made up her mind. She was just running it past me to see what I thought. My only concern was her getting in too deep, too soon. I didn't want to see her hurt. I had to admit Dave was really cool. He was from Philly. He was a nice-looking brother—six-five, brown skin with a slim build. He was a little too slim for my taste but he did have a sexy baldhead. Erika hated for anybody to touch Dave's head so I did it constantly just to bug her.

It was a typical summer in D.C., hot and humid. Hains Point was crowded as usual. The haze was hovering above the water of the Potomac River. Like most Washingtonians, I had just gotten used to the summers, but that day even I was wondering why we were out in the ninety-five-degree heat.

After driving around for fifteen minutes, Erika and I finally found a parking space. As we walked toward The Awakening sculpture, we saw Dave and Ronnie sitting on a park bench under a tree.

"Ronnie knows he is so, so fine. It should be a crime to look that good," Erika said, pulling her sunglasses down to get an untinted view.

I gave her some dap on that one. Ronnie was definitely looking fine. Every piece of clothing that had the pleasure of draping his body fit perfectly, and that day was no exception. Jean shorts and a white wife-beater T-shirt never looked better on anyone.

When we got over to them, they were laughing. Erika punched Dave in the chest and said, "What y'all laughing at?"

"Girl, what you hit me for?" he asked, lifting her off the ground.

"Put me down, Dave." He started swinging her around. People on the other side of the water could hear her screaming.

"Dave, put that fool down," I insisted.

He finally put her down.

"Damn you got a big mouth," I said.

Erika smiled. "Go to hell. Anyway, I still want to know what y'all were laughing at."

"Nothing, girl. You so nosy," Dave said.

"Forget you, Dave." She turned to Ronnie for an answer. "Ronnie, what were y'all laughing at?"

I noticed Ronnie's eyes moving up and down my body. I felt kind of uncomfortable but at the same time, I liked him looking at me that way.

"I was just commenting on the fact that I didn't know Stacey's legs were that big," he answered in a soft voice, still looking at me. Dave and Erika both laughed. I didn't find it funny.

All my life, I had a complex about my legs. I hated them. They were too big, but no matter how much I worked out, they were still big. I never had any complaints from guys though. It was a personal thing. In fact, guys seemed to like my legs. I was always getting called Thickness or something like that.

Erika had talked me into wearing one of my tennis skirts that day. She always thought my legs were nice and said that I should show them off more.

"Thank you, Ronnie," Erika began. "I tell her all the time she has nice legs but she thinks they're too big. If I had legs like Stacey's, I would have my butt in some Daisy Dukes and stiletto heels every day."

We all laughed, and Dave said, "You know you don't have no sense, girl."

"I'm serious."

"Yo, I love women with nice, big legs. That's why I made the comment. It wasn't like a diss or nothing." The more he spoke, the more I liked what I was hearing. Ronnie continued, "Man, you get some big legs locked around your back."

"You sound like you're speaking from experience, Ron," Erika teased.

Ronnie laughed and said, "Ah, let's not get into all that." He took my hand. "I just want you to know I didn't mean anything by that, Stace. It was meant as a compliment. I think your legs are absolutely beautiful."

I could feel a big smile coming over my face. I finally managed to say, "Thank you."

Since Dave and Erika were getting all lovey-dovey, Ronnie and I decided to leave them alone for a while. We found a bench near the water and sat there and just talked for a long time. He told me all about the singing group he was in called Entice. I found it fitting that he came up with the name for the group since he was definitely enticing. He and the other guys in the group—Cedric, André, and Myles—all grew up together in Brooklyn. They had been working on their demo for a while, and Ronnie hoped it would be finished some time after Christmas. He said he was going to let me hear some of the songs one day, so I was looking forward to that.

Sitting there with Ronnie, I realized how beautiful his face was. His skin was the color of butterscotch—smooth and creamy looking. His eyes were set deep. His eyebrows were thick and dark. During our freshman year, he wore his hair in a neat fade, and then he went through his bald phase. Now, he was growing it out. His hair looked so thick and soft, and it had just enough curl to it, to have the jealous brothers calling him a pretty boy. Then there were the lips…the sexiest lips I had ever seen. Ronnie had L. L. Cool J lips. They covered straight, pearly white teeth. It was almost inconceivable that someone could be so gorgeous. Something with him had to be flawed. Maybe he had messed-up feet, or maybe his manhood was small, but looking at what I estimated to be around size fourteen shoes, that was doubtful.

Since Ronnie told me his life story, of course I had to tell him mine. Not that my life, at least up to that point, had been all that exciting but it was unusual for a family to have two sets of twins in it, and he seemed really interested in everything I was saying. That was a refreshing change for me because most of my conversations with Patrick during that time centered entirely on him and the "problems" he was having with his father.

I told Ronnie all about my twin brother, Tracy, and how we had been practically inseparable since the day we were born. Tracy and I did everything together. When we were young, my parents thought it would be good for us if we went to separate elementary schools. We hated that. Every morning we would throw fits. Can you imagine my mother trying to get four little kids ready for school-two bad ass nine-year-olds and two crying five-year-olds? It finally got to a point where my parents knew the separate schools thing wasn't going to work.

My mother was kind of disappointed that Tracy and I didn't go to separate colleges. I didn't know why. I guess she thought as we got older, we would want to go our separate ways but that didn't happen. We both decided to go to Howard, had the same major and when we moved out of the dorms after our sophomore year, we even got an apartment to-gether. That summer was the first time in my life I had been away from my twin. Tracy had gotten an internship in Phoenix, Arizona, and would be gone for both the summer and fall semesters. Though I loved living by myself, I really missed having my brother there. But we still talked nearly every day, even though we were almost three thousand miles apart. My phone bill was ridiculous, but I didn't care.

My father always said Tracy was a bad influence on me, but I influ-enced Tracy just as much. My daddy just didn't realize it because I was daddy's little girl. My mother, on the other hand, wasn't fooled at all. She knew Tracy and I were like Frick and Frack. What one did, the other would do. Plus, Tracy and I really trusted each other's judgment. For example, I think men look so sexy with earrings. So, I talked Tracy into getting both his ears pierced. And if I had to say so myself, my twin was kind of fine. He always had some girl running after him. My parents didn't really care for the whole earring thing at first, but it finally grew on them, especially my mother. She was cool. Actually, my father was cool, too, but he seemed to lose some of his cool points when it came to me. He almost had a fit when Tracy talked me into getting a tattoo of a panther on my shoulder.

"Why would you do that to your body?" he asked every time he saw it.

Secretly, my mother liked it but she had to keep the peace with her husband so she didn't say too much while he was around. I knew he would have a baby if he knew I had gotten another one on my chest.

"You have a tattoo on your chest?" Ronnie asked.

"Yeah."

Ronnie smiled and said, "Can I see it?"

I had been waiting three years to hear Ronnie Morgan say something like that to me. I felt like just ripping off my shirt but I had to play it cool.

"No, boy," I answered.

"What is it?"

"It's a little elephant."

"Oh yeah, I forgot you were a Delta."

"Tracy has a panther on his shoulder, too, and a dog on his chest."

"He's a Que?"

"Please, my father would have it no other way. He ain't playing when it comes to his fraternity. My great-grandfather was a Que, my grandfather is a Que, and my father is a Que, not to mention all my uncles and cousins. Don't think he was going to let one of his sons break the family legacy."

Ronnie laughed and said, "That's deep."

I couldn't believe I was telling Ronnie so much about my family and myself. And even more unbelievable was the fact that he seemed to really want to hear it. But it was time for me to get the nitty-gritty on Mr. Ronnie Morgan.

"So, why don't you have a girlfriend on campus?"

"Well, I decided a long time ago that music was going to be my first priority. You know what I'm saying? I don't have time to be messing around with no chicken-heads."

"Excuse me, Mr. Morgan, but, ah, every girl on campus is not a chicken-head."

"Yo, they're either a chicken-head or out to get a husband, or like you…" He looked at me. "Got a man already."

"So you don't go out at all?"

"I wouldn't say that now."

"Do you know how many girls on campus are lusting after you?"

"Lusting?" he asked, chuckling.

"Well, I can't think of a better word."

"Well, I do realize there are quite a few females who *think* they like me."

"Think?"

"Please, them girls don't know me. How they gonna really like me?"

"Well then, you got a whole campus full of girls who think they like you."

"Naw, it can't be the whole campus, 'cause that would include you."

I just smiled and thought, *Yeah, but I'm not just thinking that I like you.* "You know what I mean, Ronnie."

"And how do you know this?"

"Please, I have heard what them chicks say when you walk past or when you're out on the court. Boy, you just don't know. It's girls out there who want to rock your world."

He started laughing. "You are a trip. You know that, don't you?"

"I'm serious. Me and Erika be trippin' off them. And you would not believe how many girls have tried to get all buddy-buddy with Erika trying to get to you."

"For real?"

"Hell yeah."

"Y'all girls be buggin'."

"I'm just letting you know."

Ronnie wanted to get back to the tattoo on my chest. He kept asking if he could see it. He was in a silly mood. He kept leaning close, trying to look down my shirt. I liked him being that close to me, but I continued playing it off.

"Quit playing."

"Oh, you not gonna let me see your elephant, Stace? How you gonna play a brother like that?" he teased.

"I don't go around showing everybody my elephant. Only certain people get to see it."

"So, ah, I guess only your man gets to see it regularly?"

"I wouldn't say that either."

"For real?"

"Why are you sounding so surprised?" I asked.

"I've just seen the two of you on campus, and y'all were doing some hot and heavy kissing. You know what I'm saying?"

"That doesn't necessarily mean…."

"Oh, I know. It's just that, y'all have been kicking it for a minute so I just assumed. My bad."

"Well I decided a while back that I was going to chill with that." Actually, I made that decision the previous summer.

All my life, I had problems swallowing pills. So when it came time for birth control, I couldn't handle trying to swallow pills every morning. As a result, I had to rely on the latex method—latex condoms, that is. And last summer, I found out that method was not one hundred percent.

I was always very regular when it came to my period, but one day I realized I was about a week late. I panicked. I called Erika and she brought over a pregnancy test. When I saw that red plus sign, I almost passed out. I couldn't believe I was pregnant. That type of thing didn't happen to me. The craziest thing was when I told Patrick, he was actually excited. I didn't see any reason for excitement. I had just turned twenty. I was going to be a junior in college. There was no way I could have a baby. So I decided the solution was to have an abortion. Patrick was upset, to say the least. But he let me make the decision. In hindsight, it was the worse decision I've ever made. At the time, I saw no other alternative. Well there were other alternatives but none that I wanted to deal with. Every day after the abortion, I prayed for forgiveness. The abortion is what led to my celibacy. I just couldn't bring myself to have sex anymore. Patrick was pretty supportive even though at times, it did get to him.

The only people who knew about the abortion were Tracy and Erika. The funny thing was, I really wanted to tell Ronnie the whole story that afternoon, but I knew it was too soon to share something that personal. So just as I had done every day since June 24, 1998, I pushed my abortion to the back of my mind as much as I could and went on with my day.

Ronnie still couldn't believe I wasn't having sex.

"Man, I bet that brother is upset."

"Why you say that?" I asked.

"'Cause, ah, you look like you could do a brother right."

"*Do* a brother?"

"Yo hold up. I see the sister girl 'bout to come out on me. I didn't mean anything by it. Don't start rolling your neck or nothing."

I laughed because I really was about to go there with him.

"For real, I just meant that as fine as you are—" he looked at me and licked his lips—"and as sexy as you are, you look like you could have a brother feeling lovely."

"Now what do you think your boy would say if he heard you say that to me?"

"Well, first of all, just because Pat and I play ball together doesn't mean he's necessarily my boy. On the court is one thing, but off the court...." He shrugged.

I knew what that meant. Everything off the court was fair game as far as Ronnie was concerned. I kind of liked that. I shouldn't have but I did.

"And secondly, I'm just making an observation. Don't front like I'm the only brother who said you were—" his eyes moved over my body—"sexy as hell."

"Oh, I didn't say that."

"Alright then. Just 'cause you got a man don't mean I can't enjoy the view, right?"

It wasn't like I didn't get a lot of attention from guys but being alone with Ronnie, I felt like a girl on her first date. I knew I had to be cheesing all over the place.

"Oh, that's definitely right."

He laughed as if he wanted to say something else but I guess he figured if he did, the conversation would go down a road he didn't want it to go at the moment.

"What?" I asked, trying to coax him down the road.

He just continued to laugh and shake his head. "Nothing, Stace. I'm just trippin'."

We sat around talking until almost nine o'clock. The sunset, the water, and Ronnie made for a very romantic combination. As we walked back toward my car, Ronnie took my hand. A chill went up my spine and my knees kind of buckled again.

He acted as if he was looking at my rings and bracelets but I knew what he was up to. I didn't really mind. Ronnie's hands were so soft. He rubbed my hand so gently. As we approached the car, my hand in his, I realized I was heading for trouble…big trouble.

Erika and Dave weren't at the car but I wasn't that disappointed. It gave me a few more minutes alone with Ronnie. I couldn't believe I was even thinking like that. I had a boyfriend. But right then, sad to say, Patrick was the farthest thing from my mind.

Ronnie leaned on the car. "I know you got a man and everything, Stace," he began, still playing with my rings. "But, ah, I was wondering if I could give you a call sometime." He looked at me and said, "You know, just to talk."

I smiled. As I entered my phone number into his cell phone, I knew just talking would eventually lead to more with him.

"I had a really nice time with you this afternoon, Ms. Jackson."

I smiled and said, "And I had a nice time with you, too, Mr. Morgan."

"Even though you didn't let me see your tattoo."

As Erika and Dave approached the car, I replied, "Well maybe you'll get another chance some time." Ronnie smiled and nodded.

"Have y'all been waiting long?" Erika asked.

"Naw, not really," I answered, quickly taking my hand from Ronnie.

"Well, Ron man, you 'bout ready to jet?"

"Yeah, I'm ready."

Dave kissed Erika and said, "I'll see you in about two hours."

"Alright."

"Later, Ms. Stacey."

"Later, Dave. Bye, Ronnie."

"Alright, Stace."

As they walked away, I couldn't help but shake my head. Ronnie Morgan was one fine brother. Sometimes, I couldn't believe how fine he was. Every time I looked at him, I just wanted to jump on him. And after hearing him talk about how he liked women with big legs, I wanted to jump on him and wrap my big legs around his back just the way he said he liked it.

"Put your eyes back in your head and get in the car." Erika's voice snapped me back to reality. I laughed and we got in the car. As we pulled away I said, "I was just looking. Is that a crime?"

"No but I know that look. You do have a man, you know."

"Yeah, I know," I replied dryly. "I've been telling myself that all afternoon. Shit, when we were walking back to the car, he took my hand, and I swear, if someone would have asked me my boyfriend's name right then, I couldn't have told them." Erika laughed, but I was dead serious.

"You better watch yourself. If another brother is making you forget your man's name, you might be in trouble." She didn't know how close to the truth she was.

July 21, 1999 - 11:30 p.m.

I spent the day at Hains Point with Ronnie, Erika and Dave— but mostly with Ronnie. He and I went walking and we got to know each other a lot better. He's really a nice guy. That's a plus. I mean being fine is one thing but being nice is all the better. He told me I have beautiful legs and that I'm sexy. I can't believe Ronnie Morgan thinks I'm sexy. Not that I haven't been told that before, but it felt different coming from him. He also told me how much he enjoyed talking and getting to know me better. I enjoyed it too! I realized, more than ever that Ronnie is without question the type of guy I could get with.   Now all I have to do is get rid of Patrick. (Just kidding.)

All jokes aside, I do still like Patrick but this is Ronnie Morgan.   I have wanted him for three years.   Besides, even though I still like Patrick, things with us are continuing to go downhill.   I feel bad because I know Patrick is going through changes with his father still and I need to be there for him, but the only thing I can think about is being with Ronnie.

I don't want to hurt Patrick but on the serious tip, I will not pass up an opportunity to get with Ronnie. It may sound bad but I'm not.

ms. jackson, ms. jackson

In the three years I'd been at Howard, there was never any one girl that I had really been interested in. I mean, I went out with a lot of girls, a hell of a lot, but nothing serious. Most of them were just jocking me because I played ball.

Being a captain on the basketball team did have its advantages. Pulling females was one of them. Also, having females think you're fine added to my pulling power. It wasn't like I went out chasing these girls. Many times—actually most of the time—they were right there, handing themselves to me on a silver platter. And there was no way I was going to turn down all of them.

Of course, there were a few girls who would say I was the biggest dog on campus. But I didn't see it that way. Plus, I found out girls talk a lot of smack when they're around their friends. There was this AKA from Richmond, VA who was always talking about how big a dog I was. But once she wasn't around her girls, she was all up in my face—and in my pants. I could call her at anytime, day or night, and she'd let me come over.

It's not like I wasn't honest with all the girls I went out with. I told them I wasn't trying to have a girlfriend. I had tried the girlfriend thing freshman year and it didn't work for me. Once we broke up, my fun really began.

There were a few girls here and there who started liking me after we kicked it but the feelings weren't mutual. Besides, my music was my first priority, and I wasn't going to let anything, especially some female, interfere with that.

Howard, hell all of D.C. for that matter, had no shortage of fine women. When my boys came down from New York, they wouldn't know what to do with themselves. They acted like kids in a candy store. They couldn't understand why I wasn't as hyped as they were. All those girls didn't faze me. No girl on that campus had yet to really turn my head. That was until Stacey.

Stacey Jackson was beautiful. She had the kind of beauty that caught you off guard. Everything about her was so natural that you almost didn't notice her. But right when you thought you hadn't seen her, you realized you most definitely had. She had the most gorgeous mocha-colored skin I had ever seen, lovely brown eyes and the kind of smile that made a brother melt like chocolate. Not to mention a body that could bring you to your knees. She was thick as hell! From head to toe, everything about that girl was sexy.

One of the main reasons why I never gave any of the other girls on campus too much of my time was because they might have had the looks and the body but not the mind. I was attracted to Stacey because not only was she fine but she was also smart. The girl had a 3.6 grade point average in finance. She was a Delta and vice president of the NAACP chapter on campus. She had plans for her future. She wasn't in college just to get a man like a lot of the girls on campus.

I had been seeing Stacey around campus since our freshman year. I wanted to step to her plenty of times, but two things stopped me—her twin brothers, Kevin and Devin. They had finished undergrad at Howard the year before, but were still on campus going to grad school and they made it known she was their little sister and anybody who messed with her would get his ass kicked. So for a long time, nobody really stepped to her.

Then my boy Dave finally introduced me to her after a game during our sophomore year. Man, I wanted to step to her then but she was talking to this kid, Pat, who played ball with us. Pat got on my damn nerves—more than likely because he was with Stacey. But besides that, he was always talking about his father owning his own accounting firm in Jersey. I was like big deal. My pops owned a club and two restaurants in Brooklyn.

I didn't know what to do about Stacey. I really wanted to get with her. I wasn't really trying to be ruthless but when I heard Pat was going back to Jersey for the summer, I figured I'd stay in D.C. and keep his girl company. As far as I was concerned, what he didn't know wouldn't hurt him. He didn't know what to do with a girl like Stacey anyway. She needed a real man. And I was just the man for the job.

I was on my way home from playing some ball when I decided to drive through campus. Summer school was over, and there was about two weeks before the fall semester started so I knew there wouldn't be too much action.

After running into a couple of my boys down near Ben's Chili Bowl, I headed home. I turned onto Georgia Avenue and who did I see walking her sexy self down the street, but Ms. Jackson. I made it up in my mind right then that I was going to start making some serious moves on her.

I made a quick, illegal U-turn and pulled up alongside her. I rolled the window down and leaned over the passenger seat.

"What's up, girl?"

She looked in my direction, smiled and waved. "Hey, what's up?"

As she walked toward the truck, I could see one of her big, beautiful legs peeking through the long split in her wrap skirt. I was loving the view.

One thing I really liked about Stacey was she was very sexy, but she never wore clothes that flaunted it. You'd see some girls around campus wearing bootie shorts with their butt cheeks hanging out and halters that had most of their breasts showing, but not Stacey. She wore things like the orange wrap skirt she had on, that was form fitting and gave you a little glance at what was underneath.

Stacey leaned on my truck door and pulled off her orange-tinted shades. Her beauty almost took my breath away. I had to make myself not stare. Her lips were glistening from her lip-gloss. I wanted to lean over and kiss her, but I had to take my time and be patient with this girl.

"What's up, Ms. Jackson?"

"Nothing much, Mr. Morgan. What's up with you?"

"I'm chillin'. What you doin' up here?"

"I had to drop a class and now I'm going to the bookstore."

"Oh. Would you mind if I walked with you?"

She cracked a sexy smile. "No, I wouldn't mind."

I parked the truck, and we walked down to the bookstore. As Stacey looked for her book, I stayed near the door watching her. The more I watched her, the more I began to wonder how that busta Pat got with her. She was too much woman for a small timer like him. I needed to know what she saw in him.

As we walked back toward the School of Business, I decided I would get the scoop on the two of them.

"So, ah, how are you and Pat doing?"

"We're chillin'."

"So, y'all still kickin' it hard, huh?"

"We're, ah, kickin' it…soft," Stacey replied, smiling.

Her response seemed promising. I had seen Stacey staring at me from time to time so I kind of figured there was a little something there on her part too. After our afternoon at Hains Point, I knew at least the potential was there. Pat or no Pat, I was determined to get with her. Not that I was trying to be ruthless or anything but I wasn't going to let an opportunity to get with Stacey slip through my fingers. The way I saw it, Pat should have been in D.C. handling his business.

"Can I ask you a question?" I asked. "And you don't have to answer it if you don't want to."

Stacey smiled. "Go 'head."

"What the hell do you see in Pat?"

She laughed and said, "What?"

"Naw, for real, I just want to know."

"Patrick's cool."

"Whatever."

"No, for real, when he's with me, he's totally different than when everybody else is around."

I just looked at her. She could say whatever she wanted. Patrick wasn't cool. He was a pain in the butt. Always walking around like he was God's gift to the world.

"C'mon now. That's a hell of a jump. He goes from Prince Charming with you to asshole with everybody else."

"Oh, I didn't say he was necessarily Prince Charming."

"What made you get with him in the first place?"

"I don't know. He's cute," she said, smiling.

"Please, there are probably a lot of dudes on campus who fit that criteria."

She smiled and said, "Oh yes, there are others," looking at me. Stacey could throw a sexy look at you that would tell you exactly what she meant and that look was telling me something for sure.

"For real though, Patrick is cool. It's just that he has a lot of stuff going on in his life and for the most part, that's why he acts the way he does."

"Whatever you say," was my response. He was still an asshole as far as I was concerned.

When we got back to Stacey's red 1998 Ford Mustang, I opened the door for her.

"Mmm, a gentleman," she said.

I smiled.

"You don't find too many of them around here," she continued.

"Maybe you've been looking in the wrong places." Her response was a slightly blushing smile.

"Anyway, thank you, Mr. Morgan, for keeping me company."

"Anytime."

She got into her car and quite deliberately pulled her leg inside slowly because she knew I was looking. I reiterated, "Anytime, at all." She smiled and put her orange-tinted shades back on.

As I watched her drive away, I knew for sure I had a chance to get with her. She was sending out some inviting signals, and I was definitely going to accept the invitation.

When I got back to the crib, there were several messages. Most of them were from my boys Ced, Myles and Dre. Those brothers could worry the hell out of me sometimes.

I didn't really feel like talking to any of them right then. I realized I hadn't eaten anything all day. I should have been hungry but I wasn't. I changed my clothes and lay across my bed. *Stacey, Stacey, Stacey.*

I couldn't remember the last time a girl had me tripping like that. I could still see her big, beautiful leg peeking through the split of that orange skirt. It looked so soft and smooth. All I wanted to do was run my hands over her legs. I really wanted that girl. The bad thing was I didn't know if I wanted to get with her because she was mad cool or because she was one of the females on campus who I had wanted to pull but never had. Regardless, it was on.

Fall Semester

stacey

October 5, 1999-7:55 p.m.

I have never been so tired of school in my life. I am ready to be up out of here. Tonight I am going out and really let loose. I'm gonna ask Patrick if he wants to go with me to see Chuck Brown but if he doesn't, I'm still going to go. Maybe I'll ask Ronnie. Things are really strange for me as far as Ronnie is concerned. I'm finding myself thinking about him a lot since we spent all that time together this summer. I have always thought that he was cute— well fine—but now after getting to know him better, I think I'm starting to really like him, which poses a big problem for me seeing as though I have a boyfriend.

I don't know what's going on with me and Patrick. I'm really getting confused about my feelings for him and our relation- ship. I'm not sure if the feelings I'm having for Ronnie started because of my confusion about Patrick or if the confusion about Patrick is because of Ronnie. I think it's probably a little of both.

Patrick is becoming a little too high-maintenance for me. I mean, he's always saying I'm the only person he can count on and he wouldn't know what to do if I left him. Now he's starting to get very possessive. He always wants to know where I'm going, when I'll be back.

Then every time I say anything about needing some space, he brings up the abortion. He reminds me that he was there for me through everything and even after I stopped wanting to have sex, he stuck around when a lot of guys wouldn't have. So of course, I feel guilty and everything remains the same. Lately, he's been calling me all hours of the night ranting and raving about his father and how he's been trippin' on him. I try to talk to him but it's getting to the point where there's nothing I can say to calm him down.

When Patrick said he didn't want to go with me, I did call Ronnie to see if he would go. We always got into big debates about go-go versus hip-hop. Being from New York, of course Ronnie was all into hip-hop but he hated go-go music. I would tell him all the time that before he left D.C., I was going to have him liking it.

"I just called to see if you wanted to go somewhere with me tonight."

"Where?"

"To hear Chuck Brown downtown."

Ronnie laughed and said, "Chuck Brown, huh?"

"Yeah. Do you want to go?"

"Yeah, I'll go."

"Okay then. I'll be over to get you about eleven o'clock."

"Alright, Stace. Later."

Even though technically it wasn't a date, I was running around trying to find something to wear as if it was. I couldn't wear anything too dressy or whatever because it was going to be hot as hell up in that joint but I still wanted to look...I don't know, nice I guess. I finally just settled on my blue Fila jogging suit. I wasn't going to put a T-shirt on underneath it; instead I put on my white sports bra.

When I pulled up in front of Ronnie's house, he was sitting on the steps. While he walked toward the car, I found myself studying his body. Ronnie was very muscular. He had huge arms and broad shoulders. On the top of his left arm, he had a tattoo of a basketball with the number ten inside it. I remembered seeing him raise his shirt on the basketball court. The brother had a serious six-pack working and a very sexy chest with a bull tattooed on it. His sign was Taurus—the bull. His birthday was actually four days after mine on May 8th.

My thing with men was the chest and shoulders. So I was definitely loving Ronnie's. And, he had the most perfect, cutest butt a man could have—not too big but not too small, just right. Grippable, you know what I'm saying. As if he didn't have enough going for him in the "sexy as hell" category, he was bowlegged. Now this brother had some gorgeous legs. And that night, he was showing them off. I was grateful for the Indian summer that we were having in D.C.

The smell of his Boucheron cologne filled the car as he got in. "What's up, Stace?"

"Nothing much."

I kind of looked him up and down and he asked, "And what's all that for?"

"Nothing. You just looking and smelling mighty good tonight."

"Oh, okay, thanks," he said with a slight smile.

I found myself flirting with him a lot since the summer. It wasn't like I was doing it on purpose. Most of the time it happened before I even knew it. I knew I was going to have to check that though. I wasn't trying to get busted by Patrick.

"So, you taking me to my first go-go?"

"Yeah. I can't believe you've been in D.C. for more than three years and have never been."

"Man, I ain't trying to hear that shit."

"Anyway, I know you're going to like it. Plus, Chuck plays a lot a jazzy music."

"Yeah well, we'll see."

He turned toward me and said, "So anyway, what you been up to lately? I haven't seen you around campus in a few weeks. What, your man got you on lock-down?"

"Hell no. See why you tryin' to be funny?"

"I'm just messing with you, girl."

"I've just been real busy. I had a lot of meetings to go to, some tests I needed to really study for, plus we've been having step practice every night for the past two weeks getting ready for homecoming. That's why tonight, I'm going to have me some fun."

"So I'm part of your fun tonight, huh?" His voice was so sexy. I had been noticing him flirting more too. I was starting to enjoy it a little too much.

"Well Patrick didn't want to go so I called you. I mean, I always have to go with somebody I know because I ain't going to have some dude I don't know rubbing all up on me."

"Oh, so you're going to let me rub all up on you, huh?" That caught me totally off guard. I didn't know what to say. I really wanted to say, "Hell yeah!" But I ended up saying, "Boy, you know what I'm talking about." He just smiled.

The joint was packed. I took Ronnie's hand and led him to the middle of the dance floor. I had made it up in my mind that that night I was going to push the envelope a little with Ronnie. I started dancing real close to him, and he looked down at me with surprise.

"You in D.C., baby, you gotta do it like we do it!"

"You think I can't hang?" he asked with that sexy voice, leaning close to my ear.

I inhaled the scent of his cologne and there went my knees again. "Oh, I have no doubt that you can hang," I said, licking my lips slowly.

I was flirting again but this time I really didn't care. The more Ronnie and I were together, the more I realized that I was becoming very attracted to him. Being that the brother was so fine, every girl on campus was attracted to him, but with me it was turning into more, a lot more.

"I'm not even going to go there with you, Stace," he said, kind of laughing and shaking his head.

I put my arms around his neck and said, "Oh, you think I can't hang?"

"We not gonna go anywhere near there."

"Okay." I decided to let it go—for the time being.

After getting our groove on for a while, we were both sweating like crazy. All I could think about was how good Ronnie's chest would look with little beads of sweat rolling down. The more I thought about it, the more I tried to put it out of my mind. Then it didn't help any that I could feel something poking my pelvis. Dancing as close as we were, a brother was bound to get a little excited. I wasn't going to mention it because I didn't want to start something I was not prepared to finish at that time. For some reason though, the thought of me arousing Ronnie was very exciting.

After a while, it got too hot for me. I was ready to go. Ronnie seemed to be also, so we left. The cool night air felt so good against my skin. As we walked toward my car, Ronnie pulled his sweaty T-shirt over his head, revealing those rock-solid abs that I had only seen from afar when he pulled his jersey up during basketball games. I looked at his chest and licked my lips. I wanted to reach over and run my hand over all those rippling muscles. I didn't realize Ronnie saw me until he started laughing.

"What?" I asked, trying to play it off.

"What was all that for?" he asked.

"All what?"

"All that licking your lips."

My face had to be beet red. I had never been so embarrassed in my whole life. I wanted to throw myself in front of one of the cars zipping down Sixteenth Street.

"I was just licking my lips."

He just smiled.

"It's a habit."

"Yeah, okay," he replied.

Our ride back to Southwest was pretty quiet. I was quiet because I couldn't believe Ronnie had caught me drooling over his chest. I didn't know why he was so quiet.

Ronnie reclined the seat and closed his eyes. He was rhythmically moving his head to the music of the Quiet Storm. I kept glancing at him wondering what was on his mind. As the lights from the street lamps flashed over his face, I wished I could get inside his head. Could I possibly be occupying his mind as much as he had occupied mine for all those years? That was wishful thinking on my part, but very doubtful.

Turning the corner onto Ronnie's block, a sense of sadness came over me because I knew I was quickly approaching the end of my time with him. I pulled in front of his house and turned off the engine, leaving the music playing. Ronnie slowly opened his eyes and turned his head to me.

Damn, you are so sexy, I said to myself.

"I really enjoyed the club. I gotta admit, Chuck Brown is pretty cool."

"See, I knew you would like it," I replied.

"Well I really don't know if I was enjoying him so much or if I was enjoying my company."

"Well either one is good."

"One," he said, leaning toward me and running his finger under my chin, "is much better than the other."

"Oh, really?"

The words barely came out of my mouth. I could tell by the look in his eyes, something was about to happen. He leaned toward me and said, "Most definitely," in a soft voice.

As we shared our first kiss, all I could think about was how soft his lips were. I had never felt lips so soft. Then I couldn't believe that—to use his words—we were doing some hot and heavy kissing. It was everything I dreamed it would be and more. Ronnie had this way of running his tongue over my lips and I loved it. A sister could get use to that. It seemed like we were kissing forever. Afterward, silence fell on the car again. After what seemed like an eternity, Ronnie took a deep breath.

He rubbed his lips and said, "Man. I, ah, I'm sorry about that."

"You don't have to apologize," I assured him.

"I guess having spent so much time together tonight, I was kind of caught up in the moment. You know what I'm saying?"

"Yeah. That's probably what it was. I guess I was caught in the moment too."

"I guess the moment's over, huh?"

"I guess so," I said for a lack of anything better to say.

He looked at me and said in a soft voice, "Mmm, what a moment that was."

It was some moment, one I wouldn't soon forget.

"Well I'm gonna get on up in this house."

"Okay."

He looked at me and said, "I'll see you later, Stace. And again, I really had a nice time with you tonight."

"I had a nice time too."

"Talk to you later."

"Alright."

I watched him disappear behind his door. My thoughts went back to our kiss. I ran my fingers across my lips. I would remember that night for a long time.

October 6, 1999 - 1:18 a.m.

I ended up going to the club with Ronnie tonight (last night). We had so much fun. I can't believe how much I was flirting with him. I've always liked flirting with guys but this was different. Before, if I was flirting, it was just playing around. I didn't mean anything by it, but this time I don't know.

When I took him home, we were sitting in the car and we kissed. I cannot describe the way it felt. His lips are so soft. The kiss was long and so gentle. I am just glad that we were sitting in the car because if we would have been in the house, I can't say that my celibacy would still be intact. I know I have a boyfriend and shouldn't be doing this, or even thinking this but it's something drawing me to Ronnie. I mean besides the fact that I am oh so very attracted to him, which just puts me in the category of all the other girls on campus. But I know I'm feeling something more. What am I going to do? Maybe I should go 'head and break up with Patrick. The only problem with that is I've never been good at breakups.

I'm sitting here seriously thinking about breaking up with Patrick. I can't believe this. This is the kind of shit I talk about people for and here I am. I don't even know if there's anything there as far as Ronnie's concerned. I mean it could've been just like he said, being caught in the moment. Lord, what a moment!
    I gotta shake this shit off. I ain't trying to get caught up in no drama.

I wanted to tell Erika what happened but since she and Dave had moved in together, it was hard to catch her by herself. I had to call though.

When Dave answered on the second ring, I knew I had to go to Plan B.

"Hey, Dave. What's up?"

"Hey, Stacey. How you doing?"

"I'm fine. Is Erika around?"

"Yeah, she's right here. Hold on."

Before she could get hello out good, I said, "I need to talk to you."

"What's up?" she asked, puzzled.

"I just need to talk to you."

Erika insisted I go ahead and talk but I couldn't with Dave there. "You know how nosy Dave is. You gotta come over here."

"Alright. I'll be over there in about an hour."

I was so anxious to tell Erika what happened between Ronnie and I that I couldn't sit still. I went through my apartment cleaning everything that wasn't nailed down.

By the time I finished, it had been an hour and a half since I talked to Erika. That girl was always late. Just as I was about to start cursing her out, I heard her key in the door. When she walked in, I looked at my watch.

"Forget you, girl. I said about an hour," she responded, walking toward the kitchen. "I wasn't even dressed when you called."

"Whatever. You are just slow as hell."

Erika came out of the kitchen with a glass of juice and said, "Anyway, what's up? What you gotta talk to me about?"

"Girl, you are not going to believe what happened last night," I began, as I sat on the couch.

"What?" Erika asked, sitting beside me.

"Since nobody wanted to go with me to see Chuck, I asked Ronnie."

"Ronnie...Ronnie who?" she asked, with a knowing smirk.

"You know who, Ronnie Morgan."

"Oh, really now."

"Girl why was he looking so good."

"Shit, that ain't nothing new. That brother is always looking good."

"Well, he was looking extra good last night. And, man, why did he have on that Boucheron cologne that I like."

"Yeah, yeah, yeah. Get to the damn point."

"Alright. Well when I took him back home, we were sitting in the car and...."

"And what?" Erika hated when I dragged out a story. "What, girl? Damn!"

"We kissed," I said softly.

Erika was getting ready to take a sip of juice when she heard what I said. She stopped. "What you mean you kissed? Are you talking peck or...?"

"Oh this was way more than a peck."

She started laughing. "You slut."

"Shut up."

"Ooh, let me find out you becoming a hot ass."

"Whatever."

"Anyway, how did this happen?"

"I don't know. I mean you know ever since we hung out last summer, we've started kind of flirting with each other."

"Mmm, Miss Thang."

"I just hope Patrick hasn't noticed anything."

"Forget, Pat, his silly self."

"C'mon now, Erika."

"Stacey, you can say what you want about him really being nice. I don't see it. Every time I'm around him, he's an asshole."

"Anyway. Let's just drop that."

"Yeah, let's. So what's up with that, Stace? What you gonna do about Ronnie?"

"I don't know, girl. But this shit is getting serious."

"Do you know how many girls would be ready to kick your ass right about now?" We both laughed.

"Shit, I'm thinking about kicking it myself," she said, still laughing.

"I'm telling Dave," I teased.

"Naw, I wouldn't give up my baby for nobody—not even Mr. Fine himself."

"I hear ya."

"Girl, I just can't believe, you and Ronnie," Erika said, shaking her head.

"It's not all that. It was just one kiss. No big deal."

"Child, please. You have been talking my face off about Ronnie Morgan since freshman year. Don't even front. And I'm surprised you haven't burned a hole in that brother's skin staring at him so hard."

"That doesn't mean anything. Shit, everybody stares at him. He's fine as hell."

"I don't even want to hear all that bull. Even if you think it's something small now, I have a feeling it's going to turn into a lot more soon."

"Why you say that?" I asked curiously.

"Because I know you. Oh, and just so you know, Dave asked me the other night if I thought something was going on."

"Shut up, Erika! What did he say?"

"Well he just mentioned that he noticed Ronnie staring at you a lot lately. He wanted to know if I thought anything was up. I told him no and he pretty much left it there."

"Please don't tell him, E," I begged. "I don't want something to get started over nothing."

"Alright. You know I got your back."

Erika left to meet Dave at the mall and I laid my head back against the couch. I couldn't believe it but I was starting to feel guilty about my little kiss with Ronnie. As I picked up the phone and dialed Patrick's phone number, I questioned myself, *What is wrong with you?*

Patrick answered the phone saying, "What's up girl?" He almost sounded cheerful.

"Hey, what you doing?"

"Chillin'. Why?"

"Well I ah, know we've both been kind of busy lately, so I was thinking that um maybe we could go to the movies."

"That's cool," he replied.

"Alright then. I'll be over there in about an hour. You wanna go to Union Station?"

"Sounds good. I'll see you in a little while."

Patrick greeted me with a kiss when he got in the car, which took me by surprise. We hadn't kissed like that in a while, which made me feel even worse about kissing Ronnie.

Patrick was rather talkative on the drive to Union Station. He was talking about how well his classes were going so far. It was good to see him excited about school again. Maybe things were turning around for him. I hoped so because he had really been struggling the past two semesters.

We decided to see Blue Streak starring Martin Lawrence. It was pretty funny. Not an Oscar winning movie or anything but decent. Afterward, we were both hungry so we decided to hit our favorite spot, Ben's Chili Bowl.

We got a table in the back room. I was tearing up my chili dog. They were the bomb. But Patrick wasn't really eating.

"You okay," I asked, wiping away a bit of chili sauce from the corner of my mouth.

"Um yeah."

"You sure?"

"I did kind of want to talk to you about something."

"What?" I asked.

"Well I was wondering if you would come home with me this weekend."

"This weekend? Why?"

"Um…it's ah been a year since my mom passed away and I just wanted to go up and put some flowers at her gravesite."

It was hard to believe it had been a year since Patrick's mother died. He didn't talk about her much anymore. I used to try and talk to him about his mother's death but he never seemed to want to get into it so I just left him alone.

I felt bad because my first instinct was to say I had something I had to do. But there was no way I could refuse him.

Patrick was happy I agreed to go home with him. That was all well and good for him, but on a scale of one to ten, my guilt level shot from around three straight to ten while I was kissing Patrick goodbye.

When I got back home, I plopped down on my bed and covered my head with my pillow. I didn't know what was going on with me. Though I felt guilty about kissing Ronnie, I still couldn't get him or our first kiss off my mind. The kiss was so nice. I wasn't sure if it was nice because I had been dreaming about it every night for damn near four years or because he had skills in that area. I had pretty much decided that the brother had mad kissing skills when the telephone started ringing and interrupted my thoughts.

"Hello."

"Hey, Stace. Are you busy?" Ronnie asked softly.

"Um no, I'm not busy."

"Good. I was just calling because I, ah, had been thinking about last night."

"Last night?" I was determined to play it cool. I couldn't let on that I had been thinking about the same thing.

Ronnie kind of laughed. He knew I was perpetrating.

"Yeah, you know, in the car...our kiss."

"Oh. What about it?" I asked nonchalantly.

He took a deep breath and said, "Well I just want to apologize again for kissing you. I mean I know you got a man and e'erything."

"It's no need to apologize, Ronnie. I did kiss you back."

"Yeah, you did. And why is that?"

"What you mean, why? I guess I wanted to."

"You guess, huh? Even though you have a man?"

There was nothing I could say. Ronnie sat silently waiting for my response.

"Hello?" I finally said.

"Oh, I'm still here. I'm just waiting for your answer."

"Yes, I wanted to kiss you even though I have a man."

"So is that all you want to do with me...even though you have a man?" he asked in a soft voice. He was trying to take me there but I wasn't ready to go quite yet.

"Ah, why don't we change the subject?"

"Alright, we'll change the subject... for now. Anyway, I have another subject I want to talk to you about."

"And what's that?" I asked.

"I want to know some more about this 'born-again' virginity of yours."

I laughed and said, "What are you talking about?"

"When we were down at Hains Point, you told me you decided to stop having sex with Pat, so I call that 'born-again' virginity."

I had to laugh. "You are silly."

"Naw, for real, I wanted to know how long it's been since you and your boy have had sex."

I hadn't really been keeping track but when I thought about it, I realized it had been a little more than fifteen months since the last time Patrick and I had sex. I couldn't believe it. That was actually a pretty long time. I wasn't naive enough to think that Patrick wasn't having sex, but I didn't care. That sounds bad, but I really didn't care what Patrick did at that point. As long as he wasn't all up in my face, I was cool.

I had been having sex since I was seventeen years old. You would think it would be hard to just stop cold turkey, but it wasn't. More than likely that was because Patrick wasn't that great in bed anyway. Every time we were together, he was fumbling and bumbling around like he didn't know what the hell he was doing. There were a couple of times when I wanted to say, "Just stop. Get off me and get the hell out!" But I'm sure Patrick thought he was the bomb.

"Yo wait a minute, you mean to tell me, you haven't had sex in over a year?" Ronnie asked in disbelief.

"Yep."

"Damn, how do you do it?"

"It's not that hard."

"Man, ain't no way in the world I could go without for a year. After a month, I probably would be ready to explode."

I laughed and said, "You are so silly."

"I'm serious. I couldn't do it."

It had been much easier to be celibate before Ronnie and I started hanging out. I just didn't think about it before. I kept my mind occupied with school. But Ronnie had me thinking about sex a lot more.

"You probably gave it up because Pat's weak in bed," Ronnie joked.

I busted out laughing.

"Yeah, that's it. I knew it."

I finally composed myself enough to speak. "I didn't say anything."

"A'ight then, was he weak or not?"

"Ronnie, I am not going to tell you all that."

"I just want to know. 'Cause for real, if he was handling his business and was having some fireworks poppin' off down there, it's no way you'd be able to give up sex that easily. You know what I'm saying?"

I knew exactly what he was saying. There had never been any fireworks popping off. I wanted to tell Ronnie just how weak Patrick was and ask him if he could come over and show me how it should be done. I had no doubt in my mind that he could most definitely handle his business when it came to the bed action.

I remember sophomore year, this girl who lived next door to me and Erika in Slowe Hall had been out with Ronnie and she would not stop telling everybody how good he was in bed. I swear that girl went on and on about it until school got out for the summer. Personally, I didn't want to hear about what she did with Ronnie, especially since I wanted to get with him in the worst way.

Finally, there I was lying on my bed in the dark, with him on the phone and slow jams playing in the background. But I didn't want to talk about Patrick. I thought telling Ronnie I wasn't going to talk about how Patrick was in bed would end that conversation, but I was wrong. He wouldn't let it go.

"For real, Stace, he was weak, wasn't he? C'mon, you can tell me."

"Ronnie, all I'm going to say is it was nothing special."

"Nothing special, huh? That's too bad." He softened his voice. "A man should definitely be able to give his girl something special."

"Oh, I agree."

"Maybe you don't have the right man."

"That's possible. Maybe I should be looking for another man then, huh?"

"Maybe you wouldn't have very far to look."

"Again, that's possible. Do you have someone in mind?" I asked.

"Oh, most definitely."

"Are you going to tell me who he is?"

"When the time's right, you will know."

"When the time is right, huh? Does he know my current situation?"
Ronnie asked, "The boyfriend situation or the celibate situation?"

"Both."

"Yeah, he knows. But he's confident that he can help you with both those situations."

"I didn't know I needed help with either."

"So you're saying Pat treats you the way you should be treated?"

"At times."

"Well this person that I'm talking about would treat you right all the time, in every way. And he figures after you start being treated right, you might want to go 'head and give up that celibacy thing. You know what I'm saying?"

"Ah yeah, I think so."

"Good. You keep that in mind."

While I was digesting Ronnie's words, my phone beeped. "Hold on a second, Ronnie."

"Okay."

I clicked to my other line and said, "Hello."

"What's up, baby girl?" my twin said.

"Hey, sweetie. What's up?" It was good to hear from him.

"Nothing. I was just checking up on you; making sure you were staying out of trouble."

"Whatever, boy," I said, laughing. "Look, hold on a second."

"Alright."

I clicked back to Ronnie. "Ronnie, let me call you back. That's Tracy."

"Okay. I'll talk to you later."

I normally didn't tell people who was on my other line, but I didn't want Ronnie to think I was getting off the phone with him to talk to Patrick. The only person I would hang up with him for was my brother.

Tracy just called to see how everything was at home and what was happening on campus. He loved his internship but he hated being away from Howard and his fraternity. Tracy Jackson was a Que dog to his heart. He really hated being away from his family though, especially his "baby" sister. The boy was born a measly two minutes before me, which did technically make me the baby in the family.

We didn't stay on the phone long. I was relieved he hadn't asked me who I was talking to when he called. I had never lied to my brother in my life, but there was no way I could tell him I was talking to Ronnie. Tracy knew I wasn't an angel when it came to guys but he had never known me to cheat on my boyfriends. Things sure had changed while he was in Phoenix.

my last homecoming

ronnie

I was determined to have some fun during my last homecoming at Howard. I had mad fun freshman year but after that all my free time was spent in New York with the fellas working on our demo. This year some of my boys were coming down from New York, and we were going to get ill. Dave was going to hang out with us so we met him down at the Dog House, the Que's frat house.

All the fine women in the world came to campus for homecoming. Girls came from New York, Jersey, Philly, Delaware, Virginia, and even North and South Carolina. It was fine women everywhere. Ced and Myles loved every minute of it. Dre was pissed that he was going to miss all the festivities because he had to work.

"Man, how do y'all handle all these fine women being around?" Myles asked. "I wouldn't know what to do with myself."

Dave just laughed.

"You get used to it. Plus once you get to know some of these girls, they ain't but so fine no more," I answered.

"Please I don't need to get to know them. All I need is thirty minutes," Ced said, laughing. Ced was a straight-up dog.

"I ain't even thinking about none of these girls. I got me a fine woman," Dave bragged.

"Yeah, I understand that, but you could have more than one," was Myles's answer. But Dave knew better. Erika was no joke. She would turn Howard University out if she thought for a second that he was messing around on her. Besides, Dave was really into his girl.

Now before Erika, Dave was the mack of all macks. I had seen Dave have one girl waiting for him in his dorm room and be slobbin' some other girl in the lobby. There were plenty of times when girls passed each other in the hall—one leaving, the other arriving. Erika put an end to all that.

Dave tried to continue being the mack, but she was not having it. Erika knew his reputation with the ladies so she wasn't trying to give up the poo-nani. That was Dave's excuse for the other women.

"Man, she's cool and e'erything but she ain't trying to give up the pant-ies, so I gotta get my swerve on somewhere else."

But when Ms. Matthews did finally give up the goodies, that brother was sprung. He was so whipped it didn't make any sense. Erika had him getting out of the bed at all hours of the night for a fix.

"I doubt that I could handle another girl right now. My girl can wear a brother out," Dave confessed.

We all laughed.

"I'm serious. I mean forget the fact that she is definitely all that, but that girl is a fiend. Sometimes I'm like, 'Baby, not tonight.'"

"Shit, I would love that," Myles said.

"Believe me, I was loving it the first couple months we were living together. I mean I was getting some at least twice a day. But man, you can't keep that up forever. Then basketball season started too. Shit, be-tween Erika and practice, I needed some vitamins."

It sounded funny but Dave was dead serious. There were times when that brother walked into practice and I could tell Erika had worked him out the night before.

I was trying to get into the conversation but I was a little preoccupied. There had been plenty of fine women walking back and forth but the one fine woman I wanted to see hadn't come around yet. I didn't know what was up with me. After our kiss, Stacey had been on my mind day and night. I was trying to take my boys' advice and shake it off, act like she was just another girl. But I couldn't. She wasn't.

When Stacey pulled up in front of the house with Erika, my heart began to beat faster. At that point I knew I couldn't shake it off, even if I wanted to.

"What you doin' hanging down here with the bruhs?" Erika asked me as they walked up on the porch.

"Oh, since I ain't frat, I ain't welcome down here?"

"Naw you cool, Ron. We'll allow you to hang with our bruhs," Erika assured me, patting my chest.

"Thank you so much."

From the corner of my eye, I saw Myles checking Stacey out. I knew how he was with females so I had to make sure my brother knew what the deal was. I didn't want to have to put my foot in that boy's chest so I pulled Stacey over to me.

"Stace, I want to introduce you to my boys. This is Ced and Myles. Fellas, this is Stacey."

Myles smiled. He got my point.

"It's nice to meet you guys."

"It's nice to meet you too," they both responded.

"Yeah, we've heard a lot about you." I knew Ced was about to start some shit. "A whole lot."

"Go 'head with that, man," I said, laughing off his comment.

Stacey just smiled.

Erika cleared her throat. "I know you see some other folk up on this porch."

I was so busy making sure Myles knew the deal as far as Stacey was concerned that I forgot to make the proper introductions.

"Oh, my bad, y'all. Erika, these are my boys Ced and Myles. Guys, this is Stacey's girl, Erika."

Dave's motorcycle was parked in front of the house and Erika sat on it. He gave her one of those looks like, what the hell are you doing? Now, why'd he have to do that?

"Don't even try it, boy. I am helping you pay for this damn thing, so you better chill."

Needless to say, Dave didn't like her saying it like that, especially in front of everybody, but he knew it was true. Since they had moved in together, you would have thought they were married. They even had joint bank accounts. I wasn't too sure if that was a good idea. Yeah, they were in love right then but what if the next day, it was gone. It would be a whole lot of drama trying to divide up money and everything. But Dave wasn't worried about that. He said he had finally found a woman to treat him the way he liked and he loved to death. I said more power to him. Actually, I wanted to find someone like that. Sometimes, I really thought I had.

Every time I saw Stacey, I couldn't help but stare at her. She was just so beautiful to me. I knew it kind of made her uncomfortable though, especially when other people were around. I guess she thought someone might tell Pat. I knew none of the bruhs had any love for Pat but people did talk, and things spread around that campus with a quickness. Somebody was always trying to stir up some drama. That was one of the reasons Stacey moved off campus. She didn't want everybody in her business.

"Hey, Stace, let me take you for a ride on my bike," I said.

She looked at me like I was crazy. "Naw that's okay."

"What, you scared to have something this big between your legs?" I teased. Her eyes bugged out. She was shocked by what I said but she managed to laugh it off.

"C'mon, Stace. One quick ride. I promise I'll take it easy on you."

"Shut up, boy."

"C'mon."

She finally decided to go. She got Dave's extra helmet and said, "Man, I better not get hurt."

"I would never do anything to hurt you," I assured her. She smiled one of her *Aaahh, that's so sweet* smiles.

I got on the bike. As she climbed behind me, she asked, "You haven't been drinking or anything, have you?"

"Naw, I'm cool."

"Okay."

"Hold on."

With anybody else, I would have been flying down the street, but Stacey was really scared. She was holding on tight. It felt kind of good having her arms wrapped around my waist. I knew I could get used to that.

I decided to ride down to Rock Creek Park. When I pulled up near one of the streams, Stacey asked, "Why are we stopping here?"

"I just thought it would be cool to chill here for a minute."

Stacey said, "Oh, okay," and got off the bike. She took her helmet off and caught me staring at her.

"What?" she asked.

"Nothing. I was just looking at you."

"Oh."

She put her helmet down and walked over near the water. I put my helmet on the seat of the bike and walked down beside her. She said, "It's so pretty out here."

I turned toward her. "Yes, you are."

Stacey kind of smiled. I loved making her blush. It was so cute. As I moved closer to her, I asked, "Have you missed me?"

"Missed you? What are you talking about, Ronnie? I see you almost every day."

"Yeah, but you haven't been alone with me in a few weeks," I said in a soft voice. I saw Stacey swallow hard. I loved doing that to her too. She always tried to act like she had her feelings for me under control. But I knew I could throw that off at any moment.

"Well, don't you miss being alone with me?" I asked, moving closer to her ear. She took a deep breath and licked her luscious lips. The girl had some sexy lips.

She said, "Um, Ronnie, why don't we go 'head back to campus?"

"Why don't you answer my question first then give me a kiss, then we can go back?"

"Ah, Ronnie…" Before she could finish, I kissed her.

She licked her lips and I said, "Mmm, that was nice. Can I have another one?"

"Ronnie, we really should be getting back."

"What, you trying to get back to your man?" Stacey hated for me to make comments like that about Pat.

"No, I am not trying to get back to Patrick," she answered with a little attitude.

"Your man."

"Patrick."

"Anyway, why don't you just give me another kiss?" I could tell she wanted to but she was being very cautious. I moved closer to her.

"C'mon, girl." I kissed her neck. "I know you want to give me a kiss." I kissed her cheek. "Don't you?"

"Yes."

"Well then." I kissed her again, and she finally gave in. But right when I started enjoying myself, Stacey pushed me back.

"We, ah, better be heading back."

"Alright," I conceded.

When we got back to the frat house, Stacey got off the bike and took off the helmet. "Ah, thanks for the ride." I took off my helmet and looked at her. I wanted to say, *Yeah well if you liked that ride I got another ride for you that I know you'll like,* but I didn't.

"You are very welcome." I rubbed her hand and whispered, "And thank you for that kiss." She just smiled and headed into the frat house to get Erika. As she walked away, I watched her hips sway so gracefully from side to side. *Damn she is fine,* I thought, shaking my head.

"My boy." Myles walked up behind the bike. "So that was Miss Stacey?"

I got off the bike and said, "Yeah, that was her."

"Now I see why your nose is so wide open. She is fine."

"No doubt."

"So what were you and Miss Stacey doing on that long ride?"

I just smiled. I had never been one to kiss and tell. That wasn't my thing.

Ced walked up and announced, "I am ready to get my drink on." Myles was in complete agreement. "Plus, I'm trying to get with some of these fine females."

"Well there will be plenty of females at the step show," I assured them.

"What time is that?" Myles asked.

"Seven-thirty."

"Cool. We can go get our drink on before that."

Dave, Erika and Stacey came out of the frat house. "So fellas, what we 'bout to get into?" Dave asked, rubbing his hands together.

Erika cleared her throat and said, "Ah, one of you would want not to get into much." She put her sunglasses on and continued, "Know what I'm sayin'?"

We all laughed.

"Anyway! See ya, babe." He kissed her and said, "I'll catch up to you later at the party."

"Okay."

I looked at Stacey and she turned her head to avoid eye contact. "See ya later, Stace."

"Ah yeah. See ya." She took Erika's arm and said, "C'mon, E. We gotta go."

"Okay. We'll see y'all later." Before Stacey pulled off, she gave me a quick glance. Then they were gone.

By eleven o'clock, we had gone to the step show and gotten kicked out because Myles was getting into it with some dude. I didn't even get to see Stacey and Erika do their thing with the Deltas. Needless to say, I was a little salty about that.

We did hit three or four parties around town killing time before heading to the Delta party. I wasn't really drunk but I was feeling mighty nice by the time we finally ended up at the Hilton downtown.

The room was packed. It had to be close to capacity, if not over. The party had started at ten o'clock so there was over an hour of sweat in the air. It was so dark in there that you could barely see your hand in front of your face. I was never one to dance too much at those parties. You could be getting your groove on with some female and then you get outside and she could be ugly as hell. So I wasn't trying to take any chances. Besides, standing near the deejay's table was the only person I wanted to dance with that night—Stacey. As I made my way toward her, our eyes met. Her smile told me she was glad to see me too.

"I didn't expect to see you here," Stacey said.

"And why not?"

"I just thought you would be hangin' with your boys."

"They're here. But," I moved closer to her, "I'd rather hang with you."

"Is that so?"

"Yeah. So where's your boyfriend?"

Stacey shrugged nonchalantly.

I was glad Pat wasn't around. In my state of mind at the time, I wouldn't have cared if he had been there. I would have probably still been all in Stacey's face.

"This next song goes out to all the lovers out there."

As "Before I Let You Go" by Blackstreet began, I took Stacey's hand. "Come and dance with me." Before she could say no, I pulled her out on the floor and slid my arms around her waist.

Stacey felt so good. I knew I was feeling good to her, too, because her body seemed to relax against mine. I closed my eyes and pictured us in my room, in my bed, making love. Before I knew it, I was kissing Stacey's neck. She kind of jumped but didn't stop me. After a few minutes, I guess she started getting a little nervous about it even though I knew she was enjoying it.

"Um, Ronnie, I don't think you should be doing that."

"Why? Don't you like it?" I whispered.

"I don't want to get caught up in no drama."

"It'll be alright. Your man ain't even here." Her protest, as slight as it was, ended.

Over the years, I admit, I had developed some smooth moves. For the most part they worked but Stacey was not having anything from me that night. I tried to move my hands toward her behind but she moved them back to her waist. I had to laugh.

"What are you laughing at?" she asked.

"You."

"Why?"

"Why'd you move my hands?"

She smiled and said, "Because they were where they weren't supposed to be."

"Is that so?"

"Yes, it is."

"Well I would beg to differ."

"You'll be alright."

I nodded.

"So, ah, is your man coming over later?" I inquired.

"Where did that come from?"

"It's just a question."

"I don't know. Doubt it. We had a little argument earlier," she revealed.

"Ah-ha."

"And what's all that for?" she asked.

I liked messing with Stacey about Pat, even though I knew it got on her nerves.

"I was just saying."

"Yeah, okay."

I whispered, "You know I'm just messing with you, girl. You better stop acting like that."

She sucked her teeth.

"You want me to stop?"

"Yes."

I rubbed against her slowly and kissed her on her neck again. "Do you want me to stop everything?" She swallowed hard but didn't answer. I knew what buttons to push with Stacey. "Well?" I asked.

"Yes," she answered, smiling, knowing she was lying.

"You sure now?"

"Just leave me alone, boy."

When the party started breaking up, I took Stacey's hand and we went outside. Everybody was just kind of hanging out. Even though it was almost two in the morning, people were trying to figure out where the next party was. Around homecoming there was no shortage of parties.

You could party from sun up to sun down. All I was trying to figure out was how to make some moves with Stacey.

Stacey was very apprehensive about people seeing us together. I wasn't ready for our time to end so I had to think of a way to get her away from the crowd.

"Aye, did I tell you I got a new truck?"

"No. When? What kind?" Stacey responded excitedly.

"Last week. A '99 4Runner," I stated proudly.

"Mmm, you a baller for real now."

"Go 'head wit' that. Anyway, you wanna see it?"

"Yeah, sure. Where is it?"

"A couple of blocks down."

"Okay."

I never parked my truck anywhere near a party because it was always something going down afterward. I had seen brothers get into fights and be all over people's rides. I wasn't trying to have that happen to my new truck so I parked a few blocks away. When we got to the truck, I leaned against its shiny black body and said, "So you like it?"

"Yeah, this is really nice, Ronnie."

"Thank you," I responded, staring at her. She turned her head, as usual. She hated me staring at her. Actually, I doubt that she hated it but she had to play the role.

"So, what are you getting ready to do?" I asked, moving the zipper up and down on her Delta Sigma Theta jacket.

"I don't know. Probably go home and go to bed."

"Mmm. That sounds like a plan. Can I come with you?"

"I don't think so. I think you need to go home and get some sleep."

I pulled her closer to me and put my arms around her waist. "Sleeping is the last thing on my mind right now." Stacey just looked at me. She knew I was serious. I kissed her softly and asked, "Do you want to know what's on my mind?"

"No. I don't think I want to know what's on your mind right now."

"You probably have an idea."

"Probably."

I ran my fingers through Stacey's hair. She had one of those nice layered short cuts. It was always laid. The girl was at the hairdresser every week, religiously. That was another thing I liked about her. She was a well-put-together sister. She was exactly the kind of woman I always wanted to get with. I wasn't ready to get married at that point but I had played around for three years. I was ready for a serious relationship again. The more I was around Stacey, the more I thought she might be the one to give me that relationship, despite her current situation with Pat.

"So you're not going to let me come home with you?" I asked. I really wanted to go home with her. I knew if I did, her celibacy would be history. I liked Stacey a lot but that didn't erase the fact that I most definitely wanted to get her in bed.

"I don't think so, Ronnie."

I nodded. "Well, how 'bout a little kiss before I take you back to your car?"

Stacey kind of looked around. "You know you want to." When Stacey kissed me, I knew I was right about that.

As I drove Stacey to her car, I kept thinking about what would happen if I ended up at her spot. I wanted her so bad; I had to give it one more shot.

"So you're absolutely sure you don't want me to come over tonight?" Stacey just laughed. "What you laughin' for? I'm just asking you a question."

"And I know why you're asking."

I pulled up beside her car and turned my hazard lights on. I looked at her and said, "Oh, you do? Why?"

"We both know why and that's exactly why you're not coming over."

"So you're saying if I did come over, some things might pop off?"

Stacey looked at me and kind of smiled. I knew what that meant.

"What I'm saying is, I really don't think it's a good idea for you to come to my house tonight."

"Because of Pat?" I asked sarcastically.

"Among other things."

"I still don't see what you see in that busta," I said, shaking my head.

"Let's not get into that again."

Her relationship was one topic she never wanted to get into with me because there was no way she could explain why she continued to stay with that punk. He was not all that. I guess he looked alright. He did have a lot of girls jocking him, probably more than Stacey knew about. But he was an asshole.

"I will see you later, Mr. Morgan. Thank you for the ride."

"You're very welcome, Ms. Jackson. I guess I'll go find my boys since you're not gonna let me come over."

"Well y'all have fun," Stacey replied with a devilish smile as she opened the door to the truck and got out.

We both knew she didn't want me to have but so much fun, because I knew for sure I didn't want her to be having any fun with Pat that night.

I didn't really feel like hanging out too much after Stacey left. I decided to head back to the crib and chill for the rest of the night. When I got home, Myles and Ced were already there with some female company. The last thing I wanted to do was explain to them why I was home alone, so I cut all conversation with them short and just went to my room.

As I took off my smoky smelling clothes, I couldn't believe I was in the house alone that damn early during homecoming—my last homecoming, no less.

I tried to go to sleep but between the girls downstairs talking, giggling and moaning, not to mention my preoccupation with Stacey, I really couldn't. I lay on my bed wondering what she was doing. Had Pat gone over to her crib? Could they be having sex right at that moment? Was he kissing her body the way I wanted to? Was he rubbing her breasts as softly as I would? Were her nails running up and down his back? Were her moans filling the room? The more I thought about it, the more aroused I became. Before I knew it, my hand was moving toward "Big Man." I couldn't believe it. I hadn't had to handle my own business in years. At least not since I was in high school, early high school at that. And I refused to go out like that. I forced myself to think about something else and finally fell asleep.

The homecoming game didn't start until noon, but me and the fellas were up on campus around ten-thirty. The weather was really nice. It was warm for October, around eighty degrees and sunny. We called ourselves getting on the yard early, but there were a lot of people out there. One thing I could say about students and alumni at Howard, they had mad school spirit despite the fact that we hadn't won a homecoming in the three years that I had been there.

Myles and Ced were chasing skirts, as usual. I was making my way toward the Deltas' favorite spot, looking for one soror in particular. There were a few Deltas around but Stacey and Erika weren't there yet.

After walking from one end of the stadium to the other, Myles spotted Stacey and 'em.

"Yo, man, there go your girl."

She wasn't my girl but I liked the way it sounded. We headed in their direction. Before we got over to them, Pat walked up to Stacey.

"That's her man?" Myles whispered. I just nodded.

"You should go over there and slip her the tongue and see what he does," Ced joked.

We all laughed hard because Ced had done that to a girl once. He was going out with this chick with a boyfriend while we were in high school. One day, her boyfriend came up to school and Ced saw them out near the track. That fool walked up to her and grabbed her head and started kissing her. Ol' boy almost had a fit. He was 'bout ready to jump in Ced's chest. We were falling all over the ground laughing. Needless to say, the girl didn't want anything to do with Ced after that. But he didn't care.

I watched Pat lead Stacey away from Erika. I remembered they had an argument the night before so I assumed he was trying to get back in. Stacey was leaning on a mailbox not really paying attention to what he was saying. You could tell he was pleading his case, begging and shit. Stacey was looking all over the place. She finally turned her head in my direction. I pulled my shades down and gave her a little wink. She tried not to smile, but she couldn't help it.

I was so busy looking at Stacey that I didn't even notice Erika walk up in my face. "What you lookin' at boy?" she said, snapping me back to reality.

"Get out my face, girl."

"Why you all over there?"

"Oh, you know why. What he talking 'bout?"

"He over there begging her to forgive him. They got in some kind of argument yesterday before we met y'all up at the frat house."

"Oh," I replied, looking back in Stacey and Pat's direction.

"Well, I'll see you guys later," Erika said as she headed inside the stadium. "Stacey, c'mon, girl," she yelled.

"I'm coming." She said her final words to Pat and started walking toward Erika.

Stacey was looking mighty cute. Of course she had on a red Delta T-shirt, but because it was so warm out, she had on some jean shorts. Now these weren't just regular jean shorts. These were, what I decided right then, my favorite jean shorts. They were cut off halfway up her thighs. Those big, beautiful legs were flawless. Ever since we hung out at Hains Point, I had been dreaming about getting those big legs around my back. I wasn't too concerned about the celibacy thing. I was pretty sure I could get her to change her mind on that. But there was the little problem of her having a boyfriend. But I decided if she didn't give a damn about him, why should I? I was going to get mine regardless.

I watched Stacey as she walked over to Erika. I realized that girls were pretty much the same whether they were twelve or twenty-two. They were silly, giggling creatures. Especially when it had something to do with the opposite sex. She and her friends knew I was watching. As they walked into the stadium, Stacey looked back over her shoulder and smiled. Right then, I knew she liked me watching.

I didn't see Stacey again that day. She went off with her sorors and my boys went back on the prowl. That night, we partied until dawn and the next afternoon I woke up with a hangover that was no joke. The fellas headed back to New York around three and I slept for the rest of the day.

Homecoming 1999 was pretty cool. I got a chance to just chill with my boys. We didn't talk about music all weekend. That felt good, but it also made me feel kind of guilty. If my music was the most important thing in my life, how could I not want to talk about it or work on it? I realized I could love my music but also have a life outside of it.

That weekend also gave me the opportunity to spend some more time with Stacey. And I found out that Stacey and I were on the same page as far as our relationship or potential relationship was concerned. She was a little scared to take it to the next level, but I would work on that. We were going to get together somehow. Pat's days were definitely numbered.

not another argument

"Where the hell have you been?"

"I'm sorry, Patrick. My class ran over."

"I have been sitting out here for damn near a half hour," he barked, angrily.

What the hell did he expect me to do? Tell my professor, "Could you please hurry up because my ever-growing pain-in-the-ass boyfriend is waiting for me?"

"Don't be having me waiting like that no more."

I couldn't believe he was going off like that. It wasn't like I was all that excited to see him anyway. My week had been going pretty shitty so far and the last thing I needed right then was for him to be tripping.

"Well next time, Patrick, why don't you just leave?" I snapped.

He looked at me like *What did you say to me?*

"Oh, don't think I won't."

At that point, I was wishing he would leave…for good.

"Don't start trippin', Stacey."

"I ain't the one trippin'. You are."

Things between Patrick and I had been very rocky as of late. His whole attitude was getting worse every day. The old Patrick was almost nonexistent. Now I was seeing the Patrick that everybody disliked. The "asshole," as Erika put it. It seemed like every time we were together, we ended up arguing about one thing or another.

"Anyway, since I had to wait so long for you, I gotta get to class myself. I'm out."

"Whatever."

Patrick grabbed my wrist and said, "What did you say?"

"Get off me."

"I asked you a question."

"And I said get off me," I said, attempting unsuccessfully to pull away.

He gripped my wrist tighter and pulled me in close to his body. The way he was holding me would have an onlooker thinking we were a couple sharing a loving moment but the reality was far from that.

The more I tried to loosen Patrick's grip, the tighter it became. He leaned his six foot three frame down and said, "You need to watch how you talk to me." There was something chilling in his voice.

He finally let me go and had the nerve to ask, "Don't I get a kiss goodbye?"

I turned my head without even acknowledging his question. I wasn't giving him shit. He forcefully turned my head back to him and said, "Do not ignore me, Stacey." I tried to turn my head again but he held it in place.

"You hear me?"

"Yes," I answered reluctantly through clenched teeth.

"Now—where's my kiss?"

I half-assed kissed him then he just walked away.

I was so mad I didn't know what to do. I threw my bag on the ground and sat on the bench. Who the hell did he think he was? Demanding shit. I was so pissed that I didn't even see Ronnie sit down beside me.

"Hey, Stace. What's up?"

I looked at him and said, "Oh, hey, Ronnie."

"What's wrong?"

"Nothing."

"Are you sure?" he questioned.

"It's nothing. Just Patrick getting on my nerves again," I said.

"You want to talk about it?"

"Not really."

"You sure?"

"Ronnie, I'm not trying to be rude or anything like that, but I'm not really in the mood to talk." I didn't mean to be like that toward him but I really didn't feel like talking about Patrick right then.

"So what did he do to you this time?" he asked sarcastically.

Did I or did I not just say I didn't want to talk about it? I thought. For the first time in months, I was not feeling Ronnie.

"I said I don't want to talk to about it," I snapped.

"You never do. I mean he's always trippin' but you never want to talk about it. Naw, that's not exactly true because sometimes you will talk about it, but when that happens, all you do is make excuses for him."

Ronnie did have a point there. Patrick had really started bugging. He was starting to get more and more aggressive, and I was always making excuses for his behavior. But I still resented Ronnie saying anything about it. It was nobody's business but mine.

"You know you don't deserve to be treated like that," he continued to rant.

"I don't want to hear it, Ronnie."

"You need to hear it. I mean you keep letting him do that shit. You know he don't treat you right but yet and still you just take it." Now he was snapping at me.

I couldn't believe what I was hearing. Where did Ronnie get off talking to me like that? He didn't know anything about what was going on. He didn't know everything Patrick and I had been through with my pregnancy and the abortion, then Patrick's mom dying and his father not being there for him. Patrick always said, "You are the only good thing in my life now, Stacey. Since my mom died, you're the only person I can really count on. I don't know what I would do without you." It might be silly but I really believed him. Patrick felt like when his mother died, he lost both his parents. No matter how much we argued, I didn't want him to feel like I was leaving him too. I didn't have any romantic feelings for him anymore, but I did still care about him.

I refused to sit there and listen to Ronnie go off on me like that. I picked up my bag and he said, "Oh, so you gonna run away?"

"I'm not running away from anything." I wasn't running away, I was walking.

"You keep on running, Stace. Maybe you'll run into a man who's going to treat you right."

I wanted to look back but I refused. I wasn't going to give him the satisfaction. What was going on between me and Patrick was really none of Ronnie's business anyway.

We had actually been doing okay before our trip to New Jersey the weekend before. Once we walked in the house, Patrick's demeanor changed. He was normally very confident but he seemed to shrink around his father.

Mr. Smith was sitting in the living room watching the evening news and before we got in the door good, he started in on Patrick.

"I thought you said you were going to be here by four." He looked at his diamond encrusted watch and said, "It's damn near six."

Patrick rolled his eyes and turned towards me. He asked, "You want something to drink?" ignoring his father's comment.

"Ah yeah, some water is fine."

"Alright." He rolled his eyes at his father again and walked out.

I knew right then it was going to be a long weekend. I sat on the couch across from Mr. Smith and he said, "And how are you Ms. Stacey?" His tone of voice was pleasant.

"Um, I'm doing good."

"How's school going so far this semester?"

"So far, so good."

He laughed.

When Patrick walked back in, Mr. Smith's smile faded. Patrick handed me a bottle of water and I said, "Thank you."

He nodded and joined me on the couch.

"Do I even need to ask how school's going for you so far," Mr. Smith snapped at Patrick.

He didn't respond. He just stared at the television. I glanced at Mr. Smith not knowing what to do.

"All I know is, those grades better be up this semester or that's a wrap for you."

Patrick took my hand in his and gently rubbed it, still staring at the television. I think he wanted me to come home with him more because he didn't want to be there alone with his father.

Mr. Smith always played poker with his brothers on Friday night so when he left, Patrick ordered us some pizza and we just chilled the rest of the night. Early the next morning, we got up and went to his mother's gravesite.

I had attended his mother's funeral but the headstone wasn't there at the time. But now there was a large marble headstone. It was inscribed with her full name, Patricia Anne Smith and described her as a "faithful wife" and "loving mother." Until that day, I didn't realize how young she was when she died. She had just turned forty-two.

Patrick bought some cal lilies and set them on the headstone. I wanted to give him a little quiet time so I went and sat on a bench under a large oak tree nearby. After a few minutes, Patrick joined me on the bench.

He took my hand and said, "Thank you for coming up here with me." He kissed me on the cheek. "I really appreciate it."

"You don't have to thank me."

Patrick nodded and looked back at his mother's headstone. We sat there for a while longer then went back to his house. I spent the rest of the weekend being the buffer between Patrick and his father. Mr. Smith didn't get on his case as much while I was around.

As I walked back to my car, I started resenting Ronnie's tone more and more. What gave him the right to talk to me like that anyway? Yeah he was fine but not that damn fine.

> *November 17, 1999 - 7:14 p.m.*
> *Patrick and I got into it again today. Ever since we got back from Jersey, he's been acting like an asshole. I was a little late meeting him after class and he threw a fit. He thinks this whole world revolves around him. Like I don't have shit else to do in my life but be there for him. Then to top everything off, Ronnie like bombed me out about Patrick not treating me right. I don't know what...*

I was venting in my journal when the buzzer for the front door broke my concentration. I knew it wasn't Patrick because he always tried to stay away after we got into it. I reached over and grabbed the TV remote control off the end table. I pressed three. I loved living in a building with security cameras in the lobby. That way if I didn't want someone to know I was home, they didn't.

I looked at the TV and to my surprise, there was Ronnie standing in the lobby impatiently waiting for me to answer his buzz.

I sat there gazing at my twenty-seven-inch TV. He looked so good, even in black-and-white. But, what did he want? To bomb me out some more? I picked up the phone and pressed the star button to connect to the lobby intercom.

I said, "Hey," trying my best not to sound excited to see him.

"Hey. Um, are you busy?" he asked as he looked directly into the camera.

"No, come on up."

Even though he had kind of cursed me out earlier, I was still happy he was there. I actually had been thinking about him a lot lately, probably too much.

I ran to the hall mirror. I had to check to make sure my 'do was alright. My weekly hair appointment was a few days off but the coif still looked good.

I cracked the door to my apartment for him and quickly went back in the living room. A minute later, I heard the front door shut. Ronnie walked into the living room and my heart skipped a beat. That boy could definitely make an entrance.

"Hey," he repeated in his soft, low voice.

"Hey."

I pretended I was still writing in my journal but I kept glancing over the top of the book watching Ronnie sit on the edge of the chair looking at the TV.

After a few minutes, I asked, "So, what's up?" Ronnie looked at me and said, "I just dropped by to talk to you."

"Oh," I nodded. "Okay." I waited for him to continue, but silence fell over the room again.

The weather had made a dramatic change from a couple of weeks before. Around homecoming it had been rather warm, especially for October. But this night must have been kind of cold out because Ronnie had on a black leather jacket. It fit him perfectly too. Everything fit him perfectly. Those broad shoulders of his were about to drive me out of my mind.

"You can take your jacket off, you know," I said, breaking the second wave of silence.

Ronnie smiled as he took off his jacket and laid it across the chair. He took off his Atlanta Braves cap and set it on top of his jacket. He sat down and brushed his hands over the front of his pants, as he did every time he sat down. Ronnie hated wrinkles in his pants.

Ronnie was looking very nice in his Tommy Hilfiger shirt, jeans and Timberland boots. I could feel myself beginning to stare at him so I turned my head toward the television. After a few minutes of yet more silence, I finally had to ask the brother if he had come all the way across town to just sit there.

"Naw, there are some other things I could be doing if you would like me to," was his response with that sexy smile of his. I looked at him and tried to act like I didn't know what he was talking about. But I did. When I really thought about it, I had some other things he could be doing also.

Ronnie slowly moved beside me, and my heart started pounding so hard that I thought it was going to jump out of my chest.

"Now, I do have some ideas about what I could be doing with my lips."

"Ronnie." He didn't need to be tempting me like that.

"Naw, on the serious tip, I just wanted to apologize for this afternoon. I was out of line."

"Don't worry about it."

"Naw, I'm saying, I meant e'erything I said but I shouldn't have come at you like that. You were already upset and I didn't help the situation any. So I'm sorry."

"Like I said don't worry about it."

"I do want to ask you something though." His voice lowered as he turned toward me. "Why do you let Pat do that to you?" I knew Ronnie wouldn't understand my situation so I just sat in silence.

"Don't you have an answer?"

"Ronnie, I don't feel like getting into this with you again."

"Oh, but you are getting ready to get into this with me, again." His tone was very serious. It kind of took me back. He had never spoken to me like that before.

I knew Patrick wasn't treating me right. Lord, did I know it. But I was handling the situation myself—the best way I could at that point.

"You don't deserve to be treated like that, Stacey." Ronnie's tone changed to his normal soft, gentle voice.

"Look, Ronnie, I can handle it. It's no big deal."

"He's not giving you what you need." He took my hand and inter-locked his fingers with mine. He began rubbing his thumb softly across the palm of my hand.

The first time a guy did that to me was when I was a freshman in high school. Keith Anderson was my first real crush. He was a junior, and I thought the sun rose and set with him. Every time he touched my hand, he rubbed my palm. Eventually, I asked him what it meant. That's when he told me it meant he wanted to have sex with me. That never happened and he moved onto his next freshman. Keith was the first to do it but not the last. But when Ronnie did it, a chill ran from the back of my neck to the tips of my toes. I kind of lost my breath for a moment. He was really making me rethink my whole celibacy thing.

"What are you talking about?" The words barely came out of my mouth.

Ronnie kissed my neck softly and it felt very nice. I remembered how good it felt when we were dancing at homecoming.

"Oh, you know exactly what I mean."

"Um, Ronnie, stop."

"Why?" That was a very good question.

"What about Patrick?"

"What about him? It's not like you love him."

Even though I knew that was true for some reason, I got up. "How do you know?"

"So you're telling me that you love Pat?"

"I'm saying, how do you know I don't love him?"

"I don't know. That's why I'm asking you." He looked at me and asked, "Do you love him?"

"Ronnie, you don't…."

"The answer is either yes or no."

"It's not that simple."

"Oh, yes it is." He walked up to me and said, "Have you ever thought that you might need somebody else in your life?" He rubbed my cheek. "Someone who would treat you right."

"Didn't you say you knew someone like that?"

"I most definitely do."

Those dark brown eyes did something to me. My heart was beating so fast and hard that I just knew Ronnie could hear it. When he kissed my neck again, I was just about through. My inner thighs began to heat up. I could not believe my body was betraying me like that. It wasn't my body that was betraying me, but my head was betraying my body. My body knew instinctively what to do when it was near Ronnie. It was my head that needed some working on.

I had never put myself in that type of situation before. That's exactly why I didn't let him come home with me that night during homecoming. I knew what would have happened. I had had a couple of drinks and Ronnie had been drinking too. I didn't want to be in a situation where I wasn't in control. This time though, there had been no drinking. I couldn't blame anything that was happening or about to happen on alcohol. I was supposed to be in control. But it was becoming more and more evident to me that I was losing all control where Ronnie was concerned.

"You need somebody who's going to treat you right in more ways than one." Ronnie's voice had a hypnotic effect on me. He kept kissing on my neck. I closed my eyes and found myself really enjoying his soft kisses. I was enjoying it a hell of a lot. But something snapped me back to my reality. I couldn't let things get further out of control.

"Um, Ronnie, you really gotta stop this."

He wanted to know why. I really didn't have a good reason. I just felt like that's what I was supposed to say.

"I'm not going to be able to explain a hickey on my neck to Patrick." That sounded stupid once it left my mouth.

He looked at me and smiled slyly. "Well we'll just have to do something he won't be able to see."

"As in?"

He kissed me softly and said, "As in this." Then he kissed me again.

"Ronnie, I shouldn't be doing this."

"You know you want to, don't you?"

I took a deep breath and said, "Yes but…" He slid his arms around my waist and said, "Well then." He was so smooth. Before I knew it, we were kissing.

Kissing Ronnie was so nice. It was nothing like kissing Patrick. Though he would beg to differ, Patrick did not know how to kiss at all. Since he liked to think of himself as "the man" he always seemed to be trying to prove something. But Ronnie knew he was the man. Not even the man but, a man, period. He knew how to treat a woman. He knew how to gently touch my face. How to softly lick my lips. I wondered how he learned all that. Regardless of how, I was just glad he had.

Right when I was starting to really get into it, the phone rang. I didn't want to answer it but I had to in case it was Patrick.

"I gotta answer that," I said, slowly pushing Ronnie back.

"Let it ring," he begged.

"I can't."

Trying to quickly catch my breath, I picked up the phone. And just as I thought, it was Patrick.

"What are you doing?"

I was never that good at lying. It always made me nervous. That's why Tracy always had to do all the lying when we were little. So when I answered, "Ah, nothing," I knew he wouldn't believe me.

"Why you lying?"

"Patrick, I'm not doing anything but watching TV and getting ready to get my stuff together for tomorrow."

"Yeah, okay."

I felt Ronnie's body pressing up against me from behind. He started kissing on my neck. I closed my eyes. I forgot all about Patrick being on the phone.

"Stacey—Stacey! Stacey, what the hell are you doing?" Patrick yelled.

I was all into Ronnie and his soft lips on my neck that I hadn't even heard Patrick calling my name.

"Oh, ah, I'm sorry. I was um…looking at TV."

"I don't give a damn about your little I'm sorry."

It was crazy but Patrick's nasty tone didn't bother me. What was irritating me was the fact that he was interrupting what was going on with Ronnie. Patrick was knocking my groove with Mr. Morgan.

"You would want to get yourself together." On that note, I wasn't trying to waste any more time with him.

"Look, I gotta go."

"Why?"

"Because I have stuff to do. I'll talk to you later."

Before he had a chance to say another word, I hung up.

Ronnie turned me around and without saying a word we resumed our kissing. He took the handset from me and turned the ringer off so there would be no more interruptions from the asshole. Then he turned the lights off and laid me on the couch.

Patrick always felt like a ton of bricks when we lay on the couch like that, but Ronnie's two-hundred-thirty-pound frame didn't feel heavy at all. As he started kissing on my neck again, I felt his hand moving toward my shirt. I couldn't believe what was happening. It felt like everything was moving in slow motion, like I was dreaming.

This scene had played in my head almost every night since the first time I laid eyes on Ronnie; before I even knew his name. The one big difference was there wasn't a boyfriend in my dream.

Was I getting ready to cheat on Patrick? Kissing Ronnie in the first place was cheating technically but what Ronnie's hand was leading to was definitely cheating. I realized he was unbuttoning my shirt when I felt the air hit my stomach. I wasn't stopping him. In fact, I wanted to help him.

When I felt his hand on my breast, it seemed like my body went limp. As Ronnie's fingers gently massaged by breast through my lace bra, I could feel my temperature rising. At that point, every inch of my being wanted him, but I knew that was more than I could handle right then. I wanted to resolve my issues with Patrick before going there with Ronnie. Right then, I decided Ronnie would be the one I gave my "born-again" virginity to. But when I gave myself to him, I wanted no distractions. My situation with Patrick was a definite distraction.

I knew I was going to regret it but I couldn't let things go any further. I pulled his hand down and sat up.

"Stop, Ronnie."

"What's wrong?" he asked, breathing hard from his excitement.

"I can't do this." I wanted him more than he would ever know. "I just can't. At least not right now."

He rubbed his lips. Those soft, sexy lips. Again, looking at him, I knew for sure that I was going to regret what I was doing or wasn't doing for that matter.

"Okay. I, ah, know you made a conscience decision not to have sex. I didn't mean to push."

"You weren't pushing. It's just that…."

He interrupted me with a kiss. "Don't worry. I will definitely wait."

I knew that it was time for him to leave. If he stayed one more second, I was going to stop trying to convince myself not to sleep with him.

"You really have to go, Ronnie."

"What, you don't trust yourself?" he asked, teasing. Didn't he know what he was doing to me?

"No, I really don't," I answered honestly.

He looked kind of surprised at my answer. That was probably the first time that I had ever been that straightforward with him.

He nodded. "Okay."

He pulled me up and started slowly buttoning my shirt from the bottom. I saw him kind of shake his head. He had to be thinking, *I cannot believe I'm standing here helping this girl get dressed, and I ain't even get none.*

"Well at least I got to see your elephant tattoo. I guess I'm one of those certain people now, huh?"

"I guess so."

He ran his finger across my tattoo and said, "It's cute."

"Thank you."

As I walked Ronnie to the door, I was still wondering if I was doing the right thing. I knew with everything in my being that cheating was wrong but was I turning away someone who I was really beginning to have strong feelings for, to try and be there for someone I wasn't really sure gave a damn about me or anything else anymore? Well, I wasn't going to find out that night.

"Give me a call later," Ronnie said, rubbing my arms.

"Okay."

"A'ight then, Stace."

"Bye."

He pressed his soft lips against mine one last time and left.

November 17, 1999 - 10:30 p.m.

I can't believe what just happened. Ronnie came over to apologize about what happened between us earlier, and before I knew it we were on the couch kissing. I can honestly say that things were getting ready to go to that next level. But me being the dumb ass that I am, I stopped it. I can't believe how stupid I am. Ronnie Morgan, fine-as-can-be Ronnie Morgan was in my living room, on my couch, kissing me, undoing my shirt, wanting to have sex with me and me wanting to have sex with him but I stopped it. I have to be losing what's left of my mind.

This situation is getting very sticky. Before it was all fun and games. The two of us flirting with each other, just trippin'. But now it seems like playtime is over as far as Ronnie's concerned. He made it clear tonight that he wants more. I don't know if I did the right thing but I think I made it clear to him that I want more also but just not right now. Well, when? I don't know. I guess this is just one more moment with Ronnie that I won't forget anytime soon

I hate to admit it, but sometimes I wonder if Ronnie is the dog that everybody says he is. The way I'm starting to feel about him, I would probably—no definitely—be devastated if he was just out for "the goodies" as he puts it. I can't even think about that though.

*He can't be. Then again it's kind of messed up but I would prob-
ably still give him some.*

All night I tossed and turned thinking about Ronnie. I needed to talk
to someone so, of course, I called Erika. You know you have to be tight
with someone to call them at two-thirty in the morning. Once she picked
up the phone, I could tell by her breathing that I had interrupted something.

"Um, Stacey girl, I'll call you back in a half." That girl was a sex fiend.

Erika and Dave were really getting serious. She said they had even
talking about getting married after we graduated. I couldn't believe it.
Erika was the one who never wanted to get married. "Why should I get
married? I'd probably end up getting divorced. Besides, I love men too
much to be with just one." Well, I guess Dave changed her mind on that
one. Truthfully though, they had the perfect relationship, well as perfect as
they get. Though I hated to admit it, I was kind of jealous. I wanted
someone like Dave in my life. Not that I wanted to get married any time
soon, but I wanted a good man. I really believed Ronnie was a good man,
but why in the world was I still wasting my time and energy on Patrick?

By the time Erika called back, I was almost sleep. "Sorry, girl, but you
know how it is. I was in the middle of something."

"Yeah, I know what you were in the middle of…freak mama."

"Anyway, what's up?" Erika said, laughing.

"First, is Dave around?"

"Naw, he's in the bedroom, knocked out."

"Oh, okay." I took a deep breath. "Erika, girl…."

"What's wrong?"

"Ronnie came over here earlier."

"Oh, really now? And what did he want?"

"Well Patrick and I got in another argument on the Quad and Ronnie
was there. So after Patrick went to class, Ronnie started in on me about
Patrick not treating me right."

"For real?"

"Yeah, and I wasn't really in the mood so I left. Then he came over to
apologize for the way he came at me."

"Well, that was cool."

"Yeah."

I never kept any secrets from Erika. The only thing I didn't really tell her about was how Patrick was starting to get a little more aggressive when we would get into arguments. Erika would be ready to fight so I just decided to keep it to myself. Erika had her share of drama with men so she could understand what I was going through.

Though I had called her, I wasn't really talking.

"Stace, is that all?" she asked.

"Well…."

"C'mon, girl, out with it. What's up?"

"First, I have to tell you about homecoming."

"Homecoming? What about it? I can't believe you've been holding out on me."

"You remember when Ronnie and I went for the ride on the bike?"

"Yeah."

"Well we rode down to Rock Creek Park. We were just chillin' down there for a while, and…."

"And what? Would you stop beating around the bush and just tell me?"

"And we kissed again."

"Mmm, girl. You and Mr. Morgan are getting more and more friendly, aren't you?"

"I don't know what's going on, girl. Every time I'm around him, I start buggin'."

"My, my, my. Now you know if this was me you would be trippin' off me, wouldn't you?"

"I know. Then there was the party."

"What happened at the party?"

"We were dancing and chitchatting, and girl, he was rubbing against me and, let me tell you, I was about to fall out."

Erika laughed and said, "Mmm, you had my man getting a little excited."

"You know. That's the same thing that happened when we went out to the club that first time. So anyway, after the party, we were outside just talking. And that was right after he got his new truck so he took me to see it. He kept asking if he could come over but I was like 'ah hell naw.'"

"Why?"

"Because one, we both had had a few drinks and two, if he came back here, I knew something was really going to go down."

"You think so? You've held out this long."

"E, let me tell you, I know it would have happened. Even after I said no to him, we were kissing and, girl, he was changing my mind. And after what happened tonight."

"What happened? You didn't…did you?"

"No, I didn't, but I was so close. We were lying on the couch kissing, and the next thing I knew, my shirt was unbuttoned."

"You slut!" Erika said, laughing. The girl was so stupid.

"I know. Can you believe it? That's why, as much as I knew I would regret it, I told him he had to get up out of here."

"I know that brother was mad. He probably just knew he was about to get all up in that piece."

"Naw, he was really cool about it. More than I thought he would be. You know brothers ain't down for the blue balls. But he said he would wait for me."

"Mmm. Well now you know what's on his mind for sure."

"I think I've known that for a while."

Ronnie was not the type to play games. I laughed off a lot of his small advances but I knew he was for real. I didn't know just how serious until that night.

"So, what are you going to do, Stace?" Erika asked.

I didn't know what I was going to do. If I knew that, I would've done it by then. That was why I had her on the phone at three something in the morning. I needed her to tell me what I should do, like she had so many other times in our lives. I needed to know what she thought.

"What do you think I should do? I'm so confused."

"Well I think you need to figure out what's going on. I mean do you want to stay with Pat? Are you trying to really get with Ronnie or what? Or is this just a sex thing?"

"I don't know. I've never been in this situation before. This is one of your little triangles."

"And you know it's nothing but trouble. I mean you can have your little fun with Ronnie if you want to but I want you to make sure you cover your ass. You know I got your back but we both know if Pat finds out, it's going to be mad drama."

"I know. The thing is I don't know if I want just a little fun with

Ronnie. I think I'm really starting to like him."

"More than Pat?"

"Sometimes I don't know if I even like Patrick at all anymore. Things with him are just so crazy."

"Mmm, don't tell me you're goin' from no drama to a drama queen."

"Go to hell."

Erika knew how to ease my mind when I got worked up. I finally felt like I could get some sleep.

"Look, girl, I'm getting ready to go to bed. I'll talk to you tomorrow," I said, yawning.

"Alright."

"Thanks."

"No problem."

When I hung up, I looked at the clock. It was three-thirty. That meant it was twelve-thirty in Phoenix. My brother never went to bed before one so I decided to give him a call.

"What's up, baby girl?" Tracy said, answering on the first ring.

"Hey, sweetie."

"What you doing up this late?   Something wrong?"

"No. I just called. I haven't talked to you in a few days."

"Are you sure, Stacey?"

"Can't I call my brother if I want to?"

"Yeah, I guess so."

Tracy knew I wasn't being straight up with him but he wasn't going to push the issue. I wanted to talk to him about everything that was going on but I couldn't. Instead, we talked about his internship, my classes and all the women he was going out with. By the time we hung up an hour later, even though I didn't tell him about Ronnie and Patrick, I felt better. Just talking to him made everything alright for the time being.

listen to my music

stacey

School was really been kicking my tail this semester. I couldn't wait until Thanksgiving break came. Between my classes, all my extra curricula activities, my family, Erika, and giving Ronnie more and more of my time, not to mention the mess I had going on with Patrick, a sister was about to have a breakdown.

Things with Patrick continued to spin out of control. After seeing first hand how things were between him and his father, I had been trying to be there for him a little more. I admit, since Ronnie came into the picture, Patrick and his feelings haven't been a priority for me. But I knew this was a hard time for him so I decided to put in a little more effort. So when he said he wanted to see me before he left, I agreed.

He borrowed his frat brother's car and came over. There was a time when Patrick and I could talk for hours, but things had changed considerably. We just sat in the living room watching TV. I was so tired that I kept dozing off.

"Stacey," Patrick yelled.

"What?" I snapped back.

"I come all the way over here and your ass is falling asleep."

"I'm tired. I mean, shit, you just watching TV."

"What the hell else am I supposed to do? It ain't like you trying to give up no booty."

I opened my eyes slowly and just stared at him. If looks could kill his punk-ass would have been done.

He said, "Am I right?"

"Whatever."

"Yeah, that's what I thought."

I sucked my teeth and got up.

"And where are you going," he asked.

I headed to the kitchen to get some Tylenol because he was giving me a headache. I heard his footsteps quickly coming behind me.

"Stacey, you hear me talking to you?"

"Yeah I heard you," I quipped.

"I told you before don't be ignoring me."

I said, "Whatever," and the next thing I know, I saw something out the corner of my eye. It turned out to be his hand. When he hit my face, I swear I saw stars.

I always said if some nigga ever laid his hand on me, I would try my best to knock the shit out of him. But when this happened, I guess I went into shock. It took a minute for it to register that Patrick had just hit me. I don't know why I was so surprise it happened though. When I really think about it, our arguments were leading more and more in that direction.

The whole side of my face was throbbing. He had slapped the shit out of me! I didn't cry but it hurt so bad that my eyes started watering. I just looked at him in shock.

"Oh my God Stacey, I'm sorry," he had the nerve so say.

I didn't even acknowledge his apology. I continued on into the kitchen. I put some ice in a Ziploc bag and gently placed it against my cheek. I leaned on the sink wondering how the hell I let my life get so out of control.

Patrick walked in after me and said, "Stacey."

I didn't respond.

He put his hand on my back and I moved from his touch.

"For real Stacey, I am so, so sorry. I don't know what came over me. I promise it will never happen again."

I still didn't respond.

"I'm ah—I'm gonna go," he sighed. I guess he finally got the picture.

It wasn't until I heard the apartment door shut, that I went back into the living room. I returned to my seat on the couch and turned the TV to channel three to view the front lobby. Once I saw Patrick leave the building, the real tears began to fall.

I fell asleep right there on the couch with my homemade ice pack still on my face. The phone ringing startled me out of my much needed slumber. I reached for the handset and looked at the Caller ID. It was Patrick. I definitely wasn't going to talk to his ass. Though I had wished the earlier incident was all a bad dream, my numb cheek reminded me otherwise.

After my answering machine greeting finished, Patrick started apologizing again for hitting and promising it would never happen again. He begged me to pick up. When I didn't after a few minutes, he gave up and ended the call.

I returned the receiver to its cradle. I needed to talk to someone but I could never tell Erika what happened because she would go crazy, but not as crazy as Kevin or Dev. And I didn't even want to think about Tracy finding out. He would kill Patrick. I decided I would just deal with it myself. There was no need to get everyone in a big uproar over something that happened in the heat of the moment. Patrick *did* apologize and say it would never happen again. So I was going to leave it alone.

I woke up the next day, still feeling run down. I figured I just needed some peace and quiet. I wanted to stay in and relax for the whole break. But just like always, whenever I laid down to chill, my phone started ringing off the hook.

First, my mother called making sure I was going to be home at exactly one o'clock the next day to help her get everything together. Then, one of my sorors from Atlanta needed a ride to the airport. I was ready to unplug the phone when it rang again.

"Hello," I sighed.

"Hey. How you doing, Stace?" No matter how tired I was, I didn't mind Ronnie calling.

"Hey. What's up?"

"What you doin' tonight?"

"Nothing. Patrick's gone home for Thanksgiving, so I figured I would just chill."

"Oh, well I know I've been promising to let you hear some of my music so I was thinking if you wanted to come over, I'd play some for you."

"Ah yeah. I would like that. I'll be over in about two hours. I gotta take one of my girls to the airport."

"Cool. I'll see you later."

"Alright."

As I headed to Ronnie's from Reagan National Airport, I tried to figure out why I was feeling guilty. It wasn't like I was in this nice, loving relationship and I just decided to be with someone else. I wouldn't even call what Patrick and I had a relationship anymore. It was more like a big mess.

It felt like the whole world knew what I was about to do. The thing was I didn't even know. It seemed like every time I turned to a radio station, there was a song on about cheating. *Secret Lovers. My Little Secret.* I really didn't need to hear that right then. Finally, I just turned the radio off.

I thought the silence would be better but it wasn't. That just gave me more time to think about what almost happened between Ronnie and me a couple of weeks before.

Each turn that got me closer to Ronnie's house made my heart beat a little faster. By the time I made it up the steps to his front door, I was nearly hyperventilating. I took a deep breath and said, "Alright, girl, calm yourself down." I rang the doorbell. A few seconds later, I heard Ronnie's voice from behind the door.

"Who is it?"

I swallowed hard and said, "Stacey."

The door opened and my heart started beating fast again. Ronnie was standing there with his jeans fitting loosely around his waist. He had on a denim shirt, which was outside his pants and his trademark white wife-beater T-shirt underneath that was hugging his muscular chest and abs perfectly. He was looking finer than usual. I didn't know it was even possible. But it was true.

He didn't have on shoes or socks, and I noticed how pretty his feet were. I had never seen a guy with nice feet, especially an athlete. It amazed me that everything about this boy was so perfect. There had to be something wrong or flawed with him. I couldn't imagine what it could possibly be though.

That was my first time ever being inside Ronnie's house. I had dropped him off a few times but whenever he invited me in, I came up with an excuse not to go. The whole house was nicely decorated. Ronnie said his sister and mother had a lot to do with that. After he moved in, they came down for a week and hooked him up.

The house was one of those old three-story brownstones that his father bought and had remodeled. Ronnie said if he didn't stay in D.C. when he graduated, his dad was going to rent it out.

Ronnie's bedroom was actually the entire third floor. The space use to have three bedrooms and a bathroom up there but when it was remodeled, all the walls were torn out and it was converted into one large space. It was really nice. African art was hanging from every wall. There was a gas fireplace directly across from Ronnie's king-size bed, which sat in the middle of the room. I always figured he'd have a king-size bed. When you're six-five, you do need a little space when you're sleeping. Beside his bed was a state-of-the-art entertainment system. There was a black leather couch in front of the fireplace with a mud-cloth throw hanging over the back. The plush area rug in front of the couch looked like it would feel so good under my bare feet.

It was all very cozy and romantic. All those hoochies on campus probably would have gone out of their minds if they saw it. Ronnie said he never brought any girls to his house. He didn't like a lot of people in his personal space. That made me feel kind of special.

Ronnie had incense burning on both of the black nightstands that flanked the bed.

"What kind of incense is that?" I asked, inhaling the aroma.

"Black Love."

At that moment, my mind began wandering in a direction that, for a person with a boyfriend who was standing in another man's bedroom, was very dangerous. I could just see myself lying on that bed. That was my cue to move toward the door.

"So, ah, do I get to hear some music or what?"

Ronnie laughed and said, "Alright, let's go down in the basement."

The basement was full of electronic equipment. I had never seen anything like it before. It looked like a recording studio or something.

"Where did you get all this stuff from?"

Ronnie sat down behind some keyboards and said, "My dad got most of it for me."

"Mmm, must be nice."

He smiled.

I sat down and picked up a photo album that was sitting on the glass coffee table. It was full of headshots he and the guys had taken to send out with their demos. I had to admit, all those brothers were fine.

"Entice is a good name for this group," I commented.

"Why you say that?"

"'Cause I'm saying, y'all could entice a sister to do some things."

"Don't be sitting there creamin' over my boys."

I smiled and said, "One of you is a little more enticing to me than the others." I could tell by the way Ronnie licked his lips and smiled that he liked my flirting.

"What you blushin' for, boy?" He just laughed. He started playing a melody and asked, "So what do you want to hear?"

"I don't know," I said, putting the book back on the table.

"Well I'll play you some of the songs I wrote."

I didn't even know he wrote music. In fact, I didn't know he played the piano and the drums. He had never mentioned that before. Ronnie's music seemed to be a very personal and private part of him. A part that he didn't share with many people. I was touched that he wanted to share that with me.

The very first note that came from his mouth almost took my breath away. Ronnie didn't look like a singer. He looked like a ball player. Dave always told us about him walking around the locker room singing before and after practice. But that didn't prepare me for what I was hearing.

He had one of those smooth, silky voices like Brian McKnight that was made to sing love songs. I could see him on stage with no shirt on, singing to a crowd of screaming, out-of-control women. There would be panties, bras and hotel room keys flying through the air landing at his feet. As I sat there staring at him, I could see myself being one of those women.

"I wrote a song with you in mind." That made me kind of nervous.

"It's called—" he looked at me—"Not Good Enough." Like I didn't know he was referring to my situation with Patrick.

While he was singing, I was wishing so badly that I could run out of the room but it seemed as though his voice had some kind of control over my legs and wouldn't allow me to leave.

"So what you think?"

"I, ah, I liked it."

"You see why I wrote it with you in mind?"

"Um, yeah, I think so."

He nodded and kept tinkling on the keyboard. Neither one of us said anything for what seemed like hours but actually was only a couple of minutes. The lyrics to the song kept ringing in my head.

"I have one more song I want you to hear. We just finished working on this one the last time I went home. The name of it is 'Stay Here.'"

Now that song was one that you put on when you want to get someone in the mood for a little som'thing, som'thing. Talking about slowly undressing, laying you down, and hands tracing your body. As he sang, he never took his eyes off me. I felt beads of sweat starting to form on my forehead. I was praying that he couldn't see them.

"So?" he said in a soft voice, "how'd you like that one?"

"Oh, ah," I really didn't know what to say. "I liked that one too."

"Why don't you?"

"Why don't I what?" I asked with a confused look on my face.

"Stay here," he said, continuing to play the keyboard. I knew I couldn't be hearing him right. Was he really asking me to stay the night with him?

"What?"

"Don't act like you didn't hear me."

"Oh, I heard you but I don't understand what you're asking."

"Okay," he said, getting up and walking toward me.

It seemed as if he was moving in slow motion. He sat beside me and said, "I want you to stay with me tonight." I had wanted to hear Ronnie say that from the very first time I saw him.

We had just finished unloading Tracy's things in Carver Hall, freshman year. As Tracy and I were walking back to the car, Ronnie and his dad rode past in a black Lexus. The car is what initially caught my eye. It was sweet. But then the car stopped and this tall, fine brother got out. Tracy was mad because I almost dropped the box I had in my hands when I saw Ronnie emerge. No matter how fine he was then, he had gotten even finer as each year went by. But what he was asking wasn't possible.

"Ronnie, I can't stay here with you."

"Why?"

"What do you mean why? What about Patrick?"

"Stacey, c'mon now. We've been over all this before. It's not like you love Pat." I felt his finger running up and down my arm. The goose bumps weren't far behind. "And it's not like you don't want me as much as I want you. I mean we've been playing this game with each other since this summer. Now, I think it's time to stop playing."

He began kissing on my neck and that familiar chill went up my spine. He moved closer and whispered in my ear, "Stay the night with me, Stace." The kissing on my neck and the sexy voice in my ear, how was I expected to resist all that? Patrick was in Jersey. I was alone with Ronnie in his house. The more I thought about it, I knew I had to take my ass home and fast.

"I gotta go, Ronnie." I got up and headed toward the steps.

"Let me ask you something, Stacey," Ronnie said, leaning back on the couch. He put his arms on the back of the couch and stretched his legs out. Ronnie knew how sexy he was, and I guess over the years, he had learned to use that sexiness to his advantage. "Are you attracted to me?" he asked.

He had to be kidding me. What kind of dumb question was that?

"What does that have to do with this?" I asked.

"I just want to know, straight up."

"Ronnie, you know the answer to that. But Patrick is a friend of yours and besides, you know about my decision to chill with sex."

"First of all, I told you before, Pat and I are *not* friends—we're team-mates, and yes, I know you had stopped having sex with Pat, but I also know I'm not the only one feeling some things here." He got up and took my hand. "Am I?"

"No. In all honesty, I know this has been building between us for a while. It's just that you know that I have a lot of stuff going on right now, and I don't feel like I could give myself to you totally at this point."

I couldn't believe I was actually telling him something that normally would have just been words in my journal. I wanted to be drama-free with Ronnie, but I wasn't at that time. Patrick was sending my life into chaos, and Ronnie didn't even know half the story.

He moved closer to me and said, "Stacey, whatever you can give me right here tonight, is what I want. I mean I know some of the stuff that's going on in your life, and I don't expect you to be madly in love with me or nothing." He just didn't know how close to madly in love I was right about then.

He started running his hand up and down my side, and his eyes fol-lowed his trail. "But, I want to be with you. And I have been wanting you for a long time." He looked at me and licked his lips. "Can I have you tonight?" That soft voice made it hard to say no to him.

"You're making this real hard for me."

"C'mon, Stace," he said, looking right in my eyes. My head was saying no but "okay" came out of my mouth before I knew what was happen-ing. I couldn't believe my own ears.

I was getting ready to *really* cheat on Patrick. I had never done any-thing like this before. As Ronnie and I started kissing, I realized I had never met anyone like him before. Nobody had ever touched me like he had. And, I was looking forward to letting him touch me some more as he led me back up to his bedroom.

I was so nervous. I just knew he could tell. After not having sex for so long, I felt like I did my very first time. Compared to a lot of girls in my school, I started having sex pretty late. There were girls I knew who had been having sex since they were thirteen or fourteen. It wasn't that guys hadn't tried before then, but my mother always told me not to let some

smooth-talking boy convince me to give something that special to someone who didn't love me. So I waited. It wasn't always easy either. I mean
when you're in the dark kissing, you're not always trying to hear your mom's
voice in your head, let alone listen to it.

My first time was with this guy named Tim Green. He lived across the
street from us, and we had grown up together. We both liked each other
but we didn't officially be come a couple until tenth grade. Though we
talked about it a lot, we didn't "go all the way" until the summer before
our senior year.

After we graduated, Tim went down to Morehouse College in Atlanta
so we broke up. He wanted to try and work it out but I wasn't into long-
distance relationships. We were moving into another phase in our lives. We
needed to meet new people and experience new things. Even if he had
gone to school in the area, I would have still broken up with him. It was
just time to move on, separately. We remained good friends though. You
know the type of friends who sleep together from time to time, when
neither of you is in a relationship and get that jones.

When everything started happening with Ronnie, I told Tim about it.
That was a big mistake. Tim got so jealous. We couldn't even talk without
him making some kind of smart remark. I guess he could tell I was really
beginning to like Ronnie and after all the years Tim and I had been together, he was second to someone. He could handle me being with Patrick
because he knew it wasn't that deep between us. But he knew Ronnie was
a totally different story.

As I stood there in Ronnie's bedroom, I realized he was something I
had never experienced before. I watched him as he moved around the
room cutting on the stereo, turning down the lights, lighting candles and
more incense. I started imagining what was about to happen, which made
me even more nervous. The last thing I wanted to do was ruin my first
night with Ronnie. He walked up behind me and rubbed my arms. I
could feel his hardness in the small of my back. I actually felt like my legs
were about to give out. I thought, *What the hell is wrong with you, girl? This is
what you have been waiting for since freshman year.*

"Are you alright?" Ronnie whispered.

"Um, I guess I'm just kind of nervous. It has been a while for me."

Ronnie kind of laughed and said, "Yeah that's true."

As he began kissing on the side of my neck, he asked if there was
anything he could do to relax me.

"Well that's helping."

He smiled and continued kissing me.

I didn't want to get caught up in the moment before I made sure there was some protection. Though I had recently started taking birth control pills again, I knew there were lots of other things you needed to protect yourself against besides pregnancy. Besides, Ronnie had been quite the ladies' man. I knew he had a few skeletons in his closet. I didn't want a bone to fall out and crack me over the head. I told him we couldn't do anything without protection. No glove, no love. He assured me he had it all taken care of.

Ronnie started unbuttoning my shirt and he said, "I've been thinking about this for a long time."

We had that in common because I had been thinking about it for a while myself. I was trying to stay cool but as I watched his fingers undo my shirt, I started getting very anxious.

He rubbed his hands across my stomach. Then his massive hands began gently caressing my breasts. His touch was so soft.

"I've tried to imagine what your skin would feel like—smell like, everything," he said in an almost whisper. His words were catching me off guard. I never imagined that he had thought about me in that way.

"You've been thinking about me that much?" I asked.

He moved in front of me and said, "More than you will ever know," as he looked into my eyes.

He took off his denim shirt and threw it on the chair beside the bed. He reached down and pulled his T-shirt over his head. That went on the chair too. The sight of his chest left me feeling light-headed. His body was the epitome of beauty. The solidness of his shoulders. The roundness of his pecks. The ripples of his abdomen. Even the scar right above the waistband of his Calvin Klein underwear was beautiful. I just about passed out. I knew the brother had a body but up close it was…*Mmm.*

He ran his finger over my tattoo and said, "I get to see the tattoo again."

As Maxwell played in the background, we moved toward the bed. I barely noticed Ronnie undressing me. The way his eyes moved up and down my body made me feel beautiful, more beautiful than I had ever felt in my life.

As I got up the nerve to help him take off the rest of his clothes, I let my eyes trace his body. He had to have the most perfect physique I had ever seen in my life. My eyes scanned every inch of him. And I do mean, *every* inch. I was definitely right about those size fourteen shoes and his manhood. I saw why he called it, "Big Man."

We made our way to the center of Ronnie's bed and he wasted no time getting down to the business at hand. He was marking my body with the most tender kisses. As much at he talked about being a leg man, he could have fooled me that night. The way he licked and sucked on my nipples, I would have sworn he was a breast man. I had never had an orgasm from having my breasts worked but that night I came close. Ronnie's tongue felt amazing against my skin and he knew exactly how to use it.

After adequately exploring my breasts, Ronnie took his tongue on an expedition of the rest of my body. He hung around my stomach for a little while then went on to my belly button. The next thing I knew, that brother and his tongue were like Captain Kirk—boldly going where no man had gone before. I almost lost my mind. My first oral sex experience was off the chain. I was grabbing at the sheets so much I thought I was going to rip them off the bed. Before I knew it, my body exploded with its first orgasm in fifteen months.

Ronnie was lingering between my legs, kissing on my thighs which were still trembling. I heard the foil of the condom wrapper rip and thought, *Alright now, on to the main event.*

Ronnie came back up the same path he went down. Finally, we were face to face, about to become one. He looked at me and asked, "Are you ready to feel me inside you?" His voice was so sexy. I almost couldn't respond, but I managed to nod and answer, "Yes."

I guess "born-again" virginity is closer to true virginity than both of us thought. It took a little effort but Ronnie glided himself inside me. I flinched a little from the pain. I say pain but it wasn't that bad. It was strange mixture of both pleasure and pain. And it was far more pleasure than pain!

Ronnie took my hands and stretched them over my head. That's when he went to work. I gasped for air through clinched teeth with every stroke. Soon our moves and moans were in unison.

I never truly understood what a G spot was until that night. Erika always talked about Dave knowing her spot. I could never relate because I didn't even know where my spot was and nobody had come close to hitting anything that felt like a spot. But Ronnie definitely hit my spot. And when he did, my entire body trembled. He had to know he had hit it because I couldn't help but let out a loud moan of pleasure. I would have normally been somewhat embarrassed but I didn't give a damn at that point because I had never felt anything like that in my life. Ronnie wasn't disappointing all my fantasies about him. He was the exact lover I thought he would be and much, much more. He was putting it down.

For the first time in my life, I really knew what making love was. The way he touched me and kissed me made me believe he had the same feelings for me that I was beginning to have for him. That's when I realized that the situation could really get out of control after that night.

An hour and three orgasms later, I was lying beside Ronnie with my body still tingling from the best sex I had ever had. The smell of sex, sweat and incense filled the room. It was a beautiful scent to me. One I would never forget.

"That was nice," Ronnie said, taking a deep breath.

"Nice?"

He laughed and said, "You know what I mean, girl." He kissed me softly. I knew exactly what he meant then.

He lay on his back and put his arm behind his head. He looked at me and I said, "What?"

"Nothing. I was just looking at you."

"Why?"

"Because I want to," he said.

I kind of laughed.

"No seriously, I was, ah, just thinking that was well worth the long wait."

"The long wait? How long are you talking about?"

Ronnie rolled his eyes toward the ceiling and licked his lips. I noticed he did that whenever he wanted to say something but didn't exactly know how to say it. Finally he got it out, "Since the first day I saw you."

"And when was that?" I asked, fixing the cover over my breasts and turning toward him.

"It was freshman year and there was some type of orientation going on in the gym. You and Erika were standing outside. I don't think you saw me, but I saw you. Y'all were standing near the side doors and you were leaning on the rail."

He looked at me and continued, "You had on a blue tennis skirt with a blue-and-white shirt and some white Reebok Classics. I remember thinking how beautiful you were."

He remembered what I was wearing over three years ago. I had no idea the brother was into me like that. Shit, if I had known, I sure as hell wouldn't have been wasting my time with some of those bammas I went out with over the years, Patrick included.

"Why didn't you say anything?" I asked.

"Well in the beginning, word spread fast in the dorm about whose sister you were and that you were off limits."

"What! Who said that?"

"Your brothers."

"Kevin and Devin?"

"And Tracy," Ronnie added.

"Get out of here. I can't believe they did that. And I can't believe all y'all listened to them."

"Man, nobody was trying to mess with all your brothers. Besides," he said as he kissed my nose, "I figured the right time would come along eventually."

"Is this the right time?"

"I think this is the perfect time."

Perfect. Things were far from perfect in my life. I sat up in the bed and readjusted the sheet around me. It was then that I noticed the black sheets on the bed felt like satin.

"Are these satin sheets?" I asked.

"Yeah," Ronnie answered matter-of-factly.

It was at that moment, I realized just how inexperienced I was in the art of romance. To me, real people didn't have sex on satin sheets. That was stuff for soap operas or the movies. Maybe it wasn't romance I was inexperienced at. Maybe it was seduction. I knew that playas had their own bag of tricks when they wanted to get a woman in bed. They used satin sheets, put on the soft music to set the mood and had incense burning to add to the seduction. I looked around the room—satin sheets, soft music and incense. Had Ronnie just opened his bag of tricks to get me in bed?

"What's wrong?" he asked, sitting up on his elbows.

"Are these your sexing sheets?"

He kind of laughed and said, "No. I wouldn't say that."

"Oh, you wouldn't?"

"No. I told you, I don't bring females to my house."

"So you put these on just for me?"

"Ah, yeah."

"So you were pretty sure you could get me to stay, huh?"

"Not really. But I knew it had been going through your mind, too, so I figured it was time to at least try and take it to that level. You know what I'm saying? If you said no, I would've just tried again later."

I laughed and said, "Oh, really now?"

"Yeah, you wouldn't have been able to say no to me forever," he said, smiling.

I cut on the TV and said, "Oh, really?"

"You know I'm in your head, girl."

"Whatever."

After a few minutes, I said, "You know I'm still with Patrick."

Ronnie didn't respond. He started rubbing his finger over the tattoo on my shoulder. I looked back at him. "Did you hear me?"

He just nodded. Ronnie didn't give a damn about me being with Patrick, especially since he hated the way Patrick had been treating me. I was glad he didn't know about Patrick hitting me. He probably would have tried to kill him.

"Ronnie?"

"Stacey, you already know how I feel about that. I mean like I said before, it's not like you love him. And you know better than anyone that you don't need somebody treating you like he does. So how many times do we have to talk about this?"

He was right. Patrick was the subject of far too many of our conversations. He was the last thing I wanted to talk about right then.

Ronnie sat up and put his arm around my waist. He put his chin on my shoulder.

"You need somebody who's going to treat you like a queen."

"A queen, huh?"

He kissed me and said, "Yeah, a queen. Someone who would give you any and everything you want, need and desire."

"That might be nice."

"It would be more than just nice."

I smiled.

He ran his finger over my elephant tattoo and said, "My friend, Ellie."

"What?" I asked.

"This is my friend, Ellie."

"Oh, it is?"

He leaned over and kissed my tattoo.

"Yeah," he said as he kissed me, "and I have a feeling, we're going to become very good friends."

"Oh, you have that feeling too?"

"Most definitely."

Ronnie introduced me to some things that night that just about blew my mind. I had never even done it twice in one night before. But the way Ronnie was making me feel, I probably could have gone for a third. Ronnie remembered that spot because he hit it again, and I knew I was going to enjoy having him hit that spot over and over.

We stayed up half the night talking about any and everything. I told him all about my first time with Tim and he told me about his first time with some girl named Crystal. Of course Mr. Man's first time was with an older woman. She was twenty and he was sixteen.

I was kind of shocked he hadn't had sex before that, being as fine as he was. He said he had always been taller than most guys his age, which made him kind of awkward so girls really didn't pay that much attention to him. Then the summer before his junior year, he started working out and when he went back to school, all the girls were on him.

Ronnie also told me about his ex-girlfriend, Kim. They had gone together his senior year in high school and she followed him to Howard. I was tripping because I never saw Ronnie with any girl in particular, and believe me, I was looking. Apparently, Kim wasn't really into college life so she left after the first semester. But they stayed together until that summer. He broke up with her mainly because she was in New York and he was in D.C. He didn't really want to deal with a long-distance relationship either.

"Plus, once she went back home, that girl started buggin'. I mean if she called and I wasn't in my room, I must have been with some trick. I wasn't trying to hear that bullshit all the time."

He did admit that when she left, he realized that there were too many females who wanted to talk to him for him to be tied down. He and Kim were still friends and he saw her a lot when he went home. He also said he thought she still liked him, which I didn't like too much. I had some nerve. But I couldn't help it.

The next morning, I opened my eyes to find Ronnie's muscular arm around my waist. I stretched. *Mmm, what a night,* I reminiced.

"Well good morning, Ms. Jackson." I knew right then I could get used to waking up to that voice.

"Good morning, Mr. Morgan."

"So, did you sleep alright?" he asked.

"Yeah. How 'bout you?"

"Oh, I slept real good."

Lying in bed next to Ronnie was feeling so good that I completely lost all track of time. It was almost eleven o'clock. The brother must have really whipped something on me because I never slept that late. As much as I didn't want to, I had to get up. I had promised my mother that I was going to be home by one.

"I gotta get going," I said as I sat up.

"Awe, c'mon, don't leave me. I was loving laying here with you."

I smiled and said, "So was I but I have to go home, shower, get dressed and get over to my parents'."

"Alright then. I guess I gotta let you go spend Thanksgiving with the fam."

"Thank you so much."

November 25, 1999 - 11:54 a.m.

Last night I finally did it! I slept with Ronnie! I can't even begin to describe it. Everything was so perfect. He was so gentle. I can honestly say that was the best sex I ever had in my life. He threw some stuff on me last night. That boy knows what he's doing. I still can't believe how good it felt. Last night just affirms my thoughts that Patrick was weak in bed because he's about as far away from Ronnie as it can get.

Speaking of Patrick, I really don't know what I'm going to do. I am caught up in something much more than I thought it would be. I really wonder if I'm not falling in love with Ronnie. Can this really be happening to me? I'm trippin'. I think Ronnie just whipped it on me last night and I haven't shaken it off yet. I hope I can shake it off 'cause if not, I'm in big trouble!

"Hey, Mommy."

"Hey, sweet pea. How's Mommy's baby girl?"

"I'm fine."

I loved going back home. It brought back so many memories of when I was young. My family always had a lot of fun. There was so much love in the house. My parents made sure of that.

My parents, Cheryl and Greg Jackson, met twenty-seven years ago at a New Year's Eve party while they were both students at North Carolina Central University. From that night on, they were inseparable. Then the unthinkable happened: right before their senior year began, my mother found out she was pregnant. Their parents were highly upset to say the least. They each blamed the other's child for ruining their child's life. But through it all, Mommy and Daddy knew they were in love and that they would make it together.

Since Mommy was having twins, she had to stop school before her last semester to stay on bed rest. And on February 13, 1974, the Big-Head Twins were born.

Daddy had graduated that December and gotten a job in D.C. with the Department of Education. Mommy said Daddy was a wreck having to be away from his baby boys for the six weeks she stayed in North Carolina after they were born. But once those weeks were up, she moved to D.C. with him and on May 1, 1974, they were married at the Justice of the Peace.

My mother finished her last few credits at night while Daddy watched the boys. Then when the twins were three years old, she went back to school full-time working on her master's degree in psychology. Soon after she started, she found out she was pregnant again—with twins again! Tracy and I were born three days after my parents' fourth anniversary. When we started kindergarten, my mother went back to school again and finished her master's and went on to get her Ph.D.

Daddy always said he and Mommy stuck together when everybody told them they'd be divorced in two years, and now they're getting ready to celebrate their twenty-sixth wedding anniversary. I loved that my parents had such a deep love for each other. It gave me hope that one day I'd find that kind of love.

Though I was glad to be home with my family, my mind was still preoccupied with my previous night's activities with Ronnie. My body was still tingling. There was no way I could keep this from Erika, and there was no way I could tell her over the phone. I knew she would be down the street at her parents' house.

"Where have you been, girl? I've been trying to call you all night," Erika said before she even got on the phone good.

"Right after you eat, you gotta come over here," I demanded.

"What's up?"

"Just come over here after y'all eat. I mean right after, girl."

"Alright, alright. I'll be down there."

Dinner was great, as usual. My mother could burn. Daddy and the boys ate like there was no tomorrow, as usual. Then they all went in the den to watch college football, but before long, they were all asleep.

I was clearing the dinner dishes from the table when I caught a glimpse of the full moon through the curtains on the patio doors. It was beautiful. I walked over to the doors to get a better look. The sky was crystal clear. Not a cloud in sight.

There had been many nights when I stood in that very same place and reminisced about evenings Tim and I had spent together. But on this night, my thoughts weren't of Tim. The only person on my mind was Ronnie and our romantic first time together.

I smiled, as I thought about the Black Love incense, the candles, the Maxwell CD, the satin sheets. I couldn't help but think about his beautiful body. I wanted to engrave the image of his body in my mind and I had succeeded. My heart began racing as I remembered that body touching mine for the first time.

"Stacey," Tracy said, rubbing my back and startling me back to reality. "I'm sorry, baby girl. I didn't mean to scare you. What are you over here thinking about? You seemed a thousand miles away."

"Oh, nothing really," I said as I began clearing the dishes again.

"You sure now? I mean, I could tell you were thinking about something—or someone."

I glanced at him but didn't respond. I wanted to tell Tracy about was going on with Ronnie but I had to find the right time; this was not it. He understood my silence.

"Okay. You don't have to talk to me about it right now."

I smiled. He knew he'd eventually find out what or who had my mind a thousand miles away.

After what seemed like an eternity, the doorbell finally rang. It had to be Erika. Mommy and I were finishing up the dishes.

"I'll get it," I said, dropping the dishtowel as I ran to the door. I couldn't wait to tell Erika about what happened with Ronnie. I pulled her in the door.

"Damn, girl. What is wrong with you?"

"Who is that, Stacey?" Mommy yelled from the kitchen.

"Hey, Ma," Erika called out. I wished she hadn't done that because I knew my mother was going to want to talk to her.

"Come on in here, girl, and give me my kiss," Mommy demanded.

Erika went in the kitchen, and I waited impatiently in the hall. After what seemed like forever, she finally came back. I grabbed her hand and pulled her up the stairs. We went in my bedroom, and I shut the door.

Erika sat on the bed and said, "What the hell is wrong with you, girl? Why are you trippin' like this?"

I sat beside her and said, "You are not going to believe what happened last night?"

"What?" she asked intrigued.

"I spent the night with Ronnie." I couldn't help but smile as the words came out.

Erika looked at me and said, "You are lying, girl." I just looked at her. She knew I wasn't lying.

"How did that happen?" she asked.

"He called and invited me over to listen to some of his music. I went over there and he was singing some songs for me. And girl, let me tell you, brother man can blow."

"For real?"

"Oh yes. It's like he sang this song that was saying something about not taking your love away and after he finished singing it, he asked me to stay the night with him."

"And obviously you said yes."

I smiled and said, "Obviously."

"Alright, tell me, what's in the bun?"

After both of us began having sex, Erika and I made up code words to tell each other what size a guy's private part was. A Vienna sausage in the bun was real small. A hot dog in the bun was pretty average. The guys that were really packing were foot-longs, half-smokes, etc.

"It's a jumbo foot-long, half-smoke in the bun," I stated proudly.

Erika had a look of disbelief on her face. "Get the hell out of here. Are you serious?"

"Jumbo foot-long, half-smoke," I reiterated.

"I just cannot believe he's fine as hell and packing a foot-long, half-smoke," Erika said in disgust.

"A jumbo foot-long..." I attempted to correct her but she cut me off.

"I don't even want to talk about it anymore," Erika teased.

I laughed and said, "Don't hate."

"Well how was it?"

I shook my head and said, "Erika girl, it was...."

I put my hand on my chest and took a deep breath. The mere thought of that night started my heart racing. "Whoa, I can't even describe it. All I know is it was the best sex I have ever had in my life."

"Get out of here."

"I'm serious. It felt so good. I mean from start to finish and every single minute in between. I mean he did some shit I ain't never, ever had done before."

"Downtown?"

"Downtown, uptown, across town, all around town."

"Alright now," Erika said, laughing and giving me a high five.

"Oh, and you know that spot you're always talking about Dave hitting?"

Erika laughed and said, "Yeah."

"Well Ronnie found it and hit the hell out of mine last night."

"You go, girl. You finally got somebody to do you right."

He definitely did me right. That was for sure. I lay back on the bed and covered my eyes. It really hit me that things were getting more and more complicated.

"You alright, girl?" Erika asked. I looked up at her, and she could tell I wasn't. "What's wrong?"

"Besides the obvious fact that I cheated on Patrick?"

Erika sucked her teeth and said, "I sure hope something else is bothering you because I ain't feeling the Pat thing."

"Erika, I just...I just don't know what's going on with me. I mean we always tripped about me being in love with Ronnie but after last night...."

"You really think you're in love with him? I mean, don't confuse great sex with love."

"I don't know." I sat up. "It's like, every time I think about last night, my heart starts beating so fast and all these emotions run through me. I mean I was thinking about it driving out here and all of a sudden tears were rolling down my face. I feel like I'm going crazy."

Even as I spoke, the tears began falling again. I wiped my eyes. "Look at this shit. What the hell is going on with me, Erika?"

"Stacey, you are going to have to do something. You can't keep putting yourself through all these changes."

"I know."

Erika was right, but some things are easier said than done.

last night

Dave had an aunt who lived in Alexandria, Virginia, and every Thanksgiving since we started at Howard, he had gone to her house for dinner. He asked me if I wanted to go and since I wasn't going home that year, I said yes, but I didn't really feel like going. I just couldn't get Stacey or the night before off my mind. For a minute, I thought I might be feeling guilty about Pat. But, I knew better than that. I didn't give a damn about Pat. Maybe I had stronger feelings for Stacey than I was trying to admit to myself. I rolled over and the scent of her was still on my pillow. I was tripping, laying there hugging on a pillow. Then the phone rang.

"Yo, man, you up?" Dave asked.

"Ah yeah, I'm up."

"What time you want me to roll through?"

"Oh, I don't care."

"Alright, I'll be over there around two-thirty."

"Alright, man. Peace."

All morning I sat around thinking about Stacey. I didn't think sleeping with her was going to affect me like that. I had no idea I'd be thinking about it so much. I constantly replayed that night over in my mind. I hadn't reacted like that the very first time I had sex with Crystal. Maybe that was because Crystal was nowhere near as good as Stacey. And the first time I had sex with Crystal, I had no feelings for her whatsoever. All I wanted was to get my first piece and brag how it happened with a twenty-year-old woman.

I had been looking forward to having me a big Thanksgiving meal, but I couldn't even eat. I was just kind of picking over my food when I noticed Dave looking at me funny. He was going to want to talk later, but I wasn't sure if I was ready to talk about what was going on.

After dinner, I went and sat outside on the deck. I was hoping some fresh air would help me clear my head, but as I sat there looking at the duck pond in the distance, my mind drifted back to Stacey and the night before. Everything was still so clear to me. I saw myself slowly uncovering that beautiful body of hers. Those perfectly round mocha-colored breasts, her flat stomach, wide hips and those thick legs.

The squeaking of the French door as Dave opened it brought me out of my daydream.

"Yo, man, why you been so quiet today?" Dave asked as he shut the door behind him.

"Oh, no reason."

"C'mon, dawg. What's up with you?"

"I, ah, just got some things on my mind, that's all."

"Well let me know if you want to talk, man."

I did need to get it off my chest. I had talked to my boys from home about Stacey but it wasn't the same since they didn't really know her. To them, she was just another female. They couldn't understand why I was wasting so much time on someone who not only had a man, but before last night, wasn't even giving up the goodies.

"Dave, man, if I tell you something, you gotta swear that it stays on the DL."

"C'mon, man, you know I got you."

"Alright. It's like, I'm starting to have some feelings for someone that I probably shouldn't."

"Okay, Stacey, and?" he said kind of matter-of-factly.

"Ah…" I really didn't know what to say. He caught me off guard. I just looked at him.

Dave kind of laughed and said, "Yo, man, I'm your boy. Don't think I haven't noticed who you've been spending a lot of your time with and who your conversations have been about lately." There was nothing I could say. I just didn't know it had become so obvious.

"So exactly what's up with y'all?" Dave asked, nudging me with his elbow.

"She, ah, spent the night at the crib last night."

"Get the hell out of here. What you mean she spent the night? She gave you a piece?" he whispered.

I nodded.

"I thought your rule was no chicks at the crib?"

"Yeah, I know. She got me breaking a lot of my rules."

Dave just looked at me, shaking his head and smiling.

"I saw this shit coming, dawg," he finally said.

"What you mean?"

"Man, I've been asking Erika if anything was going on with y'all for months. Ever since we were down at Hains Point. I saw the way you were looking at Stacey."

"Dave, man, I don't know what the hell's going on with me and this girl. I mean, I have thought she was beautiful since the first time I saw her freshman year. But it's like this summer, we started hanging out a lot and things just started poppin' off. Then last night…."

I got up and walked over to the banister. I started thinking back on that night. All I could do was shake my head. "Damn."

Dave laughed and said, "It was that good, huh?"

I looked at him and said, "You just don't know, man. I don't think I ever had a piece that good."

"Word? It was all that?"

"It was more than all that. I can't even describe it." I shook my head. "Dave, man, she's so different from any girl I've ever been with. And that's part of the problem."

"What problem?" he asked.

"For the past few years, I haven't let anything or anyone get in the way of my music. And I'm not saying that Stacey's getting in the way but I feel like she's becoming a priority, and I don't know if I'm ready for that. When me and Kim broke up, I made it up in my mind that I wasn't going to let no females get in my head. But Stacey is most definitely in my head."

"I don't know what to say, man. But it's becoming more and more obvious. So y'all better chill before it gets back to Pat."

"Please, the last thing I'm worried about is that nigga. I wish he would step to me. I'd tell him how his girl had to come to me 'cause he wasn't hittin' it right."

Dave laughed and said, "Boy, you know you ill."

"Seriously though, that's part of the problem. I just don't understand why she's even with his punk ass."

"Well I don't understand that either," Dave agreed.

"Then, man, on top of all that, a couple of weeks ago when I was home, I ran into Kim and some things went down between us."

"For real?"

"Yeah, man, so now I'm confused about all this shit. I mean I know I really like Stacey but she's got a man. Then here comes Kim trying to get back in the mix."

"Well what's up with her? Do you want to be with her?"

"Me and Kim are good in bed. That's about it."

"Well is it different with Stacey?"

"Yeah, I mean, I can talk to that girl for hours about anything. Plus, to be honest, I think I just slept with Kim because I was getting frustrated with Stacey. I mean you just don't know how many times I've told myself that I was going to stop messing with her because she has a boyfriend. Then two minutes later, there I am picking up the phone to call her."

"Have you talked to Stacey about all this?"

I shook my head. "Naw. I don't know what to say. I mean, what if she's really trying to stay with Pat?"

"Well if that was the case, she wouldn't be kickin' it so hard with you," Dave said.

"Yeah, I guess so."

"Have you talked to Kim about what happened with y'all?"

"Naw 'cause I know she's probably thinking we're getting back together or something and that just ain't the case. Like I said, I was frustrated with Stacey, and Kim was there."

"Well, man, you're going to have to talk to one or both of them soon."

"Yeah, I know."

Dave and I continued to talk about my situation with Stacey as he drove me home. By the time he dropped me off, I felt a little better about everything. I walked in my bedroom and turned on the lights. Everything looked just as it did when Stacey left that morning. I hadn't even made up the bed. The ashes from the incense were still laying on the nightstands. The candles were still in their same places. Stacey's perfume still faintly lingered throughout the room.

I sat on the couch and turned on Maxwell. Stacey loved Maxwell, so his CD had played all night. I knew I would never be able to listen to him again without smiling.

I looked across the room at the bed. The whole night with Stacey was replaying in my head yet again. I sat there looking at the bed. I felt like I was watching TV. I could see her freshly manicured nails running down my back, her big beautiful legs wrapped around my waist. I could almost feel her biting on my ear, on my neck. I could hear her softly moaning my name, *"Mmm, Ronnie."*

I wondered if Stacey was thinking about our night as much as I was. I decided to give her a call, but there was no answer at her place. Then I remembered she was going over her parents' house, so I paged her. I laid my head against the back of the couch and waited for her call. When the phone rang, my heart actually started beating fast. I couldn't believe I was tripping like that.

"Yeah, hello." I always got real smooth when I talked to Stacey. Plus, I couldn't give any indications that I was tripping about last night.

"Hey, boy," Stacey said in a soft voice.

"Were you busy?"

"No. I was chillin' with Tracy. What's up?"

"Ah, nothing. I was just thinking about you, so I decided to give you a call but then I remembered that you weren't home."

"Oh. So how was your Thanksgiving dinner over Dave's auntie's?"

"It was alright. But my mind was a little preoccupied."

"With what?"

"Who is more like it."

"Well who?"

"You." Stacey didn't respond. "Well you…and last night."

"Oh, I see."

"Have you been thinking about it?" I knew she had been, but I just wanted to see if she was going to try and front.

"Um, hold on for a second."

"Okay."

I heard Stacey put the phone down. "Tracy, hang this up when I get upstairs." Someone picked up the receiver. "Leave it alone until I get upstairs, boy."

A masculine voice replied, "Just hurry up, girl. Don't nobody want to hear your little conversation."

She picked up the phone. "Alright, hang up." Neither of us heard the phone hang up.

"Hang up, Tracy!"

He laughed and hung up the phone.

"I'm sorry. I had to come up in my room. My brother was all up in my face," Stacey explained.

"Don't worry about it. I know how that is. Anyway, what you mean your room? You don't live there. You ain't got no room."

Stacey laughed. "Please, this is my room and it's always gonna be."

"Oh you got it like that, huh?"

"Sure do."

"Oh, okay. So anyway, back to my question, have you been thinking about last night?"

"Yeah, I have," she admitted.

"What have you been thinking?"

She kind of laughed.

"Don't get shy now. You weren't that shy last night," I teased.

"Don't even try it."

"Naw, I'm just trippin' with you. But for real, what were you thinking?"

"I don't know. I guess I thought I would feel guilty about cheating."

"But?"

"But I don't."

"And why is that?"

"I don't know. I guess because it felt right."

"No doubt. It most definitely felt right. I guess that's why I haven't been able to concentrate on anything all day but you and last night."

I knew she was cheesing. "Quit smiling," I teased.

She laughed. "I'm not smiling."

"Yeah, okay, whatever you say."

"Maybe I'm smiling a little bit." Then, I was smiling.

"So, ah, why don't you, ah, come see me?"

"Now?" she asked.

"Yeah."

"Ronnie, for real, I would but I promised my mother I was going to stay the night and if I come back to D.C., I'm not going to want to drive back out here tonight."

"True that. I wouldn't want you to be out there like that anyway. Well what are you doing tomorrow night?"

"Nothing really."

"Well how 'bout I make you some dinner?"

"You can cook?" Stacey asked curiously.

"Of course I can."

"Mmm, a man of many talents."

"Oh, you know that," I said, laughing at the nasty thoughts in my mind.

"Anyway. That sounds good."

"What time are you coming back this way?"

"I don't know. Probably around four or so."

"Okay."

"Well I'll give you a call when I get home."

"Okay. Later, boo."

When I hung up, I realized I had never called Stacey "boo" before. Kim was the last girl I had called that. I hadn't really been serious about any other girl since Kim and I broke up. I guess after the night before, I was getting serious about Stacey.

During our pillow talk, Stacey told me how she liked to be wined and dined. "That's why I like going out with older guys because most of the time, they treat you like a lady. I mean, if they take you out to dinner, they ain't necessarily trying to get in your panties."

That wasn't completely true because I knew plenty of dudes who would expect some booty for an expensive dinner. Shit, I knew a few who would expect some for a two-piece meal from KFC.

Stacey liked to be romanced. She liked walking in the park, getting little love notes, stuff like that. I figured I'd show her that she didn't have to find an older man to give her that. I was more than capable of giving her some romance.

With Stacey coming over I had to look good. I took a shower and threw on my fly Boucheron cologne that she loved. I also knew she liked the way I looked in my jeans because I heard her talking to Erika one time when I saw them at the library.

They were on their way in as I was going out. Both were looking fine as usual. I spoke and everything and we did the chitchat thing for a few minutes. As I walked down the steps, I heard Stacey comment, "Damn, that brother look good in them jeans. Talk about wantin' to get in somebody's pants." She was whispering but I still heard her. I was going to turn around but I decided not to. I didn't want her to be embarrassed. Every time I wore some jeans after that, I waited for her reaction. She didn't always say anything aloud, but sometimes she would just shake her head and lick her lips. That was her thing, licking those gorgeous lips. She was always trying to play it off talking about, "It's a habit." But I knew better than that.

After I got dressed, I stood in front of the mirror checking myself out. *Yeah, you looking kind of good,* I thought. Then the phone rang.

"Yeah, hello."

"Hey." It was Stacey.

"What's up?"

"I just got home. I'm going to change my clothes and I should be over there in about forty-five minutes or so."

"That's cool."

"Oh, and thank you very much for my little surprise."

"You're very welcome."

I knew Stacey would like my surprise. Since she wanted some romance, I gave her a small taste of what I could do.

Music always gave me a way to convey my feelings. So I searched and searched for a song to express my feelings about the night we had shared. Finally, I found it. "Last Night" by Az Yet. That was the perfect song. Even though our night together had actually been the night before last, I knew Stacey would like it. I also wrote her a little love note. I wrapped the CD and the note with some red ribbon. I bought some roses and took the petals off. I decided I was going to spread them in front of her apartment door and put the tape and note on top of them. When I got over there I had forgotten she lived in that damn security building. Luckily someone was coming out. My first romantic mission had been successfully accomplished.

Stacey was all about being on time. Exactly forty-five minutes after we hung up, the doorbell rang. I was almost running to the door but I caught myself. I opened the door and couldn't help but smile. I had been waiting all day to see Stacey and she was finally there. I was so busy staring that I left the girl standing outside.

"I'm sorry, come on in."

"I was 'bout to say," she said, laughing.

As she walked pass, I thought, *She seems more beautiful every time I see her.* I shut the door and turned toward her. We were just standing there, neither of us saying a word. Stacey raised her eyebrows. I hoped she was about to break the uneasy silence. She did.

"I've never seen you this quiet," she joked.

"I could say the same thing for you."

"Whatever, boy."

"Anyway, your dinner is almost ready. Would you like something to drink?"

"Sure."

"I'll go get you something. You can go 'head in the den and make yourself at home."

"Okay."

I turned to walk toward the kitchen. From the corner of my eye, I saw Stacey checking me out. I loved the way she did that. She was pretty smooth with her stuff. It was really sexy. Especially, when she licked her lips. She sure could roll that tongue. She looked like she was ready to rip off my clothes.

I knew Stacey was going to be very impressed with my culinary skills. There weren't many brothers my age who could cook like I could. My father used to be a chef so I learned early how to make all kinds of stuff. But I wasn't going to reveal all my skills to Stacey at once. I decided to make something kind of simple: broiled crab cakes, with real crabmeat, not that imitation shit; sweet potato fries; and a Caesar salad. It took me a little longer to decide what to fix for dessert though. Stacey had said she didn't really like chocolate so that shot down my specialty, German Chocolate pound cake. I finally decided on a Key Lime pie.

As I made my final survey of the meal, I was proud of myself. I had prepared many-a-meal for females before but it had always been in an effort to get in their pants, and believe me, it worked every time. That wasn't my motive with Stacey though. Not that I wasn't feeling her like that 'cause I most definitely was. But, I just wanted to show her what type of man I was, how I could take care of her. I wanted her to see how a queen was supposed to be treated and that I was the man to do it.

I had a nice fire burning in the den and some Norman Brown playing on the stereo. A little jazz always set the right mood. Stacey had commented that she liked the Black Love incense. A brother took a mental note. So, of course, there was some Black Love burning.

Stacey was sitting on the couch gazing into the fire. I couldn't help but wonder what was on her mind. Was it me and our night together? Or was she thinking about Pat? I knew better than that. He had never given her what I gave her. That much I knew. Stacey told me how weak he was in bed. Well she never actually came out and told me, but she said enough. She wasn't going to just come out with it, at least not to me.

"A penny for your thoughts," I said as I sat beside her and handed her a glass of peach iced tea, her favorite. I startled her. "Oh, I'm sorry."

"That's okay," she said, taking the glass. "Thank you."

"You're very welcome. Where were you? You seemed a thousand miles away."

She smiled and said, "I was just thinking how sweet it was of you to leave that surprise for me." I knew she was going to love that. She leaned closer and planted a long, soft kiss on me. "Again, thank you."

If she only knew, that was just the beginning.

I was going all out on the romantic tip. I set the dining room table and lit some candles. I piped in the jazz from the den and escorted Ms. Jackson in. She was taken back when she saw the spread. "This is so nice, Ronnie."

"Well I'm glad you like it." I pulled her chair out for her and she sat down.

"I didn't know you were so romantic." I leaned over the back of the chair close to her ear and said, "There's plenty more where this came from." Her smile told me she liked that.

All during dinner, I couldn't help but stare at Stacey. She was trying her best not to look at me but she finally put her fork down.

"Why are you doing that?"

I sat back and smiled. "Doing what?" I asked, as if I didn't know what she was talking about.

"You know what? All that staring."

"Because, number one, you're beautiful."

"Okay, what's number two?" she asked, smiling.

"Because I want to."

Stacey just laughed and went back to enjoying her meal.

"Is that okay with you?"

She looked at me and smiled. "I guess it will have to be."

After dinner, I decided I wasn't going to waste any of my time with Stacey cleaning up the dishes. I could do that the next day, if need be. When we got back to the den, I sat down and patted the couch. Stacey smiled. She sat down but not close enough for me. I was ready to get my cuddle on. I moved closer to her and put my arms around her waist. She felt so good. I knew she liked it too by the way she sank into my arms.

"Dinner was very nice, Mr. Morgan," she said, running her finger up and down my arm.

"Why thank you, Ms. Jackson. I'm glad you enjoyed it."

"Man, I didn't know you had skills like that."

"I have many skills," I said, smiling. Stacey just laughed. "Why you laughing?"

"You are too funny, boy." I'd be funny. I'd be whatever she wanted me to be.

I loved kissing on Stacey's ears. She always giggled like a little girl. "Stop, boy. That tickles," she would say. I messed with her a lot like that the when she spent the night.

I was on her ear again when the phone rang. I was not about to let anything distract my attention from Stacey, so I let it ring.

"Aren't you going to get that?" she asked.

"Naw," I answered without missing a kiss. Whoever it was would call back if it was important. Besides, there was nothing more important than what was going on right there on that couch. The answering machine picked up after the fourth ring.

"Hey, babe."

When I heard Kim's voice, I almost had a heart attack. I was ready to jump up and cut the volume down but I knew that would look kind of bad.

"I was just calling to see how you were doing. I really miss you, babe."

When Kim finally hung up, I didn't even want to look at Stacey. I could feel her glare burning on my skin. I really did not want to go all into the Kim thing. I knew Stacey had a boyfriend from jump. Even though Kim wasn't my girlfriend, Stacey hadn't heard anything about her until we spent the night together. I decided it was best to go ahead and get it over with. So I finally looked at her.

"So, *babe*, who was that?" she asked, kind of smiling.

"That was ah, Kim."

"Oh, really now. Your ex-girlfriend Kim?"

"Ah yeah."

She nodded and said, "Ah-ha." It was hard to tell by her tone if she was upset or not.

"It's no big deal, Stace."

"Oh, I didn't say it was. Besides, what—" she looked at me and said—"or who you do is none of my business."

I couldn't believe she was tripping like that. I was going to have to put her in check real quick.

"Ah, excuse me Ms. Jackson, now I know you're not going there with me, are you?"

Her eyebrows went up and she kind of popped her neck back. I could tell by her expression she was surprised I had said that to her. She nodded and kind of laughed. Not an *awe that was funny* kind of laugh but an *oh no he didn't say that* kind of laugh. She turned back toward the fire, arms folded and legs crossed. The next thing I knew, her little foot was bouncing. That was not a good sign. I thought, *Oh hell no. I am not gon' let Kim knock my groove.*

"Look, Stace—" I gently turned her head toward me—"I'm goin' to be honest with you, when I was home a couple of weeks ago, some things went down between me and Kim."

"What kind of things? The other night type of things?" she asked.

"No, not the other night type of things. I mean it was something that just…."

"Just happened," she said sarcastically. "So, did she get the satin sheets too?"

"Stacey, I can't believe you trippin' like this. What, you think I'm trying to run some type of game on you?" She didn't respond. But that answered my question.

"Stace, I am not trying to run game. I have been nothing but straight up with you from day one. That shit with Kim happened but that's it. I'm not rolling with her like that."

I put my finger under her chin and softly pressed my lips against hers. She looked up at me with those big, beautiful brown eyes. If she only knew how deep I was into her.

"I'm sorry. I know I've been really buggin' lately. I don't have any right to trip off who you're seeing."

"I am not seeing her."

"I'm just saying. Like you said, I'm the one with the boyfriend."

I didn't want to hear that too much more either. After spending the night with her, I knew I was in deeper than I should have been at that point. The last thing I wanted to do was think about Pat's weak ass touching her. I had spent all night learning every inch of her body. From her head, down to her perfectly pedicured toes and everything in between, and I do mean everything. Just the thought of her body was getting me a little excited—well more than just a little.

"Look, we are going to end this conversation right here. I do not want to hear anything else about Pat or Kim, alright?"

She nodded.

I had to think of a way to get my mood back. Stacey was still kind of tense. I picked up the remote and flipped the CD changer to number three—Earth, Wind & Fire. I had become very knowledgeable about which songs set the right mood. If you really wanted to get your groove on you had to go back to the old school love songs. I got up and put another log on the fire then I cut off the lights. I took Stacey's hand and said, "Dance with me." She tried to act like she didn't want to but I knew better than that. I pulled her up and put my arms around her waist. She was still acting a little stank. I popped her butt and said, "You better stop acting like that, girl."

She laughed and said, "Stop, boy." She put her arms around my neck and we began slow dancing.

"By the way, those satin sheets are only for you and Ellie," I whispered in her ear. She smiled. I felt her press her body to mine.

I loved the way her body felt. This girl was taking me down a road that I didn't know if I was ready to go down yet. As I inhaled the scent of White Musk from her neck, I knew I wouldn't be able to stop the trip though. As we headed upstairs to repeat what we had done the night before last, I realized that I might not have thought I was ready to go there but I was more than willing.

merry christmas

ronnie

Stacey had been in an extra good mood the last couple of times we had been together. She was really getting into the Christmas spirit. I went with her and Erika shopping for Dave's gift, and Stacey was just like a little kid, so excited about everything. I could only imagine what she was like when she was little.

I guess her enthusiasm rubbed off on me because I went all out on her gift. It was a beautiful diamond-and-ruby tennis bracelet. I had to throw a little red in there for her sorority. If my mother ever found out I spent more than eight hundred dollars on a gift for a girl, she would have a fit. She thought all girls were just out to get my money anyway. Sometimes she was right, but not in Stacey's case. I had been looking at that tennis bracelet for months. I knew Stacey would love it but I didn't want it to seem like I was trying to crowd her. I finally decided to go ahead and get it. Stacey was going to freak when she saw it. I had just finished wrapping it when she called.

"Hey, boy," was Stacey's normal greeting for me.

"Oh, you know what kind of man I am," was my normal response. I think she liked hearing me say it, that's why she never changed what she said.

"Anyway, do you want to go see the National Christmas Tree with me?"

"Yeah, sure."

"Will you drive?" she asked.

"Yeah. I'll be over there in about twenty minutes."

"Okay."

We decided to take a carriage ride around the Mall before going to see the trees. It was a cold night but there wasn't a cloud in the sky. The stars were so bright. Stacey and I cuddled under the blanket in the carriage. We just soaked up the beauty of the night.

"I'm going home tomorrow morning," I kind of blurted out. We had been avoiding that subject for weeks.

"Yeah, I figured you'd be going one day this week."

"I really wish I could stay here, but Moms would bug out."

"Yeah well, you have to go and be with your family on Christmas. You know, be with the ones you love."

I wanted to say, "That's why I want to stay with you." But those words just weren't ready to pass my lips, though I knew in my heart they were true. I think I had known it for a while. From that first night we spent together. Possibly even from the first day I saw her outside the gym.

"Well I'll call you and you can call me," Stacey said, trying to sound reassuring.

I looked at her and said, "You know I will."

"Look, let's just enjoy tonight. I don't want to talk about that anymore. You bringing me down, man."

I laughed and said, "I don't want to ruin your Christmas spirit."

Once the ride was over, we went walking around looking at the Christmas trees. Stacey had been there a million times, but you would have thought that was her first visit by how excited she was. We stood in front of the bonfire, and then we strolled around the fifty small trees representing each state.

I was looking forward to seeing my family but I was going to miss Stacey. We had been spending a lot of time together and I had kind of gotten use to it. If I hadn't thought my mother would kill me, I probably wouldn't have gone home. That's just how much I wanted to be with Stacey.

After hanging out for a while, we went back to my crib to exchange gifts. I lit a fire for us in my room, made some hot chocolate and got some Christmas cookies my mother had sent, for us to munch on.

"Did you enjoy going down to see the Christmas trees?" Stacey asked.

"I enjoy myself whenever I'm with you." Stacey blushed like she always did. "Are you ready for your gift?"

Stacey smiled slyly and said, "Why, Mr. Morgan, you know I'm ready to take anything you want to give me."

"I'm talking about this gift, nasty girl," I said as I pulled out the box. "I'll give you that gift later on."

Stacey took the box and shook it. "Mmm, sounds like jewelry."

"Just open the box," I insisted, anxious to see her reaction.

She unwrapped the box and opened it. Her mouth dropped open at the sight of the bracelet.

"Oh, my God." She looked at me. "Ronnie, you...."

I took the bracelet out and put it on her arm.

"How do you like it?"

She held out her arm and said, "Ronnie, it's beautiful. I can't believe you got me something like this."

"Well, I knew you would love it."

"Do I? But, Ronnie, this is too much."

"Nothing is too much for you," I said, taking her hand. "This is how a queen is supposed to be treated."

She kissed me and said, "Thank you so much."

"Mmm, you are very welcome."

I was enjoying my long thank-you kiss when Stacey remembered her gift. She pulled it from her bag and sat back beside me. "If I would've known what you were buying me, I would have given you mine first, then we could have built up to yours," she joked. She gave me the box and I opened it. It was a gold necklace and a gold G-clef charm with a diamond in the center.

"This is fly. Thanks, boo."

"You really like it? I mean it's not like your gift."

I kissed her and said, "It's not supposed to be like my gift. This is your gift to me, and I love it because it came from your heart." That made her feel better because she flashed that beautiful smile. I didn't want her to feel like she had to give me gifts just because I was giving her gifts.

"Let me put it on you." She took the chain out of the box and put it around my neck. Once she hooked it, her arms rested on my shoulders.

"Thank you," I said softly. She kissed me.

"You're very *(kiss)*, very *(kiss)*, very *(kiss)*, very *(kiss)*, welcome."

I loved when she kissed me like that. As we continued to kiss, I reached for the remote control and turned on the Maxwell CD. We both knew what Maxwell meant. I told myself when Entice finally got its record deal and I got in the mix, I was going to have to thank my man Maxwell for the many nights of ecstasy he had given me with Stacey.

Stacey always fell right off to sleep after one of our private sessions. A brother with a little less confidence in his abilities would be hurt, but I knew our sessions wore her out, just as they did me. Before I went to sleep though, I lay beside her and just watched her sleep. The moonlight was falling across her eyes. She looked so peaceful. There were times I couldn't believe how beautiful she was. I couldn't believe I had wasted so much time with all those chicken-heads on campus when I could have been feeling like that all along. Even though I was tired, I laid in bed staring at Stacey for what seemed like hours. I was trying to soak up as much of her in my memory as I could. As the minutes ticked by, my heart began to ache more. The thought of being away from her was unbearable.

I finally drifted off to sleep. It had to have been around four in the morning. Even though I didn't get that much sleep, when I woke up the next day, I felt well rested. Whenever Stacey stayed the night with me, I slept like a baby.

I lifted my head and looked at the clock. It was quarter after nine. I lay back down. I had told my mom that I would be home around noon but I realized that wasn't going to happen. I reached for the phone to call home. Stacey slept like a log. Nothing could wake that girl when she was sleep so I wasn't worried about disturbing her.

"Happy holidays." My mother changed her phone greeting with every holiday. "Morgan residence."

"Hey, Ma."

"Hey, baby. Where are you?"

"Ah, still in D.C."

"What are you still doing there? I thought you were going to leave early."

"That was the plan but I had a late night."

"Okay, Ronald Jr., what time should I expect you now?" she said, laughing.

"I'm going to try and get out of here by noon."

"Alright, sweetie. You drive carefully."

"I will."

"I love you."

"I love you too."

I put the phone back on the base and turned toward Stacey. She was still fast asleep. I decided to surprise her with breakfast in bed. I got up, took a shower and went to work.

I fixed her an egg-white ham and cheese omelet, raisin-bread toast, orange juice and mint tea with honey. Most brothers don't have mint tea just sitting around their crib but Stacey liked it so I made sure she had it whenever she was over.

My mother had bought me a breakfast tray once when I was sick and she came down to take care of me. So I pulled it out and arranged everything nicely. I looked at the tray and had to admit, when it came to romance, I was the man.

I took the tray into the bedroom. Now the smell of all that food would have awakened most people, not Stacey. I set the tray on the nightstand and pulled the curtains open to let the sunlight in. One thing Stacey hated was any type of light when she was asleep. Once the sun hit her face, she frowned. Even her frowns were cute. She pulled the comforter over her head.

"C'mon, girl, get up." I pulled the cover back. I kissed her cheek. "I made you some breakfast."

"For real?" She stretched and rubbed her eyes.

"Yes, for real."

She looked over at the breakfast tray. "I don't know what to say about you," she said, shaking her head. "You're going to spoil me."

"That's what I'm trying to do."

She smiled. "Alright, I'm getting up. Let me just go wash my face."

She got up and I watched her as she headed toward the bathroom. She had on one of my pajama tops. It stopped about mid-thigh on her, which I was digging. I loved those big, beautiful legs of hers.

After sharing breakfast in bed, Stacey went to take her shower while I finished packing my things. I was trying to finish before she got out because every time the subject of me leaving came up, she got quiet. I knew it was upsetting her. I hated it myself.

The time to leave finally came. I put my bag in the truck and walked Stacey to her car, which was on the street right in front of my house.

"Well," I began, not really wanting to or knowing how to say goodbye, "I, ah, guess I'll see you in about two weeks."

"Yeah, I guess so."

Stacey began fidgeting. One minute her hands were in her pockets. The next she was putting on her gloves. Then she put her gloved hands back in her pockets. She looked down the street in one direction, then up the street in the other. But she never looked at me.

"Stace," I said, taking her hand. "I'm really going to miss you, girl." She didn't respond. I pulled her closer. "You hear me?" She just nodded. "You gonna miss me?"

She just nodded again but she still wouldn't look at me. I moved in front of her and said, "Hey." She turned her head quickly. "You not talking to me?" She still didn't respond.

I just stood there a minute not knowing what else to say. I looked down at her again and saw her lower lip trembling. I leaned over a little and saw a tear rolling down her cheek. The last thing I expected was for her to cry.

I never knew how to handle it when girls cried. I mean that's how Kim got to me all the time. She knew I would cave in if she started crying so she turned those tears on all the time. But after a while, I got hip to her game and the tears didn't work anymore.

Stacey's crying was a different story. She wasn't playing a game. I didn't want her to get too upset. I was just going home for a couple of weeks.

"Aye, boo, if you don't wipe that tear away, it's going to freeze in the middle of your cheek."

She laughed and looked at me. I wiped her cheek and she said, "I can't believe I'm being this silly. I'm sorry."

"Sorry for what?"

"I was trying so hard to not be a big baby about this."

"Girl, please, you're not being a baby." I kissed her and said, "It's fine."

"I'm going to miss you too," she said.

"I know. But it's only a couple of weeks, and I'm going to call you every day." My mother wasn't going to like it but I would deal with that later.

"Well, I'm going to let you get going. You have a long drive ahead."

"Alright."

As we hugged, I didn't want her to let go. It had to have been about twenty degrees outside but I didn't feel cold at all standing there holding Stacey.

"You better go," Stacey said, slowly pulling away from me.

I kissed her and opened her car door. She gave me one last kiss and got in. I shut the door and she started the car. Tears were forming in Stacey's eyes again. She knew I had seen them so she didn't let the car warm up too much before she pulled off.

I got in my truck and sat there a few minutes. I was so close to going after Stacey and telling her I was going to stay in town for Christmas but I didn't want to disappoint my mother. So I hit the road.

All the way up I-95 North, I kept thinking about Stacey. I didn't know if she was alright or not. I called both her apartment and her cell phone but there was no answer at either. I was starting to get a little worried so I called Dave.

"What up boy? You up in New York?"

"Naw, I'm on my way up there now. But look, I need you to do me a favor, kid."

"What's up?"

"Ask E to check on Stace."

"What's wrong?"

"It's just that she was a little upset about me leaving for the holidays."

"Oh, okay. I'll tell Erika to see what's up with her."

"Thanks, man. I'll hit you back when I get home."

"Alright. Peace."

I got home around four-thirty. I didn't see any of the Morgan family vehicles as I drove down the street looking for a parking space. Knowing my mother, she was out somewhere shopping and my father was probably at one of the restaurants. As I walked up the steps to the brownstone I had lived most of my life, I was kind of glad no one was around, that way I could try to get Stacey again.

I put my bags down and went in the kitchen to see what my mother was cooking up. Not only did my father know how to cook but so did my mom. They always joked that she taught my dad everything he knew but I don't know how true that was.

My mother had more food than the law should allow. She had the biggest turkey I had ever seen in my life. I know that thing weighed about thirty pounds. Then she had a huge ham, some lasagna, seafood gumbo, potato salad, macaroni and cheese, greens, candied yams, string beans with potatoes, and she probably wasn't even finished cooking everything. I opened the fridge and there were all kinds of desserts. I loved Christmastime in our house because we got our eat on.

I was so tempted to steal a piece of pie but my mother would have killed me so I just shut the door. Still worried about Stacey, I called her house again.

Caller ID was invented for people like Stacey. She wouldn't pick up the phone without checking to see who it was. And if your number came up Private or Unknown, you could forget about her answering your call.

"Hey, boy," the voice on the other end of the line said softly. She still didn't sound like herself.

"What's up, boo? How you doing?" I asked, relieved to hear her voice.

"Fine."

"Did Erika call you?"

"Yes, but you didn't have to get her to check on me. I was okay."

"Well I called you a couple of times and you weren't at home and you didn't answer your cell." I hated sounding so possessive of somebody else's girl, but I couldn't help it.

"I'm sorry. I just needed some quiet time to myself."

"I was kind of worried."

"Well don't be. I'm fine. Anyway, how was your drive? Was there a lot of traffic?" Stacey was starting to sound like herself.

"Naw, not really. I mean it was a little slow through the McHenry Tunnel but after that it was cool."

"So how's everybody doing?"

"Nobody's even here. My moms is probably out shopping with my sister, my father's probably at one of the restaurants and my brother won't be home until tomorrow."

"Dag, boy, that's jacked up. E'erybody was like, 'Forget Ronnie, we're out.'"

"Whatever, girl."

Stacey and I stayed on the phone for almost an hour. When I hung up, I felt good. She was still a little down but she assured me that she was going to be fine. I knew she would feel better once she got around her family.

I was lying on the couch watching TV when my mother and sister, Raina, walked in.

"What's up, big head?" Raina said, popping me upside my head. She had been doing that ever since I could remember.

"Quit playing, girl."

"Get up and give me a hug, boy," my mother demanded.

I got up and hugged her, lifting her off her feet. I kissed her and said, "What's up, sexy lady?"

"Save that ol' sweet talk for all your little female friends."

I laughed.

"I know that's right," Raina cosigned.

"Anyway."

Just as I thought, the two most important women in my life had been out shopping. I had learned more from those two about women than I ever would have on my own. They were both strong, beautiful black women, not just beautiful on the outside but on the inside also. I think that's why I was into Stacey so deep, because she reminded me of both my mother and sister in many ways.

Raina went in the kitchen and my mother started the Spanish Inquisition. "So Ronald Jr., who is this young lady that caused your late night?" she asked, taking off her full-length purple leather coat.

Purple was my mother's favorite color. She had more purple pieces of clothing than Prince ever had. Not many people could pull off some purple high-heeled boots, but my mom was working it.

"What young lady you talkin' 'bout?" I asked, trying to laugh off the question. My mother knew me too well.

"You know what I'm talking about. So who is she?" She took off her purple scarf and settled in the lounge chair. She crossed her long legs and waited for my answer.

"Ah, her name is Stacey Jackson," I admitted, trying not to smile too much.

"Stacey Jackson, huh? And where is this Stacey from?"

"She's from Maryland."

"And how long have you and she been kickin' it?"

I started laughing. My mother was funny. She was always trying to use slang. Though this instance was an exception, she usually used it wrong.

"Kickin' it?" I repeated.

"Yeah, that's right, isn't it? Kickin' it means hanging out, chillin', right?"

"Yeah, it's right, Ma. Anyway, I've known her for a while. You remember my boy Dave?"

"Yeah, that little cutie from Philly."

"Ah yeah, Ma, well Stacey and Dave's girl, Erika, have been best friends since they were shorties."

"Oh."

Raina walked in from the kitchen with a bottle of apple juice in her hand. She plopped down beside me and asked, "What y'all talking 'bout?"

I took the juice from her and said, "None of your beez-wacks." I drank some juice then handed the bottle back to her.

"Your brother was just telling me about his new friend, Stacey," my mother explained.

"Mmm, Stacey, huh? Well if you're talking about her, she must not be like them other chicken-heads you been messing with down there at Howard."

"Chicken-heads?" My mother didn't know what a chicken-head was and we weren't about to try and explain it to her.

"Never mind, Ma," Raina and I responded in unison.

"Anyway, little brother, what does she look like? Is she cute?"

"C'mon now, who are you talkin' to?" I asked conceitedly.

"Raina, you know better than to even ask Ronnie that question," my mother said, laughing.

"Naw for real, she is beautiful," I said.

I talked to my mother and sister about Stacey for a long time. I told them everything about her, except the fact that she had a boyfriend. They didn't need to know about Pat because as far as I was concerned, he was going to be out of the picture very soon.

"So when are we going to meet this girl? She sounds very nice," my mother said.

"I don't know. I'll probably try and get her to come up some time next month."

"Well I know what you need to do while you're here is tell that stupid girl Kim to stop calling here all the time," Raina interjected.

Kim had been calling me a lot at school too. But with me chilling with Stacey so much, I hadn't returned any of her calls. I knew she was going to be calling my parents trying to find out when I'd be home.

Raina and Kim had been pretty cool when I was in high school, but after we broke up, Kim would always try to get information from Raina about what I was doing or who I was seeing and my sister was not having it.

"Ronnie, she *has* been calling here every day," my mother confessed.

"She's been calling here three or four times a day." Raina was about fed up with Kim. She wasn't going to be nice much longer. "You would want to talk to her 'cause the next time she calls here, I'm going to bomb her out."

"Alright. I'll talk to her," I promised.

Just then, my pops walked in the door with some long-stemmed white roses. "What's up, man? I see you finally made it."

"Hey, Pops." I hugged him. He squeezed me tight and patted my back.

He walked over to Mom and kissed her. Not just a peck, but a long, hot and heavy kiss.

"Are these for me?" my mother asked Pops, with a sly grin.

"Of course they are."

"What's the occasion?"

"No occasion really. I just felt like getting the woman I love some roses. Is that alright with you?"

"It's definitely alright with me."

Watching how affectionate my parents were was strange because during my freshman year in high school, they had separated. My mother found out that my father was messing around with this other woman. Mom went straight ballistic. She threw my father and all "his shit" out the house.

That was a hard time for me because my father was the man who was supposed to show me how to treat women. I mean even when my brother and I were little he made us open the door for Raina and Ma. We had to pull their chairs out for them and help them with their coats. He said he was teaching us how to be gentlemen. But then he cheated on my mother. I couldn't understand how he could be telling us one thing but doing another. I stopped talking to him for a while. I felt like he not only betrayed my mother but me too.

My parents stayed apart for about two years. Slowly they started working things out. They actually started dating each other again. Pops would come over a couple of nights a week and they would go out somewhere. I thought that was kind of cool. Then right after I graduated from high school, they renewed their wedding vows. It was a big affair. The ceremony was cool because we were all in it. I was my father's best man. My brother was one of the groomsmen and Raina was my mother's maid of honor. That whole situation with my parents showed me that no matter what happens in a relationship, things can work out if you really want them to.

I called Stacey every day while I was home. Most of the time, we talked two or three times a day. We knew our phone bills were going to be crazy but we didn't care. My mother noticed I had been talking to Stacey a lot but she didn't mind me calling her. I think she could tell how much I liked her.

New Year's Eve was approaching and I hadn't made any plans yet. I knew I could always go down to my dad's club and bring in the New Year but I wasn't really sure what I wanted to do.

Kim had called me a couple of times asking if I wanted to go out with her for New Year's. I hadn't said no but I knew I wasn't going to go with her because she would take it as a sign of something going on between us.

"Hey, Ron." It was Kim's third time calling that day. I was trying to be nice but her constant calls were working my nerves.

"Oh, hey," I said dryly.

"What you doing?"

"Chillin'."

"So have you decided what you're going to do for New Year's? I mean we could have some dinner and then hit the club to dance the New Year in."

"Um, Kim, I'm really thinking I'm just going to chill at home for New Year's."

"Well, I could come over and chill with you."

"I don't think that's such a good idea."

"Why is that?" Kim was going to force me to have the conversation I had been avoiding. "What's going on, Ron? It seems like you're holding me at arm's length."

"Kim, it's just that there are some other things going on with me and I'm really not trying to give you the wrong idea."

"What are you talking about, Ronnie?"

"It's just that I've kind of been seeing somebody back at school."

"Oh, really? Well when did this start?" she asked with an attitude.

"Kim, we don't go together anymore."

"I know that. But you weren't saying that a few months ago when you were at my house, in my bed."

"I know. I was wrong for that and I'm sorry. I didn't mean to make you think it was anything more than just sex." Once the words left my mouth, I knew I shouldn't have said it that way.

"Oh, really?"

"I didn't mean it like that. It's just that I have a friend at school who I've been seeing, and I'm not trying to be with anybody else right now."

"I see. So does your new little girlfriend have a name?"

"Her name is Stacey, and she's not my girlfriend."

"Ah-ha. So she's why you haven't been calling me back?"

"Not really. I've just been busy getting ready for my finals. Plus, I've been playing ball and working on my music."

"And seeing this Stacey," she added sarcastically.

"Yeah and seeing Stacey."

Kim wanted me to sit on the phone and discuss my whole relationship with Stacey and I wasn't about to do it. It was like she was trying to talk me out of seeing Stacey and into see her again. That was not going to happen. Even if I wasn't seeing Stacey, I wouldn't start talking to Kim again.

Kim hung up mad but I was relieved. I knew the whole situation with her was my fault because I shouldn't have slept with her again but that type of relationship was over between me and Kim. I had gotten rid of my past and now all I had to do was help Stacey get rid of her present.

The last New Year's of the millennium and I didn't really want to do anything. My pops was planning the party of all parties but I didn't feel like being around all those people. My boys were talking about hitting all kinds of parties. But, all I really wanted to do was be with Stacey. I thought about going back to D.C. a couple of days early, but I had already promised my parents that I was going to stay until after the New Year. So I decided I was going to bring the New Year in with Stacey the only way possible, on the phone.

Everybody joked me. Every time I walked pass my father, he would act like he was examining my nose or something. When I asked him what he was doing, he said, "I'm just looking at how wide that girl got your nose open."

My brother was right there with Pops. Rob just shook his head every time he saw me. "You used to be my idol, player. Shorty must have really whipped something on you to have you sitting up in this house alone on New Year's Eve."

My mother just smiled every time she saw me. She thought it was cute. So did Raina.

My boys had been dogging me about Stacey ever since I told them she had a boyfriend. They kind of let up when they came to homecoming and saw how fine she was. But once I told them I wasn't going out with them for New Year's, they started in on me again. I didn't care though. I had heard all the jokes. I was still going to stay home and bring the New Year in with Stacey.

I was lying on my bed watching *Dick Clark's Rockin' New Year* waiting for Stacey to call. It was about eleven-thirty when the phone rang.

"Hey, boo."

"What's up, boy?"

"Are you going to come up with a new greeting for me in the New Year?"

"I doubt it. I like your response," she confessed.

I laughed and said, "Oh, I know you do. Because you of all people know what type of man I am."

"I most definitely do, Mr. Morgan." I loved Stacey's sexy voice. It was so seductive.

"So what are Erika and Dave doing tonight?"

"They're going to some party downtown."

"Have you talked to your man tonight?" I teased. I knew she didn't like when I referred to Pat as her man but I wanted to make sure she didn't forget that he was her man and I wasn't, for the time being anyway.

"Ronnie, why you gotta go there?"

"I'm just asking you a question."

She didn't say anything. When Stacey got upset, she completely shut down.

"Stacey?"

She still didn't respond.

"Okay, boo, I'm sorry. I was just playin'."

"Why do you always do that? You know I hate it," she said, still upset with me.

"I don't know. But I am sorry. I won't do it again."

"Don't even say that because you know you will."

"Well put it this way, I'll try my best not to. Alright?"

"Yeah, alright."

By the time we got through that little episode, it was almost midnight. In less than ten minutes, it would be the year 2000. Stacey asked me what I would remember most about 1999.

A lot of good things had happened to me that year. I had been on the MEAC championship team. My grades that year had been the best ever. I had even made the dean's list twice. I had written more songs that ever before. But there was one thing that I would always remember about 1999.

"Thanksgiving," I finally answered.

"Thanksgiving?"

"Actually, the night before Thanksgiving."

Every time I laid in my bed, I thought about that night I spent with Stacey. It was almost like her perfume was still in my pillows.

"Ronnie, c'mon now, I'm serious."

"So am I. I will never forget that night."

Stacey didn't know how to take things I said sometimes. I think even though she liked me she still thought I was just some cat with a smooth rap. I had been straight up with her regarding all the girls I had been seeing prior to her. And I admit there had been quite a few. But things with her were different. I wasn't trying to play her. I often wondered if that was the reason she hadn't broken up with Pat yet. Maybe she thought I was full of shit and was out to dog her.

"So anyway, Ms. Jackson, what are you going to remember most about 1999?"

"I guess I'll remember 1999 as the year that we got to know each other better."

"Do you think that's something you're going to remember for the rest of your life?"

"Yeah, but there are specific things that I'll always remember too."

"Like what?"

"Of course I will always remember the first night we spent together but even more than that, I'm going to remember that afternoon we spent down at Hains Point. Actually it was more so the end of the day. The sun was setting over the water and we were walking back to the car." She paused a minute and laughed.

"What?" I asked.

"I just can't believe I'm telling you this. It's embarrassing."

"You can tell me anything. Go 'head."

"Alright. We were walking and you took my hand. And when your hand touched mine, this chill went up my spine. I knew right then that something was going to happen between us. I didn't know when or where but I knew it was going to happen eventually."

"Now why was that embarrassing?"

"I don't know. It's just...I don't know. I guess I just don't want it to seem like I have some kind of school-girl crush."

"It doesn't seem like that to me."

I heard her take a deep breath.

"Stacey, do you think I'm going to hurt you? That I'm just playing some type of game with you?"

"No, I don't think that."

"Good. And I want to reiterate right here and now that I am not out to play any games or to hurt you. I would never do that to you. I hope you believe that."

"I do."

Right then the countdown to the New Year began. Five-four-three-two-one. It was the year 2000.

"Happy New Year, Ms. Jackson."

"Happy New Year to you, too, Mr. Morgan."

Spring Semester

ronnie

When it snowed in New York City, everything basically went on as usual. The "city that never sleeps," couldn't let a little snow slow it down. D.C. was pretty much the same way. Nothing ever shut down when it snowed. That's why I wasn't at all fazed by Bob Ryan's forecast of two to four inches of snow by morning. Classes might be delayed but nothing would be cancelled. Besides, there had been plenty of times when the weather forecast was wrong.

Good ol' Bob wasn't totally wrong that night. The first snow of the season actually surpassed expectations, measuring in at more than five inches.

Classes were delayed by two hours so I lounged in bed. Staring out my bedroom window, I wondered if I should even go to my classes at all. It was the beginning of the semester so I had plenty of time to make up my work. I dozed off. The phone woke me from my short nap. I picked up the receiver and looked at the Caller ID display.

"What's up, boo?"

"Hey, boy. What you doin'?" Stacey asked cheerfully.

"Chillin'. Trying to decided if I'm going up on campus in this snow."

"I was thinking the same thing. How 'bout I come over there?"

"Bet. That sounds like a plan."

I was definitely down with that. I had only seen Stacey once since I got back from Christmas break.

"Are you sure you want to drive in all this snow? I could come over there."

"I don't mind driving in the snow. I doubt that it's that bad out there anyway."

"Are you sure?" I asked.

"Yes, I'm sure. I'd rather be at your place. You know how much I like that king-size bed," she said in her seductive voice.

"Oh, so you just want to use me for your pleasure, huh?" I teased.

"You know it's not just that. I want something to eat too." She laughed, "A sister's fridge is bare."

I laughed.

"I'm just trippin'."

"No, you're not but that's okay."

"I'll be over in about an hour."

After telling Stacey to drive carefully, we hung up. I lay back on the bed and closed my eyes. I couldn't wait to spend some time with my boo. I didn't stay in bed long because my crib was a mess. Stacey wouldn't have cared but I couldn't let her see the place like that.

Just as I finished sweeping the kitchen floor, the doorbell rang. I put up the broom, gave myself the once-over in the hallway mirror and opened the door.

"Hi there." My neighbor Stephanie, from two houses down, saw my truck parked in front of the house and decided to stop by.

Stephanie had been trying to get with me ever since I moved in. She had to be around forty. I was used to older women hitting on me. And I must admit she was fine. But she was also, very married. Ever since my parents had their little marital problems, I promised myself I would never mess with a married woman or cheat on my wife. I saw what my father's cheating did to my mother. I wasn't going to put my wife through that pain.

Stephanie was persistent though. She owned a little Afrocentric bookstore not too far from our houses so she would be home sometimes during the day. Every time she saw my truck, she stopped by.

"Oh hi," I said, responding to her greeting.

"What, you were expecting someone else?"

"Actually, I was."

"One of your little girlfriends, I suppose."

I laughed.

We basically had the same conversation every time she came over. I would ask her if her husband knew she was ringing my bell in the middle of the day and she would reply, "What he doesn't know, won't hurt him," but not that day.

"Tony and I are separated."

I said, "Oh," with a nod.

"So," Stephanie said, running her finger down my arm, "what do you think about us going out for a drink some time?"

"I think separated is still married," I answered politely, moving her hand off my arm. I did it right in time, too, because, just then Stacey pulled up. You would have thought I got caught cheating or something by the way my heart jumped when I saw her drive up.

Stephanie turned and looked as Stacey got out the car. She said, "Mmm, I would have never thought you were into the thuggish type."

Stacey was looking a little out of character, but with the weather the way it was, I could understand the big ol' Howard sweatshirt, jeans and Timberland boots. She was still fine as hell though, even with the blue bandana on her head.

Stacey looked up on the porch and cracked a smile. I had told her about Stephanie hitting on me all the time. She reached in the backseat of her car and pulled out her leather book bag and her overnight bag. We hadn't said anything about her staying the night but I had no problem with it.

Stacey walked on the porch and said, "Am I—" she kind of looked Stephanie up and down and continued—"interrupting something?"

"Naw. This is my neighbor Stephanie Lewis."

"Oh, nice to meet you Mrs. Lewis," she said, making a point to emphasize the *Mrs.* part.

I was trying my best not to laugh. "Stephanie, this is my friend Stacey."

"Hello," she responded half-heartedly.

Why did Stephanie have to do that? She just gave Stacey an excuse to sharpen her claws. Like most women, she could be real catty when she wanted to.

Stacey turned to me and said, "Hey, baby." Then she kissed me. Not our normal greeting peck but a slow, tongue-y kiss. I knew she was just doing it to mess with Stephanie but I liked it nonetheless.

She wiped my lips and said, "I'll be upstairs." She cut her eyes toward Stephanie and added, "In the bedroom."

She looked at Stephanie and said, "It was really nice meeting you, ma'am."

"Okay, I'll be there in a minute."

Stacey went in the house and shut the door. I kind of laughed. She was a trip.

"So what's the deal with you and little Miss 'Around the Way Girl' there?" Stephanie asked, with a frown.

"We're friends."

"What kind of friends?" She moved closer and whispered, "The kind of friends that I want us to be?"

I stepped back. If Stacey saw that woman all up on me, my plans for the rest of our day *and* night would be ruined. "We're the type of friends you and I will never be."

She sucked her teeth and said, "Anyway, let me get back to work. And you can get back to your little company."

"A'ight then."

I shut the door and shook my head. That woman was a trip too. But if she hadn't been married and I hadn't been kicking it with Stacey, I sure would have been up in there.

I turned around and was startled by Stacey standing in front of me.

"First of all, let me just say that I am so mad that she is forty years old and looks that good."

I laughed.

"Secondly, let her call me little Miss 'Around the Way Girl' one more time and she'll find out just how around the way I can get."

"How you hear that? I thought you were going upstairs," I said, amused that she didn't trust Stephanie enough to go upstairs.

"Please. Not with that old lady down here trying to push up on you."

I wrapped her sweatshirt strings around my fingers and pulled her closer. "You know you are sexy even in a big ol' sweatshirt, jeans and Tims."

She smiled and said, "Don't try and change the subject."

I kissed her softly. "Stephanie Lewis is not a subject for me." I kissed her again, as softly as before. "Now, Stacey Jackson, that's a different story. Stacey Jackson is actually one of my favorite subjects."

She was cheesing so hard her jaws were probably sore. I loved seeing Stacey's bright smile. It was one of the things that made her so beautiful.

I moved my eyes toward her overnight bag sitting next to the steps. "What's that?"

She smiled and said, "A bag."

"What's in it?"

"Some clothes."

I smiled and nodded.

"You don't mind me bringing it, do you?" she asked.

"C'mon, now. You know I don't mind you staying here. I was just messing with you."

She just smiled.

My growling stomach was telling me it was lunchtime. "Are you hungry?" I asked.

Stacey smiled slyly and said, "Oh, you know I am. What did I tell you about that king-size bed?"

"You are so nasty." She smiled. "I was talking about food. I'll take care of that other hunger later."

My boo wanted a cheeseburger so I whipped her up one with some French fries. I even made her a chocolate shake. Stacey was so spoiled. I always waited on her hand and foot when she came over. I didn't mind though. That's what I was there for—to give Stacey any and everything she even thought she wanted. I tried to tell myself I would treat any girl I was seeing the same way, but that wasn't true. Stacey was special and I knew that.

After we ate, Ms. Jackson decided she wanted me to break out the PlayStation so she could get her butt beat in some NBA Live '99. Dave was the only person who had beaten me and that happened only once.

"So who you want," I asked Stacey as I hooked up the game.

She was taking off her boots and she said, "I want Alonzo Mourning."

I knew she was going to say that. We had gone to see the Wizards play the Heat with Erika and Dave and that girl nearly lost her mind when she saw Alonzo Mourning. I thought I was going to have to carry her butt out of the MCI Center.

"He ain't all that."

She sat on the floor in front of the TV. "Whatever. You need to stop hatin' on Zoe. He can't help it if he's so fine," she said, taking the controller.

"Like I said, he ain't all that."

Stacey looked at me like I was crazy.

I smiled and said, "Alright then, who do you think looks better, me or Alonzo?"

She kind of laughed and said, "Start the game."

"No, answer my question."

Stacey looked up at me and said, "You know I think you're finer than Alonzo." She laughed and said, "Now, start the game."

"Yeah okay."

Stacey's cell phone kept ringing. Each time it rang, she would look at it and put it back on the table. I knew it was Patrick. After the fifth time,

I was getting tired of it. "Why don't you just cut it off?"

"Because Tracy or Erika might call," she answered, still focusing on the game.

Since Patrick had, in essence, been brought up in our conversation, I decided to pose a question that had been on my mind.

"Aye, let me ask you something?"

"Go 'head," she said, still into the video game.

"Since we started sleeping together, have you ah, slept with Patrick again?"

"Why would you ask me that, Ronnie?" She still didn't take her eyes off the game.

"I don't know. I've just been kind of wondering."

Her fingers stopped moving against the controller. She turned her head slowly toward me and I knew right then, I should have kept my mouth shut.

"Oh, you've been kind of wondering if I'm sleeping with both you and Patrick?"

"Stace, I didn't...."

"No, let me make sure I understand this."

She put the controller on the floor. "I hadn't been sleeping with Patrick for over a year, then I started sleeping with you and you've been wondering if I might have started back sleeping with him for some reason?"

Stacey had a way of making things that in my mind seemed so rational sound so stupid.

"For real, Stace, I didn't mean for it to sound like that. I don't know why I even brought it up. Let's just drop the whole thing."

"Oh no, we ain't gonna drop the whole thing," she responded, with an *I'm 'bout to get in your ass* laugh.

"Now, maybe the way I've handled things with you has given you the wrong impression about me but just so you know, I am not now, nor have I ever slept with more than one person at a time. If I had been sleeping with Patrick, I wouldn't be sleeping with you now. That's not how I do things."

I was glad to hear that. I honestly didn't believe she was sleeping with Pat. But sometimes, stupid things pop in your head, especially when sex enters the picture. A man has the capacity to sleep with a lot of different women and expect them to be cool with it, but let that same man find out one of "his women" is sleeping with another man, he'd have a fit. I guess

I was no different. Every time Stacey and I had a private session, I wondered if Pat was getting a piece of *my* goodies. There was no way I could explain my feelings to Stacey and expect her to understand where I was coming from. No matter how I said it, she was going to think I was tripping.

"Alright, Stace, I'm sorry I even brought it up."

"You don't have to be sorry but since you brought it up, I want to know are you sleeping with anyone else?"

I looked at her. The player in me wished I could say yeah but the truth was, I wasn't sleeping with anyone else. I really didn't want to be with anyone but Stacey.

"Now I'm going to answer your question but you have to promise not to tell none of my boys, 'cause they might make me turn in my playa's card."

Stacey laughed and said, "You are so silly."

"Naw for real," I leaned over and kissed her. "I'm not sleeping with anyone but you."

She smiled.

"Now, let me ask you something else." I pulled her up from the floor and led her toward the steps. "How many changes of clothes did you bring?"

"Why?" she asked.

"'Cause you know how you are," I said, leading her up the steps. "You know how you sweat during our private sessions. I just want to make sure you have enough clothes for after all those showers."

By this time, we were inside my bedroom. Stacey laughed and said, "Don't even try it. You're the one who's always sweating."

I lay back on the bed and pulled her on top of me. "A brother puts in hard work."

She kissed me softly. "I know that's right."

"Well, I guess we both sweat a lot then 'cause you be working it, too, girl."

She laughed and said, "Now, I know that's right."

And with that, the session began.

Forty-five minutes later, Stacey looked at me and said, "Mmm, you know I love this king-size bed."

I smiled and said, "You're sweaty."

"So are you, Mr. Morgan."

"I know." I kissed her.

Stacey flipped over on her stomach and looked at me. "Ah, Patrick noticed my bracelet the other day."

I grabbed the remote control from the nightstand. "Oh really?" I turned on the TV and turned to my man, Matlock.

"Yeah. He asked me where it came from and I told him Tracy gave it to me for Christmas."

Stacey was getting good at lying. Every time Pat questioned her about something, she had some kind of lie to answer.

"Yeah well, just so you know, Dave said Pat's been asking him if I'm seeing anyone," I said as I watched Matlock cross-exam a dude in a wheelchair who killed his wife. I had seen that episode a million times but I would rather watch it again than talk about Pat.

"For real?" Stacey asked, surprised.

"Yeah. I don't know what Dave told him though. I think he just said he didn't know."

Stacey dropped that conversation. She turned back over and laid her head on my shoulder. She closed her eyes and I looked down at her. "Yeah, go 'head and take your nap. I know I wore you out, as usual."

She laughed and said, "Shut up. You know you'll be sleep in a minute too."

She was right. I could feel the sleep coming down on me and before I knew it, we were both sleep.

When I finally awoke from my short nap, I realized from the darkness of the room that I hadn't taken such a short nap after all. The large neon numbers on my clock read 5:58. I couldn't believe I slept that long. I stretched and turned to wrap my arms around Stacey's small waist. To my surprise, she wasn't there. I sat up.

"Stace."

There was no answer. I put on some sweatpants and a shirt and went to find her. As my eyes adjusted to the lights in the hallway, I called out to her again. Still, there was no answer. I was just about to get nervous when I heard the pots and pans banging against each other in the kitchen. I walked in and Stacey was going to town fixing dinner.

"Oh, hey sleepyhead," she said.

"Hey," I replied.

She wrapped her arms around my neck and kissed me. "You always cook for me so I decided to surprise you by fixing you some dinner for a change."

"That's cool."

"It will be ready in about fifteen minutes."

That was the first time Stacey had cooked for me. I hadn't been to the grocery store so she didn't have much to work with but she put together a spaghetti dinner that I almost hurt myself eating. Stacey was fine, smart and could cook. I felt like I had hit the jackpot.

Since Stacey had cooked, I decided I would do the dishes for her. She was happy about that since she hated doing the dishes. It was probably because being the only girl in a house of three brothers; she did more than her share of dishes. Me, on the other hand, grew up in a house with an old school, semi-chauvinistic father who thought girls did certain chores and boys did others. So my brother and I didn't do too much washing dishes. Taking out the trash and shoveling snow—yes, but dishes—no.

After I finished, I locked up everything downstairs and headed upstairs to join Stacey in my bedroom. I felt a sense of déjà vu when I walked in the room and didn't see her again. Then I noticed she was in the bathroom preparing to take her shower.

The only wall in my room was a glass brick wall separating the bathroom from the rest of the space. The wall allowed me to keep the loft-like feeling to the area while added some privacy to the bathroom, not that I needed it living by myself.

Stacey was the first girl to ever be in my bedroom so she was in turn the first girl to take a shower in my bathroom. Actually, my sister had showered there but she didn't count.

Stacey was in the shower and I was laying on the bed looking at TV. I was all into the highlights from the last night's college basketball games, when I caught a glimpse of her body behind the glass wall. I tried to return my focus back to the TV, but Stacey's silhouette wouldn't let me.

I felt kind of guilty laying there watching Stacey shower but it was so sexy. I couldn't see anything clearly but I could imagine her rubbing soap on her beautiful breasts; her cleansing my goody box; the water cascading down her big, round thighs.

Though I hadn't planned it, my bed was placed in such a way that I had good view of the mirrors over the sinks in the bathroom. When

Stacey got out of the shower, she stepped into my clear view of her then. With a big white terrycloth towel wrapped around her, she began her nightly routine.

I watched as Stacey squeezed toothpaste on to her red toothbrush, brushed her teeth and rinsed. She then pulled out her face cleansing pads and washed her face. She rinsed and put on some moisturizer. As she rubbed scented oil over her body, I wished my hands were given that job. Stacey slipped into some red-and-white pajamas. After straightening things in the bathroom, she turned off the lights.

I quickly turned my attention back toward the TV. She lay beside me and the full scent of her body oil hit me.

"What's that scent?" I asked, placing my nose near her ear. Ever since I bought her some oil back from Carol's Daughter, the girl was hooked. Stacey had a different scent for every day of the week almost.

"It's called Eleven." She giggled. "Now get away from me. That tickles."

"Girl, you smell good enough to eat. You making a brother hungry."

She laughed and said, "See you 'bout to have me saying something nasty."

"Go 'head and say what you want to."

"Naw, I'm trying to go to sleep."

I laughed and got up. "Yeah, well then you better keep it to yourself then."

She just laughed.

I took my shower and joined Stacey on the bed. We lay there watching TV for a while. When Stacey was watching TV, she was really into it. There was no talking to her. She was in another place. But I had made an important decision. I was going to give Stacey something I hadn't given anyone else before.

"Stacey."

"Huh?" she replied, not taking her eyes off the TV.

"Let me talk to you for a second."

She didn't even respond. I turned the TV off and she looked at me. "What's wrong? Why you turn the TV off?"

"I want to talk to you for a second."

"Oh, I'm sorry, sweetie." She turned toward me, giving her undivided attention.

"There's something that I've been contemplating for a while and I think I've made my decision." I opened the nightstand and pulled out the spare house key I had gotten made. "I want to give you something."

Giving Stacey her own key was big step for me. My own mother didn't have a key to my house. But I wanted Stacey to know I was getting really serious. My only problem was as much as I wanted to reveal my true feelings totally something was holding me back. My guards were still partially up. Probably because of a little thing called her boyfriend. As long as Pat was still in the picture, I couldn't open myself up too much, at least no more than I had.

I took the key off my ring and said, "I've never given anyone the key to my place before." I looked at her and she looked as if she was getting ready to cry. The girl was so emotional.

"What's wrong?" I asked.

"Nobody's ever given me the key to their house before."

"Well I guess this is a first for both of us."

She smiled and wiped away the one tear that rolled down her cheek. I placed the key in her hand and folded her fingers around it. When I looked at Stacey, I knew I had made the right decision.

new york, new york

stacey

"What are you doing this weekend?" Ronnie asked.

"Nothing really, why?"

"Well, ah, I'm going home and I was wondering if you wanted to go?" I couldn't believe he was asking me to go home with him. "I'm leaving tomorrow night but I know you have classes until after twelve on Fridays so you can get the train up then."

"Ronnie, I don't know if I can afford to go on such short notice."

"Oh, don't worry about it. I'm going to handle all that."

"Are you serious?"

"You should know by now that I don't play games."

My boy was on the ball. He had already gotten the train schedule for me. I could get the one-forty train out of Union Station and he would pick me up around four-thirty and I would ride back with him Sunday afternoon. I figured it would be fun. I called my mother to let her know where I was going. Much to my amazement, she didn't ask too many questions. Then I called Erika.

"Hey, girl, I just wanted to let you know I'm going to New York this weekend."

"For what?"

"Just to go."

"Oh. Dave said Ronnie's goin' home for the weekend."

"Ah, yeah I know."

There was a long silence on the line. Erika was processing what I said.

"Wait a minute, girl. I know you not going to New York with Ronnie."

"No, I'm not going *with* him."

"Oh, but you are going to be with him, right?"

"Something like that."

"Mmm, you *are* becoming a hot ass."

"Don't be saying that. And E, don't tell Dave about this."

"Girl, please, Dave already knows what's going on between you and Ronnie."

"And how is that? You didn't…."

"No, I didn't say anything. Ronnie told him about what happened between y'all Thanksgiving."

"Oh, my God. I ain't trying to have the whole world know."

"Stop being so dramatic. The whole world doesn't know."

"I don't know what's up with me. Ronnie has got me doing some crazy shit. I mean I'm getting on a train tomorrow afternoon going to New York to be with him. I can't even think straight anymore where he's concerned."

Erika's advice to me was to just chill and go with it. I wondered why the situation didn't bother everybody else as much as it bothered me. Then again I guess it didn't bother me enough to stop seeing Ronnie. I wasn't about to do that.

I saw the whole situation unfolding right in front of me. In fact I probably brought most of it on myself. I could tell by the way our conversations were shifting that things weren't strictly on a friendship basis anymore. If I didn't want anything to happen, why didn't I stop going out with him and calling him? Those were questions that I didn't have the answers to and at the time, I didn't really care. I was going to New York to kick it with Ronnie for the whole weekend. What I needed to do right then was pack.

Friday was not moving fast enough for me. I sat in my accounting class doing nothing but watching the clock. I was so ready to leave. Ronnie was just as anxious as I was. He called me when he got home, which was around one o'clock in the morning. He wanted to let me know he had gotten there safely. Though he was tired, he kept trying to talk. He was very excited that I was going to be coming.

"Ced and Myles said they lookin' forward to seeing you again. And Dre is looking forward to meeting you."

"Ronnie, look I'll be there tomorrow. We can talk then. Get some rest."

I finally got him off the phone that night but then he called again the next morning before I left for class.

"What's up, boo? I just called to make sure e'erything was straight for this afternoon."

I really liked how attentive he was to me. That's something I had been missing being with Patrick. Ronnie made me feel so special. For the first time in a long time, I felt like someone's girlfriend. That was really strange because I wasn't Ronnie's girlfriend. I was supposed to be Patrick's.

I had never really been on a train before. Of course I had taken the Metro around D.C. and the MARC train back and forth to Baltimore. But, being on Amtrak was a lot different. I was really enjoying the ride. The scenery was beautiful, all the trees and everything. It all seemed so peaceful. As I looked out the window, I couldn't help but think about all the things that were going on in my life right then, good and bad.

> *January 28, 2000 - 2:07 p.m.*
> *I'm on my way to New York and I'm too excited. It's not like I've never been there before but this time I'm going to be there with Ronnie. When I'm with Ronnie everything feels so right. He's like the perfect man. I know nobody's really perfect but I bet Ronnie comes damn close.*
>
> *Being with him is tripped out though. On one hand, sneaking around with him is exciting. I know that sounds crazy but it is. I mean it feels like I'm in the movie of the week or something. But on the other hand, it's terrifying. I don't know what Patrick would do if he ever found out about this. He's really beginning to scare me. He gets this look in his eyes sometimes, and I just don't know what he'll do. Then I know if he found out I was cheating with someone on the team, especially Ronnie, he would flip. He's so jealous of Ronnie. He's always talking about how everybody on campus be jocking Ronnie and his game ain't even all that. I never say anything but I want to say, "He is all that." Patrick is the one who's not.*
>
> *Anyway, Ronnie and I have been talking about a lot of things lately but he's never really said what he wanted from me as far as we're concerned. I guess for now, I'm going to leave things as they are. I just can't make a move first because I don't want to get caught out there. I don't want to tell him how I feel and have him not feel the same.*

The train ride took no time. Before I knew it I was in New York. I had no idea where I was going to wait for Ronnie. He said he would be there around four-thirty but the train was a half hour early.

I really had to go to the bathroom but I wasn't too sure about going in the rest rooms at a train station. Most of the time they weren't that clean and I couldn't stand using a dirty bathroom. I really had to go though, so I was going to take my chances. It turned out not to be that bad in there. It wasn't like a bathroom in somebody's house, but it would do. When you gotta go, you gotta go.

After taking care of business, I got a bottle of Snapple peach iced tea. Since I had some time to kill, I went over to this newsstand to see what magazines they had. As I was scanning the large variety of books, magazines and newspapers, I could feel eyes on me. I sipped my tea and tried to discretely see if I was being watched.

I saw a strange-looking guy standing off to my left. He looked like a throwback to the eighties. He was all dressed up like a broke-down breakdancer. I quickly turned back toward the magazines. I picked up a copy of *Heart & Soul* and prayed he didn't come over. But that prayer wasn't answered.

"Hey, beautiful."

I thought rappers were the only people who wore gold teeth but I guess I was wrong. That dude had a mouthful of gold. The glare was just about blinding me. I damn near needed my sunglasses.

"Hi," I responded, trying to show no interest.

I paid for my magazine and walked away. I was trying my best not to be rude because I was in a strange city, in a big train station all by myself. I guess my saying, "hi" made him think he could have a seat with me. All I could think was, *Ronnie, come the hell on!*

"So, you waiting for your husband?" Goldie asked.

"Ah, no. I'm not married." I don't know why I said that. I should have lied. The brother started smiling like he had just won the lottery. Not that I believed it could be done, but, if there was a man who could turn women into lesbians, he was sitting beside me.

"Are you getting a train out or did you just get in?"

"Um, I just got here," I answered hesitantly.

"Is this your first time in New York?"

"No, I've been here several times before."

"Where are you from?" I was starting to get tired of playing Twenty Questions.

"I'm from D.C."

"Mmm, yeah I heard D.C. had some fine women, and you definitely are one of them," he said, smiling in my face.

"You know, I am really not trying to be rude but I'm trying to read my magazine."

"How 'bout you let me take you out to dinner tonight?"

"I don't think so."

"What, you think you too cute?"

I just knew he had to be kidding. I wanted to say, *Hell yeah I think I'm too cute for your ugly ass!* Things like that always happened to me. Every time me and Erika went out somewhere, I always had some ugly dude following me around. Erika always had all the fine brothers walking up on her. But you could bet your life that all the bucked-tooth, cross-eyed, bad-breath having bammas would be rolling up on me.

I looked at my watch. It was four-thirty-five and still no Ronnie. All I knew was he had better get there soon before I had to go off on that brother.

"No, I don't think I'm too cute. I'm just not interested in going out to dinner with you."

"What, I ain't your type or something?"

That was an understatement. The whole time this dude was talking, I was looking around trying to find some way to get away from him.

Finally, there was Ronnie walking with a guy I didn't recognize right off. It looked like one of the guys in the group. It had to be Dre. I was about to have a fit because they didn't come over. They just sat down across from me.

Ronnie looked at Goldie. He smiled and raised his eyebrows. Goldie looked at him and said, "Is he here for you?"

I don't know why but I decided I was going to mess with Goldie a little.

"Ah no," I answered. I looked at him and knew at that moment that this was the ugliest brother I had seen in my life.

"I'm really not trying to be rude but I have to meet that brother over there," I said, trying my best not to smile. Goldie actually looked at me like he couldn't believe I would leave him to go talk to somebody else.

I got up and headed toward Ronnie. He smiled and rubbed his fingers over his lips.

It was obvious that Ronnie hadn't told Dre who I was because when I sat down beside him, Dre seemed very surprised.

"Excuse me, I know you don't know me," I began as I leaned closer to Ronnie, "but I saw you over here and I just had to come over and let you know that you are one of the finest brothers I have ever laid my eyes on." Dre sat there with a look of disbelief on his face.

"Oh, really, well thank you, boo," Ronnie replied with a smile.

"Are you here to pick up someone?" I asked.

"Yeah, but, ah, she's not here yet."

"She is a lucky woman."

"Oh, I agree."

I leaned closer to him and rubbed his arm.

"You know what, I wish I could have you for just one night," I said, licking my lips.

Ronnie loved that. I had been with him enough to know what buttons to push. I knew Ronnie was getting a little excited. When he kind of shifted in his seat and cleared his throat.

By this time, Dre was really tripping. He got up and walked around the bench. "This shit could only happen to this nigga," he mumbled, shaking his head. Ronnie and I were both trying our best not to laugh.

"Do you think that one night can be arranged?" I asked.

"I don't think so, boo."

Dre mumbled, "It can be arranged with me."

"Well, ah, do you think I can at least taste those beautiful, juicy lips before I go?"

"I don't see a problem with that."

Dre was looking in another direction and when he heard Ronnie say that, he looked at him as if to say, *Are you crazy?*

Ronnie and I started kissing, and Dre threw his hands up in the air. "I do not believe this shit."

As we stopped kissing a few minutes later, I slowly licked Ronnie's upper lip and said, "Mmm, thank you."

"Oh, you're very welcome. It was my pleasure."

I whispered, "It always is." Ronnie smiled.

Dre just stood there looking at us like we were crazy. Ronnie and I started laughing.

"What's up with your boy?" I asked as I wiped the lipstick from his lips. Ronnie shrugged and said, "I don't know. Why don't you ask him?"

"What's up with you, Dre?"

"How you know my name?" he asked.

"She's seen your pictures before," Ronnie answered.

Dre looked at both of us and we started laughing again.

"Man, I was straight buggin' up in here. I couldn't believe that shit. I was like 'how come no girl ever does that to me?'"

"The look on your face was so funny," I said.

"Don't be doing that to me no more."

Ronnie smiled and said, "Well, Dre, this is Stacey. Stacey, this is my boy, Dre."

"See, girl, I'm through with you already."

Ronnie laughed and said, "Alright, man, let's bounce."

As we walked to the car, Ronnie asked me how the trip was. "Oh, it was fine until I got here and Goldie over there tried to talk to me." They both laughed. I really didn't think it was funny.

"Yeah, we saw him," Ronnie said.

"I was like Ronnie, please come on."

"Oh, we were here. I saw dude when he spotted you when you walked out of the bathroom."

"No, you didn't." Ronnie started laughing and so did Dre. "How you gonna do me like that?" They just kept right on laughing. I was ready to kick both of them in the neck.

I really wanted to see the city so Ronnie decided to take me on the scenic route. New York was so cool. It had everything. I always thought it would be nice to live there, but I would have to be making mad loot. New York was expensive as hell.

I was so busy looking out the window that I didn't even notice Ronnie putting a CD in. I heard Maxwell start and I looked at him. He didn't look in my direction, but he smiled. I smiled, too, because Maxwell had become our CD. Whenever we were together, that CD was on. You would think we'd get tired of it but we didn't. I especially didn't get tired of the *Love Jones* version of "Sumthin', Sumthin'" because that's exactly when we used it—when we were doing a little sumthin', sumthin' or our private sessions, as Ronnie referred to them.

Ronnie kind of glanced at me and asked, "So ah, how's Ellie doing?" cracking a sexy smile.

"She's fine," I answered. "Can't wait to see you."

Ronnie laughed. "Oh, I can't wait to see her either."

Dre leaned toward us and asked, "Who's Ellie? One of your girls?"

We both laughed.

"Not exactly," Ronnie responded.

"Oh, it's one of them private things, huh?"

"Yeah, man, you know how that is."

"And knowing your ass, Ron, it's something freaky."

We both started laughing.

"Go 'head with that, man."

"Now, do I look like I'd be doing anything freaky?" I asked Dre. Hopefully my question wouldn't backfire on me and he'd say, "Yeah, you look like a little freak."

"Naw, you don't look like it but you've been messing with him long enough that he probably turned you on to some freaky shit." He was right about that because I had done some freaky things with Ronnie. But I must say, I enjoyed every bit of it.

"Go to hell, man," Ronnie said, laughing.

After dropping Dre off, we headed to one of Ronnie's father's restaurant, Melodies. Ronnie had come up with the name, of course. His father opened it in 1989. It was kind of like an upscale soul food restaurant. The tables were set with linen napkins and fancy goblets for water, polished silverware and nice china. It was along the same lines as B. Smith's in Washington—actually there was a B. Smith's in Manhattan too. I guess that would be his main competitor.

Melodies mixed the old-fashioned type of soul food: fried chicken, collard greens and chitterlings with more contemporary dishes. I couldn't imagine eating chitterlings on fine china but Ronnie said people did it every day at his dad's place.

"My parents are looking forward to meeting you," he said, glancing over at me, "especially since I haven't stopped talking about you lately."

"So, what did you tell your parents about me?"

"Everything."

"You didn't tell them everything about me, did you?"

"You mean that you gotta man?" He knew exactly what I meant. "Hell yeah. I told them you got me hanging on a string while you sticking by your little punk-ass boyfriend."

"Ronnie!"

He kind of laughed. Ronnie thought those little comments were funny but I didn't. We stopped at a red light and he leaned over. "You know I'm just messing with you, boo." He planted those soft lips on me, and I almost forgot what we were talking about. Even though I had been messing with Ronnie for almost four months, he still had that effect on me. And I loved it.

"I told them you were a very smart and very beautiful woman. They don't need to know the rest."

"Why do you do that to me all the time?" I asked, trying not to smile.

"I like seeing your reaction."

"You need to stop."

He kissed me and said, "You know you like it." On some levels, he was right.

I was kind of nervous when we walked in the restaurant. I hated meeting people's parents. You never know how they're going to take you. I guess that's how guys felt walking up in my house with my father and three brothers staring them down.

The restaurant was beautiful on the inside. The décor was very Afrocentric but not overdone. Everything was in earth tones and there were African accents everywhere. Someone in Ronnie's family had to be a Charles Bibbs fan because his work was on almost every wall.

"This is nice," I remarked as we walked through the dining area.

"Raina and my mom did all the decorating."

"I can tell. It reminds me a lot of your house."

"Yeah, they both think they're interior decorators," Ronnie said, kind of laughing.

A tall, slender woman with very short hair walked out of the kitchen. She was beautiful, an exotic kind of beautiful. Her skin was bronze and flawless. I'd never seen skin so smooth. She walked over to us and Ronnie said, "Hey, beautiful," giving her a kiss on her cheek.

She smiled and said, "Hey yourself."

The woman looked at me and said, "So—this is the Stacey that we have been hearing so much about."

I smiled. I didn't know how to take her comment. Was hearing about me a good or bad thing?

"Yeah, here she is. Stacey, this is my mom, Mrs. Morgan."

I couldn't believe that was his mother. She looked like she could have been his sister. Ronnie said his mother was fifty-two but I swear she didn't look a day over thirty-five.

"It's nice to finally meet you, Stacey."

"It's nice to meet you too, Mrs. Morgan. Ronnie has told me so much about you."

"Oh, he's been telling us about you also."

Ronnie laughed and said, "C'mon now, Ma, I haven't been doing all that much talking about her."

"Okay, whatever you say. Well let me go get your father and Raina. We were all wondering what was taking you so long."

Ronnie said, "I took the scenic route to show Stacey around a bit," smiling like the cat that ate the canary.

If his mother only knew what really took us so long.

After we dropped Dre off, Ronnie decided he wanted a private session before we went to the restaurant.

We turned down a small alley and I asked, "Where are we going?"

"Don't worry about it," he said with a smile.

"I thought you said we were on the way to the restaurant?"

"We are."

I just looked at him. I knew damn well the restaurant wasn't down no alley.

Ronnie turned into a small parking lot where several cars were parked. I recognized the black Lexus from our freshman year.

"Isn't that your father's car?"

"Yep."

He pulled around the side of the building and put the truck in park.

"Ronnie, where are we?"

He flipped the CD changer back to the Maxwell CD and said, "Behind the restaurant."

When I heard, 'Sumthin', Sumthin' start playing, I looked at Ronnie like he was crazy. Like I said, I had done some freaky things with Ronnie, including doing it outside on his deck but I was not about to have sex with him outside of his parents' restaurant. What if someone saw us? I would be mortified.

"C'mon Stace. Nobody's gonna see us," Ronnie assured me. He was right because it wasn't going to happen.

"Awe boo, c'mon," he pleaded. "I haven't seen you in over a week. You know how you be having me fiendin'."

I just looked at him. "Are you out of your mind?"

He sucked his teeth and asked, "A'ight then, can I at least have a kiss before we go inside?"

I was hesitant, but finally agreed. That was my first mistake.

I loved kissing Ronnie. He had seduced me with those kisses so many times that I should have known better.

My second mistake was not stopping him when his kisses moved from my lips to my neck. The little willpower I had went straight out of the window when he kissed my neck.

Now, I wasn't a freak in the literal sense of the word but Erika always said I had 'freak tendencies' when it came to Ronnie. As I was slipping my pants off in that truck, I knew she was right.

Ronnie pushed his seat back as far as it could go in anticipation of me taking the riding position.

"Are you sure nobody can see us?" I asked.

"Trust me boo, nobody can see through this tint."

I said, "Okay," and straddled him.

He smiled victoriously and I said, "I can't stand you."

He laughed and replied, "Yeah well, we'll see how you feel about me in about twenty minutes," as he started unbuttoning my shirt.

There was nothing I could say at that point because I knew he was right. Ronnie did not disappoint when it came to sex. He was far more experience than I was but I didn't mind being his student one bit. He had it going on.

It didn't take Ronnie long to get my shirt open. The former leg man had become a pro at unhooking my bra with only two fingers. He wasted no time exposing his new favorite parts of my body.

Ronnie cupped one of my breasts in his large hand. His gentle touch coupled with the expert way he used his tongue on my nipple, sent my body into a heated frenzy. I forgot all about being in the truck.

Ronnie pulled a condom out of his pocket and set it next to the gear shift. The brother showed off the strength in his abs as he raised his pelvis with me on him and somehow got his pants down.

He handed me the condom and said, "Put it on for me."

His request took me by surprise. I had never actually touched Ronnie's "Big Man." To be honest, I had never actually touched anyone's manhood before, not even Tim's and of the few guys I had been with in the six years that I had been having sex, I felt the most comfortable with him—until Ronnie.

I took the Magnum packet and carefully opened it. I took the condom out and threw the wrapper on my seat. I gently stretched the condom down his fully erect tool. He trembled a little at my touch.

I was about to add a new position to my sexual repertoire. Tim and I were straight missionary. With Patrick, I had added doggy-style and now I was about to ride the pony. Though I hadn't done it before, I was sure I could handle it. It was all in the hips and I definitely knew how to work my hips.

I slowly lowered myself on to him and our bodies became one once again. My body had gotten use to Ronnie's massiveness, but this new position came along with a new and highly intense sensation. I know it's neither biologically or anatomically possible but it felt like Ronnie was about to puncture one of my lungs. I almost jumped off him but he held me in place.

"Just relax into it boo." He started kissing near my ear and whispered, "You can handle it."

Ronnie guided my hips up and down. I've always been a fast learner so it didn't take long for me to catch his rhythm. I began grinding slowly. Ronnie's moans filled the truck. He rubbed his hands up and down my thighs and said, "Mmm Stacey, you feel so good boo."

I was working it out, if I do say so myself. I was kind of proud of myself. With every rotation of my hips, Ronnie's breathing got heavier and his moans became a little louder. "Damn," passed his lips several times. The more he moaned, the more I put it on him.

Ronnie's sexual stamina was amazing. That brother was as far away from being a minute man as you could get. I realized that was because he was normally in control. But this time, *I* was in control.

Ronnie was doing his best to maintain but he couldn't any longer. The sound that he made as he exploded in ecstasy wasn't like any I had heard from him before. I knew right then that I had him. The "Big Man" was mine. As I achieved my own explosion, I realized, he had me too. The poo-nani was all his.

As his mother disappeared behind a door marked OFFICE, I looked at Ronnie. "I can't believe that's your mother."

"Why?" he asked.

"She looks like she could be your sister or something."

Ronnie laughed and said, "Yeah, that's what a lot of people say. I have to get in Myles's chest all the time 'cause he be looking at her butt."

I laughed and said, "You know your boy is a perv."

We sat down and Ronnie was rubbing my arm. He kept telling me how glad he was that I was there. I was glad too. I knew I would really enjoy being with Ronnie that weekend without having to worry about someone seeing us.

Ronnie kept kissing on my neck. I pushed him back even though I was really enjoying it. I didn't want his parents to walk out and see that.

"Ronnie, stop now."

"Why?" He licked his lips and said, "You weren't telling me to stop a little while ago in the truck." I liked when Ronnie talked dirty but I had to play it off.

"Why don't you stop? Your parents will be out here soon."

Ronnie laughed and said, "What, you don't think they know why you're here?"

"And what exactly do you mean by that?" I asked about to cop an attitude. The last thing I wanted was for his parents to think I was just some freak he was bringing home.

"Stacey, if I'm bringing you home to meet them, they know you mean a lot to me. And, my parents are not stupid, they do know I have sex."

"Still."

"Okay, I'm going to stop messing with you."

"Thank you."

Ronnie's mother came back out of the office with his father and sister. Ronnie's sister looked just like his mother. But Ronnie's father, now he was F-I-N-E. He was so fine that when I saw him, my jaw dropped open. I saw where Ronnie got his good looks. His father was one older man that could definitely get it. Ronnie must have sensed my thoughts. He nudged me and whispered, "Quit creamin' over my pops."

I laughed and said, "Shut up."

"Ron, Raina, this is Ronnie's friend Stacey. Stacey, this is Ronnie's father, Mr. Morgan, and his sister, Raina."

We all exchanged greetings.

"Well, well, well, we finally get to meet the infamous Ms. Stacey Jackson," Raina said, smiling.

Ronnie looked at her and said, "Shut up, girl."

Raina just smiled.

"Don't pay attention to these two, Stacey. They go at it like this all the time," Mr. Morgan interjected.

"Oh, I understand. That's how my brothers and I are."

Ronnie's father patted him on the back and said, "I know you're entertaining this weekend, but I need you for a couple of hours."

"I can take Stacey past my place to drop off her things then we can go hang out for a while in Manhattan," Raina volunteered.

"Thanks, sis. I really appreciate that."

"No problem."

Ronnie looked at his father and said, "Well, Pops, Stacey's in good hands, so I'm here for you."

"Cool."

Before Raina and I left, Ronnie pulled me to the side. "Are you going to be alright?"

"Yeah, of course," I replied.

"Okay. Well here's some money." He pulled out two hundred dollars.

"What's that for?"

"Didn't you say you wanted to go shopping?"

I pushed his hand back and said, "Yeah, but I have my own money." I didn't want anyone in Ronnie's family to see him giving me money. "You know I don't need you giving me money."

"Girl, please. Take this money and get yourself something nice for tonight." He kissed me and said, "I want you lookin' fly."

I smiled and said, "Okay."

Raina said, "C'mon, Stacey. I can tell you some funny stories about my brother while we're out."

"Don't be trippin', Raina," Ronnie said.

"Anyway, c'mon, Stacey," she replied, unfazed by his serious tone.

Ronnie kissed me and said, "I'll see you later." I smiled, and Raina and I left.

We were going to just drop my bags off at Raina's apartment but I told her I wanted to freshen up after the train ride. I couldn't tell her I needed a shower after sexing her brother in his truck. I showered, changed my clothes and we headed to Manhattan.

I needed to find an outfit to wear that night. Raina said she knew I would be able to find something nice at Bloomingdale's. I didn't know what I really wanted though. All I knew was it had to be sexy. There was a good chance that I was going to see Ronnie's ex-girlfriend Kim and I wanted to look fierce. My problem was it was the dead of winter so I was going to have to be very creative to pull off sexy.

Raina suggested some leather pants. "They always work for me when I want to turn a head or two." I had never had any leather pants but I had always wanted some. So I figured there was no time like the present.

Raina and I finally found the perfect outfit. I was going to turn some heads. I bought some black leather pants that were low-cut at the waist, a black leather tie-back halter and some fly high-heeled Kenneth Cole boots. I already had a leather coat so I would be warm outside and with my halter, I would be sexy inside.

Raina and I were on our way to the food court when Ronnie's cell phone started ringing in my purse. He had given it to me in case I needed it because my phone didn't work in New York. My service was just for the D.C/Maryland/Virginia area. I got it out of my bag and said, "Hello."

A female voice on the other end said, "Hello?"

"Yes."

"Ah, who is this?"

I always hated when people call on the phone and then ask you who you are.

"Who are you calling?"

"I'm calling Ronnie Morgan."

"Well he's not here."

"And who are you to be answering his cell phone?" the unknown girl asked with an attitude.

I laughed and looked at Raina.

She mouthed, "Who's that?"

I shrugged. I didn't know who the chick on the other end was. But I knew I was going to have to put sister-girl in her place real quick.

"Ah, I'm answering his cell phone because he gave it to me. And who are you to be asking me questions?"

"Well I'm his friend, Kim."

"Kim?" I said aloud. What the hell was Kim doing calling Ronnie? He told me he hadn't been talking to her anymore.

Raina sucked her teeth and said, "Just hang up on her." I laughed because I knew Kim had to have heard her. "I can't stand that girl."

"Well, Kim, I will tell Ronnie that you called."

"Yeah, you do that. And to whom am I speaking?"

"Oh, you're speaking to Ronnie's *new* friend, Stacey."

"Stacey?"

"Like I said, I'll tell Ronnie you called."

I hung up the phone and Raina said, "She is such a pain. Ronnie told that trick to stop calling all the time when he was home for Christmas. The problem is he's been too damn nice. Let her call my mother's house one more time when I'm there. It ain't gonna be nothing nice." All I could do was laugh.

We went on down to the food court and got something to eat. We spent a few more hours tripping off Kim and getting to know each other better. Raina was really cool.

Diamonds was Ronnie's father's club. It was in a converted warehouse, and it was becoming one of the hottest dance clubs in New York City.

You could hear the music pumping from blocks away. The line to get in wrapped around the block. The club had to be the bomb to have so many people standing out in the cold to get in. I was glad we didn't have to stand out there. Raina just walked right up to the door and I followed her inside.

"Awe man, this place is off the chain," I said, having never seen anything like that club before.

"Yeah, it is pretty live in here." Raina turned to me and said, "So, are you going to be cool?"

"Oh yeah. I'll just find Ronnie."

"He's probably upstairs in the VIP section." She pointed upward.

"Okay. I'll go on up there."

"Alright, girl. I'll check you later."

She walked away and I made my way toward the steps. As I approached the bottom of the staircase, I saw Ronnie coming down.

"Hey, boo," he said, greeting me with a kiss.

"Hey."

"Alright, let's see the 'fit."

I took off my coat to reveal my leather outfit to him. His eyes widened. "Man, boo, this is fly."

I turned around slowly letting him soak in the full sexiness of the outfit. I knew the tight leather pants, plus the halter with my back almost entirely exposed would drive Ronnie wild.

"You like?" I asked, knowing full well what the answer was.

"Do I?" He hugged me and rubbed my back. "You 'bout to start an uprising in here."

I just laughed.

"Let me run your coat upstairs. Then you and I are going to hit the dance floor."

"Alright."

"And I'll show you how we do it in the N-Y-C."

"You better come wit' it," I taunted.

Ronnie put my coat up in the lounge. When he came back down, he took my hand and we headed to the dance floor. The music was cranking. We danced for almost an hour straight. Both of us needed a little rest. We made our way over to the bar and Ronnie ordered us some drinks.

Ronnie was sitting at the bar and I was standing in front of him. He glanced to his right and groaned.

"What's wrong?" I looked to my left and saw a girl walking toward us. "Who's that?" I asked.

"That's Kim."

I had been waiting all night to see good ol' Kim. She wasn't bad looking. That is if you like the tall, light-skinned, long-hair, green-eyed type. She looked exactly like I thought one of Ronnie's ex-girlfriends would look.

"Oh, I forgot to tell you she called you earlier on your cell phone," I said, smiling slyly.

Ronnie looked at me and said, "What?"

I just smiled.

Kim walked up to us and said, "Hey, Ronnie."

She didn't acknowledge my presence at all. I just laughed. I thought, *Oh this hoe wants to be like that?* I had already had two Long Island Iced Teas so I was definitely feeling nice. I was more than prepared to take it there with her.

I leaned in close to Ronnie and put my arm around his neck. I kind of rubbed my nose against his cheek, all the while, looking at Kim. Ronnie was trying his best not to smile.

"Ah, hey Kim. How you doing?" Ronnie finally greeted her.

"I'm alright." She kept looking at me like I was with her man or something.

"Oh, um, Kim, this is my friend Stacey. Stacey, this is Kim."

"Hey," Kim responded in this stank tone.

I laughed and said, "Hey."

Kim kept looking me up and down. She had to really be out of her mind. She didn't know me. I decided I had enough of her just standing there looking at me like she was crazy. I took Ronnie by the hand and said, "Let's go dance some more, baby." I pulled him away before he could say too much more to his little ex-girlfriend.

"Girl, why you do that?" Ronnie asked, laughing.

"Please, she standing up there looking stupid."

He just shook his head and said, "You are too funny."

"Alright people, these next jams are going out to all the lovers in the house."

"Is that us?" Ronnie asked, wrapping his strong arms around my waist.

"I think so," I responded, kissing him softly.

We had been dancing a few minutes, when I felt someone bump against me. I turned around and saw it was Kim. She gave me a half-assed "'scuse me" and kept dancing with some dude. I looked at Ronnie and he said, "Don't let her get to you, boo." The mere fact that she was near me was getting to me. But I decided to let it go. We continued dancing and I couldn't believe it, but the heifer bumped me again. "What the hell?" came out of my mouth before I knew it.

"'Scuse me." This time she said it with this little smirk. Ms. Kim didn't know how close she was to catching a beat down.

"You would want to watch what the hell you're doing."

The combination of the Long Island Iced Teas I drank and the fact that she was Ronnie's ex, made me a little louder than I normally would have been. Ronnie had never seen that side of me before.

"I said 'scuse me."

"I don't give a damn what you said."

"C'mon, boo, let's just go upstairs." Ronnie started pulling me away.

"Boo?" Kim said with her face all frowned up.

I turned back toward her and said, "Yes, boo. You have a problem with him calling me that?"

"I guess you can be his number two boo if you want." I was so ready to jump on that girl. If we hadn't been in Ronnie's father's club, I would have.

"Well I guess he had to move on to a bigger and better boo."

That pissed her off. There was nothing she could say. I wasn't going to let no fake-ass Chanté Moore try to carry me.

Instead of going up to the lounge and chilling, Ronnie decided it was time to take me home. He actually thought the whole situation was funny. When it was going down, I didn't think it was funny at all, but as Ronnie recounted what happened on the drive to Raina's apartment, it was kind of funny. I was still a little embarrassed though. I didn't normally act like that. I had never, ever gotten into a fight with another chick over any guy. But I knew that I could have punched that girl in her face that night. I didn't even know why. Ronnie had talked to me about other girls he had gone out with on campus, but there was something different about Kim. He said he had been in love with her. I wanted him to be in love with me, but as far as I knew, he wasn't. She had been where I wanted to be and for that reason alone, I couldn't stand her.

When we got back to Raina's apartment, Mr. Romance went to work. He turned the lights down and lit some candles. Ronnie was going to fix me a glass of wine but I had had quite enough to drink at the club. He ended up fixing us some cranberry juice in wineglasses, which I thought was cute. He lit a fire and set some big black pillows on the floor in front of it. For the next few hours, we sat in front of that fire, drinking juice, talking and listening to music. Before the night was over our talking session turned into one of our most passionate private sessions ever.

The rest of my stay in New York with Ronnie was no less romantic. He took me all over the city and showed me everything I ever wanted to see. We went to the Statue of Liberty, Times Square, Central Park and he even got us tickets to a Broadway show. Everything was perfect.

January 30, 2000 - 5:12 p.m.

I just got back from my weekend in New York with Ronnie. I had the best time with him. Whenever I'm with Ronnie, I feel so complete. He always goes out of his way to make me happy. All the time we were there, he was making sure I had a good time. He took me all over the city and showed me every tourist attraction there was.

I met his family. Ronnie's father is so, so fine. I couldn't believe it when I saw him. I see where Ronnie gets his good looks. His mother is gorgeous too. And so is his sister. I didn't get to meet his brother, but I saw pictures and he's cute too. They are just a pretty family. They look like they should be on the cover of Essence.

We had mad fun at Ronnie's father's club, Diamonds. That place was the bomb. And while I was there, I met Ronnie's ex-girlfriend, Kim. Well Ronnie introduced us but I wouldn't say we really met each other. She was acting real stank. I had had me some drinks so I wasn't even trying to go there with her. I messed with her a little since she was trippin'. I really felt like grabbing Ronnie's head and putting my tongue down his throat while she was standing there but I didn't. If Erika would have been around I know I would have because she's such bad influence on me. Just kidding. Anyway, Kim and I got into it a little but it was nothing big. Ronnie wasn't trying to deal with her so we eventually just left.

Last night, he had his father close off a section of the restaurant and we had a very romantic dinner. He went all out. There were a dozen white roses on the table, wine and everything. He even had his dad prepare the meal. I was too impressed.

I realized this weekend that I am in a little too deep. I knew once I saw Kim and my blood ran hot that I was in over my head. I'm falling for Ronnie hard and fast. I need to get my shit together with Patrick because I'll never be able to really be with Ronnie until I do.

I was getting my clothes together for the next day when the phone rang. I looked at the Caller ID. It was Patrick. I was still on my high from my weekend with Ronnie and didn't want him bringing me down, so I let the answering machine pick up.

"Hey Stacey. It's me, Patrick. Ah, I've been calling you all weekend. I know why you haven't answered or returned my calls. I'm sorry about what happened, Stacey. I didn't mean to hit you. It's just that I was kind of tired and everything. I know I've said it before but I promise it won't happen again. Please just give me a call."

happy birthday!

stacey

I had a decision to make. My brothers' birthdays were coming up and I was supposed to be going over my parents' for our traditional family birthday get-together. On all of our birthdays, we always had a big dinner and my mother would bake her special triple chocolate birthday cake for the boys and coconut cake for me. It was the bomb. As we got older, the boys were always trying to get out of it but that never worked because Daddy would get in their chest.

"This dinner means a lot to my wife, and you are not going to upset her. Because when she's upset, I'm upset. And you do not want me upset." So dinner was on.

Mommy had invited Patrick over but he didn't want to go because he knew my brothers didn't care for him. Not that they knew everything that had gone on between us, they never liked him. Kevin and Devin always said, "That bamma thinks he's the shit." Then Patrick being an Alpha didn't help his case in their eyes. They weren't really that petty to not like him just because he was in a different fraternity, but it was a convenient excuse for them.

Patrick got on Tracy's bad side the first time they met. Tracy and I both lived in the Towers West. I was always in Tracy's room chilling with him and his roommate, Joe.

On this day, Patrick happened to be visiting a friend of his that lived on the same floor. Joe always kept the door open because he was nosy as hell and had to see who was going in whose room. Tracy had his head in my lap and we were all watching *Oprah*. Patrick walked pass and saw me. He walked back in the room and said, "What the hell is going on, Stacey?"

Patrick's first mistake was just walking up in Tracy's room. His second mistake was talking to me like that in front of him.

"Excuse me," Tracy said, getting up from the bed. I knew I had to jump in quickly before Patrick opened his mouth again, and really pissed Tracy off.

"Aye Patrick, this is my brother, Tracy." By this time, Joe had risen up and was ready to fight too. "And this is his roommate, Joe."

"Oh, I'm sorry. It's ah nice to meet y'all," he said, a little embarrassed.

"Yeah—whatever," was Tracy's response. I knew then Patrick was on his shit list.

No matter how much Tracy disliked Patrick, he didn't say much about it, mainly because he knew I heard enough from Devin and Kevin. Since I knew he didn't really like Patrick, I didn't discuss our relationship much with Tracy.

I knew none of my brothers would miss Patrick being at dinner but I didn't know how they would react to me bringing someone else. They all were big sports fans, especially Howard sports, so they knew who Ronnie was. Tracy definitely knew who he was because he knew about my big crush. However, he didn't know I had started messing with Ronnie. That was my big dilemma as far as the birthday dinner was concerned. I was really starting to like Ronnie and I wanted Tracy to know.

"You are really buggin' now," Erika said when I asked her if I should take Ronnie. "You know damn well if you roll up in that house with Ronnie, all kinds of questions are going to be flying at you."

She was right. Everybody would want to know what happened to Patrick. Was Ronnie my new boyfriend? And to be honest, I wouldn't have any answers. Despite all that, I asked Ronnie anyway. I convinced myself that I could say he was just a friend from school and everyone would leave it at that.

"I'd love to go and chill with the Jackson family," was Ronnie's answer to my invitation. "But, isn't your family going to wonder why I'm coming and not your man?" he asked.

"Not really. I told you my brothers don't like Patrick. And they have no problem letting him know. Actually, they don't have a problem letting anybody know they don't like them."

Ronnie laughed and said, "This should be an interesting afternoon." That was an understatement.

When we pulled in the driveway, Tracy was outside playing with our dog, Duchess. We had her almost six years. She was a big, beautiful dog. A lot of people were scared of her but she wouldn't hurt a fly. That's why my father didn't like her. He said a Rottweiler shouldn't be that friendly to everybody. Daddy just didn't know, Duchess would bite the hell out of somebody if you really wanted her to.

When I talked to Tracy the day before, I told him Patrick wasn't coming, but I didn't tell him I was bringing someone else. He saw Ronnie in the car, looked over at me and gave me a sly smile. I smiled and shook my head. Ronnie saw Duchess and said, "Yo, Stace, I ain't even trying to get out of this car with that big-ass dog there."

"She's not going to bother you, especially with me being with you." He looked at me like *Yeah right, whatever.*

"What, you don't trust me, Ronnie?" He tried not to smile.

"Yeah, okay."

We got out of the car and Tracy said, "What's up, baby girl?"

I hugged him.

I hadn't seen my brother that much since he first got back from his internship in Phoenix. I really missed him. Going back and forth between two men and trying to stay on top of all my schoolwork, along with my sorority commitments and NAACP didn't leave me a lot of extra time.

"Hey, sweetie," I said, wrapping my arms tightly around his neck. Tracy looked at Ronnie, then back at me and smiled. He was so silly.

"Ah, Tracy, this is…um…a friend of mine, Ronnie. Ronnie, this is my brother, Tracy." They both said, "What's up, man?" and gave each other the brother-man handshake and hug.

Tracy said, "Y'all kicking some butt in the MEAC this season."

"Yeah, we're doing pretty good."

Ronnie turned his focus back to Duchess. Tracy told him she wasn't going to bother him but he wasn't trying to hear it. I decided to just take him in the house. Tracy whispered, "We are going to have to have a little talk before you leave here, sis." I just nodded.

We walked into the house and headed for the kitchen where I knew my mother was cooking up a storm. Whenever my mother cooked, she had her *Motown's Greatest Hits* CD blasting. She was singing and bopping to the music. She had gotten her hair braided since I last saw her. The braids were bouncing around right along with her.

"Mmm, look at Mrs. Jackson shaking her groove thang," Ronnie jokingly whispered.

"Shut up," I said, hitting him in the chest.

"Hi, Mommy," I shouted over the music. She turned down the music and said, "Hey, sweet pea." She grabbed my face and started kissing all over it just like she'd done all my life. "How's Mommy's baby girl doing?"

"Mommy, stop." I shifted my eyes in Ronnie's direction, and she looked at him.

"Mmm, and who is this fine young man here?" My mother had good taste in men too.

"Mommy, this is my friend, Ronnie. Ronnie, this is my mother, Mrs. Jackson."

"It's nice to meet you, Ronnie," my mother said, shaking his hand.

"Nice meeting you, too, Mrs. Jackson."

"Don't you mind my daughter. You can call me Cheryl."

Ronnie smiled and said, "Okay, Cheryl. And I just want to let you know, I was really enjoying your dancing and singing," Ronnie joked. Mommy hit him with her towel. "Go 'head with that, boy," she replied coyly.

"Ah, anyway, where's my daddy?" I asked, tripping off my mother flirting with Ronnie.

"Oh, he and the boys are down in the basement playing pool and Gina's down there watching."

"Oh, my future sister-in-law is here. Cool. We're going to go down there. I'll be back in a few minutes to help you out."

"Don't rush. I pretty much have everything taken care of."

"Oh, okay."

I had to warn Ronnie about my father. He was always trying to embarrass me when I brought people home. It didn't matter who it was, male or female. When he saw Ronnie, I knew he was going to really cut up. With Kevin and Dev being down there, it was going to be even worse.

The boys always beat my father at pool. He was not that great of a loser either. In fact, he a sore loser is what he is. My mother usually had to rescue the guys, because every time Daddy lost, he had to play "one more game."

Once we hit the bottom of the steps, I could tell nothing had changed. Dev was already messing with Daddy.

"Man, Pops, I think you should just retire your stick."

"Just rack the balls, boy, and shut the hell up."

"Yeah, Dev, he's just warming up. Ain't that right, Pops?" Kevin said, laughing.

"Y'all keep on talking." Daddy saw me and smiled. "Yeah, see now y'all are in trouble. My good luck charm is here." I hugged him and said, "Hey, Daddy."

I always loved getting hugs from my father. He would wrap his big arms around me and squeeze. It always made me feel so safe.

"Hey, pumpkin. How's Daddy's girl?" he asked in his baritone voice.
"I'm fine."

My father looked Ronnie up and down. "And who's this big nigga?"
he said through his teeth.

I hit him and was like, *"Daddy!"* I knew Ronnie heard him because he
kind of laughed. "Daddy, this is Ronnie. He's a friend of mine from
school. Ronnie, this is my father, Mr. Jackson."

"What's up, big man?" Daddy wasn't about to extend his hand. He
didn't know Ronnie so he had to play that hard role.

Ronnie smiled and said, "Nothing much, Mr. Jackson. It's nice to
meet you."

"Pumpkin, this isn't the same guy that…."

I had to shift the conversation with a quickness. The last thing I needed
was for Daddy to start talking about Patrick.

"Ah yeah, Ronnie, these are my brothers, Devin and Kevin and that's
Dev's girlfriend, Gina."

Gina and Dev had been going out on and off since they were in tenth
grade. She was real nice. Though my mother and I were close, it was
good having another female that I could talk to. Both Erika and I always
thought of Gina as the big sister we never had. Hopefully, my stupid
brother wouldn't let her get away…again.

When Devin started going to Howard, he thought he was all that. He
had to be the Mack Daddy supreme. At first Gina didn't know, but one
weekend, she came home from Tennessee State and all hell broke loose. It
was too much for me. My girl was going off on him, and Erika and I had
front-row seats.

When she went back to school, they had broken up and it was for
good, so she said. Dev tried to perpetrate like it didn't bother him but we
all knew better. He really did love Gina. Eventually, they made up. They
decided to see other people in school but still remain "together" so to
speak. When Gina graduated and moved back to D.C., they really got
back together.

"Ah, we're going upstairs to see if Ma needs any help in the kitchen,"
Gina said, grabbing my arm and pulling me toward the stairs. I hoped my
father and brothers didn't trip too much. Ronnie seemed like he could
hang though.

We sat down at the kitchen table. "Alright, I want to know what is up with this?"

I started laughing.

"What are you girls doing up here?" Mommy asked, shutting the oven door.

"I want Miss Thang here to tell me what's up with that fine, fine brother downstairs." Mommy sat at the table too. She was so nosy. Plus, she swore she was young.

"Yeah, I want to know about him too. He walked in here and I was like *Mmm*. He could make me rob a cradle or two."

My mother was too funny.

"He is just a friend. He plays ball with Dave and 'em."

They were both looking at me like "do we look stupid?" I wasn't sure if I should really tell them the whole story.

"Doesn't Patrick play basketball too?" Mommy asked.

"Um…yeah."

They both started smiling.

"You go, girl," Gina said.

"Don't trip, y'all. He's just a friend, okay? Patrick knows Kevin and Dev don't like him, so he didn't want to come. And Ronnie wasn't doing anything today so I just invited him. I thought he would enjoy coming."

"So you're saying, there is nothing going on between you two? Ab-so-lute-ly nothing at all?" Gina asked.

I couldn't help but smile. Like I said, I had never been a good liar and I couldn't even think about lying to my mother or Gina. Tracy saved me from having to answer by walking back in the house. We all looked at him. He looked down at his clothes, then around him.

"What?" he asked.

Gina laughed and said, "Nothing."

Mommy told him the guys were still in the basement playing pool. "I want to talk to Stace about that stud that she brought up in here." We all started laughing. The guys and my father came up from the basement and Gina said, "Nooo," kind of laughing.

"What are y'all doing up here? Dinner's not going to be ready for at least another hour," Mommy said.

"There are some basketball games on. We're going in the family room and check them out. If that's alright with you, Mrs. Jackson," Daddy said smiling.

"Alright, Mr. Jackson." Daddy kissed Mommy and all the men except Tracy went in the family room.

Gina said, "Trace, aren't you going to look at the games?"

"No, I told you I want to talk to my sister."

"I'll talk to you after dinner. I promise." He looked at me suspiciously but went in the family room anyway.

"That boy is something else," Mommy said, laughing.

Gina was all about the business at hand. She wanted to know exactly what was going on between Ronnie and me. "Okay, now getting back to my question, what's going on?"

"Alright, I guess you can say we're a little more than friends."

Mommy flashed one of her *I could say something but I won't* looks and got up. She said, "Well on that note, I'll get back to my dinner." She went back near the stove.

I kind of laughed and said, "Mommy."

She threw her hands up and shook her head. "You girls talk. There are some things I would rather not know details about."

Gina hit my hand and asked, "Anyway, exactly how much more is going on?"

"Just a little."

Gina pulled me closer to her and whispered, "A little, as in a kiss or as in a little sumthin', sumthin'." I laughed and Gina just looked at me.

"I know you better answer me before I go tell your brothers the little bit I do know."

"Oh, so you gonna dog me like that? I thought we were cool, Gina."

"Stacey."

I laughed again and said, "Okay, okay."

"So you and he…."

I glanced at my mother and saw that she wasn't paying a bit of attention. I looked at Gina and nodded. She took my hand again and said, "C'mon, we have to go for a walk."

We got our coats but before we could get out of the door, Devin came out from the family room. "Where y'all going?"

"We're just going for a little walk. We'll be back in a few minutes," Gina said.

He looked at me and I shrugged. Gina pulled me out the door. As we walked, Gina just looked at me, shaking her head.

"What?"

"I can't believe this. How long has this been going on between you two?" she asked.

"Well it kind of started this summer."

"This summer? Y'all been kickin' it that long and you didn't tell me?"

"It's hard to explain, Gina. It's like when Patrick went home this summer, me and Ronnie were just chillin' together a lot because he and Dave are real tight. Eventually it became obvious that there was more there."

"I want some details. How did this really start?"

"Well remember when I told you I went to see Chuck Brown back in October?"

"Yeah."

"Well Ronnie went with me and when I took him home, we kissed."

"Mmm," Gina said, smiling. I had to smile myself remembering that first kiss.

"It's like we had been flirting with each other a long time before that."

"So what happened after that?"

"Nothing really. Things just kind of went back to the way they had been. I was honestly trying my best to just stay away from him and remember I was with Patrick, but I guess I couldn't."

Gina laughed and said, "You guess, huh?"

When I told Gina about the night Ronnie came over my house and we came so close to having sex, she couldn't believe nothing happened.

"Girl, you a better woman than I am 'cause between you and me, if that would have happened to me, I really doubt that I would have been able to turn him away. That brother is fine as hell."

"You just don't know how hard it was. I mean ever since I stepped foot on campus, I have thought Ronnie was fine but I mean that was that. Then we started spending so much time together. Gina, girl, he has me doing things I never thought I would."

"What you mean, as far as sex?"

"Most definitely." I had to kind of laugh thinking about all the places I had been with Ronnie. "And girl, it is the bomb."

"Oh, I don't doubt it."

"But, it's not just that. It's like you know I have never been one for all that sneaking around stuff. But I do it constantly."

"How do y'all manage that? I mean with him playing ball with Patrick and everything."

"I don't know. I mean one good thing is Patrick doesn't have a car and Ronnie lives in Southwest, not too far from Zanzibar. So I mean I can go over there whenever I want to really. And Patrick has classes every Wednesday and Thursday night, so Ronnie's at my place then. And on the weekends if Patrick's out with the frat, which he usually is lately, I'm out with Ronnie. Plus, if Patrick ever did decide to just pop up over my house, I could just look at the monitor and act like I wasn't home."

"You go, girl."

"Gina, what do you really think about all this?"

"Well, Stace, I just think you need to decide what you want. I mean it's no way you can keep seeing both Ronnie and Patrick. Eventually, your man is going to find out or Ronnie's going to get tired of being number two."

"But Gina, the funny thing is, he's not really number two. I mean I see Ronnie way more than Patrick. You would think he was my man."

"Well you know what I'm talking about. Eventually, he's going to want you to make some sort of decision."

"Yeah, I know. I just don't...I don't know what to do anymore."

"You'll figure it out in time. But you just be careful. I don't want you caught up in no drama, girl."

"Please, if Patrick ever finds out, that's exactly what it's going to be, drama, mad drama."

"Don't let it get to that. 'Cause you know your brothers are just looking for an excuse to jump on that boy."

"Yeah, I know."

"C'mon, let's go back inside. I know one of them nosy boys will be out here pretty soon wanting to know what we're talking about."

"Okay."

Gina was right. Once we walked back in the house, there was Kevin wanting to know where we'd been.

"We were just outside having a little woman-to-woman chat," Gina answered.

"About ol' boy I bet."

"Why are you so nosy?" I asked, smiling.

"Dinner's ready," echoed from the kitchen. "Everybody get to the table." I was saved from that conversation yet again.

We all went in the dining room and sat down. Mommy nodded to Daddy to say grace. He blessed the food and my brothers went to work. Those boys could eat you out of house and home. My mother used to always get on them for acting like pigs.

"So Ron, you play basketball for Howard, don't you?" Devin asked, knowing the answer already.

"Yeah," Ronnie answered, nodding.

"The boys tell me you're pretty good," Daddy added.

"I'm okay."

"Man, you're more than okay. You gotta average what, eighteen points a game?" Tracy asked.

"Twenty-three," I said, without thinking. Daddy and the boys looked at me, smiling.

"What?" I wanted to literally crawl under the table. They all just laughed.

"So Ronnie, where are you from, sweetheart?" Mommy asked.

"Brooklyn."

"Oh, New York. Stacey, you were in New York a couple of weeks ago, weren't you?" Daddy asked. Everybody looked at me. Tracy smiled and raised his eyebrows as if to say, *Yeah get out of this one.*

"Ah yeah, I was," I answered hesitantly.

Wanting to get the conversation off me and New York as quickly as possible, I asked Gina how she liked her new job with Sprint.

"It's fine, girl," she answered, laughing. "A lot of work."

"Oh, that's good."

Kevin went right back to giving Ronnie the third degree. "So Ron, are you thinking about going pro?"

"No," he answered, shaking his head. "I've had some agents approach me but that's not what I want to do with my life."

All eyes were glued on Ronnie as he explained how he had been singing since he was very young and wanted to concentrate on getting Entice a record deal.

"For real. That's really what you want to do?" Gina asked.

Ronnie nodded and said, "Yeah, that's really all I've ever wanted to do. We've had this group for almost seven years now."

"That's cool," Gina said.

Mommy said, "Mmm, so you're fine and can sing." Daddy put his fork down on his plate and looked at Mommy. We all laughed.

"I'm just saying, Greg."

Daddy slowly turned his head toward Ronnie but cut his eyes back at Mommy. We laughed again and she hit him with her napkin.

"Anyway, Ron," Daddy finally turned all his attention back to Ronnie, "I, ah, hope you have a Plan B. I mean it's pretty hard to break into that business."

"Well, yes sir. That's why I came to Howard. I'm getting my degree in hospitality management. My family owns two restaurants back home so if this doesn't work out, I have something to fall back on."

Daddy nodded. I could tell he liked the way Ronnie had thought out what he wanted to do with his life. Everyone, including me, was impressed. Gina pushed my leg and I tried not to smile.

The dinner conversation continued but it did finally get off Ronnie. After everyone was finished eating, Mommy cleared the dishes and brought in the cakes. Everyone loved my mother's desserts. The current crowd was no exception.

Daddy was reaching for his second piece of cake when he happened to glance at the tennis bracelet Ronnie had given me for Christmas.

"Where'd that bracelet come from, pumpkin?" he asked.

Gina picked up my arm and said, "Mmm, this is nice."

All three of my brothers looked exactly like my father, but for Devin and Tracy, that's where the similarities ended, but not with Kevin. He and my dad were like two peas in a pod. For me, it was like having two fathers sometimes. Sitting at that table, was one of those times.

"Yeah, where'd you get that from?" daddy number two asked.

"Um, a friend gave it to me for Christmas," I answered.

Ronnie was rubbing his thumb across his chin and smiling.

Tracy asked, "Who, Pat?"

Ronnie started coughing, trying not to laugh. Tracy looked at him and then at me. It was at that moment that he knew who the bracelet had come from.

"Ah-ha a friend," Daddy started, "that must be some friend. Probably a friend I don't want to know about, huh?"

I smiled nervously. My father wasn't dumb. He knew I wasn't a virgin because my mother knew. I had talked to her when things happened with

Tim. That's the type of relationship I had with her. I could talk to her about almost anything, but I knew I couldn't tell her about Patrick hitting me. I couldn't tell anybody about that. It was too embarrassing. Plus, if I told her about that, I'd have to tell her about the abortion. There was no way I could do that.

I knew my mother had told Daddy about me and Tim having sex but he would never come out and say anything. Even though I was grown, I still felt uneasy knowing that he knew about me having sex.

"It's beautiful, sweetheart," Mommy said.

She gave me the opportunity to ignore Daddy's question. "Thank you, Mommy."

"Nobody said it wasn't beautiful," Kevin responded. Out of all my brothers, Kevin was the one who always got under my skin. He liked agitating me.

"What we want to know is what kind of friend gives you something like that?" Kevin continued to push the issue.

"My kind," I retorted.

"Yeah, and what did you have to give up to get that bracelet?" he snapped.

I just looked at him. I couldn't believe he would say something like that in front of Ronnie.

"Shut your mouth, Kevin," Mommy insisted.

"Thank you. You forever comin' out your mouth wrong," I said.

"Yeah, and what did you have to come out of to get that bracelet?"

"Mommy!" I whined.

"Kevin William Jackson, what did I tell you? Shut your mouth!"

Kevin kind of smiled at me and I mouthed, "I hate you."

"Well, Ronnie, do you have any brothers or sisters?" my father asked, trying to change the subject. He knew I was getting mad. Kevin and I always argued like that. He could be such a pain in the ass.

"Ah, yes, sir. I have a younger brother named Robert who's a freshman at Delaware State and an older sister, Raina, who manages one of my father's restaurants at home."

"Well I hope y'all don't act like these four," Daddy said, shaking his head.

Ronnie laughed and Tracy said, "Man, Pops, how you gonna put me in that?"

"Boy, don't act like you're so innocent just because you weren't in it this time. Most of the time it's you and Stacey against them other two." Everybody laughed except me. I was still pissed at Kevin for embarrassing me in front of Ronnie.

"Oh, so we're just the other two, huh, Pops? Devin asked.

"Yeah and?" was Daddy's response.

Kevin kept looking at me, smiling. I rolled my eyes and he laughed.

"You are not funny, Kevin." I got up. "You make me so sick." My chair fell back on the floor.

Mommy said, "Kevin!" Of course he said he didn't do anything.

"Pumpkin, sit down. You have company," Daddy said calmly. He looked at Kevin and said, "And you—get up, clear the table and start washing the dishes."

"Man, Pops."

Ronnie picked up the chair. I sat back down. I was so mad that I was bouncing my leg up and down almost uncontrollably. Ronnie rubbed my leg under the table. Slowly, I began to calm down. I couldn't believe Kevin was tripping on me like that in front of Ronnie.

Daddy continued scolding Kevin, "Since you think you're so funny, let's see how funny those dishes are when you finish."

"I can't believe I don't even live here anymore and you're still making me do the dishes."

"You still eat here enough, now do like your father says and be quiet," Mommy added. Kevin started clearing the dishes and Mommy said, "Well y'all can go 'head back in the family room if you want." Everybody got up and Tracy took my hand. "I want to talk to you." He looked at Ronnie and said, "Do you mind if I borrow your hostess for a few?"

"Naw, go 'head. I'll go chill in the family room."

"Cool."

Tracy pulled me out on the deck and shut the door.

"Trace, it's cold out here."

He walked up behind me and put his arms around me. "You'll be alright. I want to know what's up with you and Big Ron?"

I smiled and said, "What you mean?"

"You know what I mean. What happened to that fool Pat?"

"He's still around…kind of," I answered.

Tracy looked at me and said, "Oh, you living like that now, huh, baby girl?"

"Naw, not really. Things just started happening with Ronnie, and I guess I let them continue to happen."

"So what are you going to do about Pat?"

I shrugged. I honestly didn't have the answer to that question. If I did I probably wouldn't have been in that situation to begin with.

"You know this ain't you." He smiled. "It's me, but not you."

"I know. I'm always telling myself that but it's been me since this summer."

"Get the hell out of here. And you didn't tell me?"

"I wasn't trying to tell nobody. Do you know how hard it is to be going from one man to the next without anyone knowing, plus keeping your grades up?" Tracy laughed and said, "Do I? It takes skills."

"You're so silly."

"So does Ronnie know about Patrick?" Tracy asked.

"Of course, they're on the basketball team together," I answered.

Tracy laughed. "Oh yeah, I forgot. You are the woman. Got two men on the same team and one don't even know about the other. I want to be just like you when I grow up."

"Please, I don't want to do this anymore. It's too much work," I said, laughing.

"So sis, on the serious tip, what's up? You're not one to cheat so this brother must have laid a heavy rap on you."

"Trace, you just do not know."

He laughed.

"You don't remember me talking about Ronnie before?" I asked.

"Hell yeah, I remember, girl. Every time I turned around, you were talking about how fine Ronnie Morgan on the basketball team was. That's why I was trippin' when you drove up in the driveway and I saw him in the car. I was like 'she finally got with that brother.'" We both laughed.

I loved Tracy so much. He was the best friend I could ever have. I loved my other brothers, too, but I guess Tracy being my twin made everything different. I even loved my stupid brother Kevin. He just made me sick. I was still mad at him when he came out on the deck with us.

"What y'all out here talking about, ol' boy?" he asked.

"None of your goddamn business," I snapped. I whispered the 'goddamn' part. The kitchen window was right off the patio and I didn't want Mommy to hear me cursing. Kevin knew I was really mad at that point because I would never say something like that to him otherwise.

He smiled and said, "C'mon Stacey-Lacey. I know you're not still mad at me." I just looked at him.

"Man, Kev, why you do that to her in front of ol' boy?" Tracy asked. Kevin pulled me from Tracy and hugged me.

"Seriously, Stae," Kevin was the only person that called me Stae. "I'm sorry. I was just trippin'."

"Kevin, why did you have to embarrass me like that in front of Ronnie?"

He kissed me and said, "Seriously, I am sorry. You know I was just messing with you."

"Still, he's the one who bought me the bracelet and you sitting there talking all that smack about what I had to give up."

"I knew he bought it anyway."

I looked at him. "And how did you know that?"

"Please, that punk-ass boyfriend of yours wouldn't spend no money like that."

I pushed him and said, "Shut up, Kevin."

"Now don't act like he would. Pretty boy wouldn't buy nothing for nobody but himself."

"Anyway, can we just change the subject?"

"Y'all stupid," Tracy said.

Kevin pulled me back close to him and said, "Mmm, lil' sis, you must have whipped something on that brother to have him buying you a bracelet like that."

Tracy laughed and said, "You know what I'm saying? She got that brother sprung."

"Both of y'all shut up. Don't be saying that stuff."

"Kev, man, our sister must have some mad bedroom skills."

They gave each other some dap and Kevin said, "Did you whip it on him, Stae?" I had to laugh because they were so stupid.

"Don't be ashamed 'cause I have to admit, dude does look good," Kevin joked.

"For real. If I was a chick, I'd do him," Tracy added.

I laughed and said, "Y'all are dumb."

"But on the serious tip, Stae, don't be getting yourself caught up in no drama. I don't want to have to kill nobody over you," Kevin said. He could be an asshole from time to time but whenever I needed him, he was right there, no matter what. I kissed him on his cheek and said, "I'll talk to both of y'all—" I kissed Tracy on the cheek too—"later." I opened the door and Kevin said, "You hear me, Stae?" I nodded and went in the door.

I went in the family room and Devin and Gina were hugged up on the couch. Daddy and Ronnie were all into the TV. The Miami Heat was playing the New York Knicks. Daddy hated the Knicks so he was cursing at the TV, as usual.

"I wish Spike Lee would shut the hell up. He needs to be home coming up with a movie where he don't have everybody floating down the damn street."

I knew better than to disturb him when he was watching a basketball game and Ronnie was pretty much the same way. When a game was on, it was no need to even try to talk to him because he wasn't going to hear a word you said. He was the same way with his music. When Ronnie was down in that basement, he was all about the music. It was like he was in another world completely.

I sat on Devin's lap and he asked, "Did you and your brother make up?" I nodded. Gina picked up my arm and looked at the bracelet again. She shook her head and let my arm drop.

I smiled. "Don't hate the playa," I joked. "Hate the game."

"Dev, when are you going to buy me a bracelet like that?" Devin tried to act like he was all up in the basketball game. Gina pushed him.

"Oh, what you say, babe?"

"You heard me. When are you getting me a bracelet like Stacey's?" Gina asked again.

Devin looked at my bracelet and then looked at Gina. "Girl, I ain't rollin' like that." He kissed her and said, "Besides, would you rather have a diamond bracelet or a diamond ring?"

"What kind of ring are you talking about?" Gina asked.

Devin just smiled.

A commercial came on and Daddy headed to the kitchen. Ronnie looked at me and winked. I smiled. Gina pushed me and Ronnie laughed. He shook his head and said, "Y'all are a trip." Daddy came back in with two sodas. He sat down and handed Ronnie one. "Oh, thanks, Mr. Jackson."

"No problem, son."

"Where's mine, Pops?" Devin asked. Daddy didn't even acknowledge his question. He popped open his Pepsi and took a long swig. We all laughed.

"You want me to get you something, sweetie?" Gina asked Devin, trying to soothe his ego.

Devin shook his head. He didn't want anything to begin with. He just wanted to mess with Daddy.

Gina leaned close to me and said, "Why don't you and Ronnie go chill?"

"He's looking at the game."

Ronnie smiled and said, "No, I'm not really." I looked at him.

"Now I know you didn't think that was whispering," Devin said to Gina. She smiled and shrugged.

Ronnie and I took Gina's advice and went in the living room. He sat down and I closed the French doors. I sat beside him and put my legs over his. He kissed me. He said he had been waiting all afternoon to do it. So had I. Whenever I was near him, I wanted to taste his sweet kisses.

"You know, my dad really likes you," I told him between kisses.

Daddy would never come right out and tell me, but I could tell by the way he was interacting with Ronnie. He normally didn't do that. He could be very standoffish, especially with the guys who I had brought home.

"Your pops is pretty cool. Actually, the whole Jackson clan is pretty cool."

"I'm glad you're enjoying yourself."

"Well you know I always enjoy myself with you." All I could do was smile.

Ronnie always kissed on my ear when we were alone. I liked it but it tickled.

"Stop, boy."

"Don't be trying to act brand new 'cause we at your parents' house."

"Shut up."

I could tell Ronnie was in one of those moods. He started kissing on my ear again and his hands were moving up my leg.

"You think me and Ellie can get together tonight for a private session?"

"I'll see what I can do," I said, smiling coyly.

I loved our private sessions. I didn't know if I was that inexperienced as far as sex went or if Ronnie was just that good. Either way, I was whipped, sprung or whatever you wanted to call it. I had never experienced the sexual feelings that I had with Ronnie. Every time seemed so perfect. I realized it was more than just the sex though. Everything always felt perfect with Ronnie no matter what we were doing. With every day that went by, I was getting in deeper and deeper. I was starting to suspect that I wasn't just some girl Ronnie was messing with behind her man's back either. As if my life wasn't complicated enough. The last thing I needed was to fall in love.

this must be love

The Deltas were having their annual Valentine's Day formal. I had gone the year before and had a decent time. I wanted to go again, but I couldn't go with who I wanted to. Stacey, of course, was going with Pat. So I decided I would ask one of my home girls to go with me. I honestly didn't think it would be a big deal with Stacey, but I couldn't have been more wrong. When she saw me walk in with Keisha, her expression told me she was pissed.

All night long, Stacey watched every move I made. I guess she thought she was going to catch me doing something. The whole situation amused me. I thought about messing with her a little by kissing Keisha's neck or something but decided against it. I didn't want Stacey really tripping.

I dropped Keisha off around midnight, and then headed home. I was chilling listening to some Jay-Z when my cell phone rang. I knew who it was even before looking at the Caller ID.

"Hey, what's up, boo?" I said, yelling over the music and the air blowing in from my window being rolled down slightly.

"Who the hell was that bitch?" Stacey snapped.

"What?" was the only thing that I could say. I wasn't expecting all that.

"You heard me. Who was that bitch?" she repeated.

Stacey had been drinking. The only time she cursed like that was after she had a few. But I didn't care how much she had to drink. I wasn't going to let her go off on me like that.

"Yo, first of all," I began, turning the music off. "You need to calm down and check your tone."

I stopped at a red light. "And secondly, she's just a friend of mine from home."

"Oh a friend, huh?" Stacey asked sarcastically. "Did you fuck her?"

I couldn't do anything but laugh. I had never seen Stacey act like that. It was so out of character.

"Why are you are trippin'? Ain't nothing going on like that with me and Keisha."

"How you gonna throw some hoe all up in my face?"

"Stacey, I did not throw anybody in your face. And she's not a hoe."

There was no response. But I could hear her angry breathing.

"Look, you knew I wanted to go tonight. Obviously, I couldn't go with you so I just asked a friend to go with me. What was I supposed to do, not go?"

"I didn't say that."

"Well what are you saying Stacey? Because obviously I'm not understanding why you're so upset."

"What the hell you do when I'm not around is none of my business. Just don't bring that shit in my face."

"Oh, you mean the way you be kissing Pat in my face?" I snapped.

Stacey said, "Forget you Ronnie," and hung up.

I looked at the phone in disbelief. "No, she didn't." I was pissed. I dialed her number.

She answered, "What?"

"Let me tell you something right now, don't you ever hang up on me again." If it was one thing I couldn't stand, it was being hung up on.

"And before you call me trying to bomb me out about some girl, you would want to remember who has the boyfriend."

"And I've had one since last summer. What's your point?"

I couldn't believe she was trying to punk me. I really liked Stacey but my ego wasn't going to let me get punked.

"My point is, you're not mine and I'm not yours. So what I do is none of your business. Just like what you do with Pat is none of my business."

"You're right Ronnie. What you do is none of my business. Well I'm going to let you get back to your business."

"Stacey."

"And just so we're both clear, I'm saying good-bye so I'm not hanging up on you."

"Stacey."

She hung up. I was getting ready to call back again, but figured, *Hell no.* She ended the conversation so let her call back.

By the time I got home, I had calmed down a little but I was still pissed. When the night began, I had no idea it would end so messed up. Stacey and I never argued. There was no reason to normally.

Valentine's Day was supposed to be romantic. I was supposed to be with my girl. Exchange some little gifts. Have a nice dinner. Maybe go dancing. Then go home and get to the private session. But I didn't really have my own girl. Stacey and I exchanged gifts but there was no nice dinner because she was with her man. We didn't dance because I was dancing with someone else while she danced with her man. And my night was ending with me lying in my bed alone. There would be no private session.

I was so wound up that I couldn't get to sleep. I decided to try and unwind by soaking in the Jacuzzi tub for a little while. It really didn't help. I was still upset, more so because I didn't like arguing. I especially didn't like the fact that I just had my first argument with Stacey and on Valentine's Day, no less. Even though the argument wasn't my fault, I still felt like calling her and apologizing.

There was no need to continue soaking, when it was doing no good. I got out, put on some pajama pants and laid on the bed.

I was on my second round of flipping through the more than a hundred cable channels on my TV, when my doorbell rang. I looked at the clock. It was two-thirty in the morning. *Who the hell is ringing my bell at this time of night?* I thought. I headed downstairs. As I got to the bottom of the stairs, the unexpected visitor knocked on the door.

"Here I come," I called out, as I flipped on the hallway light.

The shapely figure behind the frosted glass in the front door was a familiar one.

I opened the door. "Hey," I said, emotionless. I was definitely fronting because I was very happy to see Stacey.

"Hey," she said softly.

Stacey tried to avoid looking at my bare chest, but she couldn't help herself. Her favorite part of my body was my torso. She took a deep—get your mind off his chest—breath. She slowly raised her eyes to me. They were red. Some of the redness was probably the effects of the drinking, but I could also tell she had been crying.

I moved aside, allowing her to come in. She went in and headed up the stairs to my room. I shut and locked the door, cut off the lights and followed her upstairs.

Stacey took off her red ski vest as she walked into my bedroom. She then pulled off her Reebok Classic tennis shoes. I returned to my spot in the middle of the bed. Stacey unzipped her jacket to reveal a red lace bra. I tried my best to stay cool, but it was hard...literally. She knew exactly what she was doing to me as she pealed off her sweatpants, revealing the matching red lace panties. She slowly crawled on the bed toward me and sat across my lap.

Stacey ran her finger over the tattoo on my chest. Neither of us said a word. The TV was the only sound in the room. Finally, Stacey made eye contact. "Are you still mad at me?" she asked timidly.

I cracked a slight smile. "I was—until you took off those sweats."

She chuckled.

"I'm, ah, sorry about how I was acting earlier," she said, moving her eyes back toward my tattoo. "I was way out of line." She shook her head and shrugged. "I don't know what to say. It's just that when I saw you walk in with her—"

"Stacey, there's nothing going on between us," I interjected.

She looked at me and said, "I know. I was more upset with myself for not being in the position to go with you. But, after a couple of Long Island Iced Teas, I got mad at you."

I laughed.

"And I also apologize for all the cursing. I know how much you hate that. I promise it won't happen again."

She was silent again. As far as I was concerned, we could get to the private session. She was sitting across my lap with some sexy drawers on. The last thing I wanted to do was talk at that point.

I rubbed up her thighs and said, "Stacey, we're cool. It's over."

"I just want you to know how sorry I am."

"I know you are. Like I said, we're cool." I was ready to get to it, but Stacey wanted to talk more.

"When I saw you walk in with her, my heart dropped. All I could think was you had gotten tired of my situation with Patrick, which I honestly wouldn't blame you." She looked at me. "I was scared I had lost you."

"Stacey, girl…."

"No, 'cause like you said, you're not mine and I'm not yours."

"Look, we're going to let this thing go. We both said some things that, though they might be true, didn't really need to be said in the heat of the moment." I kissed her and said, "Okay?"

She gave me a little smile. "Okay."

I kissed her again and said, "So ah, when did you get this sexy Vicky's Secret set?"

"How do you know it's from Victoria's Secret?"

"'Cause I remember seeing it in your catalog a few weeks ago."

"Well, I ordered it as another Valentine's Day gift for you. After what happened earlier, I was thinking I wouldn't need it. But I knew I had to apologize and I figured you wouldn't be able to stay mad at me for long if I came over with this on."

I rubbed her back and said, "Oh, you're right about that."

She sat up straight. "So you like?"

"Do I?"

I sat up and kissed my friend, Ellie. Stacey smelled like flowers. She always smelled good, from head to toe and everything in between. I was particularly happy about the in between area myself.

"I didn't think I was going to get to end my Valentine's Day the way I had wanted," I said, kissing on her neck.

"And how was that?"

I looked at her and said, "Making love to you."

"Well you are definitely going to end your Valentine's Day the way you wanted."

After Stacey left my house the next morning, I didn't really talk to her much. I knew she had to be wondering what was up with me. But after everything that went down between us, I knew I needed a little time away from her to get my head together. I was starting to get feelings for her that I didn't know how to deal with.

That last time we were together was a trip for me. I realized I said I wanted to make love to Stacey. I never said *make love.* Girls were quick to say they made love to some dude, but I always felt like you had to be in love to make love. I surprised myself when the words came out of my mouth so easily that night.

I was also surprised by Stacey's request of me to keep my eyes open during our session. Now, I was usually the one trying to get someone to keep her eyes open. You can drive a woman crazy staring at her during sex. But Stacey flipped the script on me. She seemed to be trying to take control and I wasn't sure if I was ready to give that up yet.

"Why?" I asked in response to her request.

"I just want to look in your eyes," she answered softly.

At that point, I couldn't refuse her.

Afterward, I lay beside Stacey, watching her sleep. I thought about what had happened during our little session. Looking in Stacey's eyes, I saw some amazing things. I saw my future. I saw Stacey walking down the aisle in a beautiful wedding dress. I saw her nursing my child. I saw us being happy for a long, long time.

Before Stacey, if someone had asked me had I ever been in love, I would have said yes without hesitation. In the beginning of my relationship with Kim, I just knew I was in love. She was my world. Even after we broke up, I still thought of her as my first love. Now, I knew she really wasn't. Nothing I felt for Kim even remotely compared to what I was feeling for Stacey. I decided it was time for us to have a talk, so I gave her a call.

"Hello."

"Hey, what's up, boo?"

"Hey, girl, what's up?" she said. Obviously, Pat was there.

"Oh, your man's there, huh?"

"Nothing. Me and Patrick are just chillin' watching some TV."

"I really need to talk to you."

"Um, yeah sure. I'll be over there later on."

"Alright then. I'll see you later."

"Okay."

I hung up and wondered if I should even talk to Stacey about how I really felt. I mean she didn't seem to be in any hurry to break up with Pat. No matter what he did to her, she still stayed with him. I often wondered how I got myself into this situation anyway.

When Stacey called and said she had just dropped Pat off and was on her way over, I started wondering how I was going to say it. Would I just come out and say, "Stacey, I'm falling in love with you?" To be honest, I wasn't completely sure if I wanted to go through with it. But before I knew it, Stacey was ringing the bell. My moment of truth had arrived.

Stacey walked in the door and kissed me. "Hey, Mr. Morgan."

"Hey," I responded softly. Stacey could tell by my demeanor that I had something on my mind.

"What's wrong?" she asked.

"Ah, I need to talk to you about something," I said, leading her into the den. We sat down. Stacey looked worried. She probably thought I was going to say I didn't want to see her anymore. At that point in time, I probably couldn't have said that if I wanted to. I took her hand and rubbed it hoping it would ease her mind somewhat.

"Over the past couple of days," I began. "I've been really thinking about what's been going on between us."

I looked into her beautiful brown eyes. That girl's eyes could make a man do just about anything.

"I understand that you're still in a relationship with Pat, but I need you to know how I feel."

I paused and Stacey looked at me like "go on." I put my head down and rubbed her hands. I tried my best to think of some poetic way to say it but I couldn't. I wrote plenty of songs about falling in love but at that moment, the words escaped me.

"Stace, I, ah…" I looked up at her and said, "I think I'm, ah…."

I always used my music to hide behind when things got a little uncomfortable for me, but I didn't want to do that with Stacey. I couldn't go out like that. I didn't *think* I was in love, I knew I was.

"You know, I was getting ready to tell you I thought I was in love with you but that's not true because I know for sure that I am in love with you."

Her eyes bugged out. I wanted to laugh, but I figured that wasn't appropriate at that time. She got up and walked toward the fireplace. She looked back at me and said, "Man." She took a few more steps and looked back at me again.

"Don't play, Ronnie. Are you for real?" she asked.

"Yes. I'm for real."

She leaned on the mantel of the fireplace and looked at me with the same response as before. "Man."

I had to laugh. She was really shocked.

"Is that all you're going to say?" I asked.

She took a deep breath and said, "I'm just trying to get my thoughts together. I mean I never, ever expected you to say that."

"I understand that. But it's been on my mind and you know I don't like anything done half-assed so I had to let you know."

"Man," was her response again. I had to admit I was expecting a little more than that.

She kind of laughed and said, "I'm sorry but that's the only thing coming to my mind right now." She scratched her neck and looked at me, smiling.

"What?" I asked.

"I want to say it again but I know you don't want to hear it."

"Look, I know this is catching you off guard."

"Off guard comes nowhere close."

"Don't feel like you have to say something. I'd rather you not say anything, than say something you don't mean."

She sat back beside me and said, "How do you know that what I'm going to say now isn't what I really mean?"

"I guess I don't."

"That's right. You don't, Mr. Morgan."

I figured the ball was in her court so I wasn't going to say anything else. I had waited a long time to tell her how I felt. I knew for months that my feelings were getting deep, but I didn't want to get hurt. Besides, I was "the man." I couldn't be acting all soft. I was determined, at least in my mind, to continue my cool act. I couldn't let her know she had me sprung like that.

Stacey was silent for a long time. She took a deep breath and finally looked at me. "Do you know what it's like to want something so bad but not really know if or when you'll ever get it?"

I really didn't know where she was going, but she finally started talking so I wasn't going to interrupt her.

"It's like, all my life, I've had this romantic idea of what being in love would be like. When I was seventeen, I thought that my whole relationship with Tim was so romantic. We had known each other since we were kids. We were each other's first sexual experience. And I *thought* he was my first love. I mean everything in my life centered around him. But then, I started at Howard. And there was this *oh so fine* basketball player from Brooklyn."

I had to smile. She smiled too.

"For almost three years, I longed to just know him. Somehow, I knew even then, that he was someone I wanted to be with. So when he tells me he's in love with me, I don't know what to do with myself. I've dreamed about hearing those words from his mouth since the day I saw him emerge from that black Lexus."

I smiled again.

"I said all that to say this—" she looked into my eyes—"I love you too."

I couldn't believe my ears. "What?"

She kissed me softly and said, "I love you too."

I didn't know it was possible to kiss that long. It felt different kissing

Stacey after telling her I loved her. I didn't know if it was all in my mind or what. What I did know was there were some more things that needed to be discussed and if that girl kept kissing me like that, I wasn't going to want to talk about anything. I had to slow it down because I could tell when Stacey eased her body across my lap she wasn't trying to slow down.

"Hold up, boo." I took a deep breath. "We need to talk some more."

"About what?" she asked still kissing on my face and neck.

"About your little situation with Patrick."

That slowed things down. Actually, it brought them to a screeching halt.

"What about it?" she asked.

"You know this changes things as far as I'm concerned."

"What you mean it changes things?"

"I don't know how long I can handle waiting for the girl I love to break up with her boyfriend."

Stacey took a deep breath and sat back on the couch.

"I'm not trying to crowd you or anything because obviously there are some things going on keepin' you there that I don't know about. But, I do know, that I need you to make a decision."

"Ronnie, I'm…."

"Do you see where I'm coming from? I mean if the tables were turned, wouldn't you need me to make a decision?"

"Yes, I would. And I promise you I'm getting myself together as far as this thing with Patrick goes."

"Alright. I'm not going to try and make you tell me something right here, right now but I want you to know that I definitely want you to make a decision. And soon."

"Alright," she said in a soft voice.

Stacey spent the night but for the first time since our first time, we didn't have one of our private sessions. Ever since that first night, Stacey and I had been flexing almost every time we saw each other. No girl ever had me feigning like that before. I always tried to play it cool though. I mean I didn't want to seem whipped and I didn't want her to think she had it like that. But whenever I saw her, before I knew it, it was on. I wasn't complaining though because it was the bomb.

As I lay beside her in the bed, rubbing her side as she fell off to sleep, I realized I had never slept in a bed with a girl without having had sex with her. To my own surprise, I wasn't tripping off it. I just loved being next to Stacey. I kissed her cheek and knew I had made the right decision telling her how I felt.

Stacey left early the next morning. She had a ten o'clock class. I went up on campus around one-thirty because I had a class at two. I was heading inside the business school when I saw Stacey and Pat standing outside the front door of the building. When Stacey saw me, she cracked a nervous smile. I was cool though. Well I really wasn't cool with seeing the girl I was in love with standing there with her boyfriend but I wasn't going to let her know that.

"What's up peeps?" I greeted the happy couple.

"What up, man," Pat responded, trying to be cool.

"Hey, Ronnie." Stacey's voice was soft.

"So what y'all up to?" I asked.

"I'm 'bout to walk Stacey to her car."

I looked at Stacey and said, "Oh, really." She looked at me and put her head down. Pat looked at her then at me.

"Well let me get on up in this building." I tried to play it off. "I'll see y'all later."

"Alright, man, peace," Pat said.

Stacey didn't say anything.

As I opened the door, I decided to mess with her a little. I turned around and said, "Aye Stacey."

She looked at me and said, "Yeah."

"When you gonna hook me up with your girl Ellie?"

Stacey smiled and said, "I'll tell her you want to get with her and she'll call you."

"Don't forget now."

"Oh, I won't."

As I went in the building, I heard Pat ask Stacey who Ellie was. Stacey told him she was one of her sorors that I wanted to get with. I laughed and went on about my day. For someone who had never cheated before, Ms. Jackson was getting good at covering her tracks.

After I finished with my classes for the day, I decided to run up to Pentagon City, which was a big mall over in Arlington, Virginia. Stacey had been talking about some Nike Air Max sneakers that she was going to buy. I decided to surprise her with them.

My cell phone rang as I got out of my truck in the parking garage. It was nobody, but Dave.

"Yeah," I answered.

"What's up, dawg? Where you at?"

"Up at Pentagon City," I said, entering the mall. Even though it was the middle of the day, the mall was still crowded.

"What you up there for?"

"I'm getting some sneakers."

"You just got some Jordan's last week," Dave chastised like he was my father.

I was going up the escalator, heading toward the third floor. A group of females were going pass the escalator and I caught their eyes. "Damn, he is fine," one girl remarked. They got on the escalator below me and I just smiled.

"I didn't say they were for me," I said. "I'm going to Lady Foot Locker."

Dave laughed and said, "Boy, you are so whipped."

"Forget you, man. Ain't nobody whipped."

"Whatever. Every time I turn around you buying Stacey something."

A nice-looking woman walked past me and said, "Mmm, how you doing?" I smiled and nodded. I watched her as she passed by and noticed the girls from the escalator following not too far behind me. I laughed and shook my head. Getting a good look at them, they had to be around sixteen or seventeen. Probably skipping school. When they saw me look at them, they giggled and ran in the other direction.

"Shit, it all started at Christmas with that bracelet, then it was some jeans here, some boots there," Dave continued teasing. "Now you headin' to Lady Foot Locker to buy her some sneakers."

Until Dave itemized everything, I hadn't realized how much I had been giving Stacey. He didn't even know about a lot of the little stuff.

"I ain't even gon' say nothing about all the damn meals you've cooked."

I laughed.

"How I know you're whipped is your ass be driving all the way from Southwest to Northeast at all times of the day and night for your little sex session."

"Private session," I corrected him.

The shoes Stacey wanted were right at the front of the store. "Could I get this in an eight and a half?" I asked the saleswoman.

"Just whipped!" Dave said.

"Why you hatin' on your boy like this?" I asked Dave, laughing.

"I'm not hatin'. I'm just statin'. For real though, if you're whipped, then you're just whipped."

"I ain't whipped, man," I said low so no one in the store could hear.

"Brothers only go out like that for one of two reasons— either they're whipped or in love."

I didn't say anything.

"So which are you, Ron?" he asked.

Dave didn't know about my revelation regarding being in love with Stacey. I wasn't about to get in that conversation with him standing in Lady Foot Locker.

"Ah, Dave man, let me get up with you later?"

He laughed and said, "A'ight, man. Peace."

As the saleswoman brought out the shoes, I saw Pat walking past with one of his frat brothers.

Damn, I thought. He was the last person I wanted to see. Pat and I didn't like each other. He didn't like me because he was jealous. I didn't like him because he had something I wanted—Stacey.

They walked in.

"What's up, big Ron?" He was so phony.

"Nothing much," I answered dryly.

His boy and I gave a what's up nod to each other.

Pat looked at the shoes and said, "These are some fly kicks. Some chick got you buying her some sneakers?" he asked, being nosy.

I wanted to say, "Yeah, your girlfriend punk." But I just answered, "They're for a friend."

"Oh, she must be some friend."

"Yeah, she is."

"Well, we're 'bout to be out." He said, "I'll catch you later," like we were boys or something. If he caught anything with me later, it would be a beat down.

"Alright, then. Later." *Much later,* I thought.

I paid for the shoes and left.

Dave and I were boys but that didn't stop us from going at it on the basketball court. I had never met anyone more competitive than me until

Dave. Every chance we got, we were on the court playing one-on-one.

"You don't want none of this, boy," I taunted.

"Come wit' it."

Swish.

"Nothin' but net, baby."

"Just take the damn ball out." Dave hated when I talked trash while were playing ball.

I could hear my pager going off in my bag. "Time out, yo."

"Hell no. Let's play," he demanded, irritated.

"Man, chill. Let me see who that is."

I laughed as I walked over to the bleachers. I opened my Nike bag and pulled my pager from my jacket pocket. It was Stacey paging me 911. She had never done that before.

"Yo, dawg, where's your phone? I left mine in the truck."

"C'mon, man, let's finish first."

"Dave, man, I need to call Stacey. She paged me 911."

He handed it to me and said "Oh, straight up?" Before I got it in my hand good, I had already finished dialing the number. As soon as she answered the phone, I knew something was wrong. She sounded like she'd been crying.

"What's wrong, Stace?" She didn't say anything.

"Stacey."

"Could you just come over please?" She sounded as if she was fighting back tears.

"I'll be there in twenty minutes."

I hung up the phone and started packing up my things. Dave kept asking me what was wrong but I was concentrating on getting to Stacey.

"Ron, man, what's up with Stacey?"

"I don't know, dawg. But she didn't sound right. I gotta get over there. I'll get up with you later."

"Call me and let me know if everything's alright."

"Bet. Peace."

I had never gotten to Edgewood Street so fast. When she opened the door, I could tell she had been crying. Her eyes were all red and her face was flush.

"What's the matter?" I asked as I pulled her close to me. Stacey was grasping something tightly in her hands.

"Tell me what's wrong, Stace." She opened her hand and showed me the bracelet I had bought her. It was broken. I knew she couldn't be that upset about a bracelet.

"Is that what you're so upset about? Girl, we can get this fixed."

She began crying again. I had no idea what was going on. It was like she was having a breakdown.

"Stacey, what's the matter? Why are you crying like this?"

"Patrick broke it."

"Calm down, boo. C'mon, let's go have a seat."

I led her into the living room and we sat down. I wiped her eyes and said, "Now, what happened?"

"He came over here and we got into an argument."

"And? What was it about this time?" I knew she was upset but this was the same old story with her and Pat.

"He was saying that I've been acting different toward him lately."

"Don't worry about it."

"I think he knows something's going on."

"Why do you say that?" I asked.

When Stacey and I were together, we very rarely talked about her and Pat. So I had no idea he had recently been making little accusations. Until that moment, I didn't know he had seen her wearing the sneakers I bought and remembered them from the store. He asked her where she got them. She told him her brother. He didn't really believe her, but let it go.

"Well, a lot of people have those sneakers. That's not a big deal."

"I know, but he was talking about my fancy little bracelet and me disappearing for days without calling him. I tried to put all that on Tracy because I know he won't approach him about it, but he's getting suspicious."

On one hand I was glad about that. Maybe that would force Stacey to make a decision about who she really wanted to be with. She continued, "He kept saying I was his and nobody else's." Then she got quiet.

"Stacey, are you telling me everything?" Tears started rolling down her face again. "What else happened?" I asked.

"He...he hit me."

She said it so low that I almost didn't hear it. But I had heard her. The words started echoing in my head.

"He hit you? What you mean he hit you?" I asked, trying to grasp what she was trying to tell me.

She just looked at me.

I got up and walked to the window. I felt like I was hyperventilating. I tried my best to calm down. But I couldn't. I couldn't believe that fool had put his hands on *my* boo.

"I can't believe that punk hit you." I sat back beside her and asked, "Are you alright?"

She nodded.

So many things started clicking for me at that moment. Pat was always yelling at Stacey. Even though I knew she loved me, she still hadn't broken up with him. It was almost like she was scared of him. That stuff had probably been going on for a while.

"Stacey, has this ever happened before?"

She turned her head toward the television. I turned it back to me. "Stacey, answer me. Has he ever done this before?"

She stood up and said, "I don't want to talk about it, Ronnie." Since she didn't say no, I took that as a yes.

I jumped up and said, "Oh hell no. You mean to tell me he's hit you before and you didn't tell me?"

Again, she didn't have a response. That was pissing me off even more. I was the one who loved her. I was the one who wanted to take care of her, wanted to treat her like a queen. But she was protecting his punk ass. I didn't know what the hell was wrong with her?

"Answer me!" I yelled.

I had never raised my voice to Stacey like that before. She started backing away from me. Her eyes were filled with fright. She had never looked at me like that before.

"Stacey, what's wrong? Why are you backing away like that?" The closer I moved to her, the more she moved away from me. I reached for her.

"Stacey."

"Don't—" she said, almost trembling.

I didn't understand what was going on. She knew I would never lay a finger on her. That wasn't the type of man I was. I continued to move toward her. She continued to move away.

"Stace, please don't back away from me, boo. You know I'm not going to hit you. I swear to God, I would never do that." As I talked to her, I moved closer to her. "I am not Pat. I love you, remember." She fell against the wall and slid to the floor, covering her eyes. I sat down beside her. I didn't know what to do. I had never seen her so...fragile. I slowly put my arm around her. Stacey pressed her head into my chest.

"I can't believe he put his hands on you. I am straight in his ass."

Stacey popped her head up. "Ronnie, I don't want you to get involved."

"I am involved. I mean I'm not going to let anybody hurt you."

"I'll handle it, okay?"

"Hell no it's not okay, Stacey." My voice was rising again. "I don't understand why you're with that punk anyway."

She didn't say anything. I had crossed the line but I was getting frustrated again. I never understood girls staying with guys who treated them like shit. But what frustrated me even more with Stacey was the fact that she had someone else in the picture—me—but she still wouldn't break up with Pat's ass.

I looked at Stacey and tears were running down her face again. The last thing she needed right then was me yelling at her. "I'm sorry, boo." I kissed her forehead. "I didn't mean to say that."

"Ronnie, please promise me you won't do or say anything to Patrick," Stacey begged.

"I honestly can't promise you that, Stacey." I was already thinking about getting my gack and taking a drive up to Northwest.

"Ronnie, please. If you love me, please let me handle this."

"Okay, Stacey," I said reluctantly. I really didn't want to upset her anymore.

"And please promise me you won't say anything to anyone about this, and I mean anybody, not Dave, not Erika, nobody."

"Stacey, I think your brothers should know about this."

"No, Ronnie. They are the last people I want to know. If they find out, they will hurt Pat."

"That's what his ass needs."

"Ronnie, please."

"At least talk to Tracy."

"No. Please just promise me that you won't tell anybody. I will handle this myself."

"Alright, Stacey." There was no need to keep talking about it at that point.

Stacey was still clutching the bracelet in her hand. I took it and said, "We can fix this, girl."

"I'm sorry."

"Sorry for what? You have nothing to be sorry for. It wasn't your fault. I'll take it and get it fixed for you, okay?"

She smiled a little and said, "Okay."

I stayed with Stacey until she fell asleep on the couch. I was going to wake her to put her in her bed, but she was sleeping too soundly. I sat there just looking at her for a while. The words *he hit me* kept ringing in my head. For the first time in my life, I felt out of control. If I had seen Pat right then, I would have tried to kill him.

I pulled a throw blanket over Stacey and kissed her forehead. I cut off the lights and locked up as I left. Then I headed home.

But before I knew it, I found myself on Euclid Street, sitting in front of Pat's crib. I watched him move throughout the house. It amazed me that he was just going about his business. He had just hit a woman. Stacey was distraught but he was cool.

As I sat there, I could actually see myself kicking in the door and beating the hell out of him. My hands were trembling. When I got that upset, there was only one person who could talk to me and that was Raina. I had to call her because I knew I was about to lose it.

"Hey. What's up?" she answered, seeing my number on the Caller ID.

"Raina, I—I need your help."

"What's wrong, Ronnie?"

"He hit her. I'm sitting outside his house, and I'm ready to go in and get him."

"Baby, what are you talking about? Who hit who?" she asked, confused by my ramblings.

"Patrick hit Stacey."

"Who is Patrick?" she asked, more confused.

"He's Stacey's boyfriend."

"Her boyfriend? Since when does she have a boyfriend?" I never told Raina about Stacey having a boyfriend.

"She's always had one."

"And he hit her?"

"Yeah, and he's probably been hitting her a lot more but I just didn't know it. She didn't tell me. But tonight she did." My voice was getting louder and beginning to tremble. "Tonight, I found out that that punk-ass nigga has been hitting on my boo."

"Ronnie, listen to me, you have to calm down."

"All I keep hearing in my head is Stacey telling me that he hit her. He put his hands on her and hurt her."

"Ron, you are so close to having all your dreams come true and you can't let this situation mess that up. If you fly off the handle with this guy, you can get yourself in a lot of trouble. Do you hear me?"

"Raina, you just don't understand. This girl means everything to me," I explained.

"So you're willing to give up everything you've worked for all these years over some chick?"

"She's not just some chick," I yelled. I could feel the coldness of a tear running down my face. "I love Stacey."

"Okay, okay, I'm sorry Ronnie. I guess I didn't realize how deep you were into her. But it's obvious that she has some things that she has to take care of as far as this other dude is concerned."

"Oh, I can take care of him right here and now."

"Ronnie, I want you to start that truck and leave." I was still looking at the house. "Ronnie, c'mon, please just leave."

Raina was right. I had too much going for me to mess it up over Pat. I started the truck and pulled off. Pat didn't know how lucky he was that night. Raina talked to me as I drove home. By the time I got there, I was cool.

"Are you okay?" she asked.

"Yeah, I'm fine. Thanks for talking to me."

"No problem. You know I'm always here for you. If you need to talk some more just give me a call back."

"I will. I love you, sis."

"I love you too."

When I got in the house, my red message light was blinking. I hit play. Stacey woke up and saw I wasn't there. She was calling to see if I was home. I sat on the edge of the couch and called her back.

"Hello." She sounded so down. She didn't even give me my normal "hey, boy" greeting. I wasn't used to hearing her like that. Stacey was always upbeat.

"Hey, boo. I just got your message."

"I woke up and you were gone," she said solemnly.

"Yeah. I wanted to stay with you but I have practice early in the morning so I had to get back. You were knocked out so I didn't bother waking you. You need to get some rest."

"Oh. I kind of wanted you to stay with me tonight."

"I'm sorry, boo. But I'll be over right after practice tomorrow. Okay?"

"Okay," she responded softly.

"Are you alright?"

"Yeah, I'm fine." She wasn't very convincing.

"Stacey, if you want me to come back over there you know I will."

"No, for real, I'm fine. I'm going to go 'head back to sleep and I'll just see you tomorrow."

"Alright then. I'll get up with you tomorrow."

"Okay."

Stacey didn't sound good to me at all. I plopped down on the couch. Why hadn't I noticed anything going on with her before? I spent a lot of time with Stacey. Why couldn't I tell something bad was going on with her and Pat? I should have been able to tell.

Never in a million years would I have imagined when Stacey and I first started kicking it that I would be going through changes like that with her. I hated being involved with drama. That's exactly why I didn't get too involved with girls around campus. There was always some drama going on. I thought Stacey would be a safe bet for no drama. I would have lost that bet, big time.

we're playing basketball!

I was glad I would be ending my college basketball career on a winning note. We had made it to the MEAC playoffs. Coach wanted to win another championship so he was showing no mercy. We had practice every day for more than three hours. By the time I was finished with that I was beat. I was thinking about going home and taking my shower but I was a little too funky for that. I was not trying to smell myself so I knew I didn't want anyone else smelling me like that.

After my shower, I laid on one of the locker room benches. I put my hands behind my head and closed my eyes. I just needed a couple of quiet minutes to myself. I was being pulled in a lot of directions and it was wearing me down. Coach was depending on me to lead the team to another championship, we were finally finishing up the demo that I knew was going to land us a record deal, my last semester of classes was kicking my butt and the situation with Stacey was draining me.

There was no doubt in my mind that I loved that girl to death. I mean she was my everything. But nothing had changed with her. She was still with Pat. I was trying to give her the time she said she needed to get herself together but I was beginning to wonder exactly how long that was going to take.

I felt a towel pop my leg and almost fell off the bench.

"What the hell is up with you, man?" I snapped at Dave.

"Yo, dawg, I've been calling you for the last five minutes."

"Oh sorry, man."

"You alright?"

"Yeah, I'm, ah, just a little tired."

"Well c'mon, man. I gotta pick E up after I drop you at the spot."

I must have been totally out of it because I did not hear Dave calling me. I got dressed and we left.

As we were walking to the car, I saw Stacey heading toward the gym. Since Erika was on the girls' basketball team she had access to the workout room, so that in turn meant Stacey had access. She worked out about three times a week. I liked that. Stacey was in excellent shape. Oh, and the girl was flexible. There were plenty of nights that I was amazed at where that girl's legs could go.

I couldn't take my eyes off Stacey. She was so sexy. I had seen her naked plenty of times but seeing her in that workout gear was really turning me on. The red spandex running pants and halter were hugging every inch of her perfect body. She didn't like her legs but they were the bomb to me. She had the sexiest calves I had ever seen and those thick thighs were...*Mmm*.

I was so busy staring at her that I didn't even notice Pat come out the door behind us. Dave noticed him and noticed me on Stacey so hard.

"Yo, man, let's bounce. I gotta get E, remember."

"Oh, um yeah." I put my shades on. "Here, I come."

I glanced back at Pat. He looked at me then over at Stacey then back at me. I cracked a sly smile then Dave and I left. I shouldn't have been messing with his head but I couldn't help it.

When I got home, I fell right to sleep. I hadn't slept that good in weeks. I was having a nasty dream about Stacey when the phone rang.

"Yeah, hello," I answered half sleep.

"Hey, boy."

I hadn't spoken to my boo all day.

"Oh, you know what kind of man I am."

"Anyway. What are you doing?"

"I was sleeping until someone woke me up."

"I'm sorry. I'll call you back later."

"Why don't you come over? I've been missing you." That was an understatement. Even though I tried to see her every day, sometimes I just couldn't. I was real busy and so was she.

"Alright. I'll be over there in about a half hour."

"Cool."

After I hung up, I fell back asleep. I must have been gone because I didn't even hear Stacey come in. She lay beside me and woke me up by kissing on my neck. I liked being awakened like that.

"Hey, boo."

"What's up, sleepyhead?" She kissed me.

"You were looking mighty sexy this afternoon," I told her.

"When?" she asked. She hadn't seen me at the gym.

"When you were on your way to work out."

"Oh yeah." She kind of laughed and said, "Yeah, Patrick was trippin' off that."

"What you mean?" I wasn't going to tell her about Pat seeing me staring.

"He was buggin'. Talking 'bout I don't need to be walking around like that having all kinds of guys looking at my butt." I laughed. He just figured I was looking at her because she had that workout gear on. Dumb ass.

"Well you were looking mighty phat there," I joked.

"Shut up, boy."

"I ain't playing. You had "Big Man" at attention."

"You shouldn't have been all on my butt."

"Well it was just out there for all to see."

"Anyway."

I was tired as hell when I went to practice the next day. Coach was really tripping with that Saturday morning practice.

"Alright, Morgan, let's get it together."

I couldn't even get in the door good before he was riding me. Like I hadn't been working hard enough. There were some other niggas he needed to be riding instead of me. Pat was one of them.

Coach had us doing some defensive drills. God had to be messing with me because Coach had Pat trying to defend me. "D up, Smith!" Coach yelled. Pat couldn't do nothing with me. But he swore he could. Not only was he weak in bed per Stacey but he was most definitely weak on the court. I didn't even know how he got on the team.

I was tripping off Pat trying to play me so hard. He really thought he was doing something. At first it was kind of funny but after a while I was getting pissed off. Before I knew it, I was going at him too.

"Yo, kid, you better back up off me," I finally said.

I kind of bumped him with my shoulder and he pushed me. Now, why did he have to do that? I pushed Pat and he fell to the floor. He jumped back up and rushed toward me. Coach and Dave ran between us.

"What the hell is going on here?" Coach asked, confused.

"I saw you all on my girl," Pat shouted.

"Yeah, and? She was looking mighty good in those running pants," I taunted. Dave was trying his best not to laugh while he held me back.

"Don't be looking at my girl like that."

"You lucky all I did was look."

Pat was trying to get around Coach but he couldn't.

"What you gonna do?" I asked, still egging him on.

"You better watch yourself, man."

"Maybe I'll stop just looking."

"You better stay away from Stacey."

"Or what?"

"Just stay away from her. That's all I'm saying."

Of course that was all he was saying. He didn't want none of me. I would have beat his ass.

Coach was too pissed. I found out just how pissed he was when he made me run twenty-five laps around the gym. Pat got the worse of it, if you ask me. He had to run twenty-five suicide drills up and down the court.

All the way home, Dave was tripping. He couldn't believe I was messing with Pat's head like that.

"Man, you are a fool. Why you messin' with that boy like that?"

"Naw, he started that shit."

Dave laughed and said, "No, you started it. You knew he saw you looking at Stacey and you all grinnin' and shit."

I laughed. Dave was right. I knew what I was doing. The situation with Stacey and Pat was weighing on me. I was ready for the whole thing to be finished. In the beginning, the sneaking around was cool. It's not like I had never been with other girls who had boyfriends, but I was in love with this girl. I didn't want to sneak around with Stacey anymore.

Dave dropped me off and headed home. When I got in the house, I saw the light on the answering machine blinking. I put my bag down and pressed play.

"Hey, Ronnie. It's me. I need to talk to you. I don't know what happened at practice but Patrick called me pissed off. Give me a call."

I laughed and called Stacey back.

"Hey, boo."

"Hey."

"So what's up?"

"What did you do to that boy?"

"What you talkin' about," I asked, trying not to laugh.

"Don't even try it. He said you were talking about I was looking good in my running pants." I couldn't hold my laughing at that point.

"Why you do that? That fool called here ranting and raving for damn near forty-five minutes."

"I'm sorry, boo. I don't know why I was messin' with him. He just got to me, I guess."

"You are sick, boy. I can't believe you did that. Then you gonna tell him he's lucky all you were doing was looking."

"Yeah, that really pissed him off," I said, laughing.

"Ronnie, he keeps saying he knows something's going on with us."

Dave had been getting on me for a while because he said Stacey and I were becoming more and more obvious.

"So, ah, what did you tell him?" I asked, regarding Pat's recent accusations.

"I told him he was trippin'."

"Did he believe you?"

"I don't know. He was like yeah okay. But he didn't bring it up again."

"For real, I'm sorry. He just caught me at the wrong time. I'm tired as hell and the last thing I needed was for that punk to be all up in my face."

"I know. I'm sorry. I'm going to handle things."

I was really tired of hearing her say she was going to handle it. She had been saying that for weeks. But I wasn't going to say anything right then because I didn't feel like getting in some big discussion about Pat.

It was our last home game before the playoffs officially began. The gym was packed. I looked behind our bench about three rows up and there were Stacey and Erika. They sat in the same place every game.

We were playing North Carolina A&T and the game was hyped. The dudes from A&T could play some ball. But of course, they couldn't handle us. By the beginning of the second half, we were up 75-43. And I was having one of my best games of the season.

Then it happened. I went up for my record-breaking rebound number nineteen and as I came down with the ball, I landed on somebody's foot. I don't know whose but I really didn't give a damn at that point. All I knew was I was lying on the floor in the worst pain I had ever felt in my life.

The gym went completely silent. Our trainer ran over to me. He asked where it hurt. It was my ankle. I could tell it wasn't broken, but it sure hurt like hell. I glanced up at Stacey in the stands. She looked so worried. She almost looked like she was going to cry.

Patrick had been watching my every move recently so I couldn't even let her know I was alright. If he didn't know for sure that I was kicking it with his girl, he clearly suspected something. But after finding out that he had put his hands on her, I really didn't give a damn if he knew. I was just waiting for the chance to pop his ass.

A couple of the fellas helped me back to the bench. Our trainer iced my ankle down and I went on to the locker room. I didn't even want to sit through the rest of the game. I showered and got dressed.

I couldn't drive myself home, so I rode with Dave, and Erika drove my truck. Even though I had the crutches that the trainer had given me, Dave insisted on helping me in the house.

Until I got to Howard, I considered Dre, Ced and Myles my best friends. We had known one another since we were shorties in the children's choir at Allen AME Church before my family moved to Brooklyn. But then I met Dave at freshmen orientation. We hit it off from jump. We both were at Howard on basketball scholarships, we both loved motorcycles and we both loved the females.

Once school started, we talked our roommates into moving in together and we became roommates. Every time you saw one of us, you saw the other. As time went on, I realized that he was my best friend. Whenever I needed him, he was there. I knew we were going to be tight forever. Erika didn't know it, but Dave had already started saving for her engagement ring and he had asked me to be his best man when they tied the knot. Of course I would be. And whenever I decided to get married, he was going to be my best man. Hopefully, we wouldn't be old, gray-haired men when that happened.

Dave and Erika made sure I was comfortable on the couch before leaving. "You need anything before we jet?" Dave asked.

"Naw, I'm cool. Thanks, man."

"No problem. I'll give you a call later on."

Erika kissed me on the cheek and said, "You take it easy, sweetie."

"I will."

Erika was way cool. She was always looking out for me. I felt bad because I wanted her to know what was going on with her girl but I had promised Stacey I wouldn't tell anyone, not even Erika.

"Oh, Stacey said she'd be over a little later," Erika remembered as she was leaving.

"Oh, okay."

About an hour later, I heard a key in the front door. Stacey walked in the living room and said, "Hey, baby," in a sympathetic tone.

"Hey, boo. What's up?"

"How you feeling?" she asked, taking off her coat, throwing it over the back of a chair.

"I'm okay."

"Does it hurt much?"

"Not as much as before."

"Man, I was sitting there and it felt like everything was going in slow motion. When you went to the floor, I was almost in tears."

"I know, boo. I wanted to let you know that I was alright but your boy has really been in my face lately."

"I'm just glad you're alright."

"How glad are you?" I smiled.

"Boy, please, you can barely handle me with two good feet. I don't want you to hurt yourself anymore."

"Don't even try it."

She kissed me and said, "You hungry?"

"No. Mr. and Mrs. Washington made sure I was taken care of before they left."

Stacey laughed. "I'm sorry I couldn't get here earlier."

"Don't worry about it."

I tried to act like it didn't bother me that Stacey was still with Pat. Truth be told, it was really starting to piss me off. What pissed me off most was the fact that she could even stand to be near somebody who hurt her. Sometimes I felt like telling her either she broke up with Pat right then or I was ghost.

When it came to confronting Stacey on that subject, I punked out every time. I didn't know what to say to her because I couldn't understand it at all. To me it was pretty cut and dry, if someone puts his hands on you, it's time for you to go. But obviously, things weren't that cut and dry for Stacey.

Stacey and I were watching TV when her cell phone rang. She pulled it out of her bag and looked at the display. She set it on the table and went back to watching TV.

"You not gonna answer it?" I asked.

"No." It had to have been Pat.

About fifteen minutes later, her phone rang again. She looked at it and again just set it back on the table.

"Why don't you just answer it?" I snapped. It was getting on my nerves.

"Alright."

She picked up the phone and said, "Hello." I could only hear her side of the conversation but I could tell he was giving her the third degree.

"I'm at Erika's."

"Because Erika's on the phone."

"Nothing, just watching some TV."

"No Dave's not here."

"Now why would he be here?"

"What are you talking about?"

"Look, I don't even feel like getting into this right now."

She slammed her phone shut and turned it off. She took a deep breath and went back to watching TV. I didn't want to upset her more but I wanted to know what Pat had said.

"You alright?"

"Yeah, I'm fine," she answered, still looking at TV.

"So what did he say?"

"He was asking me why I was calling on the cell phone. Since I said I was over Erika's, he wanted to know what we were doing; was Dave home; if you were there."

"Me? Why would he ask you that?"

"Because he's an asshole. He's been making little comments about you a lot lately."

"Oh, really?"

"Then he talkin' 'bout I think he's stupid," Stacey continued.

"What's that about?"

"I don't know. He's just been trippin' lately."

"He hasn't put his hands on you, has he?"

"No."

"Are you sure?"

"Yes, I am sure," she answered with a little attitude, like I was wrong for asking. Like she had been up front with me from jump. I let it go because I didn't want to get into an argument.

"So was that all he was saying?"

"Well then he said something about 'yeah your boy got his ass busted tonight.'"

"Stacey, does he know about us?"

"He's never come out and said it. He just makes all these comments all the time."

Now that seemed like a good time to kick him to the curb. But again, that was my thinking. I didn't know what Stacey was thinking. What I did know was I was getting real tired of trying to figure it out. I loved Stacey but I wasn't going to sit around much longer waiting for her to make a decision that didn't seem that hard to me.

I was laid up for a few days with my ankle. It wasn't too bad because between Stacey, Erika and Dave, I was waited on hand and foot. I didn't have to do anything for myself but go to the bathroom.

I had given Dave a key, so I wasn't surprised when he walked in the living room.

"What's up, dawg? How you feeling?" he asked, setting his bag down.

I was lying on the couch, watching TV. "I'm cool."

"Man, that nigga Pat—" he sat down beside me—"is a trip." He laughed and shook his head.

"What's up?" I asked.

"Yo, why were me, Erika and your girl chillin' after class, trying to decide where we were going to get something to eat and here comes his ass. So he asks us what we were up to. We said we were 'bout to go get something to eat before our next class, so he was like, 'cool, let's jet.' Man, Stacey was too through."

He started laughing and continued, "We ended up just going down to Ben's. And it's like we're all standing there trying to figure out what we were getting and out of the blue, Pat starts talking about why people cheat."

I looked at him in disbelief. "What?"

"Yes. He started asking us why we thought people cheat. And you know Ms. Mouth, Erika started getting into it with him. She talking 'bout, if a person is handling their business, there wouldn't be a need to cheat."

"What did Stacey say?" I asked.

"She ain't say nothing. But you could tell Pat was trying to pull her into it. It's like every time he asked a question, he was looking at her, like he was asking her why she was cheating. But she wouldn't even look at him. It's like he thought it was funny."

"For real?"

"Man, going by what I saw this afternoon, that brother knows she's cheating. He might not know with who, but he knows."

I just shook my head. It wasn't anything I could do about that. Stacey had to deal with that fool. If she wanted to sit there and have him play head games, that was on her.

"She needs to take care of that," I said, shrugging and turning my attention back to the TV.

"Yeah. Well I just hope this shit don't get too deep. Pat is crazy. I don't want my girl caught up in no drama."

I didn't want her caught up with Pat either, but I couldn't make her break up with him. She had to make that decision. I had to let Stacey handle her boyfriend problem on her own.

spring break

stacey

I sat in my African American Literature class, anxiously watching the clock. I couldn't believe how slowly time was passing. Spring Break was about to begin, and I could not wait.

Patrick waited until that morning to inform me that he was going to Daytona Beach with some of his frat brothers. I was positive he had made those plans long before he told me. He continued making little comments that left no doubt that he knew I was cheating. I also got the impression that he suspected Ronnie. What I didn't understand was—if he thought I was cheating, why hadn't he confronted me?

When he told me about his trip, I just about did a cartwheel, I was so happy. For weeks, I had been trying to figure out how I was going to spend some time with Ronnie over Spring Break with Patrick around. But Patrick took care of that dilemma for me.

The clock struck two, and I couldn't get out of that classroom fast enough. I was about to spend a week with Ronnie without having to worry about Patrick at all.

A lot of people had already left town for Spring Break so campus wasn't as crowded as usual. When I got to my car, there was a note on the windshield. It just read Call Me. I recognized Ronnie's handwriting.

"Yeah," he answered after the second ring.

"Hey, boy?"

"Boy? Oh, you know what kind of man I am."

The laughter in the background let me know Ronnie was with some of his friends.

"Where are you?" I asked, starting my car.

"I just finished playing a little ball, now I'm on my way to get something to eat."

"Are you supposed to be on your ankle already?"

"It's cool."

"Whatever you say. Anyway, I got your note. What's up?"

"Who you talking to, man?" a voice asked from the background, interrupting our conversation.

"Back up off me, man," Ronnie said, laughing.

"Some chicken-head probably," the voice responded.

"Did he say chicken-head?" I asked.

Ronnie laughed. "He's stupid. Don't pay no attention to him. Anyway, what you gettin' ready to do?"

"Get a manicure and pedicure."

"Oh, okay."

"I'll get up with you guys later," he called to his friends.

"So are you free tonight?" With his friends gone, Ronnie could focus all his attention on our conversation.

"I'm free for the rest of the week. Patrick called this morning talking 'bout he's going to Daytona Beach with his boys. So he won't be back until Sunday."

"Oh for real? That's cool."

"How 'bout you meet me at my place in about two hours?" I asked.

My appointment with Sheila, my manicurist, was at two-thirty. She and her assistant usually got me in and out in an hour and half.

"Why you want me to come over?" Ronnie teased.

"I need a session."

In the months that I had been seeing Ronnie, I had become much more comfortable with my sexuality. He always told me to let him know my wants and needs. At first, it was kind of hard. I mean I had never been very forward when it came to sex. I could talk a good game with Erika, but when it came down to being one-on-one with someone, I chickened out every time. But, Ronnie forced me to verbalize what I wanted.

"Oh, you need a session, huh? Well, you know I have no problem giving you exactly what you need," he said. He liked me being forward. "Alright then, I'll be over around five. I'm going to go home, hit the shower and change."

"Ah, why don't you bring some clothes for tomorrow," I said shyly.

Ronnie chuckled. "Are you asking me to stay the night with you, Ms. Jackson?"

"If you want to. I mean it's up to you."

"Well I do love waking up next to you," he said in a sexy voice.

I smiled. "That feeling is mutual."

"Alright, girl, I'll see you around five, and I'll have my clothes for tomorrow with me."

"Okay. See you later."

"Peace."

I threw my cell phone on the passenger's seat, popped in my Donell Jones CD and headed to Ms. Sheila's Nail Salon.

Whenever possible I tried to patronize black-owned businesses. But it took me a long time to find a black-owned nail salon. Asians owned most of the salons around town so I just went to them. I met Sheila in a beauty supply store about a year earlier. She had just opened her shop and was handing out fliers and business cards. I decided to check her out and had been going ever since.

Sheila finished with me pretty quickly. I got home around four-thirty. I dropped my book bag at the door and headed to my bedroom to change my clothes before Ronnie got there. But before I did anything, I had to wash my face. Oily skin was the worst. My face always felt dirty. Just as I finished washing my face, the phone rang. I answered without looking at the Caller ID.

"Hello."

"Hey, sweet pea," my mother said.

"Hey, Mommy. What's up?"

"Well, I was just calling to let you know that your boy Tim is on his way over to surprise you."

"What? He's on his way over here?"

"Yeah he and Brenda came by and he said he was going to drop in on you. That was about a half hour ago."

"Mommy, why didn't you call earlier?"

"Girl, you know how his mother is. Brenda Green stayed here running her mouth. She just left."

My mother had her nerve. She was usually right there with Ms. Green running her mouth too.

The phone beeped twice telling me someone was in the lobby. I turned on the TV to channel three. To my dismay, there was Tim.

"Oh my goodness."

"What's wrong?" my mother asked.

"Tim is here."

She had no response. The phone beeped again. I didn't know what to do. I looked at the clock on the cable box. It was four-fifty-eight. I looked back at the TV. My heart almost stopped when I saw Ronnie walk in.

"Oh no," I whined.

"What?"

"Ronnie's here too."

My mother laughed. The phone beeped a third time.

"Mommy, this isn't funny. What am I supposed to do?" I continued to whine.

"Look, you put yourself in this position. You gotta deal with it. I told you Tim still liked you, but you didn't want to listen to me."

I plopped on the bed.

"And while I'm thinking about it, I haven't said much about your little situation with Patrick and Ronnie, but you need to do something about that also. If you're going to be with Patrick, tell Ronnie. If you're going to be with Ronnie, tell Patrick. This has been going on too long."

The last thing I needed right then was a lecture. My old boyfriend and the guy I was cheating on my current boyfriend with were standing in the lobby of my building, and I didn't know what to do.

"Alright, Mommy. I gotta go deal with this. I'll talk to you later."

"Okay. Give me a call tomorrow."

"Okay." I hung up.

My eyes couldn't believe what they were seeing on the TV. Tim and Ronnie both standing there waiting for me to buzz them in.

Tim finally hung up the call phone. He shrugged. Since I hadn't answered by then, he must have figured I wasn't home. I was relieved to see him heading toward the door. Ronnie looked at him, gave a what's up nod and headed to the phone. Ronnie looked up at the camera. His sly smile acknowledged his recognition of Tim.

He picked up the phone and called my apartment. I had to answer this time.

"Ah, hey."

"Hey yourself," he said, smiling.

"Ronnie, I didn't ask him…" I began explaining.

He laughed. "I know."

"What should I do," I asked.

"Buzz me up."

I hesitated.

"C'mon, girl. Stop trippin'."

I pressed the star button. Ronnie hung up the phone and went through the glass door. I turned the TV off. I hadn't even gotten a chance to change my clothes. I quickly took off my pants, grabbed some shorts and a halter. I dressed as I went toward the door. As I got there, Ronnie knocked. I opened the door. Ronnie smiled.

"What's up, girl?"

He kissed me.

"Hey," I responded.

We went in the living room and sat down. Ronnie kept looking at me, smiling.

"Why are you doing that?" I finally asked.

"I'm thinking about you up here watching that TV trying to figure out what you were going to do." He chuckled and shook his head. "I know you 'bout peed on yourself when you saw him."

"It's not funny, Ronnie."

"The hell it ain't." He continued laughing.

There was a knock at the door.

"Who could that be?" I asked, going toward the door.

"Who is it?"

"It's Tim."

Ronnie busted out laughing. I almost fell out. How the hell did he get upstairs? Ronnie picked up the remote and said, "Go 'head and open the door, boo." *Damn,* I thought and reluctantly opened the door.

Tim said, "Hey, girl. What's up?"

"Hey, Tim. I, ah, didn't know you were in town," I lied.

"Yeah, I came home for Spring Break. I wanted to surprise you." He had succeeded at that. "I called up here earlier, but you didn't answer."

"Oh, for real? I thought I heard the phone ring while I was getting out of the shower." The lies were just rolling out.

Ronnie chuckled.

Tim looked at me and said, "Um, I hope I didn't come at a bad time."

I really didn't want to let him in because I knew how he felt about my relationship with Ronnie, but I couldn't leave him standing there in the hallway.

I took a deep breath preparing for his and Ronnie's meeting. I moved aside, allowing him to come in. I knew they would eventually meet, but this was not how I wanted it to happen. I shut the door.

"So, what's up, girl?" Tim asked.

"Nothing much," I answered, trying to figure out what I should do next.

Ronnie made the next move for me by coughing the fakest cough I had ever heard. He was going to make sure his presence was known. I had told Ronnie that I thought Tim was kind of jealous of him so he was going to make sure he flexed a little.

Tim looked at me as if to say, "Who is that?"

"Ah, Ronnie's here," I stuttered.

"Oh."

"I didn't know you were coming over, and he and I…."

"You don't have to explain anything. I should have called."

"Well, um, since you're here—I can introduce you," I said.

I could tell he didn't want to say okay, but he did. When we walked in the living room, Ronnie had his feet on the coffee table, chilling like he owned the place.

Tim recognized Ronnie right away from the lobby. He looked at me. I tried to ignore his stare.

"Ah, Tim this is Ronnie." Ronnie stood up. "Ronnie, this is Tim."

They gave each other some dap, although, Tim did it half-heartedly.

Ronnie said, "What's up, man? I've heard a lot about you."

"Same here," Tim said.

"Aye, weren't you in the lobby earlier?" Ronnie asked, trying to start something. I looked at him in disbelief.

"Ah yeah," Tim answered.

I could tell he was upset. Not only was his surprise visit ruined but he was also face to face with someone he had decided he didn't like.

Tim turned toward me. "Ah, I'm gonna jet."

"Okay."

He looked at Ronnie and said, "It was nice meeting you, Ronnie."

"Same here."

As we headed toward the door, I cut my eyes at Ronnie. He just laughed and sat back down.

At the door, I continued to apologize to Tim.

"Naw, it's cool. Like I said I should have called. But look, I'll be here all week, so we'll hook up some time while I'm home."

"That'll be cool."

"Well I'll give you a call."

I shut the door behind Tim and wondered how I got myself into such a situation. As if I didn't have enough drama with Patrick and Ronnie, now Tim had somehow gotten back into the picture. The last thing I needed was to add more drama to my current relationship situation.

What I really needed at that point was my private session with Ronnie. Tim's surprise visit had made me very tense. Ronnie knew exactly how to alleviate my tension.

When I walked back in the living room, Ronnie looked at me and smiled.

"You are not funny," I said.

"I'm not trying to be funny."

I sat beside him and said, "Yes, you are."

"So you hooking up with your boy while he's in town?" I didn't respond. "Taking away some of my quality time for your ex?"

"Ronnie," I whined.

He laughed and said, "I'm just messing with you, girl."

I wasn't in the mood to be messed with. I got up.

"For real, Stace, I'm ain't gon' say nothing else about Tim."

I began walking out and he asked, "Where you going?"

"To my bedroom," I answered, inviting him to join me with my eyes. Ronnie cracked one of his sexy smiles and followed me back to my room.

Just as I expected, our private session had more than relaxed me. As I lay in Ronnie's arms inhaling the scent of Cool Water cologne from his chest, Tim was the farthest thing from my mind. During those quiet moments, I didn't feel like I was cheating on Patrick. I felt like I was where I was always supposed to be.

That night the phone rang around three. It scared the hell out of me. Ronnie said, "Damn, who the hell is that?" annoyed by the interruption of his sleep.

I fumbled for the phone. Finally, by the third ring, I found the ON button.

"Hello," I answered, half sleep.

Patrick said, "What took you so long? Were you busy…getting busy?"

"Patrick? What are you doing calling here at—" I looked up at the clock—"three o'clock in the morning."

"I'm just checking up on you."

"You need to hang up on his dumb ass," Ronnie mumbled.

The last thing I needed was for Patrick to hear Ronnie's voice. I softly covered Ronnie's mouth. He opened his eyes. An angry wrinkle appeared on his forehead. He looked at me as if to say, *Hang up the damn phone.* I formed my lips to say, "Shhh," silently. He shut his eyes and the wrinkle disappeared as he went back to sleep.

"Patrick, I am sleep. Don't be calling me at this time of the morning trippin'."

"Are you by yourself?" he asked.

"Are you?" I snapped, getting tired of playing his mind games.

He laughed. "A'ight then. I'm going to let you get back to sleep." He didn't want to answer my question just as much as I didn't want to answer his. "I'll give you a call tomorrow sometime."

Don't bother, I thought. "Bye."

The next morning, while we were enjoying a delicious breakfast of eggs, bacon, grits and toast, courtesy of Mr. Morgan, the phone rang. I was hesitant to answer. It might have been Patrick playing games again, but after looking at the Caller ID, I saw it was Tim. I was still hesitant.

"Hello."

"Hey girlie. What's up?" he said, surprisingly cheerfully.

"Hey Tim." Ronnie looked up from his plate. "What's up?" Ronnie kind of laughed and went back to eating his breakfast.

"I was just calling to see what you were up to today. I was hoping we could hook up."

"Ah, well let me call you back and I'll let you know."

"What's wrong? You have something planned?"

"Well, ah...."

"I guess you have to check with your boyfriend," Tim snapped. "Oh no, that can't be it because he's out of town. You must have to check with your other man."

"Tim."

"Naw, that's okay. I see how going from man to man doesn't give you much time for me. I'll talk to you later, Stacey."

He hung up and I looked at the phone dumbfounded. I couldn't believe he was acting like that. I looked at Ronnie and said, "He hung up on me."

"Now you see how it feels," he joked, referring to my hanging up on him on Valentine's Day.

"Shut up, boy. You are so silly."

"Naw for real, what's up?"

"He wanted to know if we could hook up and when I told him I would get back to him, he like went off talking about I had to check with my boyfriend, but oh no, he's out of town, so you have to check with your other man."

Ronnie laughed.

"Then he talking about he sees why I don't have time for him, going from man to man."

Ronnie shook his head. "Don't worry about it, boo. He's trippin'."

That was easier said than done for me. Tim and I had grown up together. He was one of my best friends. I didn't want to mess that up. But he also had to know that things between us had changed since Ronnie came into my life.

Mr. Morgan finished his breakfast and put the plate in the sink. He leaned down and kissed me on my cheek, then on my lips. "Well look, we're going out to P.G. today anyway so I can play some ball with your brothers, so you can call your boy back and let him know you have some free time, but he ain't taking up none of my time. Ya hear?"

I smiled.

He kissed me again and said, "We'll be finished in about three hours so I want you back at your parents' house when I get here."

"You are so silly," I said, laughing.

"I ain't playing. You better be back or there will be consequences and repercussions."

"Anyway. I can't believe you're going to play ball with my brothers."

"Why? Just because they don't like your punk-ass boyfriend, don't mean they can't like me."

"Alright, on that note," I said, getting up. "I'm going to get dressed so we can go."

He laughed and said, "Yeah you do that."

When we got to my parents' house, my brothers were ready to go. They barely said hello to me. I was treated like a stepchild when Ronnie was around. I didn't mind though because that just meant they really liked him, which I loved.

After they left, I looked out the bay window in the living room to see if Tim's car was across the street. It wasn't. I was kind of relieved. I thought about calling his cell phone but decided against it. I really didn't feel like getting into it with him about Ronnie. I had pretty much made it up in my mind to avoid him for the week and just deal with him being mad over the phone. The last thing I wanted was a face-to-face confrontation.

Ronnie and my brothers came back about three hours later, all smelling nasty. As usual, Tracy grabbed me pressing my nose into his sweaty chest. "I smell good, don't I?"

"Boy, get off me." I pushed him back. "You stink."

Ronnie laughed and asked, "So what were you up to while we were gone?"

"Nothing much. I just watched TV."

Tracy smiled and said, "Oh you didn't call your boy Tim?"

I looked at Ronnie. If there was one thing I hated, it was having my business spread, even to my brothers.

He laughed and said, "Stace, I didn't tell them anything. They brought it up to me."

I just looked at him. He said, "I swear."

"He didn't tell us," Kevin admitted.

Devin said, "Yeah, your mother told us."

I should have known. My mother tells everything unless you specifically tell her not to. So I was sure, not only did she tell my brothers, but more than likely she told my father. I was going to have to hear his mouth about that forever.

After Ronnie showered and changed his clothes, we headed to BET Soundstage for dinner. It wasn't very crowded in the restaurant area, but it was happy hour so the bar was full of singles trying to mingle. A sister with beautiful, long, locs showed us to a booth near the back of the restaurant. The Soundstage didn't have the best food in town, but I liked the atmosphere. Ronnie liked this stuffed trout dish they had. He had been trying to get me out there all semester but with school in session, I was not trying to have anyone see me all cozied up with Ronnie. But with classes out for Spring Break, I figured it was safe.

I people-watched while we waited for our Buffalo wings appetizer. There were some nice-looking brothers milling around the bar. I looked across the table and knew none of them compared to my companion. All the women walking pass gawking knew it too. Ronnie was so busy watching the music videos playing on the TV in the booth that he was oblivious to all the lustful stares he was getting. I wasn't. I actually liked being with someone who attracted so much attention from other women, especially since he didn't give it a second thought.

I sipped my iced tea and turned my attention back toward the happy hour crowd. I saw a familiar face approach the bar. It was Tim's friend Jason. I hadn't seen him since we graduated from high school and was glad about it. I couldn't stand him. Actually, we couldn't stand each other. He thought he was God's gift to women. I begged to differ. As far as I was concerned, he was a big bamma.

All of a sudden, a sense of panic came over me. Tim and Jason were thick as thieves when Tim was home from school. So if Jason was there…I didn't have far to look, there was Tim.

"Damn," was the only think I could think to say.

Ronnie turned from the videos and asked, "What's wrong?"

"Tim's here."

"Where?"

"At the bar," I answered.

Ronnie looked in their direction. I glanced over. By this time, both Tim and Jason were looking in our direction. I could tell Jason was asking Tim who I was with.

Ronnie wasn't fazed by their presence. He turned his attention back to the videos. I couldn't be that nonchalant. If Jason wasn't there, I would have felt a little more comfortable with the situation but he was a bad influence on Tim sometimes. Most of the arguments we had when we went together were because of Jason.

Oh, please don't let him come over here, I thought. I was trying to be on the down low anyway. The last thing I needed was a scene.

The waitress delivered our wings and after saying a quick blessing, Ronnie dug in. I wasn't even hungry anymore. I really wanted to go home, but I knew Ronnie was not going to have that.

I tried my best not to look in their direction, but I had to see what was going on at the bar with Tim and Jason. I took a quick glimpse. I saw Jason's mouth, "No she didn't." I assumed Tim was telling him about that whole lobby incident from the day before. Jason downed his drink and motioned Tim toward us.

"Oh Lord," I said, shaking my head.

"What's wrong now?"

"Tim and his friend Jason are coming over here."

Ronnie looked at them. He kind of laughed and shook his head. "See you done hurt your boy's feelings, now he coming with some backup."

"Ronnie, please do not trip," I begged.

"C'mon now, you know me better than that," he said with a devilish grin. I knew him alright and I knew Jason. It was about to get kind of ugly.

"What's up, Ms. Lady," Jason greeted me like we were old friends, as they reached the table.

"Hey, Jason," I answered dryly. I looked at Tim and said hey to him, too, but he barely responded.

Jason moved his eyes toward Ronnie. I suppose he was waiting for his introduction. I really wasn't trying to prolong his stay at the table so I began, "Jason, this is…."

He said, "Oh, I know who this is. I've heard a lot about you, Patrick."

I thought I was going to die right there.

"Naw, man, I told you, Patrick is her boyfriend and he's out of town," Tim said, with vindictive smile.

Ronnie laughed it off because he knew what they were doing. He was always so cool. He extended his hand to Jason and said, "Naw bruh, I'm Stacey's friend, Ron."

"Oh snap, my bad, man. I'm Jason. I've known Stacey and my man, Tim here since high school."

Ronnie just nodded.

Jason saw he wasn't going to rattle Ronnie's cage too much so he turned to me. "So what's been up with you, girl? I was going to call you last night and see if you wanted to go down to Legends with us, but Tim said you were busy."

He was full of it because I never went anywhere with the two of them. He was just trying start something.

"Yeah, she was pretty busy last night," Ronnie remarked, with a grin.

Ronnie was not going to let Jason keep getting digs in without saying something. Tim did not like Ronnie's comment. I saw his jaw tense. He wanted to say something, but I knew he wouldn't. He was going to let Jason keep talking for him.

"Oh, is that so?" Jason asked, still pushing the issue.

Ronnie looked at him and said, "Yeah, all night long."

It was a little bit too much testosterone pumping for me. I just sat there pretty much speechless. I didn't know how to get myself out of that situation. I looked to Ronnie. If he stopped flexing, Jason would lose interest, and he and Tim would leave. I guess he saw the desperation in my eyes.

"Well Jason, it was nice meeting you," Ronnie began as he scooted out of the booth. He stood up. "But you'll have to excuse me."

He looked at me and said, "I'll be right back, boo."

"Alright," I said as he kissed my cheek to piss Tim off even more.

As Ronnie disappeared around the corner, I looked at the two fools. "Why the hell are y'all trippin'?"

"You the one who tripped on my boy yesterday."

I looked at Tim. I couldn't believe he was letting Jason speak for him. But I did have to set Jason straight.

"You don't know what you're talking about so you need to mind your business."

"Oh, Tim told me what was up. How you gonna dog my boy like that for some dude you bonin' on the side?"

"First of all, I don't have to explain anything to you."

"Oh, I know…" He tried to interrupt but I continued, this time turning toward Tim. "And secondly, if your boy wants to discuss what happened between us yesterday, then we can talk later."

"So he s'posed to just wait around 'til you're finished with your big boy toy, huh?"

I wasn't even going to acknowledge Jason's presence anymore. He wasn't worth the breath.

"Like I said, we can talk later."

Tim said, "What's the purpose? You pretty much let me know where I stand yesterday."

"Fine Tim, whatever." If he wanted to be childish about the situation, I wasn't going to waste my time with him any longer.

By the time Ronnie got back from the bathroom, Jason and Tim had left. He realized I wasn't in the mood to eat so we boxed up our food and headed back to D.C.

Though it didn't start off that great, Spring Break turned out pretty well. Ronnie and I really got a chance to just chill with each other. We didn't do anything special. I ended up staying at his house most of the week because his place was more fun. Ronnie had the big screen TV and every cable channel in the world. Besides, it was easier to relax since I didn't have to worry whether it was Patrick or Tim on the other line every time the phone rang.

I tried to act like the situation with Tim didn't faze me but it did. He and I had been through too much together. I waited until the last possible moment, the morning he was leaving to go over his house to clear the air.

When I pulled in the driveway, I didn't see his car. I hoped I hadn't missed him. I shut my car door and saw Ms. Green peeking through the living room curtains. Before I could reach the front door, she swung it open.

"Hey, baby." She wrapped her ample arms around me and hugged me tightly. "How have you been?"

"I'm fine, Ms. Green. I was just stoppin' by to see your son before he left."

"Oh, he's gone to the store but come on in. He'll be back in a few minutes."

I followed Ms. Green to their den, where she had been watching The View.

"You want something to drink, baby?" she asked as she plopped her wide hips on the couch. I had no doubt that Ms. Green weighed close to two hundred fifty pounds. She had always been a large woman, but she had gained weight in recent years.

"No, thank you."

She laughed and said, "I was going to tell you to get it yourself anyway. You know you ain't company."

I laughed.

"So what's up with you and my son, Ms. Thang?" she asked, turning toward me as a commercial came on. Ms. Green was never one to beat around the bush. If she wanted to know something, she would just come out and ask. When she suspected that Tim and I had started having sex, she summoned me across the street and asked us both point blank if we were "doing it." Tim was too embarrassed.

"We're ah, cool, Ms. Green." I don't even know why I lied because I knew Tim told his mother everything.

"Oh, really," she challenged.

"I mean, we had a little falling out, but we'll work it out. It's just a little misunderstanding."

"If you say so," she replied skeptically.

She went back to watching TV, much to my relief. I didn't feel like talking to Ms. Green about what was going on between me and Tim.

What seemed like an hour passed and Tim finally walked in the door. He walked in the den and his mother said, "Look who's here to see you, Tim."

He looked at me. "Hey." The normal excitement to see me wasn't in his voice.

"Hey. I, ah, just wanted to see you before you went back."

"Oh yeah. Well here I am."

At that point, Ms. Green excused herself. The tension was getting thick. I wished I could have gone, too, but I needed to settle things before they got to a point where we couldn't reconcile.

"I just wanted to let you know how sorry I am about how everything happened at the apartment last week. I really didn't want you and Ronnie to meet like that."

"Don't worry about it, Stacey. It's no big deal. I mean I shouldn't have assumed that since your boyfriend was out of town, you would be alone."

"Tim, I just don't understand why you're trippin' like this. It's not like you didn't know Ronnie was in the picture. I told you all about him."

"Well maybe he's where I've been wanting to be for the pass four years," came out of his mouth before even he realized it.

"What are you talking about?"

"Stacey, you know how I feel about you, how I've always felt about you. You know that if it were up to me, we would have never broken up."

"Tim, I am honestly sorry. You were my first real boyfriend—my first everything and because of that, you're always going to have a big piece of my heart." I looked at him. "But, things have changed. I love you but not the same way as I did four years ago."

"Do you love him?" he asked hesitantly.

For some reason, my first instinct was to say no. Not because I didn't love Ronnie but I guess because I didn't want my answer to cause Tim any more pain. But lying to him wouldn't do either of us any good.

"Yes, I do."

There was uneasy silence for a few minutes. I could hear Ms. Green in the kitchen trying her best to make noise with the dishes so we wouldn't know that she was listening. Finally, Tim said, "I guess I knew that already. I was just hoping I was wrong."

"I'm sorry."

"You don't have to apologize. I owe you an apology for the way I was acting. I was trippin' and I'm sorry." He laughed and said, "I'm especially sorry for bringing Jason into it."

"Now that, you should be sorry for," I joked.

"So are we still cool?" Tim asked, extending his arms for a hug.

Of course we were cool. I wasn't going to let a misunderstanding destroy a friendship that had lasted more than sixteen years. I did feel kind of bad about Tim's feelings for me. At one point in my life, I would have jumped at the chance to get back with him and for a while, I thought we would be exactly like Gina and Devin and get back together after college and live happily ever after. But then Mr. Morgan came along and changed everything.

handle your business

onnie and I were on my bed watching TV. He was lying across the
bottom of the bed all into some Indiana Jones movie. I wasn't
really into stuff like that but he wanted to watch it so I acted interested. I
lay there looking at Ronnie wondering how I had gotten so lucky. He was
everything that I had always wanted in a boyfriend—even though he wasn't
officially my boyfriend. Not by his choice but it seemed to be mine. I did
want to be with Ronnie. I knew that. I also knew Ronnie's patience with
the situation was wearing thin. I just didn't know how thin.

After watching Ronnie watch TV for far too long, I decided it was
time for us to do something else. I pushed Ronnie off the bed with my
feet and started laughing.

"What the…" he said, pulling himself up from the floor. "Oh, alright,
you want to play, huh?"

He jumped on the bed and I ran out of the room. He chased me all
around the apartment. I was screaming and laughing at the same time.
The people in my building probably would have been ready to call the
police if they hadn't heard me laughing so hard.

As I rounded the couch, Ronnie jumped over it and grabbed my arm.
I screamed out in pain.

"I'm sorry, boo," he said. "I didn't mean to grab you that hard."

He actually hadn't grabbed me that hard. My arm was just very sore
from where Patrick had grabbed me when we had an argument a couple
of days before.

I was dropping Patrick off at his house with no intentions of going in
but he said he needed to talk to me. Secretly, I was hoping he was going to
break up with me. That would have gotten me off the hook. No such
luck. Once he said he had talked to his father earlier, I knew it was one of
the same ol' "my father is always coming down on me" conversations. I
wanted to say, "That's because you are such a whining ass," but I just sat
there wishing I was somewhere else. Patrick went on and on about how
his father said he wasn't going to pay for his last semester of school.

"I'm saying though, it's only one more semester," he complained.

"Would your parents dog you like that?" he asked. There wasn't much I could say because I didn't really think his father was dogging him.

"Well, no." Actually, my father would have stopped paying for Cs and Ds long before then. Patrick had been on academic probation for two semesters already.

"See. See how he is?" he said, feeling he had me on his side. Then I made my first mistake.

"It's not like you didn't know this could happen. Didn't your father tell you if weren't off probation by now he wasn't going to throw good money after bad?"

"Yeah, but—"

"But you still haven't been going to classes like you should. All you do is hang out with your frat brothers." That was my second mistake.

"Whose side are you on?" he asked, getting agitated.

"I'm not on anyone's side. I'm just saying."

"Not on anyone's side?" He glared at me and said, "Well you're supposed to be on my fuckin' side," raising his voice.

"Patrick, I'm just saying," I stammered. "You're getting upset when you knew it was going to happen and you had all the power to stop it, but you didn't. You decided to spend your time elsewhere."

Patrick's eyes narrowed. I realized I probably should not have said that. I figured that was a good time for me to leave. I got up but he blocked my way.

"Are you trying to accuse me of being with someone else?" he asked angrily.

That question came out of the blue. I mean, I figured Patrick was cheating but so was I, so what could I say. Actually, I didn't really care.

"Patrick, please." I tried to walk around him but he grabbed my arm.

"Is that what you're trying to say, Stacey?"

"Please get off me. You're hurting my arm."

"Hell no. You gonna accuse me of cheating."

"I didn't say that."

"That's what it sounded like to me." He pulled me closer and said, "I'm the one who should be making some accusations."

His vice grip was beginning to cut off the circulation in my arm. But I managed to push the pain to the back of my mind because I just knew Patrick was about to tell me it was over. As crazy as it sounds, I was almost excited. That excitement was premature.

"What are you talking about?"

He laughed a mincingly and said, "You don't know what I'm talking about huh?"

"Patrick, I…."

"I think you know exactly what the hell I'm talking about."

He pulled me closer and sniffed up my neck and around my ear.

"What are you doing?"

Patrick looked at me and said, "You know, lately you been smelling a little different?"

"What," I asked completely confused. "Smelling different?"

"Yeah." He stared angrily at me and said, "You smell like another nigga."

I was completely caught off guard. I didn't know what he wanted me to say and I didn't want to say the wrong thing. So I didn't say anything.

"You smell like that nigga Ronnie."

I knew I wasn't as inconspicuous as I should have been with Ronnie. But that was the first time that Patrick ever came right out and said anything about me and Ronnie. Deep down, I didn't give a damn but I definitely didn't want a face-to-face confrontation.

"Patrick, you're hurting my arm."

He pushed me against the wall and said, "I know you haven't been giving my stuff up to Ronnie."

I couldn't even pretend not to be scared at that point. He was forcefully unhooking my belt saying, "Why don't we see if that nigga's scent is anywhere else on you?"

"Patrick stop."

He got the belt a loose and went on to the button and zipper. I continued to beg him to stop to no avail.

The more I tried to free myself from his grip, the tighter it became. Finally, I just couldn't take the pain any longer and I submitted to his demand for me to stop fighting him. Patrick out weighed me by at least fifty pounds so there was no way I could physically fight him off without getting really hurt. I have no doubt that he would have forced himself on me if I had continued to fight, but once I stopped fighting he couldn't justify it in his own mind.

When I got home, I looked at my arm. It was black and blue and very sore. I knew I couldn't let Ronnie see it because he would go off, but it seemed he was going to see it regardless. He kept trying to pull my shirt sleeve up but I kept pulling away.

"Let me see it, girl. I want to make sure I didn't bruise you," Ronnie said, genuinely concerned.

"You didn't. It's alright." He knew something was up.

"What happened to your arm, Stacey?" I could tell by his tone that there was nothing I could do but tell him the truth. He wasn't going to let it go.

"It's no big deal, Ronnie. I mean my arm's just a little bruised."

"And how did it get bruised, Stacey?" he asked, seeming to know the answer.

The whole situation with Patrick had gotten way out of control and I knew that. But I was trying to leave Ronnie out of it. I didn't want him getting in any kind of trouble because of my stupidity. I should have broken up with Patrick long before all the drama but I didn't. And I definitely didn't want to tell Ronnie about my arm. I got up, trying to avoid answering his question.

"Stacey." He was getting mad.

"Ronnie, it's just a bruise. Don't worry about it. It'll be fine."

"Let me see it."

"Ronnie…."

Before I could finish, he pulled me to him and pushed my sleeve up. He looked at my arm and then at me.

"Did Pat do this?"

There was no way I could lie to him. But the words wouldn't pass my lips either. I just nodded.

"Damn it, Stacey. How the hell did that happen?"

Ronnie normally had a soft voice. It was deep and sexy and he talked kind of low most of the time. But he was upset. That soft voice was replaced with a loud, thunderous one.

"We, ah, were having a little argument and I tried to walk away from him and he grabbed me. That's it." My voice was trembling.

"That's it? That's it, huh?" Ronnie started walking back toward the bedroom. Then he came back in the living room.

"You are going to break up with that nigga tonight," he said, visibly angry.

"Ronnie—"

"Ronnie nothing. We ain't even discussing this shit no more. You

better break up with him," he looked at me, "or else." He went back in the
bedroom, and I followed him.

"Or else? Or else what, Ronnie?" He was putting his shoes on. He
didn't answer. I wanted to get an attitude about the ultimatum but how
could I? He had been more than patient with me.

"Ronnie."

He got his jacket and stormed passed me toward the door.

"You can't leave like this, Ronnie."

"You have some business you need to handle. I'll get up with you
tomorrow after you do."

He kissed me, out of what felt like obligation and the door slammed
behind him. I had never seen him so mad. I realized he was probably
more hurt than mad.

I sat on the couch almost in a daze. I couldn't believe what had happened. The room seemed as though it was spinning. I closed my eyes and
put my head back against the couch. All my life I had tried to stay away
from drama. That was Erika's thing. She was the drama queen. Now, I
was moving up the ranks. I was in the thick of mad drama.

The thought of the "or else" Ronnie spoke of was really freaking me
out. I continued trying to convince myself he wouldn't do it. I found out
the next day, I was wrong.

I had picked up the phone several times to call Patrick and break up
with him but I hung up each time without even dialing a single number. I
told myself I didn't know what to say, but the truth was I was scared that
if I broke up with him, he would tell everyone about the abortion. The
last thing I wanted was for my parents to find out, especially my mother. It
would break her heart that I felt that was my only option.

I sat around all day jumping like a scared kitten every time the phone
rang. I lay across my bed and turned the TV on, trying to take my mind
off all my problems. I loved all those black sitcom reruns that were on in
the afternoon. *Good Times, The Jeffersons, Sanford & Son.* They always had
me rolling. I was laughing so hard at Florence cracking on George that I
didn't even think twice about answering the phone when it rang.

"Hello," I said still laughing.

"Hey."

I almost choked when I heard Ronnie's voice.

"Ah, hey. What's up?"

"Nothing."

I wasn't used to Ronnie's tone. He sounded so distant. This wasn't going to be one of our run-of-the-mill conversations.

"So, ah, what you up to?"

"Nothing really. I was just watching *The Jeffersons.*"

"Ah-ha."

There was silence on the phone. Ronnie wasn't going to just chitchat with me much longer. "So, did you handle your business?" he asked point blank.

I didn't say a word. What could I say? No, I hadn't done what he wanted me to, even though I wanted to.

"Well, Stacey?"

"Ronnie, I…" Before I could try to get some type of explanation out of my mouth, he stopped me.

"Stacey, I don't even want to hear all that. It's a yes-or-no question. Now, did you or did you not break up with Pat?"

"No," I answered in a small voice.

Again, there was silence. This time I knew the silence was disappointment on Ronnie's part. The silence broke a few minutes later and my whole world fell apart.

"Alright then, Stacey. You know what, you just go 'head and be with your little boyfriend, 'cause obviously that's who you really want to be with."

"Ronnie, you know that's not true."

"Do I? I mean I've been sitting back waiting for you to make a decision for months."

"Ronnie, you don't understand."

"Oh, I do understand. I understand that you don't want a man who's going to treat you like you should be treated. You'd rather be with some asshole who treats you like shit. But that's fine." I could hear the hurt in his voice. "Ever since we started seeing each other, all I've tried to do is give you everything you wanted, now I'm giving you what you really want, Pat."

"I don't want to be with him."

"You haven't shown me that."

"Ronnie, I love you."

"You know what, Stacey, I really don't doubt that. But you need to concentrate on loving yourself. 'Cause you don't let somebody put his hands on you like that. I don't give a damn what the reason is. You know you don't deserve to be treated like that."

There was a long pause and he continued, "Then again, maybe you don't know. But I do. And I can't sit back and watch it anymore."

"Ronnie, please. Just give me some more time."

"Bye, Stacey."

I heard him hang up but I couldn't believe it.

"Ronnie. Ronnie."

I called him back but he wouldn't answer the phone. I didn't even know why I was calling. What could I say to him? Like he said, I hadn't done what he wanted me to do. What I knew in my heart I really needed to do. I wished I could talk to someone but no one would understand, not even Erika. Lately, she had been asking me why hadn't I broken up with Patrick and gotten with Ronnie officially. I didn't have an answer for her either. She also told me Ronnie was going to get tired of waiting. I guess she was right.

April 28, 2000 - 2:38 p.m.,

My life is messed up!!!! Ronnie told me to handle my business with Patrick and break up with him. I didn't and now he's gone. I don't know why I didn't. I kept picking up the phone but I couldn't do it.

I knew this day would come eventually. Ronnie told me he wasn't going to wait around on the side forever. Me telling him I loved him didn't mean anything. I had to show him by getting that asshole out of my life. And I couldn't even do that. I must be out of my mind.

I always thought being with anybody was better than being alone but I was so wrong. Being with Patrick is like being alone, so what do I need him for? I guess the saying really is true, I can do bad by myself. But I wasn't doing bad and until an hour ago, I wasn't by myself. I had Ronnie. What's really messing my head up is, I really thought Patrick was trying to be there for me after the abortion but he knew things weren't going to work out with us so he used my guilt to keep me there. Even after falling in love with Ronnie, I can't leave Patrick. But I can't let him control my life like this. He doesn't give a damn about me. Ronnie loves me and I'm

losing him. It's time for me to handle my business. I have to get
Patrick out of my life. Whatever happens after that, I'll just deal
with. Regardless, it can't be any worse than what I've gone through
this past year with Patrick.

All weekend I sat at home calling Ronnie. And all weekend he didn't answer. I didn't leave any messages because there really was nothing more I could say. Actually, if he had answered, I didn't know what I would have said. I think more than anything, I just wanted to hear his voice on the answering machine.

That Monday, there was a program on campus sponsored by the English department. The speaker was Terri McMillan. I really didn't feel like going but she was one of my favorite authors. I had been waiting all year to see her, and I wasn't going to let what was going on in my love life cause me to miss hearing her speak.

I sat through the program not really able to concentrate on Ms. McMillan's speech. I couldn't think of anything but Ronnie. I happened to look over my right shoulder and about two rows over was Tracy. Our eyes locked. He looked upset. I could always tell because his eyes got real small and he had these two veins in his forehead that popped out in a "V" shape.

"I need to talk to you now," he mouthed.

"What?" I couldn't imagine what he wanted to talk to me about.

"Now!" He was really upset.

I didn't want to leave in the middle of program but I had to see what Tracy was so upset about. I squeezed past a few people and went out the side door. I looked around but didn't see Tracy. I walked toward another door in the front of the building and there he was. He saw me and rushed in my direction.

"What's wrong?" I asked as he reached me.

He grabbed my arm and said, "I need to talk to you now."

"What is wrong with you?" Tracy was pulling me away from the building.

"What the hell is wrong with *you*?" he finally said.

"What are you talking about?" I asked totally confused.

"Pat has been putting his hands on you?"

I was in total shock. My heart started beating fast. How did he know

about that? Then I realized how he knew. I looked across the street and
there was Ronnie leaning against his truck. I couldn't believe he told Tracy.
He promised me he would never tell anybody.

"Answer me, Stacey!" Tracy yelled. I kind of looked around. The last
thing I wanted was for the whole campus to know what had been going
on. When Tracy was upset like that, he didn't give a damn who was around.

"Tracy, please, can we talk about this somewhere else?" I begged.

"No, we cannot. We are going to talk about this right now. What the
hell is going on?"

"Tracy, it's not that big a deal."

"Not that big a deal. That mother…."

Tracy put his fists against his forehead and took a deep breath. He
walked away from me. I went after him and said, "Tracy, please calm
down." I glanced at Ronnie. He was still watching.

Tracy looked at me and said, "Has Patrick ever put his hands on you?"
I just looked at him. There was nothing I could say. "Well." His voice was
getting louder again.

I swallowed hard and said, "Not really."

"What the hell does not really mean, Stacey?" I didn't know what it
meant. I had no explanation. Tracy turned his back to me.

"That punk has been hitting on you and you didn't even tell me."

I could hear the hurt in his voice. When he turned back toward me, I
could see the hurt in his eyes. I really felt like shit then. I had kept everything to myself thinking it was best for everyone but all I ended up doing
was hurting the two people in the world that I wanted to hurt the least.

"Stace, why didn't you tell me? I had to hear all this from Ronnie."

"How was I supposed to tell you? I didn't know what to say."

"You could've told me. You know you can tell me anything. I'm your
brother—your twin brother." Tracy's eyes were beginning to well with
tears. I took his hands.

"I'm so sorry, Tracy." Now my eyes were welling up. "I just didn't
know what to do. I mean I thought I could handle it." We hugged. Tracy
was holding on to me so tight. It was like he was never going to let go.

"I'm never, ever going to let anybody hurt you again. Never," he
vowed.

I glanced over at Ronnie. He put his head down then got in this truck.
He looked at me and put his sunglasses on. Then he drove off.

Tracy looked at me and said, "I am going to kick his ass."

"Tracy, please don't do that."

"Not only am I going to kick his ass, but I'm going to get Kevin and Dev."

"No, please don't tell them," I begged.

"Nobody puts his hands on you like that."

There was no way in the world I was going to let my brothers get in any trouble because of my stupidity. I had already lost Ronnie. It was time for me to really handle the situation with Patrick. But I needed to do it on my own. I had to prove to myself that I really could do it.

"Tracy, I promise I'm going to handle this." I could see the doubt in his eyes. "Please. I need to do this myself."

"Alright, girl, damn. But I'm telling you right now, you better handle it because if you don't, I sure as hell will."

"I will. Thank you so much." I kissed him on his cheek and we hugged. "I love you so much, Trace. I promise you from now on, I will come to you."

"You know I will fight you if you don't," he joked.

I laughed.

"So," he looked at me, "I hear that you and Ronnie are a thing of the past."

Me and Ronnie's relationship, or the lack thereof, was too painful for me to discuss. So I started telling Tracy how excited I was about my upcoming graduation. He wouldn't be graduating until December because of some classes he had to make up as a result of pledging.

My attempt to change the subject didn't work. Tracy just kept repeating his initial statement. "I hear you and Ronnie are a thing of the past." He laughed and said, "I ain't got nothing but time, baby girl. You are going to talk to me if we have to stand out here all day."

"Alright, yes, we are a thing of the past. I don't know why you're asking me anyway. You already knew the answer."

"Yeah, I knew, but again, Ronnie told me. You didn't."

"I know, Tracy, but if I told you that Ronnie and I weren't messing with each other then you would have asked why and I can't lie to you. So I couldn't tell you."

"You know that brother really loves you."

That was the last thing I wanted to hear. Yes, I knew Ronnie loved me. I knew I loved him. But I also knew I was the reason we weren't together.

"Trace, I really don't want to talk about it."

"Okay. I understand. But you know I'm here for you, baby girl."

"I know."

"Does Erika know what happened?"

"Yeah. She knows," I answered, softly. "I had to tell her when Ronnie and I stopped seeing each other."

Telling Erika was hard. Before I could even get the words out to her good, I was in tears. All my life, she had been my one true confidant. There was absolutely nothing she didn't know about me—except what was going on with Patrick. I wasn't sure how she was going to react. But as always, she was there for me. She understood why I didn't tell her. She knew it had nothing to do with her. But as I expected, Erika was ready to beat Patrick's ass. Just as with Tracy, I had to promise her I would take care of the situation.

Tracy and I hung out for a couple more hours. It felt good spending time with him, just the two of us. When I got home, I damn near broke my neck trying to get in the door. I had to go to the bathroom so bad. As I ran through my bedroom to the bathroom, I saw I had two messages.

I finished my business, washed my hands and went see who had called.

"Ah, hey Stace." My heart skipped a beat. "Um it's Ronnie. I wanted to let you know that I'm, ah, sorry I told Tracy what was going on with you and Pat. It's just that, I didn't know what else to do, Stacey. I ah…I don't know. I just did what I thought I had to do. I hope you understand that and I hope you can forgive me for breaking my promise to you."

There was a long silence. I could hear him breathing though. He wanted to say more, but couldn't bring himself to.

"Anyway, I gotta go. Take care of yourself for me, okay? Peace."

I shook my head. Ronnie always ended his calls by telling me he loved me. Things had changed a lot in a few days. I forwarded to the next message.

"Aye, it's me again. I, ah, just wanted to tell you…I still love you and I always will. Remember that. Peace."

Class of 2000

Class of 2009

stacey

May 2, 2000 - 10:34 a.m.

This is supposed to be the most exciting time in my life but everything is so messed up. I mean I'm about to graduate summa cum laude from college. I've been interviewing with some really good companies that I know I'm going to get some offers from. I should be happy but how can I be when the man I love hardly looks at me anymore. I haven't really talked to him in a couple of weeks. Now I have Tracy on my back about breaking up with Patrick. I know I'm ready to do it but I just don't know how. I really don't want a big scene or anything. But I'd better do it soon or Tracy said he'd do it for me, and I really don't want that.

Then to top everything off, day after tomorrow is my birthday, and I'm not all that excited. I would be if I was going to be spending it with Ronnie, but the chances of that are slim to none. I wish I could get the nerve to call him. I just want to hear his voice. But I don't have anything new to tell him so I doubt that he'll even talk to me. I have really made a mess of everything.

Another interview was done. It had gone pretty well. After interviewing so many times, all my nervousness was pretty much gone. I felt more confident with each one. As I was getting on the Beltway headed toward I-295 from the Greenbelt Marriott, I thought about the company. It was a small black-owned consulting firm out of Atlanta. It had a great benefits package, a mentoring program and a one hundred percent tuition reimbursement program. I really liked that because I wanted to go on to get my MBA in a couple of years. I liked Atlanta too. I had been down there lots of times with some of my sorors.

The only problem with that would be leaving my family and friends. I didn't know if I could handle being away from my parents and brothers. And what would I do in Atlanta without Erika? She and I had been together almost every day since we met. How would I survive without my best friend by my side? But it was just an interview so I decided not to try and plan the rest of my life out right then.

When I approached my front door, I could hear my phone ringing. I fumbled with the keys, trying to get the door open. It might have been Ronnie calling. I got in and dropped everything on the floor. I ran to the phone.

"Hello."

"What took you so long, girl?" It wasn't Ronnie.

"Oh, I was just getting in the house."

Tracy could hear the disappointment in my voice.

"You must have thought it was somebody else."

"Ah, anyway, what's up?"

"How was your interview?"

I went through the whole interview again with him. Tracy was a detail person. You couldn't just tell him it was fine. He wanted to know what went on from the time you walked in until the time you shook the person's hand to leave.

"That sounds like it would be good for you, Stace." That made me feel good, but I kept thinking about leaving him though.

"And don't worry about leaving me. I will be with you regardless. I mean who knows, maybe I'll find something down there or wherever you decide to go." It amazed me that he always knew what I was thinking.

Since Ronnie had told him about Patrick, Tracy was calling a lot more. Every day, sometimes three or four times a day. To my amazement, he blamed himself. "If I hadn't moved out, none of this would have happened." I told him it wasn't his fault. It was mine. I could have ended things but I didn't. And I had plenty of opportunities.

I had made it up in my mind to break up with Patrick the week before I found out I was pregnant. But after finding that out, I foolishly decided I couldn't break up with him. After the abortion, every time Patrick sensed I was going to break up with him, he'd start talking about *our* baby. How old he would be, things like that. So of course, I couldn't break up with him then. It took a while but I finally worked up the nerve last year, then his mother died.

Tracy didn't want to hear all that. All he wanted to know was when was I breaking up with him.

"I'm going to, Trace. But he's not here. He's been in Jersey for the past week."

"Stacey, when his feet cross the D.C. line, you need to deal with that."

"I am."

"Promise me." He knew if I promised I wouldn't back down. I could never break a promise to Tracy.

"I promise you, Tracy. I am going to break up with him once he gets back."

"I know it seems like I'm harping on this, baby girl, but you don't know how bad I feel. I mean all our lives I've been there taking care of you. Now, this happens."

"Like I said, I thought I could handle it myself."

"We ain't even gonna talk about this no more right now." I was glad to hear that. "So what you want to do for our birthday?"

"I don't know. I don't really have anything in mind."

"So have you, ah, heard from your boy lately?" Tracy asked, referring to Ronnie.

"Um, no. I haven't talked to him in a few weeks."

"Are you alright?" he asked.

"Ah yeah. I'm fine," I lied. I wasn't alright and my brother knew that.

"Well anyway, I'll think of something for us to do, just the two of us."

I really liked that idea. I needed to just hang out with my brother and get my mind off everything that was going on. I was looking forward to it.

Patrick came back around six o'clock in the evening or at least that's when he decided to call me. I told him I needed to talk to him because I wasn't about to break my promise to Tracy, but he said he couldn't right then.

"Stacey, I can't talk to you right now. I'm on my way up on the yard for the party."

"But Patrick."

"I'll get up with you later."

Click.

I could not believe he did that. He was in such a rush just to get to a party—a party that would be going on all damn night. He couldn't even take five minutes to talk to me. I shouldn't have been surprised because he was all about self. I was trying to be discreet about everything but it was time to finally handle my business. I headed to campus to break up with Patrick wherever I found him.

The end of the year block party was always off the chain. There were people everywhere. I spotted one of Patrick's frat brothers and asked him if he had seen him. He had this scared look on his face so I assumed Patrick must have been with some girl. But of course, I didn't give a damn.

"Hel-lo, have you seen him?"

He finally pointed me toward this crowd of Alphas standing near a little homemade bar they had built on the sidewalk.

I started walking in that direction and sure enough, there was Patrick with his arms around some girl's waist. Some of his frat brothers saw me and let him know I was coming. He saw me and his arms dropped from around the girl.

"Hey, Stacey. Wha—what you doin' up here?" he stuttered. He couldn't even play it off good. If I had cared, he would have been cold busted.

"Oh, I can't come to the party?" I couldn't resist messing with him a little. Just then, Patrick's little friend decided to open her mouth.

"Ah, who is she, Pat?"

I looked at her like she was out of her mind. All Patrick's frat brothers started laughing. "Oh, shit, it's 'bout to get twisted up in here," someone said. I was not about to fight some trick over Patrick. I just kind of looked her up and down and turned my attention back to Patrick.

"Ah, can I talk to you for a second?"

"'Bout what?" he asked arrogantly.

"Can I just talk to you?" I looked around at everybody in my mouth. "In private."

"What's up, Stacey? I don't have time for all this. We can talk right here."

I laughed and shook my head. "Alright. If that's the way you want it. Fine." I looked at him and said, "It's over."

Some of the guys said, "Daammmnn."

If it was one thing Patrick hated, it was being embarrassed. He was sorry then that he didn't want to talk in private. Now everybody on campus was going to know about what was going on.

"Stacey, why are you trippin'? Is this about her?" he said, pointing to the girl he had been all hugged up on.

"Patrick, please, I ain't even worried about that trick. She can have you."

"Trick! Who you calling a trick?" she said, moving toward me.

I put my hand up to her face and said, "Don't. Please don't play yourself. I do not want to have to beat your ass out here."

Some of the guys grabbed her and pulled her away. By this time people were noticing the commotion and were moving in our direction.

"Why are you trippin', Stacey? We can talk about this later, in private."

"Oh, there's nothing else to talk about. I've said what I came to say."

Patrick took my arm and pulled me away from the crowd. "Why are you doing this?"

"Patrick, this relationship, if that's what you want to call it, is over."

"And why is that?" He had to be kidding me. I knew he didn't ask why. I just looked at him.

"What the hell is your problem, Stacey?"

"*My* problem?"

He was beginning to really piss me off acting like he didn't know why things were going down like they were. "You want to know what my problem is, you are my problem." I was raising my voice and Patrick hated that. He could embarrass me as much as he wanted but he didn't like to be embarrassed himself. "And I'm not going to put up with your shit anymore."

I felt like tons of weight had been lifted off my shoulders. I had months of anger built up inside me. If he would have just talked to me on the phone, everything would have been cool, but he didn't, now all our business was going to be all over campus. But at that point, I didn't give a damn. I was fed up with that whole situation with Patrick.

"You're tired of my shit. What shit?"

"You know exactly what shit," I said, raising my voice again.

"See why you gotta be gettin' all loud, Stacey? We can go back to your place and talk about this later," he said, trying to talk softer.

"Don't be getting all timid now. I wanted to talk to earlier but you didn't have time. You had to get up here to be with your little trick. Well now, we are going to talk about it right here."

"You need to stop trippin'."

"Oh, I ain't the one who's been trippin'. You are. I've been trying to be there for you and you've been treating me like shit."

"Ain't nobody been treating you like shit."

"Whatever. What you need to do is find somebody to teach you how to treat a woman."

Everybody said, "Damn."

Patrick was really getting embarrassed. I could see his jaw tense up and his neck was starting to turn red. "Is that so?" was the only thing he could come back with. He could always get loud with me when people were around but now he didn't have much to say. Standing there looking at him, all the things that he had done to me flashed through my head. Tracy was right. He used the abortion and his mother's death as excuses to be an asshole. That pissed me off even more. It may have been wrong, but I was going to get him back for at least some of what he put me through.

"That's exactly why I was with somebody else."

"So. That just means some other brother wasn't gettin' any either." He succeeded in getting a laugh from his boys, which is what he was going for.

I looked at him and said, "No—that means I had to go to some other brother if I wanted good sex."

Everyone busted out laughing. Guys were falling all over each other and running into the street. Patrick kept glancing at them. He was really getting mad. I would have been scared but I saw Dave standing a few feet away and I knew if Patrick did anything, he would be there. Besides, I knew most of Patrick's frat brothers and they wouldn't let him do anything to me either.

"Well others like what I got," was his weak response.

"Well all them tricks can have you, 'cause I'd rather be with a real man who can take care of business, in and out of bed."

He looked at me and said, "Oh, like that nigga, Ronnie, huh?"

I could hear all kinds of whispering in the crowd.

"She was messing with Ronnie Morgan?"

"I knew I had seen them together."

"I told you they were kicking it."

"Shit I'd dump him for Ronnie too."

"Most definitely like Ronnie. As a matter of fact, exactly like Ronnie," I answered, confidently, confirming what he already knew.

"You just talking all this shit because your brothers are probably somewhere around here."

"And? So what if I am? You're not talking shit *or* putting your hands on me because you think they might be here."

His boys weren't laughing then. Most brothers weren't down with hitting females.

I looked at Patrick and said, "And I'm going to let you know right now, they will be in your ass if you mess with me again." He looked at me and I said, "Believe that."

I walked away from Patrick feeling really good. Better than I had in months. That's when I saw Ronnie's truck pull up. *Oh Lord,* I thought. I knew Patrick was going to front on him since everybody had heard that I was messing with him.

As Ronnie got out of the truck, Patrick saw him. He started walking toward him and the crowd followed. Ronnie looked at Patrick then at me. He knew then what was up.

"I knew something was up with you and Stacey," Patrick said, walking up in his face. Ronnie pushed him back and said, "Yo, you better check yourself, kid."

"How you gonna be messing with my girl?"

"Somebody had to hit it right for her," Ronnie replied with a devilish grin. I knew he was going to go there with him. "From what I heard, she damn sure wasn't getting it from you."

People in the crowd were like, "Daammmmnn."

Everybody started laughing and Ronnie continued taunting Patrick by saying, "You are the weakest link—goodbye."

The next thing I knew, Patrick swung on Ronnie and the fight was on. It looked like some Alphas were going to jump in but Dave and some of the boys came up. Dave wasn't gonna let nobody jump his boy. As if the situation wasn't out of control enough, all my brothers pulled up in Kevin's truck. They saw Patrick and Ronnie fighting and took it as their opportunity to get some licks in. They jumped out of the truck and started punching and kicking Patrick too.

"I'll teach you to put your hands on my sister," I heard Tracy saying as he kicked Patrick.

I ran over, begging them to stop. I could hear police sirens. That was exactly what I was trying to avoid by not telling them.

"Stop, y'all! The police are coming! Please stop." I had to have been out of my mind standing in the middle of the five of them. Dave grabbed me up and said, "Girl, get out of here."

"No, Dave. I gotta stop them. They'll kill him."

"I'll handle it. Just get the hell out of here." I reluctantly left.

Dave grabbed Ronnie and pulled him into his truck and drove off.

Before the police got there, my brothers all had jumped back in the truck and left, too, leaving Patrick's frat brothers picking him up off the ground.

I was so worried about my brothers and Ronnie that I didn't know what to do. If any of them got in trouble, I would feel terrible, because it would have been my fault.

All the way home, I was calling Tracy, but his voicemail kept coming on. I just knew something was wrong. Finally, he called back.

"Yeah, what's up?" he asked nonchalantly.

"Why didn't you answer your phone? I was worried about y'all."

"I'm sorry. I took the phone off when we jumped out the truck. But we're all straight."

"So ah...is Ronnie alright?"

"Yeah, don't worry he's still as fine as ever," Tracy teased.

I laughed. "Shut up, boy."

"Naw, for real, he's cool."

"Oh, okay."

That was a big relief to me. I wanted to call Ronnie but I couldn't bring myself to. Things were over with Patrick but I knew he was still hurt by the way I handled the whole situation.

The emotional high I had gotten from finally breaking up with Patrick didn't last long. I started feeling depressed. Though, it looked like everything was looking up for me, the one thing I wanted in my life—Ronnie—wasn't there.

I was lying on the couch when someone buzzed my front door. I turned the TV to Channel 3 and saw the UPS man standing in the lobby. I picked up the phone and said, "Yes?"

"I have a package for a Ms. Stacey Jackson," he responded.

After signing for the small box, I went back in the living room to see what I had been sent and by whom. I opened the attached card and my heart leaped. I recognized the handwriting as Ronnie's. He had sent me a birthday gift.

I read the card:

> *I just wanted to wish you a very Happy 22nd Birthday!*
> *You are one of the most beautiful women I have ever known.*
> *Your inner self makes your outer beauty that much more*
> *spectacular.*
> *I know not what our future holds, but I do know that my life is*
> *that much richer because of knowing you.*

No matter what happens, always remember I love you.
Forever Yours,
Ronnie

Tears rolled down my face as I began to unwrap the gold paper from around the small box. I opened it and I couldn't believe my eyes. I had never seen a piece of jewelry so beautiful—a pear-shaped ruby stone surrounded by small diamonds on a gold chain. The tears really began to flow then. I sat there crying like a baby for almost ten minutes. I finally got myself together. I had to thank him but I was scared to death to call.

I picked up the phone. Then put it back down. I picked it up again. And put it down again. *Why are you buggin'? Just call him,* I thought.

I dialed the number. The phone started ringing and my heart started pounding. After the fourth ring, I felt relieved that he wasn't home. I could say everything I needed to on his answering machine and I decided I was going to get everything off my chest.

"Ah, hey, Mr. Morgan. I, um, was just calling, first to say I'm sorry for what happened up on campus. I didn't expect you to get caught up in that whole thing. Anyway, I'm also calling to say thank you, thank you, thank you for my birthday gift. It is absolutely beautiful. I don't know what else to say." I took a deep breath.

"I don't even know if I deserve something this beautiful from you after everything that went down. I was so stupid. I really thought I could handle everything that was going on but I couldn't and things just got out of control. You were always there for me, trying to give me everything I wanted and needed. I should have been stronger."

As I spoke to the answering machine, I began to cry again. Ronnie was the man of my dreams and I had messed everything up. If I never got him back, I was going to at least tell him how I really felt.

"I should have done what you wanted me to but I didn't. I'm sorry. You have made this the best year of my life, and I will never forget that. You made my dream of what my first love would be like come true. I just want you to know that you did show me how I'm supposed to be treated. You have now set the standard by which all others will be held and I really doubt that anyone else will be able to fill your shoes. Well that's about it." I had babbled long enough.

"Again, thank you for everything. And when you're that big star that I know you're going to be, always remember that there's a girl who you knew back at HU who loves you. Take care. Bye."

When I hung up, I felt good. I had gotten a lot off my chest. At the same time, I felt sad because I wished things with Ronnie had worked out differently.

I spent the rest of that weekend shut up in my apartment. I stayed in bed, in my pajamas not doing much of anything, but eating cookies-and-cream ice cream. I was really waiting for Ronnie to call after hearing my message. But that didn't happen.

Sunday was me and Tracy's birthday dinner at my parents'. It was the first time in my life that I didn't want to go. I didn't feeling like being around anyone. I wanted to wallow in my own misery. But I couldn't disappoint my mother.

I walked in the house and my mother was in the kitchen putting the finishing touches on dinner.

"Hey, Mommy." I kissed her cheek and she looked at me.

"Hey, sweet pea. What's wrong?" I could never hide anything from my mother. Her maternal instincts were as strong as they come.

"Nothing, Mommy. I'm alright."

She pulled me close to her. She held my face in her hands and looked directly in my eyes. I tried to pull away but she wouldn't let me go. Tears started welling up in my eyes.

"Please let go, Mommy," I begged.

"Okay, but you know you can talk to me about anything, baby. You know that, right?" I nodded.

She kissed my forehead and went back to cooking. My mother was like that. She said what she had to say, and then it was over. I wanted to talk to her but I couldn't tell her about what happened with Ronnie without telling her about what happened with Patrick, and I couldn't bear to do that. It was bad enough that my brothers, Erika and Dave knew about it. I couldn't have anyone else know.

I wiped my eyes and said, "So, ah, where is everybody?"

"Your brothers and your father are outside playing basketball, and Gina ran to the store for me."

"Oh."

All during dinner, I was quiet. I wasn't really hungry. I just sat there picking over my food.

"Are you okay, pumpkin?" Daddy asked, concerned.

"Oh, um, yeah, I'm fine." My response was not very convincing.

"You sure now?"

"Yes, Daddy, I'm fine." I managed to fake a smile.

"So anyway, how's my friend doing?"

"What friend?" I asked.

"My man, Big Ron."

I glanced at Tracy. He raised his eyebrows as if to say, "It was bound to come up."

"Ah, I, um, really haven't talked to him lately."

"Really, so what's up with y'all?" Of all the times for my father to be cool with a guy I brought home.

"Um, nothing's up, Daddy." He looked at me. He knew I wasn't being straightforward.

"I'm really not feeling well," I said, getting up from the table. "I'm going to lay down for a while."

"Alright, sweetheart. You go 'head. I'll check in on you later," Mommy said.

I went up to my old bedroom and laid on the bed. I looked around the room. My mother had left it pretty much the way it looked my senior year in high school. Most of my stuffed teddy bear collection was still neatly arranged in the corner. I had taken some of them with me. As quiet as it was kept, I still slept with a teddy bear I had gotten when I was born. Ronnie always tripped off it when he spent the night with me.

My pom-poms were on the wall. My senior prom picture with Tim was on my dresser. There were hundreds of pictures of me and Erika all over the room dating back to first grade.

Things were so carefree then. Life was so easy. It started getting more and more complicated once I really started getting involved with boys. I had no idea then the crazy things that lay ahead, good crazy and bad crazy.

I heard a knock at the door. "Come in." Tracy walked in with a slice of cake and a glass of milk.

"I brought you some dessert."

"Thanks."

He set the plate and glass on the nightstand. He lay beside me on the bed. He put his arm around me and asked, "You alright, baby girl?"

I shook my head.

"I don't know what to tell you. I know you don't want to hear this but everything will be alright."

I kind of laughed. He was right. That was the last thing I wanted to hear.

"You probably don't want to hear this either but you know if it's meant to be, it will be."

"I know," I said solemnly. I looked at him and confided, "I really love him, Tracy."

He kissed my cheek. "I know, baby girl. I know."

I pulled the necklace from inside my shirt and said, "Look what he sent me for my birthday." Tracy took it in his hands gently and said, "Man, this is nice."

I looked at it again. "Isn't it beautiful?"

"Yeah, it is."

Tracy and I just laid there in silence. He knew that's just what I needed then.

When I got home that evening, I had two messages. The first was from Erika. "Hey, girl. What's up? Just wanted to see how your birthday dinner was. Give me a call. Later."

I hit the next message button and went in the bathroom to wash my face.

"Hey. What's up, Stace? It's Ronnie."

I almost broke my neck getting back to the answering machine. I turned up the volume and sat on the bed.

"I'm sorry I missed your call. I wanted to wish you a happy birthday. I'm in New York. I meant to call you before I left but I didn't get a chance. I've been so busy that I just checked my machine and got your message from Friday. It's obvious that we need to talk face-to-face. When I get back next week, I'll give you a call and we'll hook up. By the way, Ms. Jackson, just to let you know, you deserve that necklace and much more. Anyway, I'll talk to you later. And, boo," he paused, "I love you too. Peace."

For the next hour, I sat on my bed replaying that message over and over. It was beyond silly, I know, but that message gave me some hope that things might work out with Ronnie.

The phone ringing woke me up around twelve-twenty. I must have dozed off listening to Ronnie's message. I grabbed the handset and answered.

"Hello."

"Ah, hey Stacey." I couldn't believe it was Patrick.

"Um, hey."

"I know it's kind of late. Were you sleep?" he asked.

"Yeah. But what's up?"

"Oh well, I was just wondering if I could come over tomorrow?"

"Come over?" I asked. "For what? My brother dropped off all your stuff."

"No, it's not that. I just want to talk to you."

"I don't think so, Patrick."

"Please, Stacey. I just need to talk to you. I promise that's it."

I took a deep breath. "Look, you can't come here. I have a study session on campus at ten-thirty. I'll meet you at the library at noon."

"Alright then, I'll meet you in front of the library."

When I hung up, I questioned why I had agreed to meet with the person that had caused me so much stress and pain. I guess I was curious to what he had to say.

As I sat on the library steps waiting for Patrick, I became more and more nervous. There were always stories in the newspaper of guys killing their ex-girlfriends. Patrick could have been on his way to kill me. I was glad these thoughts were only in my head because someone might think I was crazy if I verbalized them. Patrick had some problems, but I honestly didn't think he would kill me. But I guess all those women didn't think their exes would kill them either.

I saw Patrick walking toward the library from a distance. My heart started racing. Maybe I didn't know him that well. He had his backpack over his shoulder. Was there a gun or knife in it? I was tripping.

Patrick walked up the steps and said, "Hey."

"Hey," I responded.

He sat beside me and put his backpack on the ground between his legs. I kept my eyes on that bag…just in case.

He said, "I'm glad you agreed to meet me."

"Yeah well, I guess I was curious as to why you wanted to talk to me."

Patrick looked at me and said, "Well actually, I wanted to apologize."

"You want to apologize?" I asked making sure I had heard correctly.

"Yeah. I'm sorry for everything that I did to hurt you, Stacey. And this is not one of those same ol' apologies from before. I really mean it." He put his head down and continued, "I was going through a lot of shit but I had no right to take it out on you like that."

I sat in silence, amazed at his sincerity. This was the Patrick that I met years before. He looked at me and said, "I had no right to ever put my hands on you. I can never apologize enough for that."

He was right about that.

"Well, it's over now, Patrick."

"I know. I just wish things could have been different though. I hope Ronnie knows what type of woman he's got."

"I'm sorry things went down like that," I confessed. "I really didn't set out for it to be that way."

"I don't blame you for hooking up with Ronnie. If it hadn't been him, it would have eventually been someone else. I knew you weren't going to stay around too long with me treating you like that. I guess I wanted you to break up with me so I could blame someone else again for all the bad things going on in my life."

I looked at him.

"To be honest, Stacey, I've known about you and Ronnie since Valentine's Day."

"Why didn't you say anything?" I asked, confused.

"I don't know. I suspected that you were seeing someone a long time before that. I noticed all the new stuff you had. How you would disappear for days without saying anything. But what could I say? I had my own little side things going. Even though I suspected, I didn't know who it was until that night. I mean when you saw him walk in with ol' girl, your face told me everything."

All I could do was shake my head. I guess I wasn't as good at cheating as I thought.

"Patrick…."

"You don't have to say anything. Like I said, I don't blame you. I wasn't treating you right and obviously, Ronnie was. I can't hate you for finding someone to do that."

"Patrick, I tried. I honestly did. You and I have been through so much together. I wanted to be there for you. I really did."

"I know and believe it or not, I appreciate it. But I have some things I need to work out by myself and hopefully, the next time someone like you comes into my life, I'll treat her the way she deserves to be treated."

"I hope so too."

Patrick looked at his watch. "Well I have a final in ten minutes. I can't afford to fail another class. I'm already going to be here this summer."

"For real? What did your dad say about that?"

"Well he wasn't happy to say the least," he said, laughing. "But if one good thing came out of this whole situation, he and I are getting to be pretty cool again. After I told him everything that went down with you and me, he realized he hadn't really been there for me after my moms passed and we're working it out."

"You told him everything that happened with us?"

"I hadn't planned on it but he had come down that day Ronnie and your brothers worked me over. So when I got back to the crib, he wanted to know what was going on with me. So I told him everything that happened between us, including the baby and about hitting you. So now we're working things out."

"Well I'm glad about that."

He got up and picked up his backpack. "Well let me get up out of here."

I stood up.

"Again, I'm sorry about everything," he said, looking into my eyes.

"Like I said, it's over."

"Well—I'm sorry about that too." He kissed me softly and said, "Take care, Stacey."

As I watched him walk across campus, I knew Patrick really was sorry. Not only sorry for the way he had treated me, but also sorry that he lost me.

May 8, 2000 - 5:30 p.m.

Well the Patrick Smith chapter of my life is officially over. He and I had a nice talk this afternoon and cleared the air. He apologized for everything and I accepted his apology. I had planned to curse him out but I realize that would have done no good. I daydreamed of hurting him the way he hurt me, but I don't think it's in me to do something like that. Besides, I still believe deep down Patrick is a good person. I honestly wish him nothing but the best.

With that chapter shut, I'm praying I can reopen my Ronnie Morgan chapter. I'm a little more optimistic after hearing his message a few days ago. Hopefully, we can put all my drama behind us and move on with our lives—together.

no place like home

had finished my last final as a Howard student. I was happy to be done
but I was also beat. All I wanted to do was hit my bed and stay there for
a few days. The only place for me to recoup was home. I would be away
from everything that had gone on with Stacey, and I'd be able to rest.

Raina was sitting on the couch looking at a *Black Enterprise* magazine
when I walked in the door. She might as well have moved back in as much
as she was there. Her relationship with my parents reminded me of Stacey's
with hers. They were both daddy's girls and both were best friends with
their mothers. If Raina wanted to move back, there would be no problem. My parents wouldn't mind a bit. The same was true for Stacey. My
mother probably wouldn't mind me moving back, but Pops would be
like, "You can stay for a few months until you find an apartment, but a
man should have his own."

"Damn girl, you're always here," I greeted Raina, jokingly.

She laughed. "Shut up, boy."

I kissed her on her cheek. "You might as well save your money and
give up that apartment 'cause you're never there."

I put my bags down at the bottom of the steps.

"Anyway. What you doin' home? I thought you had finals this week."
Raina said.

"I finished up early so I decided to roll up here for a few days."

"Oh. Well you know your mother will love that."

I sat beside my sister. I remembered how we went through a phase
where it seemed like we couldn't stand each other. We loved each other
but couldn't stay in a room for more than five minutes without arguing.
But that was a long time ago.

I put my arms around the back of the couch and stretched out my
legs.

"So have you decided if you're coming back here after graduation?"
Raina asked, putting the magazine on the coffee table.

"Yeah. I probably will. At least for a little while," I answered.

"So what does Ms. Stacey think about that?"

I tried to change the subject by getting up and heading to the kitchen. "Man, I'm hungry."

"Ronald, Jr. why are you trying to change the subject?"

I looked back at her, as I pushed open the kitchen door. "I'm hungry, girl. A brother's been on the road for almost five hours."

I went in the kitchen. Raina followed. She wasn't about to let up. "What's up with you and Stacey now?"

"Why do you think something's up?"

Raina sat at the kitchen table. "Spill it, boy," she demanded.

I recounted the whole story to Raina as I ate a turkey sandwich. She couldn't believe Stacey was going through all that drama.

"She looked so happy."

"Well she was happy…with me."

"Oh, you the man, huh?" Raina teased.

"Naw, I'm not trying to come off like that."

"I'm just playing with you."

"Raina, I was doing everything to show her she didn't have to put up with that shit. I mean, I showered her with love notes and flowers. I was always hooking up the romantic meals. Giving her little and big gifts, just because. I wanted her to see how she was supposed to be treated, but she still stayed with Pat."

"Well, it's not always that easy to walk away. I'm sure she understood everything you were doing for her, but there was obviously something keeping her with this guy. Something more powerful than her wanting to be with you."

"Yeah, well after I saw that bruise on her arm, I told her she had to handle her business or I was gone. The next day when I talked to her and she hadn't broken up with him, I was so pissed. I think I was mad because I felt like she was picking him over me."

"Ronnie, I doubt that she sat down and thought about the two of you and said 'oh, I'd really rather be with this guy that's beating my ass.'"

"Yeah, I know. But, I also knew I had to pull back and let her really deal with that situation."

"It's obvious that she broke up with him, so why are you here instead of with her? Didn't you say her birthday was this weekend?"

I took a deep breath and said, "With everything that was going on with Stacey and trying to study for finals—I am so drained. I sent her a gift, but I just needed to get away from everything for a few days. When I get back, we'll see what happens."

After driving four and a half hours and emotionally reliving the Stacey situation with Raina, I was ready for some sleep. I went upstairs to what used to be my bedroom. Actually, it was still my room, but my mother had gotten tired of my *Jet* beauties collection wallpapering the walls. She had the room painted but everything else remained the same.

I lay across my bed and closed my eyes. Before I knew it, I was sleep. This wasn't a regular sleep—this was a bomb could go off and I not wake up sleep.

I finally came out of my hibernation at ten-thirty the next morning. I had slept more than thirteen hours. I felt rejuvenated. I took a long hot shower, dressed and headed to the kitchen. Sleeping that long gave me a hell of an appetite.

There was so much food in the refrigerator that I couldn't decide what I wanted. The phone rang.

"Hello," I said, still looking for something to eat.

"Hey, Ronnie," Kim said. "What you doin'?"

"Tryin' to find something to eat. How'd you know I was here?"

"I saw Myles last night and he told me."

"Oh."

I was going to kick Myles's butt for telling that girl I was home. The last thing I needed was Kim bugging me while I was there.

"Aye, how 'bout I treat you to lunch?"

"Um, yeah okay." I wasn't about to turn down a free meal. "Where you want to go?"

"How 'bout Sylvia's?"

"Alright. I'll meet you there in about an hour."

Kim hesitantly said, "Okay." I knew she wanted us to ride together but I wasn't trying to give her too much time. She was the type to take any little act of kindness as me wanting to be with her.

When I got to Sylvia's restaurant, Kim was already seated. As I approached the table, I realized I had no feelings whatsoever left for her. It felt strange to come to that realization because of our history. She was my high school sweetheart. I was supposed to always love her. But sitting down in front of her, I wasn't sure if I ever really loved her at all.

"What's up, handsome?" she greeted me.

"What's up?" I responded, feeling guilty about my lack of feelings for her. "You been waiting long?"

"Naw, I just got here about five minutes ago."

I said, "Oh okay," and picked up the menu.

Kim was sitting there just looking at me with a weird smile on her face.

"What's wrong?" I finally asked.

"Nothing. I'm just glad we're getting a chance to spend some time together. The last time you were home, you had company."

Oh, here we go, I thought. Every time I was around Kim, she had to say something about Stacey.

"Speaking of your company, I heard you and Ms. Thang aren't kickin' it no more."

I looked at her and said, "And who told you that?"

"Myles," she responded.

That brother had a big mouth. I was going to have to watch what I told him.

I drank some water. "Yeah well, as usual, Myles spoke out of turn."

"What you mean? You and her are still seeing each other?" Kim asked with a disappointed look on her face.

I shifted in my seat. I didn't want to talk about Stacey, especially with Kim. I looked around the restaurant trying to find something to turn the conversation toward. Luckily, our waitress came over to take our orders.

I ordered the smothered pork chops and Kim ordered the fried chicken. When the waitress left, Kim asked, "Well Ronnie, are you and Stacey still seeing each other or not?"

"Look Kim, Stacey and I are just going through some stuff right now, but we're going to work it out."

Kim sucked her teeth and turned her head.

I looked at her and asked, "What's all that for?"

"Nothing."

I laughed. "Whatever."

Kim turned back toward me and hissed, "I just don't understand what you see in that girl."

"And you don't have to."

"I guess not," she snapped.

We sat in silence until the waitress brought our food. My pork chops were looking delicious. I blessed my food and dug in but Kim was still sitting there looking pissed off.

"Aren't you going to eat?" I asked in between bites.

"I've lost my appetite."

"Why are you trippin', Kim?"

"I'm not trippin'."

I was not going to let Kim's little attitude mess up my meal. I was too hungry. Plus, she was being silly. I couldn't believe she was mad because I was still seeing Stacey, which at the time, really wasn't true but she didn't need to know that.

The waitress came back to the table and asked, "How is everything?"

"Mmm, it's good," I answered. "Could I get a piece of peach cobbler?"

"Sure, no problem." She looked at Kim and said, "Ma'am, how's your meal?"

"It's fine," Kim snapped. The waitress sensed her attitude and just walked away.

I was trying to eat as fast as I could so I could get the hell out of there.

"Ronnie, I want to be with you again," Kim blurted out. I almost choked on my last bite of pork chop. "You're graduating next week. You could move back here and we could get back together."

I sat back in disbelief. That girl was really serious. It was like she had been planning for us to get back together for a while.

"Kim, that's not going to happen."

"Why not? Aren't you moving back here?"

"Well yeah, but…."

"We both had our time to see other people, and now I'm ready to be with you. I've never stopped loving you, Ronnie."

I didn't know what to say. All I could do was sit there dumbfounded. She had really caught me off guard. I didn't want to hurt her but there was no way we were getting back together.

"What's the problem, Ronnie?" Kim asked.

"I told you, Stacey and I are working through some things."

Kim looked at me as if she was hearing that for the first time. "What are you saying Ronnie?" Kim's voice was getting louder. We were in the wrong place to have that conversation.

"Look, let's just go talk about this someplace else."

"Naw, I'm cool. I just want to know what's up with us."

"What us, Kim? We broke up more than three years ago."

"But we've also been seeing each other on and off during that time."

"Not since I started seeing Stacey."

Kim looked at me and said, "Are you trying to tell me you're in love with her?"

I looked at her but didn't respond. She knew what that meant.

Kim sat there just looking at me. After a few minutes of awkward silence, she said, "Well Ronnie, I wish you and Stacey the best."

She got her purse and stood up.

I said, "Kim."

"No, I'm for real. I'm happy for you. Look, I forgot I'm meeting someone in thirty minutes. I'll give you a call."

I knew she was lying but I didn't push. She kissed me on my cheek and quickly left. I didn't feel like eating my cobbler after all that. I had the waitress box it up. Then I paid the bill and left.

I felt bad for Kim. She really had it in her head that we were going to get back together and live happily ever after. Raina told me she was taking my niceness as me still caring for her but I wouldn't believe her. She was going to rub my nose in the fact that she was right.

ronnie

I was surprised to have a message from Tracy when I got back from New York.

"What's up, dawg? This is Tracy. Could you hit me back at 301-555-2370? I need to ask you for a big favor. Peace."

A favor? What in the world could Stacey's brother want from me? Well he was going to have to wait for a while because a brother was tired and was going to get his nap on.

I woke up about two hours later and took a shower. I was going to be in for the night so I put on my mad comfortable, raggedy gray sweatpants and a T-shirt. I still hadn't thought of anything Tracy might have wanted from me so I decided that the best thing to do was to call him back to see what was up.

"Talk to me."

"What's up, man? It's Ron."

"Hey, man. What's up?"

"Nothing much. Sorry I'm just getting back to you but I was in New York."

"No problem, man. Stacey told me you were out of town."

"So what's this favor you need?"

"Well Stacey's been kind of down lately so me and my brothers decided to give her a surprise graduation party to cheer her up."

"O-kay," I said, wondering what that had to do with me.

"Anyway, I was thinking that it would be real cool if you and your boys could come and do a song."

I thought that would be cool too. I had sung for Stacey, but she had never seen the group perform.

"When is it?"

"This Friday. I know it's kind of short notice but…" Tracy tried to explain.

"Naw, that's cool. I'll call the fellas. I know they'll do it as a favor to me."

"Man, this is going to blow her mind." That was true. "It's going to be at Martin's Crosswinds over in Greenbelt."

"Yeah, I know where that is."

"Erika's supposed to get her there around eight-thirty so I'm thinking you can do your thing after we have dinner."

"That's cool."

"Do you need me to talk to Martin's about any type of equipment or anything?"

"Naw, we got all that covered."

"Cool. She is going to freak out when she sees you."

I hadn't had a chance to talk to Stacey since I got back. She obviously had gotten my message but we hadn't hooked up yet to discuss our future.

"Hopefully, we can sit down and talk some things out."

"She hasn't really talked to me about anything but I do know that she's been really beating herself up about how she handled everything."

"Yeah, I know. We gonna have to get all that straight."

"Well she's gonna be happy that you want to."

I had to laugh. "Tracy, man, your sister is—" I tried to think of the word to describe how I felt about Stacey, but I just couldn't. "I don't even know what to say."

"I know, man. That was just an out-of-control situation. Now y'all can see what's up because let me tell you, dawg, that girl sho 'nough got a Jones for you."

I laughed. I had me a Love Jones for Ms. Jackson too. "Yeah, we'll see how it goes."

"Alright then, man. Hit me back if anything comes up."

"Alright. Peace."

It was going to be cool to surprise Stacey. I didn't know what song we would do. I didn't want to do any of our original stuff because I didn't want it to come out and people have already heard it. Having decided not to do something original, I had to find the perfect song to cover. Maybe Maxwell. But then again, some of his notes were a little out of my range. Dre sounded exactly like Maxwell but since this was for Stacey, I wanted to be the one to sing to her.

I talked to the fellas about the party and they were down. They said they'd come down on Thursday so we could go over whatever song I chose.

For the next two hours, I went through almost every CD I had trying to find the perfect song to sing to Stacey. It had to tell her everything in my heart. After that song, I didn't want her to have any doubt about what I was feeling.

As I was looking through all my music, I came across Dru Hill's first CD. Now that CD was the bomb! When I heard the first single "Tell Me," on the radio, I knew I had to buy it. The harmony those brothers were kicking was tight.

I popped it in and continued my search through the rest of the CDs. I was thinking about "You" by Jesse Powell. That was a pretty good song. Stacey would like it. But I wasn't really feeling it. "Before I Let You Go" by Blackstreet. We had danced to that at homecoming. But the song really didn't say what I wanted to.

In the background, I could hear "Never Make A Promise" playing. I went and turned it up. As I listened, I knew that was the perfect song for Stacey. I never had truly been in love until I met Stacey. I would never hurt her. I definitely would never hit her. And I was going to do everything in my power to make her happy and give her everything she wanted. I couldn't believe how perfect that song was. I didn't have to look any further.

I called the fellas and told them what song I had chosen. They agreed it was perfect. Then I went to work. I recorded the track into my system and filtered out the vocals, leaving only the instrumentals. I looped the first fifteen seconds to extend it to sixty seconds because Tracy said he wanted some introduction time with the music playing. Then I roughly ran through it a couple of times. I had to admit it sounded pretty good, even without the fellas. When they got there, I knew it was going to be tight.

My next task was to find something to wear. I couldn't decide if I wanted to wear this bad cream linen suit I bought when I was home or if I wanted to go a little more casual. I had some baggy leather pants that would be cool but I was leaning more toward the suit. Raina had found me some phat Stacy Adams shoes. I just needed to go up to Georgetown and find me a hat to go with the outfit. The right hat would set it off. I wanted to take my flyness to the next level so I needed some new specs. I had seen some nice black-framed glasses with yellow tinted lenses. My suit, hat and those glasses would drive Stacey out of her mind.

When I woke up Friday morning, my stomach was in knots. Actually, it felt like there were a million butterflies in it. That really tripped me out because I never got nervous. I mean I was used to being in front of large crowds from playing ball. It wasn't even that I was nervous about singing in front of people. I had been singing since I was seven years old. It was because I was going to be singing for Stacey, more importantly, to Stacey. I hadn't really talked to her for a couple of weeks. So these were going to be my first face-to-face words to her in a while.

We got down to Martin's around seven o'clock. Tracy was there early making sure everything was in order. He met us at the front door.

"What's up, fellas?"

"Tracy, these are my boys, Ced, Dre and Myles. Fellas, this is Stacey's twin brother Tracy." They all greeted one another in the normal brother-man fashion.

Tracy gave me the once-over and said, "Damn, Ron, you got G'd for baby girl, huh?"

"Go 'head with that, man," I replied.

"No doubt. Your sister got my man's nose wide open." Myles added his two cents.

"Anyway." My nose was definitely wide open, but we didn't need to keep talking about it.

"Oh, he got my sister's nose a little wide too." They all laughed.

"Anyway, let me quit messing with you. Where did you guys park?" Tracy asked.

"On the side of the building," I answered.

"Cool. Well y'all can come check out the room."

We followed Tracy into a large banquet room. It was huge. I was a little concerned about the acoustics in the room.

"Can we check out the sound system? I want to see how everything sounds before a lot of people get here," I said.

"Yeah, sure. People probably won't start coming in for another half hour or so."

We were surprised that the sound system was actually pretty good. All the mics worked fine. I knew because I went to each one and checked and rechecked them. My third time around, Dre said, "Ron, man, why don't you sit down and chill."

"For real, kid, you done checked e'erything and it's all fine," Ced said.

"I know I'm buggin' but y'all don't understand."

"We understand that tonight's real important to you, but it's going to be fine so just chill out," Dre assured me.

They were right. I sat down but that didn't control my nervous energy. I fidgeted with my suit jacket, straightening and restraightening my collar. I ran my hands over the front of my pants legs making sure there weren't any wrinkles. I wiped off my shoes.

I happened to look up and the guys were looking at me. "What?" I asked, as if I didn't know. They laughed and just shook their heads.

Slowly people began to arrive. We left the banquet room and hung out in the lobby. The fellas were walking around more than I was because Tracy didn't want any of Stacey's friends to see me. I agreed. Besides, I needed to be by myself for a while to get my head together. What I really needed was a drink. A little Hennessy or JD would have calmed my nerves, but I never drank before performing.

As it got closer to Stacey's arrival time, I got more nervous because I knew I was only minutes away from seeing her. I saw Mr. and Mrs. Jackson coming in. Tracy told me the only people who knew I was going to be there were Erika, Dave and his brothers so I would have to wait to say my hellos.

Tracy came racing through the lobby doors. "Okay, everybody, they just pulled up." He ushered the few people still in the lobby inside and had everybody quiet down.

Erika led Stacey in blindfolded. When I saw her, she took my breath away. I didn't think it was possible but she seemed more beautiful than I had remembered.

She had on some Capri jeans. And man, they hugged her hips and thighs perfectly. She had on an orange halter, covered by a waist-length jean jacket and some orange strappy high-heeled sandals. Her toes looked freshly pedicured, with some shimmering orange polish. She was also wearing a beautiful orange head wrap. Her makeup was flawless. Everything about her was flawless.

"C'mon, now E, where are we?" she asked.

"You'll see in a minute," Erika answered.

Erika guided her pass me. She was so close that I could have touched her. And I wanted to so bad. I could smell the scent of her Angel perfume. All I could think about was later that night my boo was going to be back in my arms.

Erika led her into the banquet room and there was a thunderous roar of "Surprise." I heard Stacey scream. I couldn't see her but I was sure she was in tears. She was a sucker for stuff like that.

As the party truly got going, everybody sat down for dinner. The guys went in the back of the room where Stacey couldn't see them and ate. I wasn't hungry at all. I wasn't as nervous as I was before, but I never could eat before I sang.

Tracy walked out in the lobby. He handed me a microphone and said, "You ready, dawg?"

"Yeah, I'm ready."

"Okay, your boys are in place behind the curtain in front so I'm going to go in and say a little something and then cue the music and let you do your thing."

"Cool."

Tracy went back in. I took a deep breath. I moved near the rear doors. He got one of the mics and said, "Is everybody having a good time so far?" The crowd shouted, "Yeah."

"Well right now, on behalf of my brothers and myself, I would like to take this time to let our baby sister know how proud we are of her." Everybody said, "Aahh." Tracy cued the music and said, "Stace, we wanted to do something very special for you tonight, something that you would always remember, and we know you're going to like this. In fact, you're going to love it."

I began singing as I walked in. Some girls near me kind of screamed. Everyone started turning around trying to see not only what the commotion was but also, where the singing was coming from. I saw Stacey turn around in what seemed like slow motion. Our eyes met. She was definitely surprised. I saw her eyes welling up with tears and before I knew it, the water works were in full effect. I glanced around and not only was she crying but so were Erika, Gina and Mrs. Jackson. I just smiled and shook my head.

Halfway through the song, I walked over to Stacey and took her hand. I pulled her up. I led her to the middle of the floor and put my arm around her waist. At that moment, I realized how much I had missed holding her.

When the song was over, we just stood in the middle of the floor holding each other. Everybody was clapping but it seemed like the room was silent and Stacey and I were all alone.

"I love you, Ms. Jackson," I whispered in her ear.

"I love you, too, Mr. Morgan."

Tracy had hired a deejay, so the party was kicking into high gear. I had provided some romantic music, now it was time to get to some booty shaking. Stacey and I hadn't really noticed any change in the tempo of the music.

As the floor filled with people ready to get their groove on, we remained in our own world. We continued to dance slowly, even on the fast songs. Every now and then, I faintly heard people saying how much they liked the song, but I wasn't really paying much attention to anyone but Stacey.

"I can't believe you're here," Stacey beamed. I had never seen her so happy. "And you actually sang a song to me in front of everybody."

"Well, I needed a way to get my boo back and Tracy gave it to me."

"You never lost me. I was trying to figure out a way to get you back."

"You never lost me either."

Stacey smiled. I hadn't seen that smile in a while. I missed it.

"Oh, happy belated birthday."

"Thank you."

"I got you something too," she said excitedly.

"You didn't have to do that. I got your card."

"You know I had to get you something. I sent the card just to let you know I hadn't forgotten but I found you a really nice gift."

"You're all the birthday gift I need."

"I'm sorry I couldn't spend it with you."

"Don't worry about it. I was planning on staying in New York, but I came back here and me and Dave hung out."

"I bet Ms. Kim was upset about you leaving before your birthday," Stacey teased.

"Actually, we kind of got into it when I first got home."

"About what?" she asked, stroking the back of my neck.

"Well, she had this big future for us planned out."

"Us?" Stacey asked.

I laughed. "Yeah. She was thinking after graduation, I'd move back there, we'd get together and live happily ever after. I had to let her know, that was never going to happen."

"Well, I'm glad you let her know."

I smiled and said, "Don't sharpen the claws. I took care of it."

"Well I'm glad." She kissed me. "Because this boo is going to be around for a very long time."

"I know that's right," I said, rubbing her back.

"So, ah, what were you planning on doing after the party?" I asked.

"Nothing really. I was probably just going to go home."

"Would you like some company?"

"Of course."

Both Stacey and I were rather anxious to get back to her place. We wanted to be alone. After mingling for a while, we finally snuck out. We ended up getting back to her apartment a little after midnight.

"Have a seat. I'm going to go get your gift," Stacey instructed.

"Yes, ma'am," I joked.

Stacey came back with this neatly wrapped gift. With everything that was going on, I honestly didn't expect her to remember my birthday, let alone get me a gift. But she did. I unwrapped the package and opened the box. She had bought me a leather-bound notebook with gold trim.

"It's for you to keep the songs you write in."

"Man, Stace, this is the best." I gave her a kiss and said, "Thank you so much, boo."

"You're welcome."

She looked at me and said, "I'll be right back."

"Alright."

Stacey went into her bedroom and shut the door. I knew it was on then. I hadn't been with Stacey in more than a month so I was more than ready. I had never gone without sex that long before. I could've had some during that time but I wasn't going to go out like that. I knew Stacey and I were going to work everything out. I was actually being monogamous. I never thought I could do it but I guess I just had to find the right girl. And Stacey was definitely the right one.

After a few minutes, the bedroom door opened. Stacey came back in the living room. She had changed into a purple camisole and some purple paisley pajama pants. She took my hand and said, "Come with me, Mr. Morgan."

"Where are you taking me?" I teased.

"To heaven," she said, turning off the lights.

I smiled and said, "Oh, I've been there with you before."

She just laughed.

In the time that Stacey and I had spent together, she had picked up a few pointers on romance. Her room was illuminated only by candlelight.

There had to have been twenty or more all over the room. I made a mental note of that effect because it was nice. She had two large sticks of our favorite incense, Black Love, burning on each of her nightstands. There was soft music playing and Ms. Jackson had bought some red satin sheets.

"Where did these come from?" I asked.

"I bought them a little while back. Since you liked satin sheets so much, I had to make sure we had some here too. I know black is your thing but I had to go the red route."

"Mmm, I likes."

Stacey opened the French doors to her balcony. I heard rain hitting the balcony rails. She took off my suit jacket and laid it across her chaise longue. She turned the music up and pulled me close to her. We danced slowly. Stacey put her forehead against my chest and exhaled. I knew how she felt. We had been through a lot. She deserved to exhale.

"Did I ever thank you?" she asked, softly.

"Thank me for what?"

She looked up at me and said, "For being everything that I always dreamed you would be."

"Well I guess I should be thanking you for the same thing then."

She smiled and put her head back on my chest. We continued to dance and soon the foreplay began.

We slowly undressed each other. Stacey's body was more beautiful than I remembered. We moved from vertical foreplay to horizontal in the middle of Stacey's queen sized bed.

As usual, Stacey smelled so good. This time her aroma was of peaches and cream.

I kissed down her body savoring every inch. She had a surprise for me when I reached her belly button. Since our last time being together, Stacey had gotten her belly bottom pierced.

"When did you get this," I asked running my finger over the new jewelry.

"It was a birthday present to myself. Can you see what the charm is?"

I shifted my body so the candlelight would illuminate the charm and noticed it was the number ten.

I looked up at her and she smiled. "You like?"

"Oh yeah." I licked around her new belly jewelry and said, "I really like."

I continued my journey South. I hadn't tasted Stacey in a while and was anxious to feast on her goodies.

I dined like I was eating a five course meal. Stacey begged me to stop. Not because she didn't like it but because she just couldn't take the intense explosions that her body was experiencing.

I wanted to do something a little different during this session but I wasn't sure how Stacey would feel about it. But I figured it wouldn't hurt to ask.

I kissed my way back up her body, lingering around her breasts for just a little while longer. I kissed her neck then up to her ear.

"Can we do something different this time?"

"Like what?"

"Can I go raw," I whispered.

She looked at me and said, "What?"

"C'mon Stace. I just want to feel you." I kissed her softly and said, "I mean *really* feel you."

"Ronnie I don't know."

"Don't you trust me?"

"You know I do. But…."

"Let me just feel it a little. I'll pull out before I cum."

I couldn't help but laugh at myself. I knew Stacey had probably heard that before. She laughed too. I hadn't used that line since I was in high school.

"Seriously, I haven't been with anyone else since before we first kissed and before that, I always wrapped it up."

I could see Stacey was starting to weaken. I started sliding it in and she kind of jumped.

"Please," I mouthed.

She finally consented. I slowly finished my entry. I had to pause for a second. Stacey felt so good that I almost couldn't take it. I composed myself then made love to Stacey like never before.

I thought the first time Stacey and I were together was all that, but making love to her that night was incredible. Forget the fact that I hadn't had any in a while. It was more than that. Stacey and I just seemed to be made for each other.

I had never been with someone who I wanted to please so much. My job was to make sure my boo was satisfied. I wanted her to fall off to sleep with a smile on her face—which she did every single time. It wasn't one-sided because Stacey made sure I was well taken care of. So I went to sleep with a smile on my face also.

For some reason, Stacey always seemed to talk more openly when we were lying together after one of our private sessions. I guess if you've just given yourself to someone that intimately, it's a natural progression. Her openness made me open up. I had been far more honest about my feelings for her, with her, than I had ever been before. I trusted Stacey unquestionably. I had never trusted girl like that.

"You know, um, Patrick's not graduating tomorrow," Stacey said out of the blue. I had no response. I really didn't give a damn.

"He, ah, called me a couple of days ago." Stacey was good for using a buffer statement when she didn't really know how to bring up a subject. "And he asked if we could meet somewhere and talk."

I looked at her. After everything he had done to her, I just knew she didn't want anything to do with him.

"I know you probably disagree but, I met him and we had a long talk."

She was right. I disagreed but it wasn't my decision.

"Oh, really? So what did that fool have to say for himself?"

"He was just saying that he was sorry for ever putting his hands on me and that he realizes that I wasn't the problem, he was."

"No shit," I responded sarcastically.

"And he was saying that he appreciated everything that I had ever done to support him and that he hoped you know what type of woman you have."

"I've always known what type of woman you are. It was his dumb ass who didn't know," I snapped.

"Calm down, boy. I'm just telling you what he said."

"I'm sorry. But you know how I get when it comes to him."

"Yeah, I know. But Patrick has some issues."

"Everybody has issues, Stacey, but that doesn't mean you hurt other people to make yourself feel better."

"Yeah, I know."

"Can I ask you a question, Stace?"

"Yeah."

"Why did you stay with him for so long? I mean you had so many reasons to break up with him, the least of which being that he was putting his hands on you. Even after we started kickin' it, you still stayed. I just need to understand why."

Stacey took a deep breath. She turned her head toward the balcony and just stared into space.

"Stacey."

"There's something that I have to tell you and I just pray it doesn't change the way you feel about me," she said with her eyes still fixed on the rain falling outside the balcony doors.

I had no idea what she was about to tell me but I couldn't imagine anything changing how I felt about her.

"Two years ago, I, ah, got pregnant by Patrick."

Now that was a bit of a surprise. I would have never in a million years thought she was going to say that.

"Pregnant?" I asked, basically trying to convince myself that I had heard wrong.

"Yes, pregnant," she replied, still focusing on the rain. "At the time, I had just turned twenty and I knew I wasn't ready for a baby. Maybe if I had been with a different person, things would have been different."

"So you didn't have the baby," I asked.

She slowly turned her head toward me and answered, "No. I didn't have the baby."

"So you had an...."

She turned away again. "Yes. I had an abortion," she said softly.

That was deep. I didn't know what to say or if she even wanted me to say anything. What I did know was her disclosure hadn't changed how I felt about her a bit.

"At the time, I thought that was the only thing for me to do," she continued. "And there's not a day that goes by that I don't regret that decision. It's not that I think I was ready for a baby. I should have just dealt with the consequences. But I didn't."

"Well in situations like that, you don't always use the best judgment. Your emotions sometimes cause you to make decisions that you end-up regretting. But at this point, all you can do is try not to make those types of mistakes again."

"You're the only person besides Patrick, Erika and Tracy who knows about it," she confessed, finally turning toward me. I could tell by her eyes, this was very painful subject for her.

"As close as my mother and I are, I couldn't tell her. She would have been so disappointed. I mean, she always told me how when she found out she was pregnant with Kevin and Devin people were trying to get her to have an abortion. She said she wouldn't know what her life would be like if she hadn't had her babies." Tears began filling her eyes. "I can't let my mother know I wasn't as strong as she was."

I wiped her eyes and said, "Stacey, you know your mother loves you to death and though she may not agree with what you did, she would be there for you. Maybe someday, you'll be able to talk to her about it."

"Maybe."

I gently kissed her hand. "I'm glad you felt like you could finally tell me."

"The funny thing is I wanted to tell you about everything when we were at Hains Point last summer 'cause that was the real reason I stopped having sex. After the abortion, I just couldn't bring myself to do it. I kept thinking I was going to get pregnant again. Then as you and I got closer, I knew something was going to happen eventually, so I decided to go 'head and try the pill again."

"You started taking birth control pills again, just for me?"

It might sound stupid but I felt honored that Stacey would do something like that for me. I knew how much she hated taking pills.

"Well yeah. Like I said, I knew where things were heading. Plus I figured if I got pregnant on the pill, God would be trying to tell me something, and I would handle it much differently."

I just nodded.

"Remember back in March when I kind of disappeared for a few days?"

"Yeah," I answered.

"Well, sometime in the beginning of March would have been the baby's first birthday and when that really hit me, I kind of lost it for a while."

I had known so many girls that used abortion as a birth control. It was no big deal to them. But having an abortion was a big deal for Stacey. I was with her those couple of days in March. She was feeling the emotional effects of her abortion almost two years later.

"Again, I wanted to tell you then. You looked so worried."

"Worried? Stacey, worried doesn't even come close to what I was feeling." I looked at her and said, "To be honest, I was scared to death. I had never seen you like that. It was like your spirit was broken, and there was nothing I could do."

"I know. I'm sorry I put you through that. I thought I wanted and needed to be alone, but when you showed up, I was really glad you were there."

Tears started forming in her eyes. "It's like, at one of the lowest moments in my life, you were there to hold me. For two days, you just held me. And at that time, that's exactly what I needed." The girl was about to make me shed a tear.

She wiped her eyes and said, "So anyway, to answer your initial question about why I stayed with Patrick so long, the abortion had a lot to do with it, then when his mother died last year—"

"His mother died?" I interrupted. That was news to me.

"You didn't know his mother died last year?" Stacey asked, surprised at my ignorance.

"No. He never said anything about that."

"That is so crazy. I mean why wouldn't you tell your teammates that your mother died? She had breast cancer."

"Awe man, that's messed up."

"Anyway, after she died, he and his father just didn't get along, and he would always come to me for support. Then things started getting worse with him and his dad, which made things worse with us."

Stacey was staring into space. "I felt like I could handle it myself. I didn't want anybody to know what was going on. I couldn't believe that I was in that situation anyway. I never imagined that I would let someone treat me like that."

It was bad enough that she had to go through that once. I didn't want to make her relive it now that it was over.

"We don't have to talk about it anymore, boo."

"No, I want to try and explain it to you."

"Okay."

"I had every intention of breaking up with him. I honestly did, especially when things started heating up between you and me. I know it sounds stupid but I kept thinking if I broke up with him, he'd be all alone. His father was so caught up in his own grief from losing his wife that he wasn't there anymore. As far as Patrick was concerned, he had lost his baby, then his mother, then his father. I didn't want it to seem like on top of everything else, he was losing me too."

"Stacey, there was no way you should have had to take on all that responsibility."

"I know but then he started changing on me. Most people already thought he was an asshole, but with me he wasn't until his mother died. I didn't know how he would react to my breaking up with him. Patrick just seemed like the type of guy who would become a stalker or something. And I didn't want to have to walk around looking over my shoulder, wondering if he was going to jump out and really hurt me. Plus, I rationalized everything in my mind. I told myself he had actually only hit me a couple of times. I knew he had been seeing other girls so I didn't really have to see him. Besides," she looked at me, "I had you. Everything that he wasn't, you were. Everything that I didn't get from him, I got from you."

"That was no way to have to live, Stacey. You didn't have to go through all that with him."

"I know that now. But at the time, I thought that was the best way to handle it. I didn't want you or anybody else getting caught up in my mess."

"Well that's all over now." I kissed her and said, "You ain't gotta worry about me hittin' but one thing—the skins."

"You are so nasty."

"And you know you like it."

"Anyway."

Before I knew it, Stacey was asleep. As I lay beside her watching her sleep, I noticed how at peace she finally looked. I hadn't realized or paid attention to all the stress that had been on her face before. But now that it was gone, I could see the difference. I promised myself right then that Stacey would never have stress like that again. Not as long as I was around.

I should have gone home that night because I needed to give my place the once-over before my family got there the next day for graduation but I had to stay with Stacey. I had been going to sleep every night wondering when I was going to be lying next to her again. That night had finally come, and I wanted to make it last as long as I could.

My sister's was the first college graduation I had ever been to. It was so long. At least at Raina's, I could get up and walk around, but I couldn't get up at my own. So there I sat, tired and bored to death.

My cell phone vibrated.

"Hello."

"I am bored as hell dawg," Dave said, talking low.

I laughed. "You ain't the only one. Plus, I'm ready to go to sleep, man. I'm tired as hell."

"Yeah, I bet you are after your first night back with Stacey."

"You know what I'm saying? A brother didn't get much sleep last night."

Dave asked, "So what you got planned after this?"

"Man, my parents brought a truckload of food with them. You gotta come through."

"Oh I'll be there. You know I gotta come see sexy Mrs. Morgan," Dave said, laughing.

"You stupid, man."

"Man, your mother is fine as hell."

"Go 'head with that, man."

Talking to Dave had at least gotten me through the keynote speaker. They were finally calling people up to get their degrees. That was a show in itself. There was a brother named Greg Franklin graduating who had been a junior when I came in. That brother did back flips all over the stage. If I had been in school that long I probably wouldn't have even come to graduation. I would have asked the school to just mail me my degree.

As I watched people I knew walk across the stage, I began thinking about my four years at Howard. Jessica Gray was my biology lab partner. She was the reason I got an A. James Harrison played ball with me sophomore year. His parents made him quit the team when his grades dropped. Jamie Iverson was crazy. We went out once. I thought she was cool. But then she started stalking me. Everywhere I went there she was all up in my face asking what was up with us.

"Stacey Lynette Jackson."

Her name was a beautiful melody to me. You could hear her family going wild in the stands. As she walked across the stage, I was really shocked we had made it through that last year. I almost lost my mind dealing with that whole situation with her.

I had been out with so many girls on that campus—so many girls that I pretty much lost count. But Stacey Jackson was never far from my mind, even before I met her. There was something about that girl. I knew somehow I was going to have to get with her. When that day finally came, she was everything—I mean everything—I thought she would be. If I learned nothing else at Howard University, I learned what it felt like to be really loved. Loved so much that is was unexplainable. I guess I also learned that your first love doesn't always come when you're in high school. Mine didn't come until my senior year in college.

hotlanta or bust!

stacey

June 12, 2000 - 3:35 p.m.

After everything that I've been through over the last three months, never in my wildest dreams would I have thought my life would be this great. I just received another offer letter in the mail. A lady from this company called yesterday with verbal offer and overnighted the official letter. That's a total of six!!!! This one's from a firm in Dallas. I have others from two different firms here in D.C. Then there's a firm in Chicago and two in Atlanta. All of them are really good offers, especially for someone coming right out of college. I mean the lowest salary is $39,500 a year!!!! That's from the firm in Chicago and the cost of living is probably the highest there. Well I'm not really sure about Atlanta. The cost of living has been going up there since it's become the place to be for blacks. But I'm pretty sure I don't want to live in Chicago. It's too damn cold there. I went for my second interview in February and I thought I was going to die. I have never in my life been that cold.

I really don't know what I'm going to do though. I've lived here all my life so a change of scenery might be good. But I would miss my family. But it's not like I couldn't visit. And I've been with Erika all my life. I don't know if I can handle being away from her. Then there's Mr. Morgan. Things with us have just gotten back on track, and I don't want to lose him. He's still trying to get his music career going so since he's finished with school, he's going back to New York. He keeps telling me everything will be fine between us but I don't know. If I stayed here, I'd only be four hours away. That way I could still see him. This is a big decision. I'm going to go talk to Mommy and Daddy. I'm not going to mention Ronnie because I don't want a lecture from Daddy about letting a man make decisions in my life.

"Where is everybody?" I yelled, walking in the front door of my parents' house.

"We're in the den," Daddy called out.

I went in the den, and my parents were watching the news. I waved my latest offer letter around and said, "Look-a-here." Daddy took the letter and began reading it.

"Which firm is this, sweet pea?" my mother asked.

"The firm in Dallas."

Mommy frowned. "Dallas? That's kind of far away, isn't it?" I knew she wasn't going to like that. "You have two offers here, right?"

"Baby, she has to go with the best offer," Daddy said.

Mommy sucked her teeth.

"You can't keep the girl under your wings all her life."

"I'm not trying to keep her under my wings, Greg." Mommy was getting upset. In her mind, she was losing her only daughter and she thought my father should have been more understanding. Daddy was trying to understand but he really thought I should take the best offer. He didn't look at it like he was losing me but I was just moving into the next phase of my life.

"Baby, look, I didn't mean it like that," Daddy said, moving next to Mommy on the couch. "It's just that this is a big decision for Stacey and it's going to affect her life in ways we don't have to live with. She should make this decision without anyone's influence."

"I'm not trying to influence her." Mommy looked at me and said, "Am I doing that?"

"No, you're not. It's just a hard decision for me. On one hand I've lived here all my life so going somewhere else, anywhere else is exciting. But then again, I would miss y'all. And I don't know if I can handle being away from my brother."

"Pumpkin, you are a strong woman. You can handle anything you put your mind to, and no matter where you are we're always with you. If you need us, we'll be just a plane ride away."

"I know, Daddy, but it's still hard."

"I know but just weigh your options and make the best career decision." He looked at my mother and continued, "And whatever your decision is, we're going to support you."

Mommy laughed.

"Yes, we will sweet pea. Like your father said we'll be just a plane ride away."

"And Stacey Lynette Jackson—" my full name, he was getting serious—"I know how you feel about Ronnie," *Oh God,* I thought, "but you have to do what's best for you in the long run. Right now, you're in love but you can't live your life for him."

"I know, Daddy."

Even though I said it, I knew if Ronnie asked me to stay in D.C. to be closer to him, I would without hesitation. It had taken me four years to meet and fall in love with Ronnie. Well it didn't take four years for me to fall in love with him because I was in love from day one. There was no way I was going to give that up, no matter what my father said.

"Well I know your father doesn't care to know, but what does Ronnie say about your job offers?" Mommy asked.

"To be honest, he pretty much says the same thing as Daddy. He wants me to do what's best for me. I mean he says we'll just work it out somehow."

"He's a very good man," Mommy said, smiling.

I smiled.

"Yeah, he's okay," Daddy joked.

Mommy pushed him playfully. "You know you like him," she said.

"I know. He is a very nice young man."

I was glad to hear Daddy say that. I knew Daddy liked Ronnie because of the positive way he interacted with him. But, it felt good to hear it.

As I was backing out of my parents' driveway, my cell phone started ringing. I pulled it out of my bag.

"What's up, boy?"

"Where you at?" Ronnie asked.

"Ah, hello. How are you doing?" I said, teasing him for not greeting me properly.

"I'm sorry, boo. How you doing?"

"I'm fine but you know I was just messing with you."

"Where are you?" Ronnie asked again anxiously.

"I'm just leaving my parents'."

"Why don't you swing by here? I got something I need to talk to you about."

"Something good or something bad?" I asked, turning on to Central Avenue.

"Boo, this is something very good," he answered excitedly.

"Well I got something to tell you too."

"Good or bad," Ronnie asked, mocking me.

"I really don't know yet. Right now, it's just news."

"Okay, well we'll talk."

"Alright, I'm on my way. I'm hungry though. I was thinking about some fried shrimp from The Wharf."

"Well how 'bout you come here first and we'll walk over after I tell you my news?"

"Alright I'll be there in about a half hour."

"Alright, boo. I'll see ya."

I didn't know what kind of news Ronnie could have. He said it wasn't bad but that didn't stop me from worrying.

I rang the doorbell. I still had my key but rarely used it. I continued trying to figure out what Ronnie wanted to talk to me about. I was getting nervous. What if he was moving to L.A. to work on his music? None of my job offers were near there. What if he thought we should stop seeing each other? Even though he said it was something good, he was the type to say it would be the best thing for me. I didn't want that.

He opened the door and said, "Hey, boo." He kissed me.

"Hey." We kissed again.

"So what's this news?" I asked, wanting to get it over with.

"You go first."

"Well I got another job offer."

"Congratulations, boo," he said, kissing me again. "I'm proud of you, girl. So where is this job?"

I looked at him and said, "Dallas."

"Oh," Ronnie responded softly.

"But you know, I haven't made any decision yet," I assured him. "Anyway, what's your news?" I asked, changing the subject.

A broad smile came across his face. "Well—" he walked toward the stairs—"somebody else here got an offer also."

I was confused. I didn't know he was interviewing. He said he was going to concentrate on his music for at least three years and if it hadn't happened he was going back to help his dad run his businesses.

"A job offer? I thought you were working on your music?"

"I didn't say a job offer." He was being evasive.

"What are you talking about, Ronnie?"

"I—well, we—got an offer from LaFace Records." I just looked at him. "Boo, we got a record deal!" he exclaimed.

"What! Oh, my God." I ran over and jumped on him, wrapping my legs around his waist. "Congratulations!"

I kissed him.

I was so excited. He and the guys worked so hard to get that contract. Ronnie would spend hours in his basement writing and rewriting songs. He was determined to write the perfect song, the one that was going to get them a recording contract.

Ronnie gently put me back down on the floor. "Let me ask you something, didn't you have some job offers in Atlanta?" he asked.

"Yeah, two actually."

"Are they good offers? I mean are they offers that you're considering seriously?"

"Yeah. One of them is a very good offer. In fact, it's probably my number two choice."

"Well, after talking to some of the people at LaFace, I found out that most of the producers they want us to work with are in Atlanta." I just looked at him. "I know I've been telling you to do what's best for you and I still want that. But if there's a good job for you in Atlanta…."

"So you're saying you want me to take the job in Atlanta?" I asked. I wanted to make sure I understood correctly. The last thing I wanted to do was jump to conclusions.

"Yes. That's exactly what I'm asking you to do."

"Um…" I really didn't know what to say. My mind was saying yes but I knew there were other things to consider.

"You don't have to answer now. I know it's a big decision."

"It should be, shouldn't it," I said, laughing a little.

"Naw, for real, think it over for a while. Make sure it's really what's best for you."

"Okay. I will."

"C'mon. Let's go get you some of that fried shrimp."

"Okay."

I didn't stay at Ronnie's that night, even though since we had gotten back together we spent almost every night with each other. I needed some time to think about everything that was going on. My father was not going to like me going to Atlanta just because Ronnie was going to be there.

That I already knew. My mother wouldn't like me going to Atlanta at all. That I knew also. Since Erika had been with Dave, her whole perspective had changed. She was ready to follow Dave to the ends of the earth. So she would tell me to pack my bags for Atlanta. I didn't really know how Tracy would feel about me going so far away though. I needed to talk to him.

"Talk to me."

"Are you busy?" I asked Tracy as I put my car in park outside his apartment building.

"Naw. I'm just chillin', watching a flick. Why, what's up?"

"I just pulled up. I need to talk to you."

"Alright."

When I walked in Tracy's apartment—of course I had my own key— he was lying on the couch, still looking at TV. He looked at me and said, "Hey."

I threw my keys on the coffee table. "Hey."

I lifted his feet and sat down. I put his legs on my lap and put my feet on the table. I laid my head back against the couch.

"So what's up wit' cha?" Tracy asked.

I turned my head toward him and said, "I got another job offer today."

"Really? Which company?" Tracy asked enthusiastically.

"Channey Consulting in Dallas."

"You go, girl." I managed to give a half smile. "I'm really proud of you."

"Thanks."

"You alright?" Tracy asked with a confused look on his face.

I guess he figured I should have been at least a little excited. And I really was. I mean I had no idea I would have all those job offers. There were plenty of people who would have loved to have my job dilemma coming out of undergrad. But my big dilemma wasn't really concerning the job but what to do about Ronnie and our relationship.

"It's just that I didn't know this decision would be so hard," I replied, finally answering Tracy.

"Well you just have to sit down and really think about what's best for you."

"I know."

We sat in silence for a while. It really wasn't completely silent because

Tracy was now watching ComicView on BET, so he was laughing every now and then.

"Ronnie got a record deal," I said, finally breaking my silence.

"Straight up? That's cool. With what label?"

I looked at him and said, "LaFace."

"Well I guess I know what job offer you're leaning toward," Tracy said, laughing.

"I really want to be with him but Daddy keeps saying…."

"Baby girl, I know what Daddy says but if you want to be with Ronnie, go for it. I mean it's not like you're really following him. You have two good job offers there. You can get your own place. It would be the same as if you went there and got a boyfriend. You'd be handling your own business."

"I know but what if things don't work out?"

I knew the music industry was a crazy business to be around and not many people in the business had histories of long-lasting relationships.

"If things don't work out, at least you tried. You took the chance and you'll have no regrets." He smiled and said, "Then you can just move back here with me."

I smiled

"Stacey, on the serious tip, if you want to go to HotLanta, go for it. What does Ronnie say about all this?"

"He asked me to take one of the jobs in Atlanta."

"Well, I don't see what your dilemma is."

"I know. I mean it's like when Ronnie asked me to take the job in Atlanta, I would have had my bags packed and ready to head south right at that moment. But then Daddy's voice popped in my head."

"Girl, you gotta make this decision for you and nobody else," Tracy said, shaking his head. "I mean you're the one who's going to have to live with it."

"But, I'm also going to miss you." I could feel tears beginning to roll down my cheeks. Tracy sat up and put his arms around me. He wiped my eyes and said, "Baby girl, don't worry, if you ever need me, I'll be right there."

"I know."

"Mmm, you know there are some fine women in the A-T-L." It was just like my brother to be thinking about all the women he could get.

"But what about Erika? She's my best friend in the world."

"And she always will be."

"Tracy, I've never had to do anything alone in my life. One of you has always been there with me. I'm scared."

"First of all, you won't be alone this time either. Ronnie's gonna be there. And second, you would be fine even if he wasn't. You're a lot stronger than you give yourself credit for. Besides, you know that loud-mouthed girl is gonna be racking up frequent flyer miles coming to see you."

"I know," I said, laughing.

"Seriously though, are you going to take the job in Atlanta or what?" Tracy asked, cutting off the TV.

After thinking about everything one more time, I said, "Yeah. I'm going to take it."

"Good." He kissed my forehead. "Good."

Telling my father about my decision to take the job in Atlanta was one of the hardest things I ever had to do. I tried to leave out the details about Ronnie being in Atlanta. My father did ask me how I arrived at my decision though. I told him all the good points about the company. Everything would have been fine if my mother wouldn't have been there. She had to ask again what Ronnie thought about me moving to Atlanta.

"What does Ronnie think?" I repeated, trying to stall.

"Yes, that's what I asked you," she said, not falling for that trick.

"Well um, he…" Then I thought of another stall tactic, which would also lead me to finally answer Mommy's question and tell Daddy about Ronnie being in Atlanta. "Oh, I forgot to tell y'all the good news."

"What good news?" they asked in unison.

"Guess who got a record deal?" You would have thought it was me from my excited tone.

"Ronnie got a record deal?" My mother was almost jumping out of her chair.

"Yes."

"That is so wonderful," Mommy said. "After hearing him sing to you at that party, I knew it was going to happen for him."

"I'm going to have to call my man and congratulate him," Daddy said. "What label picked him up?" The moment of truth had arrived.

"Ah, LaFace Records," I answered nervously.

Immediately Mommy knew why I was so nervous. Her favorite singer in the world was Babyface. She would travel all up and down I-95 to see him in concert. So of course she knew the record label he helped start was based in Atlanta. She had been a fanatic for a while so she had schooled my father on every Babyface fact there was. I knew it wouldn't take him long to put two and two together.

Mommy was obviously cool with it. She didn't say a word. She just sat there with a grin on her face, watching me nervously fidget around the kitchen.

I opened the refrigerator and began surveying the inside for something, anything. I wasn't really hungry or thirsty but it allowed me to avoid the conversation a few minutes.

I had just picked up a Dr. Pepper when my father said, "Wait a second." I closed my eyes. Two and two had been put together.

"Stacey, I have a question for you." I swallowed hard and shut the refrigerator door. "What's that?" I asked, opening the can, which was visibly trembling in my hands.

Mommy kind of shot Daddy a look. Then he looked at me.

"Oh, never mind."

That was very strange. Daddy got up from the table and kissed my mother. Their eyes met lovingly. My mother rubbed his cheek and smiled. There was obviously something going on between them that I wasn't a party to.

"Well, ladies, I have some work to finish up." He kissed me on my forehead. "Let me know what you need for your move, okay?" He kissed me again and walked out.

I looked at my mother and said, "Why didn't he say anything?"

"Because, sweetheart, there comes a time in every parents' life when they just have to trust their child to make their own decisions."

"And you're alright with me going to Atlanta?"

"Do you want to know if I'm alright with you going to Atlanta or with you going to Atlanta to be with Ronnie?"

I looked at her and said, "With me going to be with Ronnie."

"You know, I would have reservations if you didn't have your own job lined up and you were going to rely on Ronnie to take care of you. But this isn't that type of situation."

"I know you love Ronnie and besides, you're young. Have some fun. Take some chances."

I hugged my mother. She always had the right words at the right time.

"And who knows, maybe twenty-five years from now, you'll be sitting with you and Ronnie's daughter telling her the same thing."

I laughed. "Well I don't know about that, Mommy."

Secretly, I had dreamed about that from the first day I saw Ronnie. Once I found out what Ronnie's last name was, I began writing my first name with his last. Stacey Jackson-Morgan. Stacey L. J. Morgan. Mrs. Ronald Morgan, Jr.

I had gone as far as to start making up names for our children. Our son would be named after his father, Ronald Steven Morgan III. His nickname would be Tré. We would have a daughter. I hadn't really nailed down a solid name for her yet. I was kicking around Veronica Lynette Morgan or Veronica Stephanie Morgan. I thought we could call her Ronni. It was really ridiculous. But I knew every girl in the world did the same thing with her first love, so I didn't really feel too silly about it.

Everything had worked out better than I had planned. My parents were supporting my move to Atlanta, even though they knew Ronnie was a big factor in my decision. Tracy gave me his blessing, not that I doubted he would. Devin and Kevin weren't all that happy with me going so far away, but they supported my decision too. And so did Erika. Both she and Dave had taken jobs in Raleigh, North Carolina. So my best friend wasn't going to be too far away after all.

I felt very proud of myself. I had made an adult decision regarding my job and my relationship with Ronnie. Now, I had decided that I had to tell my mother about my abortion and what had gone on with Patrick. I never kept things from her and it was weighing on my heart. Though I had made the decision, it took me a couple of days to work up the nerve to actually do it.

I called my parents' house. My mother answered. "Hey, sweet pea." She always looked at the Caller ID.

"Hey, Mommy. Um, what you doin'?"

"Nothing really. Just catching up on some reading."

"Oh. Where's Daddy?"

"He went to play golf."

"Oh. Okay." There was an awkward pause on my part. "Well, I'm going to come out there, okay?"

"Yeah, that's fine."

"Alright then. I'll see you in a little while."

"What's wrong, Stacey?" Mommy asked with growing concern in her voice.

"I, um, just need to talk to you about something," I replied nervously.

"Okay. I'll be here."

"Okay."

I hung up and wondered if I could go through with telling my mother everything that had been going on in my life the past few years. I knew Ronnie was right when he said she would love me regardless, but I worried if she'd lose respect for me. I didn't want that. But, she had worked hard to build an open and honest relationship with her only daughter, and I wasn't going to mess that up by keeping this secret from her.

I walked in the house. Everything was silent. Even though my brothers and I had all moved out, we were still in and out of the house a lot so something was always going on. On rare occasions, my mother got the house to herself. She loved that quiet time.

I found my mother in her usual reading spot, in the sunroom. It was her favorite room in the house. She decorated it in a pastel yellow. Mommy thought yellow was a calming color, plus she wanted a tropical decor. The furniture was nice, even though I personally didn't really care for wicker. But out there it fit perfectly. There were lots of plants around the room and the two ceiling fans really completed the tropical feel.

Mommy raised her head from her book when she heard me approach.

"Hey, Mommy," I said.

My mother pulled down her reading glasses and said, "Hey, sweet pea."

I kissed her on her cheek and sat down beside her. "I hope I'm not interrupting your quiet time." I smiled and said, "I know you don't get that much of it."

She laughed and said, "No sweetie, it's fine."

She closed her book and turned all her attention to me. Since I told her I had to talk to her, she was going to let me talk.

I was hoping my drive over would calm my nerves about our impending conversation but it hadn't. I was still scared, but there was no turning back.

I took a deep breath and said, "Mommy, I need to talk to you about some things."

She sat up from her relaxed position and set her book on the table.

My tone told her our conversation was going to be serious.

"I don't know how to tell you."

"Tell me what, baby?" she asked, taking my hand. "You know you can tell me anything."

I looked at her and said, "The summer before my junior year, I, um—" I put my head down—"I, ah, had an abortion."

My mother didn't say anything.

I slowly raised my eyes toward her. There were tears in her eyes. Just as my heart sank from the sight of her tears, her lips parted in a smile.

"Thank you," she said, wiping away her tears.

"For what?" I asked, confused.

"One of the nurses from the clinic called here the day after to verify your mailing address. I guess you put this number down as your home number by mistake."

I was horrified. How in the world could I have made such a mistake? What if my father had answered the phone?

"Why didn't you say anything," I asked.

She shrugged. "Because, I figured you would tell me when you felt the time was right."

"You knew I would tell you?"

"I hoped you would. I hoped I had built a strong enough bond between us that you wouldn't feel like you couldn't tell me."

I felt the coolness of my tears on my face. "I'm so sorry, Mommy. I didn't mean to let you down. But I was so scared. I didn't know what else to do."

My mother wrapped her arms around me. She rocked back and forth as she had always done to comfort me. "Baby, I love you more than anything on this earth, and no matter what happens I'm always going to love you."

"I wanted to come to you when I first found out I was pregnant, but I didn't want you to be disappointed in me."

"Stacey, why would I be disappointed in you? You do recall how old I was when I got pregnant with your brothers."

"I know but you and Daddy were in love."

"So. Pregnant is pregnant. I could have very well been in your situation." She looked at me and said, "Don't think that having an abortion didn't cross my mind."

"But Mommy you told me that when people were saying you should have an abortion you told them you couldn't do that."

"Yes, I did. But that was after I had already made my own decision. I wasn't going to let anyone else tell me what I should do with my body."

"I wish I could have been that strong."

"The situations were very different, Stacey. Please don't beat yourself up because you didn't make the same choice I did. You did what you thought was best at the time. I may not agree with it, but I don't necessarily have to. I can't live your life."

"Mommy, there's not a day that goes by that I don't wish I'd handled things differently."

"And baby, you will probably live the rest of your life like that."

I nodded in agreement. I had no doubt that, just as I had since that rainy day in June, I would always regret that decision.

"I have something else I need to tell you."

"Alright," she said, taking a deep breath. "I don't know if I can handle your visits. They're too emotional."

I kind of laughed. She was right about that. And I knew it was about to get more emotional.

"I have to tell you about something that was going on with Patrick."

"I already know you were cheating on him."

"Well it's not that."

"Okay, what is it?" she finally said.

"After Patrick's mom died, he started going through some changes and things between us started going downhill. We were arguing a lot and…."

"Stacey…I hope you are not telling me that that boy put his hands on you."

I looked at her with no response.

"Is that what you're telling me, Stacey?" she said, raising her voice.

"Mommy, please don't get upset."

"Don't get upset." She got up and started pacing. "Don't get upset. Some little nigga put his hands on my baby and you're telling not to get upset?" My mother had a Ph.D in Psychology but she was from Northeast, DC and the hood came out out every now and then.

"Mmm-hmm," she said going to get the phone. "Let me call your brothers." She started dialing and said, "We'll see if his little ass wants to hit on them."

I took the phone from her and said, "Mommy, they already know."

"They know? Well does Ronnie know about this?"

I nodded and sat back down.

"Stacey, I don't understand. How did this happen?"

"Things just started escalating with us and before I knew it, it was out of control. Then Ronnie came in the picture. He didn't know what was going on for a long time. When I finally told him, he wanted me to break up with Patrick, but it wasn't that easy. I mean I was still dealing with my guilt about having the abortion and Patrick used that to keep me there."

I put my head down and continued, "After a while, Ronnie couldn't take it anymore and he ended things between us."

My mother sat back down beside me.

"The whole time, Ronnie kept trying to convince me to talk to Tracy but I wouldn't so he ended up telling him. And that's how Kevin and Dev found out. And that's how eventually Patrick did get his butt beat by all four of them."

"Well good for him. That's what he deserves. Putting his hands on my baby."

I laughed.

"Stacey, seriously, you've been through a lot in the last couple of years, do you think you need to talk to someone, a counselor maybe?" I knew Mommy was going to put on her Dr. Jackson hat sooner or later in the conversation. "I could get you a list of counselors in Atlanta."

"I really feel like I'm okay. But I promise you, if I ever need to talk to someone, I'll call you for the list."

She smiled and said, "Okay." She kissed me and hugged me tightly.

My mother decided to have a barbecue for me before I left. She wouldn't call it a going away party because she didn't want to get too emotional about it. There were so many people there; all my family, all my sorors from campus, Erika, Dave and of course, Ronnie.

I was glad to get the chance to hang with Erika before I left for At-lanta. She and Dave had been back and forth to North Carolina finding an apartment and getting their new life started so I hadn't seen her too much. Dave joked that he knew their phone bill was going to be "crazy high" with Erika and me being away from each other for the first time in our lives. I had already made it up in my mind that I was going to have to budget more money for the phone bill. Our lives would be different but we promised each other to not let the distance come between our friendship. Plus, Raleigh was only an hour away by plane and if push came to shove, it was about six hours away by car.

I was busy throwing down on my third bowl of my mother's famous seafood gumbo when Erika came over saying she needed to talk to me about something. I had no idea what it could be. I reluctantly put my bowl down, instructing my father not to let anyone touch it. I knew when I got back it was going to be gone because he was going to eat it, but I left it anyway and followed Erika into the house.

"What's up, girl?" I asked, shutting the door behind me.

"Well you know Dave and I just got back from Raleigh," she began.

I nodded.

"And while we were there, something happened."

"I know y'all didn't break up."

"Please, girl. I don't even think so." She raised her left hand to my eye level and said, "How 'bout this happened."

I couldn't believe I was looking at a big ol' rock bling-blinging in my face. I pulled her hand closer and asked, "Is this what I think it is?"

"It sure is," she answered, cheesing like the Cheshire cat.

Simultaneously, we let out a high-pitched scream of excitement. We were hugging each other and jumping around when my parents, brothers, Ronnie and Dave ran in the house.

"What's going on?" my father asked.

I pushed Erika's hand toward them and said, "This."

My mother was the first to grab her from my clutches. "Congratulations, sweetie. I'm so happy for you." She hugged Dave and said, "And for you too, baby."

He smiled and said, "Thanks, Mrs. Jackson."

Everyone was so happy for them, but no one more than me. All our lives, Erika and I had talked about finding "Mr. Right." She found him in Dave. I knew Ronnie was my "Mr. Right" but marriage was nowhere in our immediate future. But I wasn't going to let go of that dream.

The move to Atlanta was so hectic. I had to get everything out of my apartment, and then say my good-byes to my family. It was really an emotional couple of days for me. I cried for almost three days. But once I hit the city limits of Atlanta, I knew I was going to survive. But I wasn't sure if I'd survive apartment hunting with Ronnie.

There were a lot of apartments I liked but Ronnie was so particular about where *he* thought I should live. After a while though, I just wanted a place to live. I was tired of looking. I'm sure I would have found an apartment much sooner if he hadn't been with me.

I saw so many apartments that I would have loved to live in but most were out of my price range. Ronnie told me to get any apartment I wanted and he would help me out, but I didn't want that. I didn't want to be dependent on him.

We finally settled on a nice two-bedroom apartment in Doraville, which was a little north of the city. My commute downtown was going to be hell but I really liked the apartment. Besides, it was close to the MARTA and there was plenty of shopping in the area.

Ronnie was happy because I let him buy me some bedroom furniture as a graduation present. I loved that he wanted so badly to do something, anything to make me happy. And I was happy. I was the happiest I had ever been in my life. I had successfully completed college. I was getting ready to start a great job. And, I was in a relationship with the most wonderful man I had ever known. After all I had been through that past year, things were looking up for me.

> *July 15, 2000 - 9:04 p.m.*
> *I just finished unpacking my last box in my new apartment. Lying here on my brand new king-size bed, thanks to Mr. Morgan, I can't believe I'm really in Atlanta. When my senior year started, I had my mind made up that I was going to get me a job in D.C., but plans definitely change. Me and Ronnie being together was never part of any of my plans, mainly because I never thought he would take a second look at me. When in reality, he was just as interested in me as I was in him.*
>
> *Sitting here thinking back on my college "career" at Howard, I realize that I learned so many things outside of my classes. My*

whole college experience was full of lessons to be learned. The most important lessons came during these last two years.

I learned from having an abortion that some decisions you make haunt you for the rest of your life.

I learned from Patrick that you really don't know how you're going to react to a situation until it happens to you. I never thought I'd let any man abuse me, but I did. I continue to think back on that whole situation, trying to make sense out of it, but I can't. I don't know why he changed on me. He was a nice guy when we first met, but something changed. I also learned from that situation that I might never truly understand why things happened like they did.

I learned from my parents that there's a time in your child's life when you have to just trust that you did your job and your child will go forth and make good decisions. I also learned that I could survive without my parents and brothers, especially Tracy, being beside me. I miss them but I know I'm going to be fine here.

Mr. Morgan taught me the biggest lesson of all. Ronnie taught me what real love is all about. He showed me how I deserve to be treated by a man. He loves me so much that he was willing to let me go when I was going back and forth with Patrick. Not because he really thought I wanted to be with Patrick but because he wasn't willing to stand by and watch me be treated like that. And he knew I was the only person who could get me out of that situation.

I realize life has no guarantees. There's no way for me to know if our relationship will last a year or twenty years, but I do know no matter what happens between us in the future, I will always love Ronnie for showing me what true, unconditional love is. Any man who may come after Ronald Steven Morgan, Jr. won't have an easy road to travel that's for sure!